TRAPPED

P9-DCP-620

Fifteen blocks from his apartment, John pulled the car abruptly to the side of the road, prompting a chorus of horn blasts from behind. *What was he doing?* As soon as the body was discovered, Rolf's associates would begin hunting him, and the first place they'd look would be his apartment. He should have driven to Steve's precinct house, only a short distance from where he had been held in Brooklyn, but hadn't been thinking. Manhattan had seemed distant and safe then, less so now.

John pulled the car back into traffic and found a parking space down the street near a pay phone. He'd played investigator, but there was a dead body to deal with now and somebody had tried to kill him. He had to lay everything on the table—Steve would know what to do.

John rummaged through the glove compartment for tissues, found a paper napkin and scrubbed his face of blood using the rearview mirror. He zipped his jacket to hide his bloodstained shirt, then walked to the phone. He dialed Steve's number with an unsteady hand praying he'd be there to answer the call.

"Hello." It was Steve.

"Steve, it's me," John said barely above a whisper. He knew his voice sounded strange—his jaw muscles were already starting to swell.

"John . . . that you?"

"Yeah. . . . I found something. I've got a lot to tell you. I—"

Steve interrupted. "Hold it for a second, let me shut my door." The line went silent for a moment before Steve spoke again. "John, forget that stuff now, you are in trouble, big trouble, my friend. I shouldn't be telling you this—they'd strip me of my badge—but hell, I'm going to anyway. The department's about to issue a search warrant for your apartment."

JAMES KOEPER

EXPOSED

AN ONYX BOOK

ONYX
Published by the Penguin Group
Penguin Books USA Inc., 375 Hudson Street,
New York, New York 10014, U.S.A.
Penguin Books Ltd, 27 Wrights Lane,
London W8 5TZ, England
Penguin Books Australia Ltd, Ringwood,
Victoria, Australia
Penguin Books Canada Ltd, 10 Alcorn Avenue,
Toronto, Ontario, Canada M4V 3B2
Penguin Books (N.Z.) Ltd, 182–190 Wairau Road,
Auckland 10, New Zealand

Penguin Books Ltd, Registered Offices:
Harmondsworth, Middlesex, England

First published by Onyx, an imprint of Dutton Signet,
a division of Penguin Books USA Inc.

First Printing, July, 1997
10 9 8 7 6 5 4 3 2 1

Copyright © James Koeper, 1997
All rights reserved

 REGISTERED TRADEMARK—MARCA REGISTRADA

Printed in the United States of America

Without limiting the rights under copyright reserved above, no part of this
publication may be reproduced, stored in or introduced into a retrieval system, or transmitted, in any form, or by any means (electronic, mechanical,
photocopying, recording, or otherwise), without the prior written permission
of both the copyright owner and the above publisher of this book.

PUBLISHER'S NOTE
This is a work of fiction. Names, characters, places, and incidents either are
the product of the author's imagination or are used fictitiously, and any resemblance to actual persons, living or dead, events, or locales is entirely
coincidental.

BOOKS ARE AVAILABLE AT QUANTITY DISCOUNTS WHEN USED TO PROMOTE
PRODUCTS OR SERVICES. FOR INFORMATION PLEASE WRITE TO PREMIUM MAR-
KETING DIVISION, PENGUIN BOOKS USA INC., 375 HUDSON STREET, NEW YORK.
NEW YORK 10014.

If you purchased this book without a cover you should be aware that this
book is stolen property. It was reported as "unsold and destroyed" to the
publisher and neither the author nor the publisher has received any payment
for this "stripped book."

FOR LORRAINE . . .

With thanks to my wife; Ed Stackler; Mel Berger; Pat Maloney; Charles Brown; and Wayne Davis, who, through their comments and insight, helped make this book what it is.

1

Sheets of rain from the dull gray sky beat rhythmically against the squad car's roof. Helluva lousy day to die, Michael thought, as he switched off the car's ignition and turned to his partner, Officer Raymond O'Hern. "You want to handle this one?" Michael asked, less than optimistically

Ray didn't budge. "Wouldn't want to hog all the fun."

Michael stared a moment through the rain-splattered windshield, then pulled the collar of his slicker tight at the neck and opened the car door in resignation. "Thanks."

Ray smiled. "Any time."

The curious, huddled under umbrellas, their faces flashing red and blue in the squad car lights, parted in silence as Michael hurried past them into the three-story brick rooming house. Ray stayed behind to cordon off the front of the building and await the arrival of homicide.

A musty stale smell, like a drawer where wet clothes were accidentally stored, struck Michael as he entered the rooming house. He followed the matted trail in the brown shag carpet from the entrance to the front desk, where an old stooped man, thin with leathery skin, greeted Michael in a thick Russian accent, identifying himself as the desk clerk who discovered the body and phoned the police.

"Thirty years I have been here and never has something like this happened. It is very bad. Very bad. The streets are not safe anymore, and now here. It is no good," the old man muttered as he led Michael up the steep, dimly lit staircase.

Along the stairwell, from the confines of cheap wooden picture frames, faded faces of czars and czarinas and other pre-1917 Russian nobility stared blankly outward, a vestige of the Russian immigrants who had been settling in the Brighton Beach neighborhood of Brooklyn since the turn of the century.

The desk clerk led Michael down the second-floor hallway to the accompaniment of muffled strains of classical music and extended groans from the floorboards. He stopped in front of room eight.

"Don't touch the doorknob," Michael said as he pulled a handkerchief from his pocket. "Anybody gone in besides you?"

The old man shook his head as Michael draped the knob with the handkerchief and pushed open the door. The room was dark except for a faint patch of light thrown on the floor by the room's one window. Michael flipped the light switch.

Clothes and personal belongings were strewn everywhere: five empty dresser drawers piled in one corner, pots, plates, and silverware in another. The mattress on the rusty, metal-framed bed had been slit, and yellowish fatty stuffing tossed about. Someone had torn the place apart looking for something.

An otherwise modest and nondescript room. Small—just the bed, the dresser, two chairs, a cheap table with a cooking plate, and a small, older-model refrigerator.

"The body's in the bathroom?" Michael asked.

The desk clerk nodded. "In the tub."

"Stay here. Don't touch or move anything. Got it?"

"Yeah."

A number of the tenants now stood in the doorway in T-shirts and drab pants, their blank, staring faces reminding Michael of the pictures along the stairwell.

"And keep them out of the room," Michael said, pointing to the tenants, before walking toward the bathroom.

As a twenty-year veteran, Michael had seen scores of corpses: a suicide victim, his head blown off by a shotgun blast; a husband and wife crushed in a head-on with a semi; gang members disfigured by knives, guns, and baseball bats; a three-year-old girl pulled from the East River. Necessity had long ago trained him to ignore the horror of the things he saw. He reacted to corpses from a purely clinical perspective: cause of death, time of death, evidence. Ignoring the smell had not come as easily—the smell of a decaying body brought a primal response beyond his control. A hint of that odor hit him as he neared the bathroom. Maybe only a few days, he thought. Not pleasant, but not too bad.

The body lay facedown in the tub, stripped to the waist. An old, heavy-set man, almost bald, with a fringe of closely cropped white hair. The pale gray skin, purple-blotched, hung in waxy folds that collected and spread out from the body along the tub like a stick of butter left out on a summer day.

What remained of the old man's face lay partly covering the drain in a dried pool of blackish-brown blood. Michael bent over to take a closer look at the bullet entry wounds in the back of the head, and the stench hit him. He retched once involuntarily, stood, took six or seven long slow breaths, then bent again to continue the inspection.

Three bullet holes, grouped together—professional, execution style. Michael's sense of smell hadn't been wrong; he estimated the body had been there three to four days. No evidence of a struggle. The old man's open eyes were cloudy, dry, and lifeless; they spoke neither of horror nor surprise. Perhaps resignation, Michael thought.

Michael didn't touch anything; he would leave that for homicide.

The tenants and the clerk stared at him when he returned to the other room, waiting childlike for some declaration, some assurance, that things were now under control.

"Okay, back away, back away. I've got to seal this room off now." Michael repeated the words in Russian. "Detectives will be up any minute to take down your statements."

As if on cue a voice boomed down the hallway. "Hey, Boris, what do we have?"

Michael didn't have to turn to identify the speaker—the only person who called him Boris was Detective Steve Mayer. They had known each other since the third grade; Steve tagged him with the nickname sometime in high school.

With his red-brown hair, stout build, cheap brown, wrinkled suit, and well-lined and, when it had to be, hard face, Steve Mayer looked like a cop. Acted like one too—one of the best in Michael's estimation.

Michael waved Steve into the room. A young detective accompanying Steve stopped at the doorway and began clearing the hall.

"Old man in the tub, Steve, name's Peter Olgov. Shot three times in the back of the head. Looks like he's been dead three, maybe four days. Apartment's obviously been searched."

Steve scanned the room and nodded, then walked into the bathroom. A moment later he walked out, shaking his head. "Damn nasty business. Looks kind of professional."

"Sure wasn't a heat-of-passion shooting. Facedown

in a tub, nice and tidy. I wonder what the old man could have been up to?"

Steve shook his head. "Who knows. Anything been touched?"

"Just by the desk clerk; he found the body. Old man hadn't paid his rent and the clerk checked on him."

"You go through any of this?" Steve asked, pointing to the belongings carpeting the floor.

"No. Just got here. Checked the body and that's it."

"Okay, we'll handle it from here. Camera and print boys should be up in a moment. Just copy me on your report." Steve glanced over at the young detective he had arrived with and reconsidered. He placed his hand on Michael's shoulder, leading him toward the bathroom.

"Michael," Steve whispered, "before you go, do me a favor, huh? The kid in the hall—name's Drew Hartley. I don't think you've met him before. New to homicide, just made full detective a couple of months ago. A bit of a pain in the ass, but I think he'll come around. I'm going to have him question the tenants. Think you could do the rounds with him? Help him out? You know how they can be around here. A few words of Russian might soften 'em up."

"Sure. Any way I can help."

"Thanks. I'll have someone tell Ray what you're up to."

Michael walked into the hallway and up to the young detective, sizing him up before speaking. Expensive suit, flashy tie, stylish haircut, cologne. A lot to learn, Michael guessed.

"Detective Hartley . . . hi, Officer Michael Sarikov. Steve thought I might be able to give you a hand questioning the tenants. I speak Russian pretty well."

Hartley took Michael's outstretched hand hesitantly. "Okay, Sarikov, Detective Mayer's the boss. He wants a beat cop to tag along, it's his call. But hold the

Russian—I'm not going to accept any 'I don't understand' shit from these people. You just take notes and try to stay out of the way, okay? Think you can handle that?"

A *bit* of a pain in the ass? Obviously Steve hadn't given Hartley his due. Michael overdid a smile. "I'll certainly try, detective."

The next hour and a half were uneventful. Michael and Hartley started on the rooming house's third floor and worked their way down. Michael wasn't surprised to find most of the tenants reluctant to volunteer information—in Russia the police were to be avoided, not collaborated with. Hartley's brusque mannerisms didn't help; they learned very little. Peter Olgov lived alone in the apartment, didn't have any children or friends that anyone remembered. Kept pretty much to himself, not overly friendly. He was employed, when employed at all, as a dishwasher in one of the local Russian restaurants.

No one suggested a possible motive for the murder. No one admitted seeing or hearing a thing.

The small and dirty apartments, furnished with worn-out odds and ends, depressed Michael. The impression left by the tenants was worse—the effects of poverty and futility obvious. No matter what their age, they looked squeezed of life. Most were Russian and had probably come to America with dreams of building a new life in the land of opportunity. Michael imagined those dreams, if not snuffed completely, now flickered only dimly.

It struck close to home. His parents had rented an apartment in a rooming house much like this when they immigrated to America. They never moved out. His mother died during childbirth with John, Michael's younger and only sibling. His father died eighteen years later of cirrhosis of the liver, a pile of IOU's to local bars and liquor stores his only estate. He never wrote more than a smattering of English, never held a steady job, never lived to see Michael graduate from the academy or John complete college.

The occupants of the last apartment—an older couple frightened that the killer still lurked in the building—had never met Peter Olgov and knew nothing about him. Hartley excused himself abruptly.

As the door closed behind him, Hartley shook his head in disgust. "Crazy old birds. A fucking waste of my time. Should have left it all to you, Sarikov," he said as he started for the front desk.

Michael mouthed a profanity to Hartley's back.

A few of the tenants weren't home, and Hartley left messages for them to call the station.

Was the man a fool? Hadn't he realized over the past hour and a half that the local Russian immigrant population were not keen on involving themselves with the police? There would be no calls. Michael said nothing—Hartley had made it clear his help was neither needed nor appreciated—but made a mental note to stop at the rooming house again sometime within the next week to follow up on his own.

By the time Michael and Hartley returned to room eight, the body had been removed by the coroner's office, the room had been photographed and dusted, and all the detectives other than Steve had left. They exchanged information quickly, Steve directing his comments at Michael, a fact not overlooked by Hartley.

"Don't think we have much on this one. You tell me you've got nothing, nobody heard or saw a thing or knows anything about this guy, and on our side it isn't any better. No fingerprints other than the victim's and the clerk's. We're gonna run a check on the clerk, but I'm guessing he's clean. No sign of a struggle. No lucky breaks: no skin under the guy's nails; no muddy footprints on the bathroom floor; nothing. Someone searched the room for something, but if it was here, they've got it, because we didn't come up with a thing. His personal papers are gone—no wallet, no mail, no bills, no letters, nothing. Motive? No idea. Robbery would seem to be out . . . from the look of this place, there wasn't much to steal. A gang hit? The Russian mafia? Could be, but why? I doubt if this guy messed around with drugs. There's still ballistics, but this all looks so clean I'm not holding out a lot of hope."

Leaving Hartley to parrot Steve's analysis, Michael nodded without comment and checked his watch. Ray, if he hadn't fallen asleep, would be getting antsy—time to get back on patrol. "Need me for anything else?" he asked when Hartley finished.

Steve clapped a hand over Michael's shoulder. "No. Thanks for the help."

Michael nodded and headed for the door. Homicide wasn't going to solve this case. No chance. Not that anyone would care; in a few weeks probably nobody would even remember the old man.

2

Michael and Ray cruised slowly down Coney Island Avenue in the heart of Brighton Beach. The off-and-on rains of the past week had blown out to sea, leaving in their wake a beautiful sunny day, which, besides the writing of a couple of traffic tickets, had been completely uneventful.

Ray shifted uncomfortably in his seat, tugging at his trousers. "Jesus, I'm getting fat," he complained. "What's this crap about pinch an inch anyway? I can pinch a good half a foot." He demonstrated on his ample stomach. "Let's start running every morning, Michael. Let's really get in shape again, like when we were rookies. What do you say?"

Michael glanced at his partner. When they started on the force they had been in terrific shape. Michael hadn't changed much. His sandy blond hair now hosted a few streaks of gray over the temples, and his face had grown leaner as the years had burned off the last traces of baby fat, but Michael took pride that at thirty-nine his stomach was still washboard tight and he could keep up with any of the rookies on the basketball court. He stood 5 feet 11 inches, but his well-muscled upper body made him appear taller. He had aged well.

Ray, on the other hand, had let himself go. A big man, six-three and large-boned, he carried more weight than even his frame could disguise. He had given up playing basketball, as well as most other forms of exercise, long ago.

Michael shook his head. "You're the one full of crap, Ray. I'd take you a bit more seriously if you didn't have a half-eaten doughnut on your lap."

Ray looked at the doughnut noncommittally, then took another bite. He didn't bother swallowing before speaking. "It's universally expected: a cop's gonna eat a doughnut now and then. I just believe in exceeding expectations."

Michael couldn't help laughing. "You deserve a medal. Too bad they don't make us old-timers run the fitness course; I'd love to see the round mound attack the wall."

"Hey, hey, hey, what's so damn funny? I could still do it. Give me a few weeks to get out the kinks, and they'd be calling me ol' greyhound O'Hern again, clearing walls in a single bound. Fucking-A right!"

Ray looked again at his stomach, and his enthusiasm ebbed. "Hell, who am I kidding? I'm getting old; we're all getting old, all the old gang. Even your brother. John must be, what thirty-three now?"

"Thirty-four."

"Shit, we all fart dust. What the hell's the use?" The last mouthful of doughnut disappeared down Ray's throat. "I saw his byline the other day."

"John's?"

"Yeah. In the *Post*. Something about the black market for food stamps. I think I've still got it if you want me to bring it in."

"Sure. Why don't you. I must have missed it."

"Kid can write," Ray added.

Michael shrugged. "I gave him some pointers."

"Now who's full of crap?"

"Okay, greyhound O'Hern." Michael chuckled. "I'll declare a draw. Now it's time to make a stop." Michael turned off Coney Island Avenue and headed east.

"What's up?"

"You remember the old man, Peter Olgov, shot in the head at the rooming house on Clayton?"

"Right, from last week. In the bathtub. What about him?"

"I talked with Steve the other day. He told me they've come up with exactly nothing so far. No prints; no leads. They're starting to wind down the investigation."

"What of it?"

"I told you about Steve's assistant, Detective Hartley, didn't I?" Michael asked.

"Right, I remember. I met him for a moment when we were leaving . . . that was enough of an introduction."

"Yeah, well he's been in charge of the investigation, but he's got his head so far up his ass I doubt if he'd know a clue if it was standing in front of him."

No points for originality, but Ray laughed obligingly nonetheless. Michael so rarely made off-color comments Ray made sure to applaud every attempt, like a parent encouraging the first stumbling steps of a child.

Michael continued. "He made it clear he didn't have much use for my help, but I might just give it to him anyway. A few tenants weren't home last week, and I'll bet he never followed up on them. It's Sunday today; they might be in."

"That's not our job, partner. We're beat cops, remember. Leave it to the dicks."

"That'd be leaving the job to Hartley, and that jerk'd never do it."

"You're talking reprimand if the dicks find out you've been messing in their turf." Ray tapped his finger on the dashboard for emphasis.

"Don't worry. If it blows up in my face, I'll take

the heat. You can stay in the car. Hell, I'm just doing the job the way it's supposed to be done."

"And it'd be awful fun to come up with something to throw in Hartley's face, wouldn't it?"

"That too," Michael acknowledged.

"Okay, partner, but stop by Tony's on the way. If I'm gonna have to sit in the car by my lonesome, might as well have a slice or two of Brooklyn's best to keep me company."

Michael just smiled.

The rooming house on Clayton looked worse in daylight—the graffiti, broken windows, and chipped paint no longer obscured by darkness. Ray waited in the car with two slices of pizza while Michael went in.

The desk clerk, the same one on duty last week, recognized him and appeared surprised, almost jittery, Michael thought. The clerk wasn't sure, but thought the residents of rooms three, five, and twelve, the ones gone last week, might be in today.

Michael proceeded alone up the narrow dark stairs.

Room three turned out to be occupied by a crusty old man who showed only his head and shoulders around the edge of a half-closed door. The teeth he still had were stained cigarette yellow, and when he haltingly answered Michael's questions with a pronounced Russian accent, a small line of drool started from the corner of his mouth. Michael smelled the anesthetic odor of alcohol on his breath.

Yes, he knew of the murder. No, he didn't know the man personally. Yes, he had seen him a few times, but that was all. No, he hadn't seen or heard a thing. No, he lived alone and he knew nothing else and wanted to get back to the television show he was watching, and with that started to shut the door. Michael didn't stop him.

A young couple, in their early thirties Michael

guessed, answered the door of room five. They left Russia a little under a year ago, Michael discovered, but when Michael started speaking Russian, they stopped him. They were in America now, they said, and must learn to speak English if they were to get ahead. They had heard of the shooting and wished to help, unfortunately they knew nothing about Olgov. They were, however, more than happy to question Michael about the murder—were there any leads? who did he think did it and why? why was America such a violent place? Michael soon left.

An older woman, in her mid to late sixties, opened the door of room twelve after asking to see Michael's badge through the peephole. Michael said he was investigating the shooting of the man in room eight, and the old lady invited him in.

The woman's room was the first that looked livable, almost cozy in fact. Cheap and sparse furniture, but spotless. All the old lady touches: frilly drapes, embroidered tablecloths, small ceramic statues of dogs and cats, oval-framed pictures of probably long dead relatives. An oasis of care.

The old lady, Mrs. Banovich, spoke excellent English. "I was shocked when I heard. Shocked. I've put a double lock on my door since it happened and don't open it up for anybody . . . except you of course, officer."

Michael waited patiently for an opportunity to break in with questions, but it didn't come as Mrs. Banovich continued to recount her safety precautions and every incident of robbery or theft affecting her or her friends in the last dozen years. Finally, she got around to the victim.

"Oh, I knew Mr. Olgov, not well mind you, but as well as anybody here I guess. Once every month for the last year and a half or so, on a Sunday, he would join me here for dinner. Said I cooked the old-country dishes just like his mother used to."

"What can you tell me about him?"

She paused, cupping her hand over her mouth and looking past him. "Just bits and pieces, really," she said, finally. "Things he talked about: Tambonezh, his hometown in Russia; the beautiful winters; ice skating; the smell of cut hay. Memories from his youth."

"How about the present?"

"Rarely came up."

Michael cocked his head.

"I think he preferred the past," Mrs. Banovich explained. "It must have been a happier time. That's why I really can't tell you much about him. I have pictures, though, from his childhood—would you like to see?"

Michael started to shake his head, but Mrs. Banovich charged off to the bedroom without waiting for a response. She returned with an old wooden box, about the size of a shoe box, full of photographs.

"These are his. He would bring them up to dinner now and then to show me. He never tired of looking at them. He brought the box up, oh, maybe three Sundays ago I think, and left it. I really don't know what to do with it now . . . I suppose you should take it. He never spoke of any family, but maybe somebody will show up to collect his things."

Mrs. Banovich pulled the first photograph from the box and passed it to Michael.

Time to end this. Michael had thought the old lady would come back with a couple of pictures, not a shoe box full. "M'am, I'd like to go through these with you, but I'm afraid I just don't have the time. My partner's waiting for me downstairs, and we're due on another call. Just a few more questions, okay?"

She nodded soberly. "Of course, officer."

He asked the questions, but Mrs. Banovich really

didn't seem to know much about Olgov beyond his childhood days in Russia. She had seen and heard nothing, could think of no motive for the murder, and confirmed Olgov to be of limited means, whose only employment was as a part-time dishwasher in a nearby restaurant. Hartley hadn't missed much by failing to follow up.

Michael rose to leave and Mrs. Banovich opened the door for him, wooden box in hand.

"Please take these, officer. He might have family."

Michael waved her off, but she persisted. "He told me these pictures were worth a fortune to him, the most important possessions he had. They mean so little to me in comparison."

Michael had hoped to escape without the photographs, but resistance, he saw, would be wasted effort. He took the box and promised to deliver it to the proper hands, which he knew would be a dusty shelf in the basement of precinct headquarters, where it would sit for a time before being incinerated.

The desk clerk heard the good-byes through the thin wooden door and scurried down the hall with his broom. He was sweeping at the other end of the hall when Michael exited the apartment.

Michael stared in his direction, but the desk clerk kept his head down, avoiding Michael's eyes, and in a moment Michael started down the stairs. The clerk waited until he heard the front door open and close, then hurried to an old rotary dial telephone mounted on the wall.

3

Michael slid the key into the lock and twisted. Tumblers clicked quietly.

He turned the knob. A gentle push and the door swung open. Before proceeding, he listened. All clear, the only sound a radio playing in the next room. He noiselessly shut the door behind him, refixed the lock, then moved forward carefully, planning each footfall to avoid betrayal by a creaky floorboard. He stopped when he saw the woman in the kitchen.

She was slicing vegetables with her back to him. Young, early thirties; about five feet six inches tall; slim build; shoulder-length brown hair pulled back from her face in a ponytail. She wore sweat pants, a polo shirt, and running shoes.

He ducked behind the wall separating the dining room from the kitchen and tightened his grip on the gun in his right hand. A clear shot from ten feet away, he couldn't have asked for more. Deciding on a head shot, he aimed the gun carefully, his hand rock-steady. His face betrayed no remorse as he pulled the trigger.

Kelly jumped as a stream of water hit the back of her head. She turned quickly, startled, but saw nothing behind her. She examined the ceiling. Nothing dripping. She stood still a few moments, alternately feeling the wet spot on her head and looking at the ceiling. Finally, she shrugged and resumed slicing vegetables.

Almost immediately water again sprayed the back of her head.

She spun—nothing. She rubbed her right temple, confusion clear on her face. Suddenly, her eyebrows arched. A glance at her watch and her mouth turned up at the corners. She filled a glass a quarter full of water, turned, and waited.

Sporting a huge grin on the other side of the wall, Michael barely restrained laughter building deep in his chest—nothing made him happier than reverting to childhood. He would let Kelly puzzle a while longer, then fire again. How long would this continue? Would he have to fill the squirt gun at the bathroom down the hall before she finally caught on?

After a long minute, gun raised, Michael peeked around the corner. He was greeted by a glass of water to the face.

Kelly darted off. Michael caught up with her in the living room, cornered her between the couch and an end chair, and scooped her into his arms. She laughed uncontrollably.

"Serves you right," she managed after catching her breath.

Michael sputtered once in reply, then carried her resolutely down the hall. Not until he turned into the bathroom did Kelly realize what he planned.

"No, Michael . . . really. Come on, put me down." She clutched ineffectually at the door frame as they passed into the bathroom. "This isn't fair. I've got my watch on . . . my good watch."

Michael ignored her and stepped into the shower stall. "You have five seconds to take your watch off, that's all. One . . . two . . ."

"C'mon Michael, let me go, this isn't funny!" Three kicks with no results.

"Three . . . four . . ."

"No, Michael. Please . . . I'm going to get mad."

"Five." Michael bent to turn on the water.

"All right, here's my watch," Kelly said, quickly stripping it off.

"Better toss it out, time's up."

She tossed the watch onto the bathroom rug as Michael turned the faucets.

When the cold spray hit her, Kelly let loose a barrage of invectives; Michael's response was not what she intended—he laughed.

"Look at me," she sulked, hitting him weakly on the chest. "You attacked me first . . . a surprise attack! I simply defended myself . . . and now look at me!" She faked a pout, but couldn't hold it long. It spread to a wide grin.

Michael hugged her to him and buried his head in her shoulder. Wet sweats, wet hair, sputtering for breath, and she still looked beautiful. He turned his back to shelter her from the shower. "You look pretty good to me. Real good, in fact," he murmured as he nibbled at her neck.

"Oh no, you don't. I'm getting out. I was in the middle of preparing dinner."

"Perhaps I can convince you to let that wait a bit." His teeth found her earlobe.

"Not in this freezing water you can't."

Michael set Kelly down, but kept one arm firmly locked around her waist. His free hand spun the hot water faucet. "How's that?" he asked, steam beginning to rise.

"Better," she said, grinning mischievously, her index finger tracing the line of buttons on his shirt. "Now exactly how did you plan to convince me, Mr. Sarikov?"

"First, I thought I'd help you out of those wet clothes," he whispered hoarsely, the scent of her, taste of her, intoxicating.

"Then you'll explain?" she whispered back.

"Exactly."

Kelly shrugged. "I suppose it's the least you could do."

Michael hiked Kelly's polo shirt slowly up over her shoulders, head, and up-stretched arms. Her lean, well-toned body shivered reflexively. Michael moved her directly under the hot spray, and the goose bumps on her shoulders soon melted away under his caresses. He untied the draw string to her sweat pants, slid them to her ankles, and pulled each foot free. His fingers trailed lightly against the back of her legs as he straightened, then he pulled her to him.

"My turn," said Kelly as she unbuttoned Michael's shirt and stripped it from him. Her hand followed the matted chest hair that disappeared in a thin line down his pants. She peeled down his jeans and let them drop to the shower floor. He stepped out of them and kicked them aside.

Kelly rubbed a bar of soap between her hands, producing a thick lather. She knelt and began cleaning him, starting at his feet, taking her time. His breath came hard; he lost himself gradually as thought succumbed to sensation, and finally to urgency.

Long after Kelly had slipped from the shower, Michael remained under its spray, his eyes closed, luxuriating in the warmth, glad to have this wife, this house, this life, to come home to.

After dinner and a nighttime stroll, Michael grabbed a beer and sat down in the den with the box of photographs the old woman had given him. Kelly sat on his lap and planted a kiss on his forehead. "What have you got there?" she asked, pointing to the box.

"Work, sort of."

"What do you mean?"

Michael told Kelly about Mrs. Banovich and, leaving out the gorier details, the old man, Peter Olgov.

"Sounds sad," she said.

"Yeah, I thought so, too. It's as if these photographs are all that's left of his life. Dreams, hopes, memories, just junk now. Nobody wants them. Made me think of Dad."

Kelly kissed him again on the forehead. "Want to talk about it?"

"No. You know all about Dad. It was just . . . seeing that rooming house, seeing the way the old man lived, it brought back memories. Kind of put me in a melancholy mood."

Kelly rubbed Michael's shoulders for a few moments in silence. "I'm going to bed. You coming?"

"Not yet. Just want to glance through these." Michael gestured toward the photographs.

"Okay. Don't stay up too late."

"I won't hon'. Call me when you get under the covers and I'll tuck you in."

Tucking Kelly in amounted to more kissing than tucking, after which Michael returned to the den. He wasn't sure what to do with the photos; probably shouldn't have accepted them in the first place. There didn't seem to be any relatives to give them to, and the police evidence room certainly wouldn't want them. Maybe he should keep them if for no other reason than respect for an old man's life. His father had left no childhood photos from Russia; these could be surrogates.

The photos were old black-and-whites, dog-eared at the corners—looked at many times. He took the first from the box, held it up reverently. A family: a young man and a woman with a small child, perhaps Olgov as a baby. He set the photo on the table and picked out the next.

There were photos of a small drab house, a colorless village, and oxen pulling wagons with large wooden wheels; photos of a wedding attended by a small boy dressed in shorts and a vest; and more photos of the same boy at various ages surrounded by, Michael guessed, his relatives: elderly men and women with wide toothless grins and dark eyes wrapped in deep wrinkles.

When Michael finished, he sipped the last of his beer and stared blankly at the wall. He thought of his parents, and of the grandparents he never knew, and how different his life would have been if his mother and father had not jumped a freighter for Finland and from there to Sweden and on to America. Hard to imagine—the lifestyle captured on film appeared so alien.

He restacked the photos, lifted up the empty box to replace them, and heard a dull thud. Something within the box had slid from side to side. A glance inside confirmed it was empty, but another shake again brought the muffled thud. There was definitely something hidden inside.

Michael placed his hand against an interior side of the box. The depth ran from his fingertips three-quarters of the way up his palm. The outside depth ran at least an inch and a half farther, more than the thickness of the wooden bottom would account for.

His curiosity aroused, he examined the box closely. Two screws on each end caught his attention—they served no apparent purpose. He went to the kitchen, rummaged through a drawer clogged with old coupons, pencil stubs, and matchbooks, and returned to the den with a screwdriver. With the four screws removed, he turned the box upside down. A firm shake and the bottom, a false bottom, fell free and clattered onto the floor. Another stack of photographs followed.

Michael had expected to find old documents, money, or jewelry, not more photographs. He picked up the stack and removed the rubber band around its middle. The photos, a stack about a quarter inch high, were old, gray, and faded, like the others, but the corners were flat—they had not been handled often. The first one was of a proud young man in a Russian military uniform. Michael was pretty sure he recognized the young man from the other photos—Olgov, in his early twenties at the time, Michael guessed. The young man in the photo appeared capable and confident; he would have been shocked to know what fate had in store for him.

Why had Olgov hidden these photos? Michael wondered. To keep his military service a secret? Understandable—neither U.S. immigration officials nor Russian expatriates regarded the Russian military highly.

The next photo was of a Russian officer—young, wearing glasses, a soft face and weak chin.

Michael was not expecting the following photo. He'd seen similar pictures in books and on television, but in his living room, on a three-by-five print, the unsettling impact was magnified. Two men clung to a barbed wire fence, staring into the camera lens. Their eyes haunting, sunk deep within hollowed-out sockets. Bones in their faces and arms clearly defined, wrapped by a taut sheath of skin. Skeletons clinging to life, loosely clothed in threadbare pants and pullovers with vertical blue-gray stripes.

A concentration camp.

Michael's chest tightened involuntarily. He turned the photo over and looked at the next. A barracks, if that term could apply to the pictured wall of dark shelflike compartments, the floor of each covered with a thin layer of hay. Six faces, all alike, sunken eyes and shaved heads, stared at him from within two of the compartments. One man's face, circled with a red marker, demanded Michael's attention. In the foreground stood a soldier in uniform—*Olgov*.

No wonder Olgov had kept the photos hidden. Michael's estimation of the man turned from pity to disgust.

The next photo showed what looked to be the main gate of the camp and proved Michael had judged too swiftly. Three words were posted over the entrance: "Arbeit Macht Frei." Michael knew the meaning: "Work will make you free." A Nazi concentration camp slogan.

History had always been one of his stronger subjects. He knew the Russians had liberated most of the Nazi concentration camps of Eastern Europe in the final months of World War II. Olgov, then, was not a jailer, but a *liberator*. The things he must have seen. The Nazis had tried to destroy the haunting evidence, but the Red Army's advance had come too rapidly. They rolled into the camps, shocked by what they found—surviving inmates, the walking dead, mere shadows, and worse, the actual dead, piled beside sheds of shoes, spectacles and hair the Nazis had run out of time to burn. And Olgov was there.

A man, from the waist up, in the next photo. Michael thought he recognized the man and flipped back two photos, to the one of the barracks and the face circled in red—the same face, he confirmed. In this photo the man stood, barely, against a barbed wire fence, overwhelmed by a ratty prison uniform that perhaps once fit, but now appeared many sizes too large. Michael could clearly make out a tattoo on the man's forearm. A number, a brand, like cattle.

Michael flipped the photo over, prepared to proceed to the next, when its back caught his eye. Written there, in blue ink: "Jacob Greene," and beneath that, a telephone number with a seven-one-eight area code—the Bronx, Brooklyn, Queens, or Staten Island.

The possibilities shot through Michael's mind. Was Jacob Greene a Holocaust survivor? Had Olgov kept in contact with him? Had an enduring bond formed between this Jacob Greene, a survivor, and Peter Olgov, a liberator?

Four more photos. The prisoner circled in red, Michael could now recognize him, was in the first three. He recoiled at the last. A pile of bodies, worn-out forms deprived of their final dignity. A jumble of torsos, arms, and legs with hips, elbows, and knee joints the most discernible feature.

The box contained one more thing: a newspaper clipping, dated 1974, from the *New York Times*. "Dinner for Holocaust Survivors to be Held," the caption read. The short article announced the dinner and listed the honorees: Holocaust survivors from the New York State area. Michael scanned the list for Jacob Greene's name, but didn't find it.

Michael thought of his younger brother. John always looked for the offbeat, the story that required a little digging—he might be interested. A young, proud Russian soldier, a liberator of a concentration camp, a lifelong friendship with a camp survivor, a gray, wasted life in America ending in a rooming-house bathtub. Perhaps Olgov's story deserved to be told.

He looked again at the telephone number of Jacob Greene and wondered if it was current. One sure way to find out—call the number in the morning.

Michael restacked the photos and set them back in the box. He would keep them—there was nothing here for the evidence room. He finished his beer and headed for the bedroom, hoping the photos wouldn't follow and haunt his dreams.

4

Pavel poured himself his fifth cup of coffee of the night; there would be more before morning. He arched his spine and stretched. His back was killing him—a product of the cramped quarters, though nearing fifty didn't help, he supposed. No room to stand up in the damn van, and he'd already been cooped up in it for six hours. Pissing in a coffee can, helluva way to spend a night.

Pavel's partner, Rolf, a pair of earphones on his head, aimed a parabolic dish with a pistol grip out of the van's window at the Sarikovs' bedroom window. He played with a dial on the compact piece of electronics.

The listening device functioned without the need to physically plant a bug. The principle was simple: sound waves in a room caused windowpanes to vibrate, the parabolic dish recorded the vibrations, and a receiver translated the vibrations back into sound. Given the means, reception was remarkably clear.

Rolf took off his earphones and put down the dish; he hadn't heard anything since the cop went to bed over an hour ago. "Looks like no more showers tonight," he announced. "Too bad."

Pavel didn't laugh; he found his younger partner wholly unfunny, and disturbing in a way he couldn't put his finger on. He checked his watch; his orders were to call no matter what the time. He picked up a cellular phone with an encrypted scrambler and dialed a number. After four rings, a curt "hello" sounded over the line. Pavel followed standard intelligence procedure and asked for Vasili. He, Rolf, Vasili, each had covers, other identities by which neighbors, utility companies, friends, even, in the case of Vasili, the news media, knew them. Pavel knew Vasili's deep cover name, but didn't use it—that someone could intercept the call was unlikely, not impossible.

Vasili picked up the phone a moment later. There were no pleasantries.

"It's Pavel. The cop's gone to sleep."

"He still has the box?" Despite his age, Vasili's voice still held power and authority.

"Yes."

"You've learned what it contains?"

"Family photographs." Pavel took pleasure in reporting this. He had, after all, questioned Olgav in person. If the box had contained anything other than family photographs, he would have had a lot to answer for.

"How do you know?" Vasili demanded.

"That's what the cop told his wife."

"The wife looked at the photos?"

"No, she went to bed; he stayed up and looked through them alone."

There was a momentary pause. "So we don't know *for sure* whether or not he found anything else?"

"No. Not for sure." But if you would have been there, Pavel thought, and seen the way Olgov spilled his guts, you would know he told us everything.

Vasili fired another question. "Has the cop contacted anybody?"

"No. No calls, no visitors."

The line fell silent again. Pavel knew better than to break the silence—Vasili wasn't one to hold conversations; he gave orders.

Vasili's voice came, finally, slow and forceful. "Stay the night. I want constant surveillance, understand?"

Overly cautious, it seemed to Pavel, but he didn't argue. "Yes, sir."

"Perhaps he doesn't have what we're looking for, but we won't take any chances. You and Rolf have prepared contingency plans as I requested?"

"Yes." Pavel went on to outline the plan. Vasili interrupted repeatedly, questioning assumptions, raising contingencies.

"Adequate," Vasili granted when Pavel finished. "Call me in the morning after the cop wakes."

The line went dead without a farewell. Pavel set the receiver back on its base.

A long, cold night in cramped quarters to look forward to. No use complaining—Pavel had done it many times before. He filled in Rolf, then volunteered to take the first shift. Rolf would relieve him at three A.M. Sipping his coffee, he stared, rarely blinking, at the Sarikov house.

5

Michael had a hard time sleeping—the concentration camp pictures filled his thoughts. He tossed during much of the night, drifting off late, two or three in the morning.

When he woke at six-thirty, feeling decidedly unrested, Kelly was already up. He followed the smell of coffee to the kitchen.

"What are you doing up so early?" Michael asked.

"Morning, honey." Kelly sat at the kitchen table with the morning paper. Her day as a schoolteacher normally didn't begin until eight. She rose and pecked him on the cheek. "Don't you remember? Teachers' meeting, got to be in an hour early. I didn't want to wake you; you were sleeping like a rock."

"Yeah, finally. I didn't sleep all that well last night, kept waking up."

"Poor baby." She ran her fingers once through his hair. "Anything bothering you?"

Michael recounted his discovery of the box's false bottom and the photos hidden underneath.

"That's really strange," she said.

"I thought so too, but it gets stranger. The photos? They were of a concentration camp."

"From World War II?"

"Yeah. Nazi camps . . . and inmates. Some pretty graphic. They didn't help my sleep."

Kelly paused for a moment, then moved to the dishwasher and loaded her coffee cup. "I was about to say I'd like to see the photos, but actually I'm not so sure I would."

Michael nodded. He grew up enjoying suspense and horror films, but gave them up on marrying Kelly. She had nightmares. No matter how far-fetched or how unrealistic a film, she woke the next morning complaining of dreams. If the photos had affected even his sleep . . .

Michael took a seat at the kitchen table and switched the subject. "I'm thinking of giving John a call. There might be a story here."

"Good idea . . . say hi from me. And remind him about Sunday. How about pasta with seafood: shrimp, calamari, and scallops? Think John would like that?"

"John likes anything you make."

Kelly smiled and gently butted her forehead against his. "Jealous?"

A private joke. Michael started cooking for his father and John at the age of nine. Nobody assigned him the task, it just wasn't being done. Sometimes his father would think to buy groceries, more often not, so Michael took over that responsibility as well. He begged his father for money, searched his pockets for lose change, and somehow scraped up enough for meals. But it wasn't pasta with seafood; most of the time it was awful. They laughed about it now. John loved to recount famous Michael creations, usually containing potatoes, cut-up hot dogs for special occasions. Whenever Michael and Kelly invited John over for a meal, John playfully insisted on one rule: Kelly cooked or he stayed home.

Michael faked a frown. "Hell, yes, I'm jealous. Almost twenty years now and he hasn't given me the chance to redeem myself."

Kelly laughed, then kissed him. "Look, I've got to run; I'm a little late already."

"Okay hon', I'll see you tonight."

Michael sat unmoving in his chair, sipping coffee well after Kelly left. The Brooklyn phone book lay to his side, and on impulse he flipped to the G's, curious to see if a Jacob Greene was listed. A half page of "Greenes," none with the first name "Jacob," but some with the first initial "J." He left for the den, returning with the photo with Jacob Greene's name and telephone number on its back. The eyes of the man were still haunting, even in the light of morning.

Michael ran down the telephone numbers of the dozen or so "J. Greenes," and, unexpectedly, matched the number from the photo's back. His heartbeat accelerated. A short time ago unreal and unimaginable, the photo was now firmly linked to the present.

The questions of last night returned. How had photos from a World War II concentration camp found their way into Olgov's possession? Why were they hidden? Were the camp prisoner pictured and the Jacob Greene living in Brooklyn one and the same? Curiosity bit.

Michael reached for the phone, but hesitated before lifting the receiver. What did he plan to say: "Hi, I was wondering if you were ever in a concentration camp?" The wall clock provided an excuse to delay— pretty early to engage a complete stranger in conversation. He decided to give himself a few minutes to put his thoughts in order; meanwhile he'd wake his brother—an old tradition.

In some ways John Sarikov looked like a younger version of Michael. Perhaps a little less rugged, a little leaner, maybe an inch shorter. His hair was also sandy blond, but without the streaks of gray. Like Michael, blue eyes framed by heavy eyelids and high broad cheekbones provided his face's focal point. Broad shoulders and well-toned muscles were a product of regular weight lifting, a habit continued from years past when he tagged along with Michael and his friends to local gyms.

What distinguished the two brothers wasn't as easy to specify. Maybe it was in their facial expressions, maybe in the way they carried themselves. John seemed aloof and guarded, while Michael was an open book—what you saw was what you got.

John heard the phone ring first in his dreams, then Barbara nudged his shoulder and he realized he would have to answer it. Pushing aside the clutter on the bedside table, he glanced at the clock through half-closed eyes.

"What time is it?" Barbara asked, groggily.

"Six forty-five."

"Your brother," Barbara said, shaking her head, her eyes still shut. "Believe it or not, once upon a time I actually slept past seven on a regular basis."

John mussed Barbara's hair without comment. Michael was his only family. At times the early calls could be a bit of a nuisance, but then brothers were entitled to be a nuisance now and then. When John was young, Michael would put him in a head lock or give him a jab on the arm, now he called at six forty-five—it was the same thing. The day Michael started calling later would be the day John worried they were drifting apart.

John picked up the phone. "Hello."

"Rise and shine, bro, rise and shine. You're going to miss the best part of the day."

The same line, every time. Oddly comforting, this one disturbance he could count on. "Speak for yourself. I've been up for hours," John lied unconvincingly in a gravelly voice.

"Yeah, right. It's about time you got on a decent schedule. Kelly and I've already jogged our five miles."

More than likely true, John realized. When they were young, Michael used to make him run in the mornings. Would run behind, egging him on. Two miles, three miles, along Brighton Beach's boardwalk. Now Kelly ran with him. "Good for you two. I'm about to limp to the coffee maker and might make it as far as the medicine cabinet for an aspirin."

"No wonder you always sound worn out."

"Couldn't have anything to do with the hour, could it? Six forty-five, all of five hours after Barbara and I hit the sack?"

"Tell Barbara hi if she's awake."

John set the phone on his chest. "Michael says hi."

"Ugghh," Barbara groaned and wrapped a pillow around her head.

John got back on the phone, smiling. "Barbara thanks you and wishes you all the best. She can't tell you how much she appreciates your early morning calls."

Michael laughed. John shared it as he curled the fingers of his free hand in Barbara's short brown hair.

"What's going on with you?" John asked.

"Nothing, same old stuff, busting crack rings, shoot-outs, that kind of thing."

"Right."

Barbara said he and Michael never really talked. She said they cracked jokes and laughed, but didn't know the first thing about what really happened in each other's life. He supposed she was right, but it didn't bother him. Maybe, in fact, that was one of the best things about his and Michael's relationship: it didn't matter what was going on, only that they were always there for each other—a constant.

"We still set for Sunday?" Michael asked.

"Barbara and I'll be there, if she forgives you by then. What do you want me to bring?"

"How about a bottle of white wine; we'll have the

rest. Oh yeah, I might have something for you when you come . . . something you might want to look into."

"What?"

"Came across it yesterday. A story with an unhappy ending; some powerful photos. Human interest. Could be pretty good. I'll tell you about it Sunday."

"Couldn't I just write about the crack rings and shoot-outs?"

Michael laughed again. "I'll tell you about those too."

After comparing the relative merits of the New York Giants and New York Jets, they hung up.

John snuggled against Barbara's sleeping form, kissing her neck until she stirred and began to softly grind her hips into his.

"Perhaps I can convince you my brother's early morning calls aren't all bad," John whispered.

She stretched, catlike, and whispered in return: "You can certainly try."

After talking to John, Michael's mind again focused on Olgov's photos. He glanced at the clock on the wall: almost seven, still early. He could wait until he got to the precinct—or, hell, why not now. Ask for Jacob Greene, wing it from there and satisfy his curiosity.

Michael dialed the number and waited. After the fifth ring a man answered, startling Michael. Somehow he hadn't expected anyone to answer the number, a relic of the past as old as the photos, as dead as the old man in the bathtub.

"Is . . . is Jacob Greene there?" Michael asked.

"This is he," a raspy voice with a German accent answered.

Michael's mind went momentarily blank. Should he say he was calling in connection with a murder investigation, or tell the truth: the real reason for the call was haunting photographs that had stuck with him through the night.

Michael fell back on his official role and instantly regretted the defensive posture it forced Greene into.

"Mr. Greene, sorry to bother you so early. My name's Officer Sarikov. I'm with the New York City Police Department, and I have a few questions I'd like to ask you."

"Police? . . . I have done nothing."

"I know you haven't, sir. It's in regard to one of our investigations. Your name has come up."

"How would my name come up in an investigation?" Greene asked. "I have done nothing. There has been some mistake."

"No one is accusing you of anything, sir. Just a few simple questions."

The line fell silent, and then, "What do you want to know?"

"A man, an old man, died about a week ago. He had your name written down among his things. His name was Peter Olgov. Did you know him?"

The line went silent again, the pause uncomfortably long this time. Michael could hear heavy breathing on the line.

"I said have you ever heard of a Peter Olgov?" Michael repeated.

"What did you say your name was?"

Greene's voice sounded all at once cautious—*why?* "Officer Michael Sarikov."

"You are a police officer?"

"That's right."

"And you work out of what precinct?"

"Brighton Beach."

"And your badge number?"

"It is a simple question, sir, do you know this man or not?"

"I have been told to always get the badge number of anyone who says they are a police officer."

Michael impatiently read off his badge number. *"Now,* do you know this man, Mr. Greene?"

"No . . . no, that name is not familiar. I do not recognize it."

After twenty years on the force Michael had a pretty good idea when someone was holding back, and this guy was far from smooth. He decided to throw out some additional information and gauge Greene's reaction. "Peter Olgov had your name and phone number written down on the back of a photograph . . . a photograph of a Nazi concentration camp prisoner . . ." Michael heard Greene's quick intake of breath. "Why do you think he would write down the name and number of a stranger?"

"How should I know? I tell you, the name is not familiar. I do not know the man. And now I must go. Do you have other questions for me?"

Before the last question Greene sounded evasive; after it Michael sensed fear. *What was he hiding?* Something strange too—Greene hadn't asked questions. Innocent people always do. They might ask about the photo, or about Olgov. Who was he? Was he wanted by the police? Why had he written down their name and number? Was he dangerous? Someone who vigorously denied allegations without questioning circumstances usually did so for a simple reason—they had no questions. They knew all the answers already.

"I don't have any further questions for you at this time, Mr. Greene, but someone else from the department may give you a call."

The prospect of further questioning seemed to alarm Greene. "Ja, ja, ja, but I will be able to tell no more. I have told you everything . . . I do not know this man. Now, if there is nothing more . . ."

"That's all for now."

"Then good day, officer."

The line went silent and Michael let the receiver drop from his ear. The call surprised him—not at all what he had expected. Greene was lying; he knew Peter Olgov, Michael would bet on it. The "why" wasn't as obvious. More than likely just an old man afraid of getting involved, but then again there might be other, darker, explanations for the old man's fear. One way or the other, before Michael passed this story on to John, Greene would have to be checked out.

Michael copied down Jacob Greene's name and telephone number on a scrap of paper. He'd pass it on to Hartley; questioned in person, Michael had a hunch Greene would come clean.

He stuck the photograph in the phone book, marking the page with Greene's listing, then started for the bedroom to get dressed.

6

Vasili, his wrinkled, pale face and thin legs standing out in sharp contrast to the purple silk robe he wore, pushed the omelet away. His mind kept drifting toward the time, robbing him of his appetite. He checked his watch—still early. They'd call when they knew something. He picked up the *Wall Street Journal* folded to the side of his plate and tried, unsuccessfully, to digest the morning's news.

His eyes drifted above the paper, toward the sculpture garden and pool in the back lawn, but remained unfocused. He pulled the thick-lensed glasses from his face, hooked a stem over his lower lip, and reviewed the facts. Olgov's threats had been specific. He said he had evidence he could send to the police, the papers. A lie? Perhaps, but a voice somewhere inside him beat out an alarm. That would have been a huge bluff for so small a man.

After fifty years, that this should surface now, of all times. It could not, *must not,* disrupt his plans.

The cellular phone to his side rang, and he reached for it impatiently. "Yes?" he answered.

Pavel's voice, serious, careful: "Our policeman's been up for a half hour . . . We may have trouble."

Of course we do. My voice has been telling me that it is not over, not yet. "What?"

"He may have stumbled onto something. Someone we thought dead and gone."

"Am I supposed to guess?" Vasili asked, irritated and sarcastic.

"Of course not; I apologize. It is just that the news is somewhat hard to accept. Olgov told us he had evidence . . . hard evidence he could take to the newspapers. Besides his word, we didn't know what he had. It's possible Olgov's evidence was more damaging than we ever imagined. The Jew may still be alive."

Vasili jolted upright in his chair. He knew instantly to whom Pavel referred. *The Jew, still alive?* His first thought was no, impossible, the Jew had died long ago. *Or had he?* Doubt crept in with his next thought: Olgov could have been a traitor even back then. If Olgov had disobeyed orders, the Jew could have been spared.

"How do you know?" Vasili demanded.

"I don't, not for sure, but Sarikov just called a telephone number he found among Olgov's things, from the box he removed from the rooming house. He talked to a Jacob Greene."

Jacob Greene—Vasili considered the name. Yes, the similarity was obvious. *Could he have been hiding here all these years?* First Olgov, now the Jew.

Pavel continued. "We recorded the number Sarikov called. It's in Brooklyn."

"What did they say?"

"Sarikov asked Greene if he knew Peter Olgov. Greene said no."

"Perhaps your conclusion is hasty, then."

"My gut tells me Greene lied. I think he knew Olgov, and my guess is Sarikov thinks so too."

"Let's assume your *gut* is correct," Vasili said impatiently. "I still don't follow your logic. Why do you think Greene and the Jew are one and the same?"

Another pause, then Pavel's voice, humble now: "I told you last night the box Sarikov removed from Olgov's rooming house had family photographs in it.

This morning Sarikov told his wife he found a false bottom to the box. He discovered more photographs underneath . . . of a concentration camp."

Pavel's orders had been to find Olgov's evidence, destroy it, then eliminate Olgov. Vasili's formidable temper began to flare. Pavel had failed him badly. "Olgov's evidence?"

"I would assume so."

Time enough later to deal with Pavel. "Go on," he said.

Pavel quickly continued. "Greene's name and telephone number were on the back of one of the photographs . . . of a prisoner."

Then it *was* possible. After fifty years, why were things unraveling? He leaned forward in his chair and balanced his massive head on the first two fingers of his left hand. "I see. Troubling. It seems we may have another loose end to deal with . . . first Olgov, now this Greene."

"I'm afraid so."

"What about Sarikov, what does he know?"

"Hard to say. He's seen the pictures, but what can they mean to him? I think he understands little, if anything at all. He did, however, warn Greene to expect further questioning. If Greene is the Jew, and Sarikov gets him to talk . . ."

"Then we must make sure Greene talks to no one. Do I make myself clear?"

"Yes."

"Now tell me again, everything you overheard, beginning with last night. I want to know what Sarikov has learned, what his wife knows, what his partner knows." As Pavel spoke, Vasili plotted possibilities. This time *all* risks must be neutralized. With Greene there was no question what must be done. Sarikov, his wife and partner? Vasili had yet to decide.

Vasili stopped Pavel's monologue abruptly. "Repeat that," he ordered.

"I said Sarikov called his brother, some sort of writer, maybe a reporter. Said he had a story for him, a human interest story, with pictures. That's it—he didn't go into detail on the phone, but I'm pretty sure he meant Olgov's photographs."

The decision had suddenly become self-evident. Damaging or not, he couldn't take the chance of the photos falling into the hands of the newspapers. "Most unfortunate for Officer Sarikov. Is there anything else?"

"No."

"Sarikov is still at home?"

"Yes. He's showering. I'd guess he'll be leaving for work soon."

"Your recommendation?"

There was a pause on the line. "We investigate Greene's background, and if we determine—"

"No," Vasili interrupted harshly. "Greene will be dealt with this morning. Continue."

Pavel's voice faltered momentarily. "The wife, brother, and partner are extremely low risk. Higher risk to take them out."

"And Sarikov?"

"He may be a significant risk, but he's also a New York City police officer. I'd suggest polling the Collegium."

Vasili held his anger in check. *Inane, Pavel. Inane.* "Then five hours from now, after I've polled the members, after Sarikov has made it to his precinct and talked, I'll be ready to take action. The only problem will be by that time the matter will be completely out of my control. No. I will act now, while I'm still able."

"Sir, I understand your concerns, but I respectfully suggest a decision of this magnitude be left to the Collegium."

The knuckles of Vasili's right hand went white as he tightened his grip on the receiver. Vasili knew what was happening to the organization. Since the USSR's collapse, the power structure had shifted. The new leaders of Russia had stripped many old-line KGB officers of their rank and position within intelligence. In the resulting chaos the legitimacy of rank was not as clear as it once was, nor was the certainty of swift punishment for disobedience. But the agents under his direct control *would* follow orders unquestioningly. Now more than ever that was imperative. "I repeat: by the time I consulted the Collegium the damage would be done. That can not be allowed. *No one* must learn of the Jew."

"Others may not agree. And it may not be the Jew. I feel it is my duty to—"

"Your duty," Vasili barked, "is to obey orders. There is no time to consult the others, *period.* If it is not the Jew, it will not be the first time an innocent man has been sacrificed for our cause. I have decided. There will be no further discussion. *Do you understand?"*

". . . Yes," Pavel answered meekly.

"Good, then let's move on to particulars."

In measured tones they discussed options until, finally, Vasili was satisfied. He then asked Pavel to hand the phone to Rolf.

Vasili had followed Rolf's performance closely over the last year. Impressive. A clear allegiance to Vasili, and strength to back it up. Given Pavel's failures, it was clear Pavel had outlived his usefulness, and would have to be dealt with severely, as a warning. Perhaps Rolf was ready to fill his shoes.

Vasili repeated his orders to Rolf, including one set of instructions for him alone.

7

Jacob Greene sat in his darkened bedroom, back to the wall, one hand curled in the gray shock of hair topping his thin, drawn face, the other clenching a glass of water that had done little to alleviate the dryness of his throat. His bare, shallow chest, coated with a fine sweat, heaved rapidly. His reaction to the phone call had been guttural, even after so many years. He had hung up panicked, locked and chained the front and back doors, closed every blind in the house, and taken refuge in the dark.

The same thought kept racing through his mind: they had tracked him down, were coming to get him— *again*. Such thoughts were ludicrous, he knew, but his heart ignored reason.

Of course he remembered Peter Olgov. How could he forget, as much as he might want to? And Olgov evidently remembered him, if the police officer who called had told the truth and was in fact a police officer. Greene couldn't take any chances—which is why he had asked for the officer's badge and precinct number. He had no intention of volunteering information about Peter Olgov to a complete stranger.

When his heart slowed, he would call the precinct and ask for this Michael Sarikov. He would check the officer's badge number, check his story, find out how much the officer knew, if anything. If the information didn't check, or he felt the officer was concealing something, he knew what he must do: run, change his name, disappear into another city, another country. He had done it before.

8

When Ray drove up to Michael's house at 7:45 A.M., Michael was already outside on the porch, waiting for him. The two car-pooled, and Ray rarely arrived on time when it was his turn to drive.

"You're late," Michael said as he hopped into the passenger seat of Ray's Chevrolet.

"Yeah. Overslept. Went over to a friend's for a small party. A few too many beers, I guess."

Michael nodded. If a party had beer, Ray could usually be counted on to have a few too many.

Ray pulled away from the curb. "What about you, do anything last night?"

"Nothing much. Spent time with Kelly. I did come across something interesting, though. Remember that box I picked up yesterday?"

"Right, from the flophouse. Fifty-fifty on cash, right buddy?"

"Sorry, no such luck." Michael proceeded to fill Ray in. "Some of the photos were sort of gruesome."

"Goddamn Krauts." Ray punctuated the statement by punching the accelerator. He drove too fast, a common affliction among cops. "I don't think we gave 'em nearly enough of an asskicking . . . the Japs either. We win the war; fifty years later they buy the world. Go figure."

Michael ignored the characteristic outbreak. "One photo had a name and number written on its back. I called the number for the heck of it. A Brooklyn number. The man I talked to sounded evasive when I mentioned the dead guy. Smelled sort of fishy. I think I'll give the number to Hartley, see if he wants to follow up."

"Watch out, partner. When Hartley and the detective boys find out you've been trespassing on their turf they'll train their sights on your ass."

"If the lead goes anywhere, they're not going to mind. Anyway, what am I supposed to do?"

Ray shook his head. "Your problem is you get bored sitting on your fanny, writing traffic tickets and drinking free coffee. You don't know how good you got it."

Ray was right; Michael was bored with his job. He still drove a beat at thirty-nine, for Christ's sake. Okay, plenty of thirty-nine-year-old cops drove black-and-whites, but he wasn't just any cop. He was intelligent and damn good at his job. He also had ideals, an attribute that had probably cost him a detective's shield thirteen years ago.

Michael had testified against a fellow police officer, a well-connected thirty-year veteran accused of brutality; the force ostracized Michael as a result. There were split-second decisions that had to be made on the street, times when following the spirit of the law took precedence over following the letter of the law. Michael understood that. Not many on the force lost sleep over some rapist or mugger being treated with less than kid gloves, but there were limits, and this cop had crossed the line repeatedly. Michael did what he had to do, broke the code of silence, and accepted the consequences.

The first time he put in for a detective's shield the department turned him down flat. Excellent test scores, some glowing recommendations, but behind the scenes: a hatchet job—memories in the department were long. He applied every year thereafter for seven years, each time with the same result, and then gave up.

"Maybe you're right," Michael conceded.

"Of course I'm right. Hey, who else in this world is lucky enough to ride around all day with a guy like me?" Ray turned momentarily to beam at Michael.

Michael smiled. "If I'm so lucky, why—" Screeching tires interrupted Michael as the car in front of them slammed on its brakes.

"Watch it, Ray!" Michael yelled, bracing his arms against the dashboard.

Ray couldn't stop in time. Their car fishtailed and plowed into the back of the car in front. The impact jerked Michael and Ray forward against their shoulder straps, but left them uninjured. Both cars came to a complete stop.

"Dammit." Ray slammed his hand on the steering wheel and turned toward Michael. "Did you see that? That *asshole* passed me, then hit his brakes." He turned off the ignition, opened the door, and stormed out, still swearing. Michael followed.

Pavel, alone in the lead car, checked his rearview mirror. The cops' car had been stopped, and he could see Rolf approaching in the van a block and a half to the rear. He stepped from the car; his dispassionate expression turned instantly angry. He yelled at Ray. *"Are you blind?* A dog ran across the street, didn't you see it? Look what you did to my car."

"Listen, buddy, look what you did to *my* car," Ray countered. "You can't just slam on your brakes . . ."

"Me? You're the one that ran into me! I want the police . . . I'll get the police."

"We *are* the police." Ray pulled out his badge, silencing Pavel momentarily.

Rolf parked the van behind Ray's car, blocking its retreat. He stepped from the vehicle and walked toward Pavel, Michael, and Ray. "Everything okay?" he asked. "Need any help?"

Michael, who had so far stayed out of the argument between Ray and the other driver, turned to the approaching man and was struck by a sense of familiarity. He couldn't remember where, but he knew him from someplace. "No . . . I think we're fine. Just a fender bender," Michael answered.

Rolf walked to Ray's car, bent over, and felt the dent on the front bumper. He returned to Michael's side and whispered as he pointed at Pavel, who once again engaged in a shouting match with Ray. "Old man screw up?" It disturbed Michael to feel the man's hot breath on his neck.

"Look here," said Pavel, evidently overhearing. "I did nothing wrong. It was his fault." Pavel pointed at Ray. "I've driven for almost thirty years and *never* had an accident . . . *never* a dent on my car, *and now look!*"

Pavel scanned the street as Rolf positioned himself behind Michael and Ray. Clear of traffic for two blocks. He shot a quick glance at Rolf, tipping his head almost imperceptibly, then turned toward his car, feigning an examination of his fender. When he turned around again, he had stopped yelling, his expression had changed—now blank and deadly serious—and he aimed a 9mm handgun in Michael's and Ray's direction.

"Don't move," Pavel ordered in a steady voice.

Michael's hand froze halfway to his service revolver as a gun muzzle pressed his spine from behind. The man from the van, he realized.

"What the hell—" Ray began before Pavel cut him off in a calm, commanding voice.

"Gentlemen, you are going on a ride with us. Don't struggle, don't yell, or . . ." Pavel shrugged.

"We won't hesitate. It would be better for you if you cooperated."

Michael felt a surge of adrenaline. His mind raced. A planned hostage situation, two armed men. *Why?* He looked toward Ray, who trembled slightly, his faced drained white. In contrast, Michael felt no fear, not yet anyway.

"What do you want?" Michael demanded.

"Later we answer questions, now we take a ride," Pavel answered.

Michael detected a bit of accent. Eastern European, perhaps.

Pavel frisked Michael and Ray quickly and expertly, removing their service revolvers while Rolf covered them. He then scurried to the back of the van and opened the swing doors as Rolf motioned Michael and Ray inside. So far no one had driven by.

Michael placed his earlier feeling of familiarity—he hadn't remembered the man, he'd remembered the van. On the porch this morning, while he waited for Ray, he'd noticed a similar van parked down the block.

"We're police officers," Ray said. "Abducting police officers is—"

A gun barrel to the back of Ray's head silenced him. "We know who you are, fat boy," Rolf said, his voice chilling.

"In the van, now. *No more talk!*" Pavel commanded.

Michael's mind plotted possibilities: he could run, he could lunge, he could refuse their orders. In each case he reached the same conclusion: little chance of escape, high probability of death. The two men appeared willing and able to use their weapons if provoked.

Without resistance, Michael and Ray stepped up into the van. They were motioned to sit on a bench bolted to its interior, then the men got in behind them and shut the doors.

"Gentlemen," Pavel said, "I'd like you to remain very still while my associate secures you to your seats. No sudden moves. It is not our intention to harm you in any way. Is that clear?"

"What do you want?" Michael asked.

"To ask you some questions, that is all. Do exactly as we say and you will not be injured."

"You have questions, ask them, but we're not going to let you tie us up," Michael said.

"Unacceptable. If you resist, I—make no mistake about it—will not hesitate to use this." Pavel gestured with the gun. "Do you understand?"

"You're not going to—" Ray began before the barrel of Rolf's gun dug into his stomach.

"The man asked, do you understand?" Rolf said.

Both Ray and Michael nodded grudgingly. Rolf handcuffed them to the bench, ratcheting the cuffs far tighter than necessary, and began duct-taping their legs together.

Michael studied the men, committing their descriptions to memory. The older man, the one involved in the accident, appeared about forty-five to fifty. Five feet, maybe eleven inches, tall. Medium build. In good condition. Looked intelligent. Thinning brown hair, round glasses. Blue-green eyes. Brown slacks, off-white jacket. The other man looked younger, maybe thirty to thirty-five, Michael guessed. Black hair, slicked straight back. Six one and lean. Brown eyes. Black jeans, brown leather jacket and gloves. His face was angular, mouth and lips cruelly thin. Of the two, he made Michael the more uneasy.

Michael scrutinized the interior of the van next. He already knew the van's license plate number; he had glanced at it as they were being shuttled inside. No windows; an overhead light lit the rear compartment.

Some sophisticated-looking electronic gear stowed in the front of the compartment that he couldn't identify.

Michael was bothered by his freedom to study the men and the van. *Why hadn't he been blindfolded?* Either a very stupid move or an indication his abductors were not concerned with eyewitnesses, a possibility Michael preferred not to consider.

Rolf finished securing Michael and Ray, jumped from the van, and shut the doors. A moment later the van pulled from the curb.

"We have only a short drive," Pavel said. "Please remain quiet . . . no heroics."

Michael glanced at his watch to time the drive, reminding himself to note turns, approximate distances, and unusual sounds in hopes of retracing their path. Trained for this type of situation, his one concern was not to miss anything, a clue or an opportunity, especially now, when only one gunman watched them.

Ray broke the maddening silence. "Where the fuck are you taking us?"

"I asked you to be quiet," Pavel answered.

"I don't care what the fuck you asked us to do . . . where the hell are we going?"

Pavel pulled a cylindrical metal object from his pocket and began to screw it onto the end of his handgun's barrel. A silencer, Michael realized.

"Please, Officer O'Hern. If you do not remain quiet, I'll be forced to use this. It would be most unpleasant."

Ray rocked back and forth, perspiration showing on his forehead and upper lip. Michael could see the man wasn't bluffing, but oblivious to the danger, Ray opened his mouth to speak again.

"Ray!" Michael stopped him. "*Ray* . . . look at me."

Ray looked over, eyes wide, pupils dilated.

"Partner, take it easy . . . keep quiet like the man said . . . everything's gonna be all right."

Ray stopped rocking, cast his eyes down, and made

an effort to slow his breathing. "Yeah," he muttered after a pause. "Yeah."

Twenty minutes later the van stopped. Michael heard a fence open, then the van drove a short distance and stopped again. This time it sounded as if a garage door was raised. The van drove forward once more, a few yards this time, then the engine was killed. The van doors opened, Rolf entered, uncuffed and untaped them, and ordered them out.

Michael examined the surroundings. A large room, shipping crates, fork lift—some sort of warehouse. He tried unsuccessfully to make out the shipping labels on the crates.

Rolf directed Michael and Ray to two chairs in the center of the room; he handcuffed their arms behind their backs and secured their legs to the chairs.

Michael instinctively tested the restraints. Pavel smiled thinly at his efforts, speaking only when Michael accepted the hopelessness of his position.

"Gentlemen," Pavel said, "now for the reason you are here. I would like your cooperation on a few questions. A week ago you were called to the scene of a murder. An old man named Peter Olgov. Do you remember?"

The question stunned Michael. *What could the death of the old man have to do with this?* Ray sat mute; Michael answered truthfully. "I remember."

"Yesterday you returned to the rooming house and left with a small box. You remember that?"

"Yes," Michael replied. "How did you—"

"Just answer the questions, please. What was in the box?"

"Photographs. Just photographs."

"Of what?"

"They were Olgov's. His family, his relatives. What does any of this have to do with—"

Rolf, who had been standing between Michael and Ray, lashed out quickly and savagely, hitting Michael hard across the face with the back of his hand.

Pavel, clearly irritated, waved Rolf off. "My hot-tempered friend is not as patient as I am, as you see. It would be best for you if I ask the questions and you answer them. Where's the box now?"

A small trickle of blood started from Michael's lower lip and dripped off his chin. "At my house," he answered as he licked the salty-sweet blood from his lips and glared at the man who had hit him. He would have given anything at that moment to be untied and left alone with him for a few minutes.

"Where in your house . . . exactly?"

"In the back den, on a table."

"And all the photographs are there, you have removed none?"

"No . . . they're all there. Look, what do these pictures—" Rolf again backhanded Michael across the face.

"Rolf!" Pavel barked, and Rolf stepped away with a scowl. "Do not make things hard on yourself, Officer Sarikov," Pavel continued. "Answer my questions, nothing more."

Michael now had the name of the younger man—Rolf. When he got out of this, he very much looked forward to meeting Rolf again.

Pavel turned to Rolf. "Call them and tell them where to find the box."

Rolf nodded and entered a glassed-in office space. He left the door open, and Michael could make out most of the conversation.

"This is Rolf. We've got them. . . . No, no problems. You can take care of the Jew. . . . Yes, he says it's at his house, in the back den, on a table. . . . Yes . . . okay, call us when you've finished." Rolf hung up, then exited the office.

"All set?" Pavel asked.

"Yeah," Rolf replied.

Pavel directed his next words to Michael and Ray. "Now we wait. We will be called when the photographs are found."

Michael looked at Ray and found him hyperventilating. He wanted to pass on words of encouragement, but the younger man, Rolf, remained behind them and would not, Michael felt sure, require much provocation to strike again.

An hour later the phone rang. Pavel received the short message. "Gentlemen," he said to Michael and Ray after hanging up the phone, "we found the box of photographs where you said it would be. That is good. I appreciate your honesty. Just a few more questions and we'll be done. I must know who else you have told about the photographs."

Sound certain, Michael told himself. "Nobody . . . I only got them yesterday."

Pavel shook his head sadly. "Come now, Officer Sarikov, surely you told someone. We must know before we can release you."

"Nobody. I'm telling you the truth."

"Now, now, please cooperate. . . ."

Rolf drew near to Pavel, then dropped a step behind him. With a single practiced motion he withdrew a stiletto from his pocket and snapped its blade into place. In a quick movement he cupped his hand over Pavel's mouth, bent him backwards, and drove the point of the stiletto up through the base of Pavel's skull. There is a small opening in the human cranium at the uppermost part of the back of the neck, a circular passageway into the brain for the spinal cord, and Rolf's thrust found this passageway, and with two twists of the knife, followed by a spasmodic jerk, Pavel's body turned limp and crumpled upon itself as Rolf dropped it to the floor.

Michael and Ray sat in shocked silence during the swift and ruthless attack, real fear gripping Michael for the first time. The older man had seemed the more reasonable of the two. Now they were at the mercy of a man who had dramatically demonstrated his capabilities.

Rolf wiped the knife blade clean on Pavel's lapel and turned his attention toward Michael. "This one," he gestured toward Pavel's body with the blade—"argued with orders. Not a smart decision on his part. Now it's my turn to ask the questions, to give orders, and we'll see how fucking smart you are. Who have you told about the box?"

"Nobody," Michael said, willing his voice to stay controlled.

"You are lying."

"I'm not. I've told nobody."

Rolf bent down, his face only inches from Michael. "Once more, who else have you told about the box?"

"Nobody."

"You should always tell the truth," Rolf said as he turned from Michael and gently touched the stiletto's blade to Ray's cheek. "It's not nice to lie." He slowly dragged the knife point across Ray's face, tracing his features, stopping behind Ray's right ear. He looked back at Michael. "Do you promise to tell the truth from now on?"

"I haven't told anybody. I swear it."

Without warning, Rolf jabbed the knife forward piercing Ray's ear, then tore outward. A low, growling scream escaped Ray's clenched teeth as he strained against his bindings. For an instant Michael wasn't sure what had happened, then the blood came from the severed flaps of flesh, streaming from the wound down Ray's neck and onto his shirt.

"You son-of-a-bitch, *you son-of-a-bitch!*" Ray howled.

"*God dammit,* what do you want?" Michael shouted over Ray's cries. Until Rolf had killed the other man, until he had cut Ray, it had never occurred to Michael that they wouldn't get out of this situation alive. Of course he would live. He was a survivor. The truth was now apparent. Rolf had no intention of letting them go. When Rolf finished the questioning, he would kill them, and Michael could do nothing about it.

Rolf gently lifted Michael's head up from under the chin. His thumb caressed Michael's cheek. "It's very simple, you tell me everything you know about Peter Olgov and the photographs, and everybody you've talked to about them. I will know if you are lying. If you do not cooperate, I continue with your partner, many more small cuts, until you cooperate . . . or until I start on you."

"Shit, Michael, what is he fucking talking about . . . tell him if you know anything, dammit *tell him,*" Ray shouted, near hysteria.

"Yes, Michael, tell me. Can't you see your partner is in quite a bit of pain already? We wouldn't want to make it worse, would we?" Rolf began tracing Ray's other ear with the knife.

"What do you want to know?"

"Your wife . . . how much does she know?"

"Nothing."

"You are lying to me again, Michael." Rolf did not hesitate. Ray gave out a sharp cry as blood poured from his other ear.

"My ear, God, my ear, *my ear,*" Ray screamed, tears now rolling freely down his face.

"Stop it," Michael said. "She doesn't know a damn thing!"

"I think you're lying . . . but don't worry, we have plenty of time to learn the truth."

Rolf left Ray's side and removed something from a briefcase on the floor. He moved behind Michael, took

Michael's fingers and pressed their tips against something. Then he did the same with Ray. He was taking prints, Michael could see, but why?

Rolf finished and returned the papers to the briefcase. Ray sobbed incoherently, his head a bloody mess, his dark blue shirt now stained purple to the pocket.

Stay alert, Michael thought—he could still get out of this. Tell almost everything, but protect his wife and brother. But God, Kelly and John didn't know anything anyway, nor, for that matter, did he.

Michael worked the cuffs back and forth along his wrists. Every cop knew stories of prisoners pulling out of cuffs when it seemed impossible, some tearing skin or breaking bones in the process. It could be done. Just pull harder, as hard as necessary—they weren't going to walk out of here alive otherwise. He'd gotten out of tight scrapes before; he would now. Just stay alert and wait for the opportunity. It always came. It had to.

"I repeat, Mr. Sarikov, you talked to your wife, correct? Please answer, Mr. Sarikov!"

Michael sat mutely, any answer the wrong answer.

Rolf approached Ray again, who began shaking his head and screaming. Rolf grabbed Ray's hair and pulled his head back until he stopped struggling, his wails turning to whimpers as Rolf again traced his face with the point of the knife. He jabbed upwards this time, punching the knife point up and through Ray's left nostril.

Through Ray's screams Rolf spoke again to Michael. "We will see how much you know . . . but I'm afraid to find out everything, I can't stop with your dear partner. I'm afraid it's simply a fact of nature that truth is sometimes relative to one's own pain."

*   *   *

Rolf fingered the bloody blade of his stiletto and looked at the slumped figures tied to the chairs. O'Hern had died quickly, like a stuck pig, but not Sarikov. Only semi-conscious, but still alive. Rolf felt Sarikov's pulse at the wrist. Still strong, but there was nothing left to learn from him. In fact, it seemed neither of them knew much to begin with. That didn't bother him; he hadn't been cursed with a weak stomach. He did what he had to do and often enjoyed his work, sometimes dreamt of it at night, found it exciting, especially with the strong ones like the cop in front of him. They all became submissive eventually; he enjoyed the conquest.

Rolf admired the strong cheekbones, the defined chin, and the muscled neck of the cop. He grabbed Michael's hair and pulled down, jerking Michael's head backward, his face toward the ceiling. Michael's mouth gaped open, and his eyes rolled back under their lids.

Rolf bent over Michael. He thought for a moment, then whispered in Michael's ear. "Your wife will miss your showers together. Perhaps you wouldn't mind if I fill in for you."

Rolf's words had the desired effect. The words sunk into Michael's consciousness, and he thought of Kelly; his eyes stirred.

Good, Rolf thought, Sarikov would die in fear. He pressed his lips hard against Michael's, his mouth open, and pushed the knife point firmly against Michael's chest just under the sternum. He had killed in this manner many times before, when others weren't watching.

Rolf slowly applied pressure to the knife and watched Michael's eyes until they widened, then rammed the knife powerfully up and under Michael's ribs toward his heart. There was a quick inhalation of breath, and a gasp muffled by Rolf's mouth, then a gradual exhalation, like a tire with a slow leak. Rolf inhaled Michael's last breath, then, when the body fell limp, let Michael's head fall slowly backward, separating their lips.

Rolf withdrew the knife, covered with blood, and wiped it clean on Michael's pant leg.

9

The doorbell rang. Kelly peeked out through the living room window and her face went instantly blank. Michael was over an hour late, and three policemen stood on her front porch; she knew one of them, a good friend, Steve Mayer. Every cop's spouse knew what that meant. She felt faint and sunk to the couch. Maybe they would just go away, and when they were gone, everything would be okay. Michael would come home soon; nothing could hurt Michael.

The doorbell rang again.

Kelly rose unsteadily and opened the door. Steve quickly introduced the two other officers and stepped into the house. His face revealed all Kelly needed to know. She didn't break down, though tears welled up in her eyes. Not her Michael. Not him. With his laugh, with his smile, with their love. It wasn't possible.

"Kelly . . ." Steve started, then saw she instinctively knew, and put his arms around her as she began to cry. "Kelly . . . I'm sorry, God, how I'm sorry." He couldn't think of anything else to say and held her as her body shuddered.

Kelly had once comforted the wife of another cop killed on duty. The pain of the young woman had been real and sobering, yet seemed so distant. It was simply not something she believed could happen to her. She began to shake, then tried to talk, but words wouldn't come. Finally, she managed "How?"

Steve paused uncertainly, then whispered the answer, his eyes cast on the floor. "Ray and Michael were murdered. We don't know much more than that right now. We don't know who did it; we don't know if there were any witnesses."

Ray too. Both dead. Murdered. Numbing and impossible to believe. "Poor Ray . . . Oh God . . . Oh God, why? Why?"

"I don't know why . . . but we'll find out, I promise you we'll find out. I called your parents before I came, told them what happened; they're on the way."

"John. I've got to call John."

"I've already done that. He wasn't in, but I left a message. If the station doesn't patch him through soon, I'll try again. Don't worry about calling anyone else, let your parents handle that. . . . Kelly, I don't have to tell you what I thought of Michael. Right now I wish it had been me, I really do."

Kelly wished everybody would leave—she wanted to cry for Michael alone. Cry for her loss, for their love, for something wonderful that was no more. She didn't want pity, not now. *Oh, why didn't they have kids?* They had waited so long. Next spring, they had finally decided. Why did Michael have to leave without giving her a small piece of himself to look at every day, to hug, to hold, to remember.

She struggled to contain herself. They would not leave until she did. "Thank you, Steve . . . for coming . . . for being here. How did he die?"

Steve hesitated.

"Was he shot?" she prompted. "I've got to know."

"No . . ." Steve hesitated, then finally managed the word. "Stabbed."

Kelly's tenuous grasp on control deserted her. She choked back a scream, unable to think of that, not now, not soon, maybe someday, maybe never. My poor Michael, why couldn't I have been there to hold his head, to wipe his eyes, to tell him everything would be okay, to say good-bye, to kiss him one last time. *Why?*

Steve put his arms around her. "He was a good man, a good friend, and a good police officer. I don't know why this happened to him, why it happened to Ray. I'm sorry . . . I'm sorry," he repeated as he rocked her slowly back and forth.

God, Steve felt like shit. He knew Michael, knew Kelly, knew how much the two of them meant to each other. Kelly needed so much right now, and he had so little to offer. What could you say? "Everything will be okay." Well, it wouldn't be, not for Kelly, not for a long time.

We both thought you were superhuman, buddy. Invulnerable. Since I was a kid I believed that.

Steve fumbled uncomfortably through the next fifteen minutes until his wife, Nancy, and two other police officers' wives arrived, then he escaped to another room to compose himself.

Steve loathed what he must do next, but it was an order. It was the reason the other two cops were along. He had argued with his captain that they should wait for a more appropriate time, but had been overruled. He'd almost told the captain to shove it, but knew the captain would just have found someone else to do the job. If it had to be done, better under Steve's supervision than a stranger's.

Steve walked into the kitchen, where the four women sat around the table, one of them with her arm around Kelly.

"Kelly . . . I hate to ask you this now," Steve whispered. "We'd like to look through Michael's things . . . see if we can find any leads . . . anything at all that could help us."

Kelly nodded. "I'll show you to his study."

"No, you stay here. I know my way." He put a hand

on her shoulder, then left the room. He had lied, and didn't feel good about it. The captain had not ordered him to search Michael's things for leads; he had ordered Steve to look for incriminating evidence. The whole fucking thing stunk.

Steve led the two cops to the bedroom and study, and they began a careful search of each. Steve knew there were a number of cops on the take, but couldn't believe it of Michael or Ray. They might cut a corner or two now and then, but they were clean, Steve was sure of it. He had grown up with Michael. They came from the same neighborhood, had gone to the same school, played stickball together, decided to become cops together years ago when still in high school.

Steve walked out onto the front porch to smoke a cigarette. His large hands felt clumsy as he fumbled with a match. He wasn't about to join the search—there was nothing to find. To look meant to doubt, and Steve never had a doubt in his life about Michael.

10

John arched the grapefruit-sized foam basketball toward the small hoop stuck with suction cups to the window of his apartment; it bounced off the rim and fell through. He had retrieved the ball and set up for another shot when the phone rang. He made no move to pick it up.

The answering machine clicked on after four rings. The caller identified himself as Steve Mayer. John wouldn't have recognized the voice—they ran in different circles these days, though he knew Steve and Michael had stayed close. Steve asked John to get back to him as soon as possible, said it was urgent.

John fired another shot at the basket, this time he missed. Maybe Steve's call was urgent, but John had important business of his own to attend to. Steve would have to wait. He checked the wall clock: 4:45 P.M. Just a few minutes now.

John again retrieved the basketball, but this time flopped on the couch next to the telephone. His left hand rhythmically compressed the foam ball as he watched the clock, expectant, not nervous.

The apartment was small, only six hundred square feet, but the address was right: the upper East Side, only a few blocks from Central Park, and the view was excellent: an impressive wedge of midtown. The white walls and cabinets, the subdued gray couch and chairs gave the apartment a fresh, modern look. The rent left a sizable dent in his income, but he suffered the expense gladly. Of all the places he had ever lived, he felt most at home in this neighborhood with its young bankers, lawyers, and executives. Besides, his career finally showed signs of taking off.

He could write, no one questioned that any longer, but his real strength surprised even him. As one editor put it: "You cling to a story like a goddamn snapping turtle." Assignments came regularly now, so did advances. When he'd left the *Herald* for free-lancing three years ago, part of him feared he'd be in for a humbling lesson, but so far it'd be hard to complain. And, he thought, as he felt the first flutters of butterflies, if the next call went according to plan, he'd be on his way to a whole different plane. A player.

John checked the wall clock again. Show time. He ran his hand through his medium-length blond hair and took a deep, slow breath before dialing a number from the *Yellow Pages*.

"Thank you for calling Delta Air," an agent answered, a slight twang to her voice.

"Hello," John said. "I'm calling to check on the departure time for flight 407, leaving Jackson for New York City."

"Let's see . . . that flight has already departed Jackson, sir. It left at 4:30 P.M."

"Good, just wanted to make sure it got off on time. I'd like to confirm a return flight then, New York City to Jackson, flight 235, this coming Thursday. Reservation for a Charles Fullem."

"Just a moment, sir . . . Yes, that reservation is confirmed. Anything else, sir?"

"No, that'll do it. Thank you very much." John disconnected, then punched in a new number.

"Baker and Potts," the receptionist answered.

"Charles Fullem, please," John said, his voice calm,

tone authoritative. Damn, he couldn't help thinking, he was good.

"Just a moment, I'll connect you."

"Charles Fullem's office," a secretary answered seconds later.

"Yes, may I speak to him?"

"I'm sorry, sir, he's out of the office."

Sound important and sound disturbed, he coached himself. "He's left for New York *already*?"

"Yes sir, he has."

"*Dammit,* he said he'd call me before he left." John mentally counted to three, letting the silence punctuate his outburst, before demanding: "Where can I reach him in New York?"

"He'll be staying at the St. Regis."

"What time does he get in?"

"Just a moment, sir, let me check his itinerary . . . I would guess he'd be checking in around nine."

"Hell, that's way too late." John paused. He had learned the power of silence—like a vacuum, people rushed to fill it.

"May *I* help you, sir?" the secretary said after a few seconds.

I was hoping you'd ask. "I don't know if you can. Charlie said he was going to have some junior associate working with him . . . I can't remember the name . . . fax me the Birchwood Hills proposal. I haven't received it. I checked with your fax department, but they said nothing was sent."

"That would be Patrick Finch."

John dropped the basketball and grabbed a pencil. He scribbled the name on a legal pad and underlined it twice. "Right, Patrick Finch."

"I can connect you with him if you'll hold."

"Please."

A few moments later the voice of Patrick Finch

came meekly over the line. "Hello." Young and un-certain—perfect.

"This is Rodney Chappel of Dabney, Bell and Roth-child. I've been waiting two hours now for the fax of the Birchwood Hills proposal."

"I'm sorry . . . ?"

"The fax. Charlie . . . Charles Fullem . . . told me before he took off to New York he'd have you fax me the proposal, and I haven't received it. You are Patrick Finch, *aren't you*?"

"Yes . . ."

"And you are working with Fullem on Birchwood Hills, *right*?"

Finch snapped to this time. "Yes, sir."

"Then what's the hold up?"

". . . I'm sorry . . . sir, I . . . I never got the message from Mr. Fullem," Finch said, his voice wavering.

"Fuck," John said angrily. "Excuse me, but when I talk to Charlie tomorrow, I'm going to give him an earful." He paused again, this time to give Finch the opportunity to cover his boss's ass.

"Mr. . . . ?"

"Chappel."

"You're with . . . who?"

"Dabney, Bell and Rothchild in New York, pulled in as special counsel to the lending syndicate."

"Mr. Chappel, I'm sorry about the screw-up."

"Damn, Charlie's not due at the St. Regis till nine. What the hell am I going to do in the meantime?" *Come on, Finch, bite.*

"Mr. Chappel, I have copies here. If you'll give me your fax number, I'll be glad to fax it out to you."

Good boy. Now land him. "You've got a copy . . . the proposal, the supporting documents?"

"Ah . . . supporting documents?"

"Yeah, the subscription agreements—the contracts from the investors."

"Right. . . . I think Mr. Fullem has those in his office."

"In his office? Charlie said you'd have everything ready to go."

"No problem, sir. It'll only take me a few minutes to put it all together."

Bingo. "Terrific. You're a lifesaver, Patrick. A real lifesaver. Sorry if I got on your case a bit. Charlie said you were an ace, and he wasn't lying."

John felt only a twinge of guilt as he read off a fax number. According to his informants, this deal was shady all the way down to the lawyers. Probably too young, too innocent, to be culpable, Finch was nonetheless up to his neck in slime—just as well he found out sooner rather than later.

After hanging up, John again held the receiver down only for a second before dialing another number.

"*New York Herald,*" the other line answered.

"Walt Donaldson, please," John said. John used to work with Walt at the *Herald.* They first met as new hires, both assigned to the metropolitan news desk. Rivalry had turned to friendship after the first few months. They found they enjoyed each other's company and, more important perhaps, competition no longer made sense—John had clearly shown himself to be the superior reporter.

"Just a moment, sir."

A moment later a crisp voice answered. "Donaldson."

"Walt . . . John Sarikov, here. Do me a favor, huh?"

"I'm just fine, thanks for asking."

"Glad to hear it, now about the favor; I—"

"How's that sexy girlfriend of yours, hot shot?"

"You're married, remember? For your information, she's fine. Now let's get to the favor."

"All right . . . *if* it's something simple."

"I can always count on you, Walt, can't I?"

"For my good buddy, anything, as long as it's—"

John interrupted. "Yeah, I know, as long as it's simple. This is. A fax is going to be coming in at your offices for a Rodney Chappel of Dabney, Bell and Rothchild. Could you notify your communications center and pick it up for me? It's important."

"Jesus, John, when the hell are you going to get your own fax machine? They're not expensive anymore, you know."

"You know me . . . stuck in the dark ages." True, actually. Barbara programmed his VCR and installed his word-processing computer software. Not that he couldn't have figured those things out, he just couldn't be bothered. Same with a fax machine, one more thing he'd have to learn to use.

"Right. What are you up to, anyway?" Walt asked. "Nothing that could get me into trouble I hope."

John smiled to himself. Walt was a helluva good guy, but he was like so many others: just one of the mass of mice scared of his own shadow. "Don't worry, Walt. I'm just conducting . . . minor subterfuge."

"I'm always worried when you label something minor."

"Okay, okay. You can take a peek, *if* you agree not to do a thing with it until after I give you the thumbs-up."

"What am I going to see?"

"I'm not sure, but I hope you see Senator Wilcox's name plastered all over places it shouldn't be."

"Senator Wilcox . . . Wilcox? . . . from Alabama?"

"Close—Mississippi. I got a line on a land transaction down there. Someone's been singing in my ear for a few weeks now, telling me Wilcox's been pushing for all sorts of congressional approvals on the deal. Funny thing is, he hasn't bothered to mention he and a few of his cronies hold a good-sized stake in it. I just did some fishing for hard evidence, and if what comes over your fax line is what I think it might be, I may have enough to go to print."

"Sounds interesting. Call you back when the fax comes in; we'll talk over how we're going to split the byline."

"Yeah, right. Thanks, Walt." John hung up the phone, excited. He pumped his fist, then scooped the foam basketball from beside him on the couch and launched it toward the hoop—everything he touched seemed golden. Forget the local crap he usually dealt with; this was big-time investigative journalism. If Finch came through, if the story panned out, any number of publications, maybe even television, would be pounding on his door.

A celebration was in order. He and Barbara. They'd start with a few drinks, then he'd take her to dinner— it'd been a while since they'd gone out some place nice, just the two of them.

He looked down at himself. Jeans and a polo shirt. That wasn't going to cut it. He started for his bedroom closet. He pulled a charcoal suit from its hanger, pleasantly surprised when he tried it on to find the pants loose at the waist. He looked at himself in the mirror and approved. Jogging, riding his bike, and hitting the gym regularly had paid off. A slightly different lifestyle than when he rode the copy desk at the *Herald*.

As he changed back into his jeans, John began structuring the lead article in his head—damn good stuff, he couldn't help thinking. Explosive. The kind of thing he always hoped he'd be doing. Woodward, Bernstein, *and Sarikov*? He laughed at himself.

John's thoughts were interrupted by the phone; he grabbed it impatiently off the bedside table. "Walt?"

"John . . . no. . . . It's Steve Mayer." Steve's voice sounded toneless.

"Steve, great to hear from you. Boy, it's been a long time. How's everything?"

"I left a message earlier. . . ."

"Been out," John lied. "Just walked in this minute. What's up?"

"It's about Michael. . . ."

"Yeah?"

". . . I'm at Kelly's now. I think you should get over here."

"Why?"

Steve didn't answer, and suddenly John's throat tightened. "Why, Steve?" he repeated. "What about Michael?"

"There's no easy way to tell you this, John. . . . Michael was murdered this afternoon."

Steve continued, but with each word the roaring in John's ears grew louder. The receiver slipped from his ear; he found it hard to breathe.

"John . . . *John,*" he heard, and managed a weak reply. He said very little as Steve went on, unable to form words, let alone an intelligent question. He sunk to the bed. It felt as if someone tightened bands around his chest.

"You gonna be okay?" Steve asked.

"Yeah."

"Don't drive anywhere, okay? You take a taxi. . . . John, you take a taxi, okay?"

"Yeah."

John hung up the phone, neither sad nor angry, only numb. He had heard the words, but couldn't accept them.

Murdered. Michael, murdered.

Dazed, eyes moist, he sat unmoving on the bed for over five minutes until the ring of the phone reached through to his consciousness. It wouldn't stop ringing; absently, he picked up the receiver.

"John?" It was Walt.

"Yeah."

"It's coming in. . . . The fax, John. It's coming in.

I took more than a little peek at what we got so far—
it looks fucking hot. *Fucking hot.*"

Fax? John's mind took a moment to focus. He muttered something: nonsense.

"Hey, buddy, sound excited. This is great stuff, but
we gotta move on it before the rest of the hounds
pick up the scent."

Michael murdered. ". . . Huh?"

"I say we gotta move on it."

". . . It's all yours, Walt."

"What the hell's the matter with you? You sound
strange. What do you mean it's all mine?"

Blood pounded out the message in his ears: Michael's dead, *Michael's dead.* "Take the story. I'm
out." John killed the line and headed for the apartment door.

On the street, he started walking, anywhere, it
didn't matter. No matter how many times he shook
his head no, the phone call wouldn't go away. Steve's
words echoed again and again in his mind. His only
family. His brother. Michael wasn't the same as everybody else. He was strong and good and everybody
liked him. And someone had taken him away.

Unprepared for the loss, unsure he could handle it,
John began to run. It felt better, as if he were out-
distancing the news, outrunning the pain and anger.
Sooner or later, however, he had to stop.

11

After talking to John, Steve again retreated to the front porch. He lit his fifth cigarette of the afternoon, hoping to calm his nerves, anxious to leave. Why didn't the cops he brought with him finish the hell up so he could get out of here? Kelly's parents would arrive any minute, then John would come. They'd all look to him for answers he didn't have.

How many times had he brought up retirement with Michael? A half dozen? A dozen? They'd both put in twenty years on the force, enough for a pension. It wasn't enough to make you rich, but it wasn't half bad either. You took another job and collected two incomes—plenty of cops did it. Why hadn't they?

One of the cops stuck his head out the front door. "Steve, you better get in here."

Steve let the cigarette drop from his mouth and crushed it underfoot. "What's wrong?"

"We found something."

"What?"

"It's not good. You better take a look."

Steve followed the officer to the back study, a knot tightening in his stomach.

The other officer turned when Steve entered the room. He indicated a manila envelope he held in his hands with a handkerchief. "I found it taped to the bottom of one of the desk drawers," the officer said and pointed at the desk. "That's what was inside."

Spread out on the desk were the envelope's contents. Steve looked, careful not to touch anything, and couldn't believe what he saw. He turned on the two officers, grabbing the closest by the collar and backing him up against the wall.

"Did you plant this? you son-of-a-bitch! If you planted this, I'll kill you."

The officer hit the wall with a thud, and his eyes went wide in shock. "Steve! Geez, Steve, let go of me! We didn't plant anything. It was there, honest, it was right there, like I said, when we looked."

Steve eased his grip. The man's eyes registered surprise and hurt—Steve could see he told the truth. "Okay . . . okay." Steve released him and moved away. He owed the officer an apology, but couldn't think of that now, not with what lay on the desk. It couldn't be what it appeared. Not with Michael. Impossible.

Steve thought of burning the envelope and its contents, but realized it was too late. The other cops wouldn't go for it. No way to cover this up.

Did it really matter, though? There had to be some logical explanation—the envelope was a plant, or its contents legit. One way or the other Michael would be cleared. Michael would not, could not, be involved in something criminal.

Steve turned to the officer he had pushed against the wall. "Sorry, Jimmy . . . it's just . . . Michael was a good friend. I find this hard to take."

"It's okay . . . don't worry about it."

Steve looked again at the things on the desk. They would have to be removed to headquarters.

It was time to get out of here. He didn't want to be around when John and Kelly's parents arrived. He needed time to think before answering any of their questions. "You guys about done in here?"

"In this room and the bedroom, but we have the rest of the house."

"Not now you don't; we go back to headquarters. The captain can send a team later, when Kelly's gone."

The two men looked at each other. They knew the captain had ordered Steve to search the entire house.

"I *said* we're out of here," Steve ordered.

The officers shrugged and collected the envelope and its contents, sealing them in a plastic pouch, then left the house and headed for the squad car.

Steve called his wife into the living room.

"How is she?" Steve asked.

Nancy looked up at him, her eyes red. "Oh, Steve . . . it's awful . . . Michael . . ."

Steve hugged her and ran his hand down her hair.

"I keep thinking what if it had been you . . . Christ, what if it had been you?" she said.

"I know . . ." he said, wiping a tear from her eye. "Look, I've got to go now. I'm not doing any good here. I need some fresh air. Can you stay until her parents get here?"

"Of course . . . but John will want to see you."

"I know he will, but . . . there are some things I want to have time to look into. Could you leave word for him? Tell him sorry, I had to go. Have him call me tomorrow morning."

"What is it, Steve? What's going on . . . searching the house?"

"I'll tell you later . . . tonight. Just tell John to call me. Love you."

The sun warmed Steve's face as he stepped onto the porch. Fall approached rapidly, but today summer had made a last grand appearance. White clouds drifted lazily across the sky, two children rode furiously by on their tricycles with bright red, white, and blue streamers trailing from the handlebars, and Steve had just lost his best friend.

Steve lit another cigarette and approached the squad car with the two waiting officers. He sent them on. There was a subway stop a dozen or so blocks away, and he decided to make it back to precinct headquarters on his own. He felt like walking.

12

Michael and Kelly's house looked as it always looked: grass neatly cut, basketball lying on the side of the driveway near the back door, garage beginning to peel in a few places—Michael's fall project. Part John's home also: where he spent Christmas Day, Thanksgiving, Easter dinner, summer barbecues. When he rang the doorbell, John half expected Michael to answer. He didn't.

"John . . . oh John. I'm so sorry," Kelly's mother, Mrs. Dailey, said as she clutched him.

John returned the hug, managing to keep his voice steady. "Me too."

Mr. Dailey appeared behind Mrs. Dailey. "John . . ."

"I know." John replied. Their handshake turned into an embrace.

"How's Kelly?" John asked.

Mrs. Dailey's face changed. Her mouth dropped; her voice cracked. "I guess as well as you can expect. She's been very quiet. There were some policemen's wives here, and she had me send them away. She doesn't want to talk to anyone. Hasn't cried much; just asked to be left alone."

"Where is she now?"

"Out back on the patio," Mr. Dailey answered.

John hugged them both again, then walked through the house to the back screen door. Kelly sat with her back to him in slacks and a T-shirt. The sun was beginning to set, and what had been a beautiful day had succumbed to the first chilly night of fall, but Kelly didn't seem to notice the cold.

John opened the door and walked onto the patio. "Kelly," he said softly.

She turned her head. "John . . ."

She started to rise from the chair, but John stopped her, laying a hand on her shoulder. He pulled a stool next to her, then took her hand in his. Her fingers closed tightly, desperately, around his. John noticed a tear rolling down the side of her cheek, then another, and another. He felt the tears welling in his own eyes and bit his lip.

John felt no compulsion to talk; he knew Kelly loved Michael and was left with a huge hole in her life. They wept softly, looking at each other, looking away, looking at the ground. In a strange way he felt more comfortable than he had since the news of Michael's death—Kelly understood the extent of his loss, no one else could.

John looked up at the trees ringing the back yard and finally spoke. "I don't know what to say . . . what others can say to me. I can't feel better now. He was my big brother and made everything in the world better."

Kelly squeezed his hand in reply, then they sat in silence, lost in private thoughts.

John thought of Michael and their father, remembering the first and only time they fought. Michael had come home to find John crying softly to himself, his face bruised, one eye beginning to blacken. Michael needed no explanation; he knocked their father to the ground and threatened worse if he ever touched John again. Only fourteen at the time, Michael was physically no match for their father, but John was never beaten again. Michael, on the other hand, was, whenever their father drank too much, which was often. Michael never once fought back to protect himself.

A stupid thing to think of, John thought, as more tears streaked his face.

John thought of college, at Cornell. Even on full scholarship, his father had opposed John going. *Smart kids go to that school; you won't make the grades; you'll flunk out; what a waste of good money and time*—John remembered all the tender words of encouragement he more than half believed. He decided to join the police force instead, as Michael had, but Michael wouldn't allow it. John had brains, Michael said, and could do better. Only when he made the dean's list his first semester at Cornell did John realize he was not trapped in the same aura of failure that enveloped his father.

"I'll be back tomorrow," he said, cutting short the memories. "Call me anytime tonight if you need to. For anything at all."

Kelly squeezed John's hand again as he got up. She had said nothing, but both knew everything had been said that needed to be. John walked back into the house.

Her parents were in the living room, talking. They rose when John walked in and once more expressed their grief. John nodded. They mentioned Steve had left word for John to call him in the morning, and John nodded a second time, part of him anxious and part of him horrified to learn the details of Michael's death.

Mr. Dailey brought up the funeral. He wondered what arrangements, if any, the Police Department would make. John didn't know, but said he would check with Steve.

After promising to return the next day, John hurried

from the house. As he turned up his jacket collar against the cool night air, he thought of Michael, cold and unmoving in the morgue. Anger momentarily displaced sorrow, and his mind turned to revenge.

13

When he heard who held for him on his other line, Richard DeLuca quickly got rid of the first party. Great police work hadn't elevated DeLuca to the position of police commissioner; his looks hadn't either, although DeLuca proudly sported a full, albeit gray, head of hair at fifty-eight, and with a creatively tailored suit looked almost trim. Politics had accounted for his rise to power: saying the right things to the media at the right time and in the right way; behind-the-scenes handshakes; conference rooms of cigar smoke; knowing who to support and who to turn his back on. DeLuca excelled at it, and knew enough not to keep this particular caller waiting.

DeLuca answered with an upbeat "Good evening," as he leaned back in his chair and kicked one foot onto the mahogany desk.

"Good evening, Richard. How are you?"

"Terrific. Just terrific." DeLuca meant it—life was good. "Yourself?"

"A bit concerned actually. I've heard we had some unpleasantness this morning."

"You mean the two officers?"

"Yes."

"A tragedy." DeLuca said it matter-of-factly.

"With the mayor's reelection campaign in full swing, I would say that is an understatement."

"I'm not sure I follow you."

"What I'm saying is the department's reputation's taken a beating all year—it won't help things with the electorate to have the story of two crooked cops splashed on the front pages."

DeLuca was impressed. "Your sources *are* good, aren't they? How'd you know about the crooked part—nothing's been released on that yet."

"I make it my business to know things *before* they're released. Are my sources accurate?"

"Yeah—seems pretty clear both were on the take."

"You up to speed on this one, Richard?"

It sounded to DeLuca like more of a warning than a question. "Pretty much, why?"

"As I said, I'm concerned with the political fallout. I'd like you to keep on top of things, keep me informed of any developments."

"You think it's that important?"

"I wouldn't be calling if I didn't."

"We were going to staff this one pretty heavily anyway; you want me to turn on the full-court press?"

"That is exactly what I don't want you to do. I want . . . the mayor will want . . . a low-key approach. We don't want a lot of attention. To be frank, Richard, I wouldn't mind if this case were dead and buried."

"But—"

"My sources tell me the evidence on the two cops is overwhelming. Are they right?"

"Wel-l-l, yes, so far anyway."

"Then is there any need to push things? We're not talking about two of New York's finest here—we're talking a disgrace we'd all just as well forget."

"It'd be hard to just turn my back on an investigation. . . ."

"Of course it would, Richard. Don't get me wrong, I'm not saying don't do your job. I'm just saying let's admit up front we have a couple of bad apples, then staff your investigation accordingly. To be honest with you, I'm worried that a full-court press, as you call it, might uncover other embarrassments—it would be a very inopportune time to make such discoveries. Let's take our lumps on this case, get the damn thing out of the papers, and move on so we can go into the elections without a millstone around our neck. After the election, if you're still interested, by all means continue the investigation—root out corruption wherever you find it."

"I guess . . . if you think that's the best way to handle it."

"I do."

DeLuca paused. The rank and file wouldn't like it, he didn't altogether either, but the caller had a good head for these things, not to mention the mayor's ear. "I mean . . . you're right, of course. The evidence and all, they're as guilty as sin. Hell, it pisses me off—two of *my* men taking payoffs. Maybe the best thing for all of us *would be* to let everything blow over quickly."

"My thoughts exactly, Richard," Vasili said.

14

The message from John had been waiting for Steve when he got to the precinct that morning, over an hour ago, and still he stalled, hoping the investigators would call with news. Finally, he started for Hartley's office to check in person, the second time that morning.

When homicide chose Hartley to head the investigation of Michael's and Ray's deaths, Steve had thrown a fit. The captain gave him a fair hearing, but said matter-of-factly the issue was out of his hands—Hartley had evidently caught a superior's eye. Since when, Steve wondered, had the department decided to reward inexperience and bad judgment.

Hartley busied himself with paperwork as Steve approached his desk. Obviously enjoying his new status, he didn't acknowledge Steve's presence until Steve cleared his throat.

"I don't have a shit lot to tell you right now," Hartley said. "They're still lifting prints from the things you found at Sarikov's, and I won't get the preliminary lab report on the van the two were found in until this afternoon."

"No other leads?"

"Nothing that tends to exculpate the two, if that's what you mean. You were a friend of Sarikov's, right?"

"Yeah."

"You ever have a clue he might be dirty?"

"The man wasn't dirty, okay?"

Hartley raised his hands, palms out. "Sure, anything you say."

Fucking bastard, Steve thought to himself. "Look, I'd appreciate a call as soon as you learn anything."

"I'll let you know."

Steve had run out of excuses. When he returned to his office, he picked up the phone and dialed John's number. John's hello sounded lifeless.

"John . . . there are some things, well it's hard for me to say . . . things I don't want Kelly to know." Steve didn't go into details; he realized he needed to do this face-to-face. "Can you meet me somewhere tonight? A drink to Michael, and I'll tell you everything then." Almost everything, he thought. He wouldn't tell John the coroner confirmed Michael and Ray had been tortured; he wouldn't describe what was left of Ray's face; and he wouldn't pass on the words of the note found with the bodies: *Greedy pigs get plump and fat, and plump, fat pigs get butchered.*

"Yeah, I can meet you."

"Let's say Paddy's, seven o'clock, okay?"

"Seven o'clock, yeah. I'll call if there's a problem."

"Good. How's Kelly?"

"As you'd expect, but she's strong. She'll be okay; it's just going to take a while. I'm going over there now with my girlfriend."

"How're you doing?"

"I'm mad. He was . . . was better than all of us. Get them, Steve. Whoever did this, get them."

"We will. Tonight, seven o'clock?"

"Yeah, I'll be there."

John got to Paddy's early. He couldn't stay in his apartment any longer. The four walls penned him in, left him alone with a loss he wasn't able to deal with.

Kelly's hadn't been any better; he'd left Barbara there at three o'clock. He'd found the hand holding, the hugging, the ineffectual efforts at comfort, intolerable after a time. Kelly had been worse than yesterday; she cried quietly almost the entire time. That made it even harder; John knew he could do nothing for her.

John was on his second beer when Steve arrived. They embraced quickly, then Steve took a seat next to him at the bar. "It's been a while," he said. "You look good."

That was a lie; John knew he looked like shit. Not a moment of sleep since getting the news. He debated small talk, but given the circumstances the idea seemed worse than silly. "What happened?" he asked.

"Dammit, I'm sorry. Today I feel like walking out that door and away from this job. It just doesn't make any sense. I never saw Michael going this way."

"What happened?" John repeated.

"We don't know much. We got a phone tip that we should check out a van abandoned off the Long Island Expressway, and when we opened it, we found the two of them . . . both dead."

"Who did it?"

"We don't know."

"Clues?"

Steve shook his head. "Not yet."

"Do you have any idea why?"

"We don't know that either . . . not really." Steve motioned the bartender over and ordered a bottle of beer. He took a long drink before continuing. "I don't know how to tell you this, but I'm going to have to. Better from me than from somebody else. I don't believe any of this, this stuff I'm about to tell you. None of the guys who knew Michael and Ray do . . . but you gotta know what we found. Dammit, I don't know where to start."

Steve took a deep breath before continuing. "Okay,

first, I want you to officially identify Michael's body tomorrow morning. I told the detective on the case I would ask you to do it—really should have had you in to do it today. We need someone from the family. Not Kelly. She couldn't take it, but not for the reasons you might think. They were cut up, John. Cut up real bad."

John fought to control his breathing. He somehow managed a nod.

"Anytime in the morning . . . just come to my office." Steve paused before continuing. "There was a note left with the bodies. I don't believe it, but I'm filling you in, okay? It said . . . it said Michael and Ray were on the take, for drugs, and tried a shakedown for more cash. That's why they were killed . . . the note said."

"That's a lie! That's a damn lie, Steve."

"I know it is." Steve looked at his beer.

"Michael never took a thing . . . never would. Don't tell that to Kelly. Nobody better tell that to Kelly. Nobody can possibly believe that."

"John, I *don't* believe it. Look . . . I gotta tell you this. We found some other things . . . things that don't look so good. Michael had $10,000 in cash and $10,000 in bearer bonds in his study, taped to the bottom of his desk drawer."

"That's crazy. Someone put it there, planted it. It's a frame-up."

Steve picked at his beer bottle's label. "We found some other things too—some off-shore bank books from the Cayman Islands. Two accounts, $15,000 in each. They've been open for two years. We found similar things in Ray's house. I got a report from the fingerprint department just before I left . . . they found Michael's and Ray's prints, and only their prints, all over the things."

Think rationally, John told himself. "Were the accounts in Michael's name?"

Steve nodded. "We don't know yet if the bank has a signature on file; we're having the account papers sent here. Someone else could have set up an account in Michael's name, but the fingerprints, everything, looks bad."

John's head slumped to his chest.

"John, I think this thing stinks; I think it smells, but I gotta tell ya . . ." Steve paused. "I've heard the force might not give a burial with honor. It's political, and it's shit, but somebody's got to break it to Kelly. I heard a rumor and confirmed it. I didn't want to be the one to tell you, but you had to know."

"That's ridiculous," John said, bewildered. "Michael's been on the force . . . almost twenty years. They can't do that. Do you know what that would do to Kelly?"

"It's fucking political, John. The captain, the commissioner, don't want to be involved in this . . . the papers somehow got wind of the corruption aspect and . . . hell, they're going to paint one awfully black picture. You gotta prepare Kelly. I know it stinks, but I don't think the department's gonna stand by Michael on this one."

"But it's all a lie! He was a cop, one of their own."

Steve finished his beer, and signaled the bartender for another round. "You're nuts if you think the politicians stick by the cops in this city. They don't give a fuck. I'm pissed off, and a lot of the other cops that knew Michael and Ray are pissed off, but I don't know what I can do. I talked to the captain; he told me the commissioner somehow got involved in this one and the decision was out of his hands."

"This is going to kill Kelly . . . I'll call the commissioner myself if I have to." John's voice took on a desperate tone. "Steve, if you can find the killers, find who did this, you can prove a frame-up. Are there any leads, any leads at all?''

Steve shook his head. "Nothing. We traced the van. Stolen from Queens a few weeks ago. No prints. No witnesses. We found Ray's car abandoned. Again, no prints, no leads. I'll tell you the truth. I don't know how hard the department's gonna try on this one. The case is an embarrassment to them, one they want behind them.''

"What do you mean?''

"I'm sorry . . . I'm going to do all I can, but I don't head investigations. I don't think they're gonna put a lot of manpower on the case.''

"This is Michael, Steve. They *can't* let this blow over. They'll find something if they look. You know that.''

"Yeah, I do . . . at least I don't think Michael and Ray were on the take. But if this is a frame-up, whoever arranged it was thorough, professional. They've tied things up pretty well. I'm not sure if the force put every man they had on this damn case they'd turn up anything. Anything at all.''

The bartender delivered a new round of beers. John drank a third of his in silence. When he spoke again, his tone was calm but determined. "Remember the time, when we were kids, I think you guys were maybe thirteen or fourteen. You played stickball every night. The other kids wouldn't let me play, remember? I was five years younger. Everybody said I was a lousy hitter . . . you even said I was a lousy hitter. I *was* lousy. But Michael stood up for me. He said I was as good as any of them; he knew it was a lie, but he said it. I was his kid brother, and he stood up for me.''

The hint of a grin crossed Steve's face for the first time that evening. "I remember . . . you were lousy.''

"Yeah, well every afternoon, for weeks, Michael took me to the alley and pitched balls to me. For hours at a time. He would always pitch . . . never took a turn hitting. Then he twisted some arms and got me in one of the games. I still wasn't the best hitter, but I wasn't lousy, and I always got to play after that. I don't know why I thought of that . . . so long ago. It just sort of came to me. Steve, all through my life Michael believed in me. He never gave up on me. And I'm not giving up on him now."

Steve and John had two more beers. They didn't talk much more about the investigation, they talked of the past, some recent, but most old, when they were kids, when everything was simple and an adventure. They told stories they had told many times before from a golden, almost mythical, time. The time they had climbed on top of the school and been caught by the police; the time they had got lost on the subway and ended up in the Bronx; the fights they had gotten into; the games they had played; the girls they had liked. The best times of their lives.

15

A second limousine pulled onto the shoulder of the road behind Vasili's and shut its headlights off. Aleksei Denisov, a tall man with brooding eyes, dressed in a dark suit and black overcoat, stepped out, glanced swiftly behind him, then started forward. Vasili pushed open the back door of his limo, then slid to the far corner of the backseat. Aleksei entered, shutting the door behind him. He did not waste time with pleasantries.

"It was a rash act, my friend."

"It was a *necessary* act, Aleksei," Vasili replied coolly. As a member of the Collegium, Aleksei was, ostensibly at least, his superior, and out of respect for his position, Vasili should have addressed him as Aleksei Aleksandrovich—his first name followed by a derivation of his father's first name. If Aleksei noted the slight, he did not let on.

"It was necessary to kill two New York police officers?"

Vasili ignored the question and pointed instead to the limo's bar. "Have a drink, comrade. Relax, you're agitated."

"Damn right, I'm agitated. I got pulled from a meeting to hear this from Nicholas. *From Nicholas*. Now I have to rely on Nicholas for my information?"

Vasili did not apologize. "I had to protect myself."

"Killing cops brings all sorts of unwanted attention."

"In this case it won't. I've handled things; don't worry."

"It is my nature to worry. We must be very careful; we are at a critical juncture. The plan was to keep a *low* profile and build our strength, give our opponents no justification for moving against us until we are ready. *Then* there was this Olgov, *now* the Jew, Pavel Garishov, and two cops . . . all without Collegium approval. You know there are some on the Collegium looking for any excuse to oppose you—why have you made it so easy for them to find one?"

"And if I have, so what? They are spineless old men bickering among themselves as their empire crumbles."

Aleksei shook his head. "Don't underestimate them—they still have teeth."

"Not for very much longer. The wolves, comrade, are howling at the door."

"Better, perhaps, if the wolves would wag their tails and be let in to lie by the hearth—then rip out the master's throat in the dead of night."

Behind a smile, Vasili assessed Aleksei. Not as strong as he hoped. This was nothing, a mere bump in the road—things would get much rougher. A chief union negotiator with a nice wage and plenty of kickbacks, maybe Aleksei was *too* comfortable. Perhaps Vasili had picked the wrong ally. "You worry too much, Aleksei. They grow weak. Without the USSR, where is their money to come from? where is the discipline? how long before the organization splinters and dissolves under their watch? Leadership should be, *will be,* yours and mine."

"Then why jeopardize the future?"

"I was *protecting* the future. I—my operations—are the future. You know the figures. Your share, my share, millions tucked safely away in Caribbean banks. All in only six months of operations. I saw the future—

was the only one with guts enough to grab it. Give it a year, and we'll control the rest of the Collegium."

"I agree, *so give it that year.* No more foolishness, please. No more tempting fate." Aleksei wiped his forehead with a handkerchief. "You have made the Collegium—even some of your supporters—nervous by your actions."

Vasili's eyes narrowed. "Including you, Aleksei?"

". . . I have never had any reason to lose confidence in you, comrade," Aleksei answered cautiously.

"Good, then I repeat—I had no choice. Tell the others not to be nervous. It is over."

"I may tell the Collegium to expect no further incident?"

"Yes."

"And the repercussions from the killings?"

"There will be none; I've seen to that."

"None?"

Vasili held his temper in check. Who was Aleksei to cross-examine him in this way? "You have my word," Vasili said with a finality Aleksei could not miss.

"Very well—I'll pass on your assurances to the Collegium. Lie low a while and we'll weather this storm."

"With sails unfurled, Aleksei—*with sails unfurled.*"

16

Steve stopped outside the door. "You all right, John?"

It was all John could do to nod. He stared at the glass panel on the door, not wanting to go farther, the word MORGUE glaring at him in black block letters—cold and impersonal, but very real.

"This isn't easy for you, I know that. It isn't easy for anyone, but the law says we have to have someone identify the body. Just remember, identify the *body*. That isn't Michael under the sheet in there. Michael is gone. He lives up here"—Steve pointed to his mind—"and in here"—Steve pointed to his heart. "That's just a shell in there. Just a body. Something that housed Michael. Don't forget that; it will make it easier. You set to go?"

John wasn't. He felt like a little kid again, tagging along with Michael and his friends on some adventure, scared and anxious to go home. He remembered how Michael would take him aside at those times while the others murmured "sissy" in feigned whispers. Michael would always say the same thing—"stay close and everything will be all right"—then would ask John if he was ready to go on. John answered Steve as he had always answered Michael. "Yeah, let's go."

John expected the morgue to be antiseptic, all polished chrome and white tile. Instead, the walls were yellow cement block, cracked and chipped. The floor was concrete painted a dirty brown. The unkempt look of the place upset him.

A grotesquely fat man creaked out of a chair when the door opened, his hand combing the surviving strands of long black hair over the top of his bald pate. He wore a lab coat that barely surrounded three-quarters of his girth and hosted ink blotches under the breast pocket.

Steve whispered to the man, who nodded and scanned the array of large stainless steel doors covering one wall—like refrigerator doors, but smaller and square. The man opened one and cold wisps of air curled out. A body lay inside, resting on a shelf. John could see the shape of feet draped by a white sheet.

The man pulled on the shelf and its runners responded with a reluctant squawk. John had an irrational impulse to yell at the man. His brother lay on that shelf and deserved better. Adjust the runners! Oil the track! Michael was in there!

The man in the lab coat prepared to pull back the sheet from the corpse's face. It wasn't Michael lying there, John told himself over and over again, repeating Steve's words, just his body. No matter how it looked, he could handle it; it would stay out of his dreams.

John tried to blot out what he saw next. The cuts were horrible, but not the worst part—Steve was wrong about that. The worst part was the skin, like plucked poultry's but with a bluish tinge, and the eyes, like the eyes of a fish caught, thrown on shore and left to rot. No spark of life left.

Michael's body lay there, and John identified it as such, but that thing, that piece of meat on a refrigerator shelf, was not his brother. Michael was somewhere else, somewhere better, or nowhere at all, but he was not trapped in that cold, horrible figure.

Steve led John outside. They leaned against a squad car in silence, John's face drained white.

Steve held out a pack of cigarettes. John took one with shaking hands even though he had given up smoking years ago.

Steve lit one himself. "How're you doing?" he asked.

John took long breaths between draws on the cigarette. "I'll be okay."

Steve put an arm on John's shoulder. "Sorry you had to see that."

John nodded.

Steve knew the answer to his next question, but asked it anyway. "Department call you about Michael's funeral?"

"Yeah, this morning. They're graciously paying for a portion of the burial, but because of scheduling problems, they won't be able to provide an honor guard."

"I heard. It's a fucking shame the way things are turning out. I can tell you a lot of cops are upset . . . I tried, John."

"Yeah, thanks. I know you did your best."

"I heard you tried to call the commissioner."

"News travels fast. I called his secretary. He wasn't accepting appointments, once he heard my name, that is. I'm driving to City Hall straight from here. I'm going to sit in his office until he comes out. If that doesn't work, I'll try applying some pressure—I've got an appointment to see the head of the Policeman's Benevolent Association at 3:00 P.M. I guess it doesn't matter to Michael anymore, but Kelly deserves better."

Steve nodded.

"What about the investigation?" John asked.

"A detective named Hartley is heading it up."

"He any good?"

Steve grimaced. "Let's just say he's a rookie detective and leave it at that. He's running the show pretty much on his own."

John tilted his head and looked quizzically at Steve. "This is a cop killing, Steve. Normally all the stops are pulled, aren't they? There's never any shortage of manpower."

Steve shrugged. "Honestly, I can't explain it."

John could, at least he could guess. From the department's point of view any other course was a loser, he supposed. If the department investigated aggressively, whether they found the killers or not, the story of two dirty cops would stay in the headlines, and there was always the possibility of uncovering other embarrassing incidents of corruption. Whether Michael and Ray were innocent or not was irrelevant. The whole thing stunk.

"Anyway," Steve went on, "I talked to Hartley this morning to see if there was anything new to tell you. Nothing. No evidence of who did the killing, no witnesses, no fingerprints. But it's early—give it some time."

"Yeah," John said, unconvinced.

Steve engaged John in fifteen minutes of small talk for which John was grateful—it eased his mind away from the body that lay beneath the white sheet. When his hands stopped trembling and he felt competent to drive a vehicle, John started for City Hall.

17

A pained expression crossed the face of Commissioner DeLuca when he heard who waited for him in the outer office—John Sarikov, the younger brother of one of the two slain cops. He wanted, DeLuca knew, full police honors at his brother's funeral. DeLuca felt for the young man, but it wasn't going to happen. Things had been made pretty clear to him—bury this case quickly—and nothing Sarikov said could change that. A funeral with honors would only aggravate matters.

The evidence had proved out—two cops on the take. Maybe an unanswered question or two, but not a case to risk political capital. He had received sound advice: better to turn a cop and show your clean hands than be portrayed by the media as part of a cover-up. He had no intention of allowing the young man an audience.

DeLuca left Sarikov waiting in his outer office for two hours before it became obvious the hint wasn't being taken. He picked up his phone and buzzed his assistant. "John Sarikov still out there?" he asked.

"Yes, sir."

"Dammit. Okay, I've got to get to the luncheon with the City Planning Commission. I'll leave through the back exit. I won't be coming back this afternoon."

"All right, sir."

"And Mark?"

"Yes, sir?"

"For the next few days, this Sarikov stops in, he calls, I'm out. Got it?"

"Yes, sir."

Marty Fogliano, head of the Policeman's Benevolent Association, put an arm on Sarikov's shoulder and steered him from the office. It was 3:10 P.M. He would have liked to cut off their meeting earlier, but for appearance's sake had decided to wait a full ten minutes.

"I'll personally look into the matter, Mr. Sarikov," Fogliano said at his office's threshold.

"You'll call the commissioner? Like I said, he wouldn't even talk to me."

"We'll consider every appropriate avenue of appeal. I promise you that."

"I'll hold you to that promise, Mr. Fogliano. My brother deserves this."

"That's why we're here, Mr. Sarikov, to go to bat for the rank and file." Fogliano gave Sarikov a last pat on the back. "Again, what happened to your brother and Officer O'Hern, you have my deepest sympathy. The entire force mourns with you. Now if you'll excuse me, I've got to be ready for a conference call that should be coming in any minute. We'll be in touch."

Back at his desk, Fogliano sipped his coffee. There was no conference call, and there would be no call to the commissioner. He would assign a staffer to pass the news to Sarikov: the matter was out of their hands. In truth, the association could apply plenty of pressure when and if it wanted, but Fogliano had no intention of going to the mat on this one. In his mind Michael Sarikov didn't deserve a burial with full police honors, not because he believed Sarikov was a dirty cop, but because Sarikov had testified against another cop a few years back. At the time he had tried to intercede with Sarikov on the other cop's behalf, arguing the morale of the department would suffer from the well-publicized case, but Sarikov didn't budge in his testimony. Dirty or not, in Fogliano's eyes that made Sarikov guilty.

He put the matter from his mind and turned to other business.

18

The casket was closed. The mortician had tried his best, had stitched together the many long slashes on Michael's face, but the results were far from satisfactory. Without going into details, he had strongly advised a closed-casket wake. No one had objected.

John preferred the closed casket. The idea of pumping Michael full of embalming fluid, dressing him up, and putting him on display seemed grotesque—like a stuffed animal on exhibit. Now there would be no excuse for the inane comments so often made—he looks so natural, he looks so good. No he doesn't, John would have wanted to yell, I saw him in the morgue, and I can't get the picture out of my mind. The gray-blue skin; the cloudy and unmoving eyes. He's cold and he's dead.

A crowd of forty or so filled the funeral parlor, more had come and gone. The police brass had stayed away, but a number of cops had paid their respects. John knew only a few of them, in each case casually. They all had good things to say about Michael, and many privately expressed their displeasure with the department's actions. John appreciated their support, but wondered if all were sincere.

Although Kelly looked tired, she handled herself well. She, John assumed, like him, wanted only for the day to end. Until then she would hide her pain under a brave veneer.

John ducked out early. He apologized to Kelly before leaving, but she said she wanted to get out of there as soon as possible herself.

Once in John's car, Barbara rested her head against his shoulder. He circled her with his right arm and squeezed, going through the motions of intimacy but feeling strangely distant from her, as he had all evening. "Barbara . . ." he started guiltily. "I'm going to take you home, okay?" She looked up sharply, hurt and surprised, and he went on after a moment's hesitation. "I think I need to spend some time alone."

She nodded and squeezed his hand. "If that's what you need, I understand."

She didn't, of course, not fully; John could see that in her face, but he didn't elaborate on his emotions. He kissed her on the forehead and started the car.

After dropping Barbara off at her apartment, John drove around the city for the next couple of hours with a six-pack of beer to keep him company. Yellow cabs streamed beside him as he rushed to beat stop light after stop light, going nowhere. He strayed into a dangerous neighborhood and stayed, cruising the streets, almost daring someone to mess with him. Anyone who did would get a lot more than he bargained for.

After midnight, without incident, he swung into a parking spot near his apartment.

He slept restlessly that night, although he put himself to sleep with the better part of a fifth of Jack Daniel's.

The burial was the next morning. Dark blue suits, black dresses, dark sunglasses, black limos, a young, beautiful widow. Classy, like in the movies, John thought, bothered that something so strange occurred to him.

He went through the church service and burial on automatic pilot, shaking hands of people he hadn't seen in years, smiling and acting composed. A few times he joined a circle of people and conversation halted uncomfortably, leading John to imagine they had been gossiping about Michael and rumors of drug money.

There was no honor guard, no official police presence—both the police commissioner and the head of the Policeman's Benevolent Association had effectively brushed him off.

John was second, after Kelly, to place a yellow rose on Michael's casket. More followed, then the funeral ended, and people started to leave. John sent Barbara ahead with some friends to the obligatory post-funeral lunch at Kelly's. He found a tree to lean against and waited long after the last guest left.

From a distance he watched the cemetery workers lower the casket into the grave and fill the hole with dirt. In a few days they would fix a red marble stone at the head of the grave, then roll fresh sod over the newly packed dirt and water it. When they finished, Michael's grave would look like every other grave in the cemetery. In a few weeks, from a distance, no one would be able to tell its age—as if Michael's grave had always been there, as if Michael had never lived.

The funeral offered no catharsis for John. When he cleared Michael's name, John would consider him buried; until then he had only one thought—someone owed him a huge debt, and he intended to see it paid.

19

Nicholas Anayev, at seventy-five the oldest of the six men in the wood-paneled study, broke his eyes from the Potomac, which flowed lazily at the foot of the gentle, manicured slope of the club's backyard. How had it come to this, he wondered, as he assessed his comrades—all but two old and gray like himself.

To his immediate right sat Grichko—a baker's face, doughy with red cheeks. Under cover as deputy director of the Russian UN mission, he had served as the KGB's New York station chief for thirty years. Once perhaps the purest idealist in the room, he now itched to be free of his responsibilities, more interested in retirement annuities and the moves of the Dow Jones Industrial Average than the business before the Collegium.

Kozlov, an unimposing, frail man who showed his age, sat at the opposite end of the table from Nicholas. As foreign chief of the successor to the TASS news agency, he oversaw a substantial team of agents—over two-thirds of the TASS staff were once connected to the KGB. His primary responsibility was counterintelligence: monitoring Russian expatriate activities and infiltrating Russian émigré organizations. Lately, he disregarded most of his duties in favor of attending charity balls with his jewel-bedecked wife.

Popova sat to Kozlov's right, dressed in the soft pastels favored by golfers. Ostensibly a counsel at the

Russian embassy in Washington, D.C., he acted as co-ordinator of Russia's scientific and technical intelligence efforts. If Russia intended to compete in a capitalist world, technology transfers from America were essential. Little, however, of Popova's work involved industrial espionage anymore. More often than not he spent his days in corporate boardrooms, negotiating import-export contracts.

That left only the two young sharks, Yuri and Aleksei. They lacked the subtleties that came from age, but made up for it with ambition. Yuri, whose cover was as a fellow at a foreign policy research institute in Boston, served as Nicholas's chief deputy. Before it disbanded, he had been assigned to the KGB's infamous Department V, charged with plotting assassinations and sabotage within the United States to be carried out in the event of war. His chief attribute was loyalty. Not so with Aleksei.

Nicholas looked to the tall, dark-haired young man chatting amiably with Popova. Aleksei served as deputy in charge of illegals: deep cover agents, such as Vasili, posing as American citizens. Aleksei was the only member of the Collegium with a deep cover himself—Christopher Stills, a prominent New York labor negotiator. Nicholas couldn't read Aleksei's brooding eyes, but knew they concealed an enemy. Vasili's pawn, and a formidable foe in his own right, Aleksei had one trait Nicholas hoped to exploit: an affinity for cautious behavior.

Nicholas looked to the Potomac again. The six of them in this room, the Collegium, so named in honor of the former ruling body of the KGB, oversaw Russia's dwindling intelligence efforts in the U.S.—Grichko, Kozlov, and Popova, three once proud and effective KGB operatives who now cared more for capitalistic opportunities; Yuri and Aleksei, the heirs of a dying breed; and himself, a very tired old man.

It was as it should be, Nicholas knew. Time for all of them to bounce grandchildren on their knees and forget the insanities of the past. Almost no activities these days. The struggle was over, and though they hadn't won, why did it seem they had?

Yes, for the most part he approved of what was happening—the time had come for their organization to slowly disappear—but a danger presented itself. With the USSR no more, the Collegium members disengaging, a power vacuum had developed. Vacuums, Nicholas knew, had a tendency to be filled, and he didn't like who eyed this one.

The meeting was already scripted in Nicholas's head. No use delaying—a good leader knew when to accept his losses. He called the meeting to order and turned his attention immediately to Aleksei. "You have talked to Vasili on behalf of the Collegium?"

"Yes, Nicholas Nikolaievich," Aleksei answered.

"And passed on our extreme displeasure?"

"I did."

"His reaction?"

"Respectful. He regrets not consulting the Collegium before he acted and asks our forgiveness, but circumstances dictated a quick response."

Asks our forgiveness? Nicholas doubted that very much. "How so?"

"If he had delayed in his actions, he risked compromise."

"And what of the risks to the organization?"

"With all deference to the Collegium, he believed such risks to be negligible."

Nicholas saw the color rising in young Yuri's face. He tried to wave him off. *Delicately, delicately,* he wanted to whisper in the young man's ear, but wasn't given the chance.

Yuri's indignation flared in his words. "He *killed*

two police officers and thought the risks to be negligible?"

"Yes," Aleksei answered, eyes narrowed at Yuri. "Given the exigencies, in his opinion the risks were . . . acceptable."

Yuri turned toward Aleksei in a mocking glare. "Since when does Vasili decide what are or are not acceptable risks? Did I miss the meeting at which the Collegium abrogated that power? Or have we ceded Vasili special rights?"

Control yourself, Yuri, Nicholas thought, *I have no time to baby-sit children.* He separated the sparring pair with a question to Grichko. "You have checked with your sources at the Police Department?"

"Yes."

"And what do they say?"

"Everything Vasili told Aleksei is accurate. The police are already winding down the investigation. I cannot bring myself to condone Vasili's action, but it does seem unlikely we will suffer any repercussions."

Yuri interjected himself again. "Then Vasili has the luck of a fool."

Aleksei ignored Yuri and directed his speech to the table. "Do we turn on a comrade so quickly? Where is the return of the loyalty he has always shown us? I, for one, count Vasili as a valuable comrade *and* a good friend. I support his actions."

"Loyalty?" Yuri persisted. *"We all* know the business he is entering. *We all* know the people he is associating himself with. Where is the loyalty in such actions?"

Nicholas interrupted harshly. Time to rein Yuri in. "I did not call this meeting to discuss Vasili's business affairs—I called it to discuss his orders to eliminate two New York city police officers. It *will* remain limited to that subject."

"Fine," Yuri said, refusing to be chastised. "If we are all to bury our heads in the sand, then I will confine my comments to his instant actions. Our rules of conduct are clear. Vasili has put us all in jeopardy; he deserves to be sanctioned. I call for a vote."

"I myself," Aleksei said, "would *welcome* one."

Nicholas turned to Yuri. "I'm *sure,* Yuri, a vote will *not* be necessary. Let me repeat for the record: we are very displeased with Vasili's actions, but a warning has been passed. Vasili has promised us the matter has been contained, and we will hold him to that promise, but I do not believe at this time that sanctions would serve the Collegium's purposes. Does *anyone* object to this finding?" Nicholas held his stare on Yuri, and the room remained silent.

Time to mend fences; time to play teacher. The meeting over, the members dispersing, Nicholas found Yuri and offered him a ride home. Yuri curtly accepted.

Alone with Nicholas in the rear of the limousine, Yuri, his round face reddened with anger, wasted no time squaring off. "What was that in there, Nicholas? Why did you cut me off? Why wouldn't you allow the vote?"

Nicholas set his hand on Yuri's shoulder. "Why, Yuri, are you so anxious to fight a battle you are sure to lose?"

"I have never known *you* to run from a fight."

Nicholas watched the countryside roll past through the window, wondering if perhaps Yuri was right. Was he running? No, he reminded himself, just biding his time. "I choose my battles."

"And this one wasn't worth fighting?" Yuri asked.

"I called the meeting, remember. It served its purpose; we have voiced our displeasure. What would we have gained by forcing people to take sides?"

"Let them show their colors. Let them declare themselves, friend or enemy."

Nicholas shook his head. "I know the direction the Collegium leans; I don't care to push them over the edge. You heard, even Aleksei welcomed the vote—he saw what you didn't."

"We *must* draw the line—take a stand."

Nicholas nodded. "But not today."

"Do I hear you correctly, old friend? Are you losing your stomach?"

"You know me better than that, Yuri. My stomach is intact, but so is my brain."

"Then explain. We are patriots, not drug smugglers, pawns of criminals."

"Patriots? No. No longer. We are businessmen, fathers, grandfathers. We deal with stockbrokers and lawyers now. We still come to the meetings because we must, but the zeal is gone. The ideas that once fueled us are—" Nicholas decided to be blunt—"bankrupt and obsolete."

"And Vasili is to be our future? A million dollars worth a week, uncut, that's what my sources say he's bringing in."

"I know, but we must have . . . a healthy respect for the facts."

"And they are?"

"One, we cannot expect the other members of the Collegium to support us."

"You paint the picture too darkly."

"Do I? No one is eager for conflict. They would see it as a threatening distraction. *But,* if they are to be dragged into a fight, they will take great pains to be on the winning side. Who can we count on? Grichko and Kozlov are cowed by power, whoever has it. Popova? He does not support Vasili, but won't jeopardize his business interests or family. Plus, I've heard they are all . . . let us say more than a bit intrigued by the business opportunities Vasili pursues. Aleksei, as we know, is in Vasili's pocket."

Yuri started to object before the truth closed in on him. Nicholas continued. "Second, Vasili has powerful friends. Us against them, as the situation stands now, we lose—there will be little if any help from abroad."

"We get close enough for a bullet, and it doesn't matter how many friends he has."

Nicholas shook his head. "Walk through the streets of Brighton Beach. What do you notice that you didn't see even a few years ago? Limousines parked outside nightclubs. Men in flashy suits, models on their arms. The first signs of money—most of it from drugs. Lots of it. You've noticed it, I've noticed it. Do you think our associates haven't also? Then look at our own situation. Only the highest priority assignments get attention from Moscow. The flow of money is now down to a dribble. Do you doubt that there will be many in our organization who'll want a piece of the pie? who'll see Vasili as a visionary? We take him out now, without the approval of others on the Collegium, for the sole reason that he is smuggling drugs, and we'll start a war."

"I can't believe—"

"*I guarantee it.* And don't think the combatants will be limited to our organization. Have you forgotten who Vasili has been working with? Do you know the amount of money involved? If the Collegium is not united, do you seriously think the Russian mob will desert him? Believe me, as things stand now, they'd align with Vasili and throw their weight against us."

"They wouldn't dare."

"You *know* they would. Look at Russia. Hardly a cow is butchered, an apartment leased, a business transaction conducted without a mob payoff. Politicians, business executives are being slaughtered in their homes. They have shown fear of nobody. *Nobody.*"

Yuri shook his head slowly. "What is your plan then?"

"I have none."

"You suggest we do nothing?"

"I still have some influence in Russia, which perhaps I can wield to our advantage, but on the whole, for now, we wait. For an opportunity. Vasili may yet overstep his bounds."

"You don't call killing two New York City police officers overstepping his bounds?"

"I do, others don't, though he raised some eyebrows—a good sign. Vasili's alliances *can be split,* but it will take the patience and the sure stroke of the diamond cutter. I want peace; above all else I want peace within the Collegium, and then nobody will dare interfere with us. We will be free to retire gracefully and gradually from a business that no longer has a place in this world."

"And in the meantime Vasili gets stronger every day."

"Unfortunately."

"And all we can do is wait?"

Nicholas shrugged. "Vasili may be content to run his newfound empire and let us watch over the sunset of our own."

"Do you believe that?"

Did he *wish* to believe that—yes. *Did* he—no. Nicholas knew Vasili was strengthening his forces every day; when they were overwhelming he would strike savagely. "No, I don't."

A long silence followed, after which Yuri spoke, the combativeness gone from his voice. "Are we about to lose control?"

Nicholas looked to the Potomac. He should be at the riverbank now, perched in a chair, a straw hat covering his bald head, watching his grandkids sail and swim. He was an old warrior, tired of battle, tired of conflict. He turned back to Yuri. "I think it's clear . . . we already have."

20

Wearing one of John's oxford shirts, unbuttoned, and nothing else, Barbara reappeared from the bedroom. She picked up the two empty beer bottles in front of John and carried them to the kitchen; his eyes followed the long, trim line of her legs. After turning off the television, she nestled against him on the couch and began stroking his hair.

"It's getting late," she said after a few minutes, offering herself but not pushing.

John turned from her, toward the window of his apartment, physically excited by her touch in spite of himself. For three weeks now, since Michael's death, Barbara had wanted him to open up, but he couldn't—there was nothing inside of him anymore, just a bottomless pain he didn't care to probe. Sex wouldn't heal that pain, he told himself, half afraid of finding the opposite to be true. Might he laugh again? Might he again delight in the smell of Barbara's hair and the feel of the curve of her back? Might he lose the sadness he felt—a betrayal of Michael and all Michael had meant to him?

"I need you to hold me tonight," Barbara whispered. "I think maybe we both need to be held."

Barbara's words stirred an anger in him—a dark anger he knew to be irrational but which he couldn't repress. She actually thought she could help him cope?—that she could so easily compensate for Michael's death?

He looked at her without speaking. The same face, well proportioned with a ruddy outdoors look; hair cut short, pageboy style; pronounced lines around her mouth and eyes that she didn't bother to hide. Beautiful, by any standard. The same woman Michael and Kelly had repeatedly and good-naturedly pushed him to propose to. The same intelligent woman he had fallen in love with—so what had changed? Why would he pull away from someone he loved at a time like this? What was happening to him?

Barbara's hand left his hair and caressed his cheek, then his chest. He bit his lip, both aroused and irritated. As her hand sunk lower, the anger rose within him, supplanting love and passion with raw carnal desire.

Suddenly and forcefully, John pushed Barbara onto her stomach. Poised on one elbow over her, he reached for his belt, thinking only of satisfying the need growing within him. For the first time since Michael's death he made love to her—or perhaps a more accurate characterization would be he fucked her, for John expressed little love.

Afterward, now in bed, he lay in the darkness, staring at the ceiling, Barbara coiled in a fetal position beside him. Disturbed and embarrassed by the violence of the act, he wondered if tomorrow, and the day after that, and after that, until he came to grips with what happened, it might be the same.

John rubbed a stand of Barbara's hair between his forefinger and thumb and apologized to her sleeping form under his breath. She didn't deserve this.

He'd met her almost a year ago at a cocktail party thrown by a mutual friend, and spent most of the party in constant debate with her. Someone made the mistake of bringing up politics, and John and Barbara soon held center stage. They didn't agree on a single subject that first night, except one both felt but neither voiced: they were fiercely attracted to each other. At one in the morning the host and hostess brought them their coats and, to their embarrassment, they realized everyone else had already left. At two, when the coffee shop they had moved to closed, John walked Barbara home and was invited up to her apartment. They talked until four, then she offered him her fold-out couch, and he accepted. Sometime later he woke to the rustle of covers and found her beside him. Even opposing ideologies, they found, could cooperate in certain matters.

She had turned out to be everything John had ever hoped for, so why was he driving her away? She had done nothing wrong, was simply the closest one to him, the only one he could strike out at.

One thing, and one thing only, was on his mind—revenge, as if revenge would somehow bring Michael back to life. All other thoughts and emotions were clogged by a feeling of impotence—impotence in preventing what had happened to Michael, in seeking revenge, and in dealing with his emotions. Perhaps, John thought, that explained tonight.

He lay still for another twenty minutes, his brain working too hard for sleep to come. Quietly rolling from bed, he did what he had been doing most nights since Michael's death—he went to the kitchen, poured himself a tall glass of gin over ice, and turned on the television. Sometime in the middle of a movie he drifted off and woke up on the couch the next morning to find Barbara had already let herself out.

His head hurt from the gin. No wonder, he thought, examining the bottle—three-quarters empty. A stubbly beard and dark-ringed eyes greeted him in the bathroom mirror. He looked like shit. Two glasses of water brought a queasy feeling, and he sat on the toilet seat, head in his hands. An urge to run to the kitchen and stop his head's pounding with more liquor gripped him. He started, but when he got to the kitchen he took bacon and eggs from the refrigerator instead—a memory of his father drinking vodka for breakfast had stopped him. He had hated his father for that weakness and couldn't bear the thought of repeating it.

John was surprised by how much he ate; his body seemed to absorb the food. When finished, he went to the bedroom and fell almost instantly to sleep. He woke again at two in the afternoon, even then feeling only half alive.

Time he took care of himself again. He'd be no help to Kelly or anyone else if he continued to abuse himself. John resolutely threw on a pair of sweats. A few minutes later he carried his bicycle out of the apartment on his way to Central Park.

The light outside blinded him at first, a result of last night's liquor and one of those rare days in New York City when the sky was blue all the way to the building tops, without a rim of haze. He rode slowly through the crowded streets to the park, a green sanctuary from the city's daily headaches.

Once within the park's borders, John began to pump hard along the road that looped inside the park's perimeter set aside on certain days and hours for bicyclists, in-line skaters, and joggers. He fell into the rhythm of the cyclist in front of him, a young blond woman with a red, full-body Lycra suit. The even pace allowed his mind to wander, and soon it focused on Michael—an unwanted effect he remedied by increasing his speed to clear his mind. He cut sharply to the right and passed the woman.

The hum of his chain consumed him as he passed rider after rider, determined to let no other thoughts invade.

One rider, a young man with a classic cyclist's build, long legs, strong calves, large thighs, wouldn't be passed; when John tried, the cyclist increased his speed and nosed ahead. An irrational anger flooded John; he accepted the silently offered challenge. Here was an opponent he could see, a tangible foe who could be overcome. He followed the cyclist closely, less than a foot separating their wheels. After a minute or so the cyclist, almost imperceptibly, glanced back, betraying his interest in their undeclared contest.

They neared the largest hill in the park. John pulled out from behind and unleashed a reserve of energy. The cyclist responded by lowering his head and raising his body off the seat for maximum leverage, but John was already beyond him and stretching his lead. His celebration was short-lived—his breathing came hard under the fevered pace, and his smooth efficient strokes disintegrated into undisciplined side-to-side motion. Raw determination kept him ahead, then he hit the steepest part of the hill and, simultaneously, a wall. His breathing accelerated alarmingly, and a heavy leaden sensation spread in his legs.

The cyclist passed him halfway up the hill, John unable even to pretend a challenge. By the top of the hill he crawled along, and the woman with the red Lycra suit passed him.

John pulled his bike to the side of the road and slumped exhausted against a tree trunk, his shirt soaked with sweat tainted with the smell of the poisons he had been pumping into his bloodstream. Too much gin; too little sleep.

His muscles throbbed, his lungs ached, and it felt good to feel something, anything, other than what he had been feeling.

John's breathing slowly returned to normal. When the cramps in his legs subsided, he remounted the bike and pedaled slowly home, no longer concerned with the pace of other riders.

The time had come, John decided, to get back into the game. Waiting for something to happen was killing him. A trained, experienced investigative reporter, he possessed talents that should lend themselves to a criminal investigation. He would talk to Steve in the morning to learn the current state of the investigation. If the police had come up with nothing, he'd step into the ring.

21

"The truth, Steve." John looked him in the eye. It had been three weeks since Michael's death; good news, bad news, it was time he got the straight story.

Steve shut the office door and returned to the chair behind his desk. "The truth? They haven't come up with a thing. Not a fucking lead; not a hint of a lead. That's the truth."

John expected the answer. If there had been news, he wouldn't have had to hunt Steve down to learn it. "Then they're not looking hard enough."

"Maybe not," Steve replied frankly.

"What about the accounts in the Caymans?"

"Opened in the names of Michael Sarikov and Raymond O'Hern. No signatures on file."

"That's suspicious, isn't it?"

"We've been told it's not all that unusual down there. The banks don't ask many questions where deposits are concerned."

"So anyone could have opened those accounts?"

"Yes . . . but no one's come up with a reason why anyone other than Michael and Ray would have."

To John's mind it was obvious. "To frame them."

"Good theory, but what's the basis? Why, John? Who would frame them, and what reason would they have?"

No answers to that one, not that he knew. But there was one, somewhere—he just had to find it.

Steve rose from his chair and looked out the window. He wet his lips. "John . . . this is hard for me to say, but it must have crossed your mind—I can't lie and say it hasn't crossed mine. I want you to think about it. This job can suck. It really can. You work your ass off, maybe get shot at, maybe killed, and what do you get . . . a mediocre salary, a small pension, and the respect of nobody anymore. Hell, the media paints you as a goddamn villain; meanwhile punks pull in six, seven figures running dope. You can't stop the flow, not even the feds can, so what do you do? Some figure it might be better to at least regulate the supply— let it come in from guys who don't lace everything with PCP's . . . who don't push to kids."

"I don't like where you're going with this, Steve."

"I've known cops, good cops, who've taken money. It happens. I don't want to say it, I don't think it, but it could have happened to Michael."

"No way. No way!" Even as John spoke, words heated, face red, deep inside he debated the same possibility. *Could Michael have? Was it possible?* "It was a set-up, period. I don't want to hear anything else. No doubts."

"What about the evidence: the fingerprints, the money, the note? Dammit John, I'm not saying I believe it, but Michael was human . . . it happens, it's possible."

"*No* . . . it's not."

Steve backed off. "Okay . . . okay, sorry."

John cooled down. He had lashed out too harshly perhaps, but what hope remained if even Steve had doubts. "Were Michael and Ray working on anything that could have made enemies for them?" he asked as if the previous subject had not even been broached.

"We checked that—doesn't seem so. Michael and Ray rode a beat. No long-term cases . . . a few small arrests, tickets, crime scenes, that's about it."

"The arrests—anybody who would have held a grudge? Anybody who just got out of jail?"

"It's been looked into. Investigators didn't come up with a thing."

Again, John expected the answers. He brought up the real reason for his visit. "Can I ask a favor?"

"Name it."

"A copy of Michael's and Ray's logs for the last two months?"

"Sorry, that I cannot do. Departmental property. Couldn't let them out the door."

"Make copies for me then."

"Geez, John . . . I could get in real trouble here."

"Look Steve, level with me. I think someone framed Michael. Does the department? The cops on the case, are they trying to prove Michael innocent, or has the department already found him guilty?"

Steve gave an embarrassed shrug, all the answer John needed.

"I need those files," he repeated.

"What are you doing, John? You're not a cop. What are you going to see in the logs the department didn't see?"

"Hey, I do this kind of thing for a living, remember? Maybe I won't find anything, but at least I'll have tried. I owe Michael that."

"I could get my ass in a sling for this; I want you to understand that." Steve drummed his fingers on the desk. "Okay, dammit. You sit here. I'll do the copying myself. You tell no one; you show no one. You got it?"

"Yeah, got it."

"You better. . . . Give me half an hour; I'll have copies for you."

After a long hot shower John settled on the couch with the log books. He hesitated before opening Michael's, feeling oddly invasive. Putting emotions aside, he opened the log and sank into the easy flow of Michael's writing.

Each investigation, each stop, was recorded. He hadn't realized how much paperwork police work involved. DWI stops, speeding stops, a burglary, an illegal U-turn, a speech to the local high school on drug prevention. Reports and more reports, each leading inexorably to Michael's last day.

Three hours after he started, John finished and rubbed his eyes. An uneventful string of unrelated events. Michael and Ray were involved in two murder investigations; in neither case could John fabricate a tie-in with their deaths.

In the first, Michael and Ray were called to the scene of a drive-by shooting in Coney Island. Automatic weapon fire killed a youth on his family's front stoop. No one saw the car's license number, and no one came forward to identify the killers. The parents of the dead boy denied he was involved in gang activity, but friends of the boy told a different story. Michael and Ray spent two hours at the crime scene before homicide took over.

In the second, Michael and Ray were the first on the scene of a murder in a rooming house in Brighton Beach. They found an old man in his bathtub, shot three times in the back of the head. Michael and Ray turned up no clues, no leads, no witnesses. Again, after their initial investigation, homicide took over the case.

Reluctantly, John admitted Steve was right. Nothing he read indicated Michael and Ray had been working on anything explosive—something that might have led to murder. Nonetheless, John started on Ray's log, hoping to discover some fact or observation Michael hadn't recorded.

John grew quickly disappointed. Ray's descriptions were shorter, less well written, sloppy. John knew Ray well enough to see his personality reflected in the writing style. He finished Ray's log in half the time of Michael's.

John stared at the two logs. He had hoped for at least a fragment of a lead to grasp to. It had been stupid to get his hopes up. Even if a clue hid somewhere in the logs' pages, how could he possibly identify it? What incident? A traffic ticket? A burglary? Something Michael described innocuously? Maybe the clue he sought was recorded in a log from three months ago, a year ago, five years ago.

Was he beaten so soon?

John did what he swore he wouldn't: filled a glass with ice and gin, and, before he could talk himself out of it, took a healthy drink. Two glasses later he no longer cared about his promise to himself.

22

After four rings John's answering machine clicked on. He listened, bleary-eyed, from the couch, having taken to screening all his calls. Too many missed deadlines and angry editors.

John recognized Kelly's voice. She sounded out of it—understandable considering her message. She planned to sort through Michael's things in the morning, would appreciate John's help. John didn't pick up the phone. He would shower, let himself sober up, then call back. He couldn't refuse Kelly, but didn't look forward to carving up Michael's possessions.

Kelly met John as he drove up her driveway. She greeted him cheerfully, but John guessed her pale and drawn visage more accurately reflected her state of mind.

"Thanks for coming," she said.

"Glad to help."

Her eyes floated away from him. "What a beautiful day it is."

John looked at the sky, surprised to find it was; he had hardly noticed. Probably only the low sixties, but the sun felt warm on his face.

Kelly's face took on a wistful expression. "You know what Michael and I would have done on a day like this? Jumped in the car and taken off. Had a picnic somewhere. Or hot dogs at a roadside stand, it didn't matter. Michael refused to sit inside on a beautiful day."

"Well then, why don't we take his advice? How about a walk?" John suggested. "God knows I could use the fresh air."

Kelly wavered and John guessed why—for the same reason she'd taken a leave of absence from work: she found staying in the house easier. No neighbors to run into, no whispers to ignore. Safe.

John pressed, and Kelly gave in. As they strolled, they exchanged small talk: the weather, current events, what each had been doing. John told a funny story about a mutual friend, and Kelly laughed. The time passed quickly.

It felt good, here, with Kelly, John thought. He didn't feel so alone. They ended up walking for over an hour, partly because they enjoyed themselves, partly because they dreaded the chore that awaited them.

John's light mood changed as they entered the house. Of course it made sense for her to pack away Michael's things, give the things she didn't want to charity—Michael's possessions would only remind her of his death and mire her in depression. But did that imply *they would never be okay, never be happy, until they forgot Michael?* She wouldn't want that, and neither did he.

They started in the bedroom. Kelly brought in three empty large cardboard boxes, one for things she wanted to keep, one for John, and one for the Salvation Army.

Part of John wanted everything of Michael's: sweat shirts, golf clubs, basketball, high school letter jacket. He couldn't stand the thought of Michael's clothes heaped in a great pile of used clothing in a thrift shop, being picked at like bones by scavengers.

Another part of John wanted nothing to do with

Michael's belongings. It seemed akin to grave robbing. Funny, when Michael lived, John never thought twice about borrowing, or as more probable with brothers, stealing, Michael's clothing. Now that anything he owned was for the taking, John balked at the thought. Maybe it would be best to burn it all—a great funeral pyre.

John settled on things of sentimental value: the letter jacket, some of the sporting equipment, a few T-shirts, photos of their father and mother. Kelly handed him a small wallet that he opened to find Michael's police shield. He tucked it in his pocket.

Kelly kept only a few of Michael's clothes, sort of odd things: an old sweat shirt, a baseball cap, an overcoat. She kept one pair of Michael's running shoes in the closet. A strange reminder, but fitting. Her small shoes flanked by his large pair, as it should be, as it always had been. When they finished, Kelly began moving some of her clothes into Michael's closet.

"Funny," she said, "I always complained to Michael I didn't have enough closet space in this house . . . well, now I do." She wept for the first time that afternoon. John held her, first tentatively by the wrist, then around the shoulders. She regained her self-control after a few moments, apologized needlessly, and they started on Michael's papers.

Years of accumulated receipts and bills. They discarded all but the most recent, which they boxed and stored in the attic. Most of the rest was junk: a warranty card on a stereo long since discarded, a fishing license from seven years ago, old shopping lists. They set aside all the important papers, the insurance policies and investment records Kelly might have to refer to.

John found a stack of birthday cards from Kelly to Michael, dating back to before they married. Kelly hadn't known Michael saved them. John couldn't help thinking the pile should have grown much thicker.

The Police Department had sent Kelly two boxes that held the contents of Michael's desk and locker. Two medium-sized boxes, not much to show for a twenty-year career.

Reports and forms crammed the first box. John sifted through them rapidly. Letters and bills, mainly, and photos of a sailing trip Kelly and Michael had taken off Sag Harbor earlier in the year. Painful to look at—Kelly and Michael appeared so happy. John put them back in their pouch. Three framed pictures were in the box, one of Kelly, one of Michael and Kelly, and one of Michael and John as little kids. John vaguely remembered when the last picture was taken—Michael was teaching John to ride a bike, running alongside as John pedaled. John slipped the picture of the two of them into his box.

He came across three handwritten phone messages dated the day Michael died, a reminder life went on even in the face of death. One concerned the precinct's basketball game the following night, one was from a Sgt. Scott, whoever he was, regarding a fund-raising activity Michael had volunteered for, and one was from a Jacob Greene. It was marked "returning your call regarding Peter Olgov."

John stopped at this last message. He couldn't place either of the names, but they seemed vaguely familiar, or at least the second one, Peter Olgov, did. He had come across the name sometime in the not too distant past, he was certain of it, but couldn't remember when. He tried to dig the memory from his mind, but the effort chased it away. He stopped trying, knowing it would come to him eventually, and set the message aside.

The second box contained things from Michael's locker: a windbreaker, athletic tape, gym shorts,

T-shirts, toiletries, common everyday things that took on an uncommon importance in John's eyes.

John stacked the boxes of things neither he nor Kelly wanted in the garage for pickup by the Salvation Army—Michael's life, neatly boxed, neatly disposed of. He then joined Kelly at the kitchen table for a cup of tea.

The message from Greene continued to gnaw at him, prompting his next question. "Kelly, have you ever heard of Jacob Greene?"

"Jacob Greene? No. Doesn't sound familiar. Why?"

"In the boxes from the department I found a phone message from him. He returned a call from Michael. I couldn't place the name. How about a Peter Olgov?"

"Olgov. Olgov. Sounds sort of familiar. Who is he?"

"I don't know, it sounded familiar to me too. The message from this Greene concerned Peter Olgov."

"Michael may have mentioned someone named Olgov. I'm not sure."

It came to John suddenly—Michael's log. That's where he'd read it, just last week. *What was the context?* His mind clicked again, and he had it. The murder investigation of an old man. John wasn't sure of the name, but it could have been Peter Olgov. "I think I remember now. From Michael's police logs . . ."

Kelly's eyebrows arched. "Police logs?"

"Yeah, I got a copy from Steve. Don't tell anyone—he's not supposed to give anyone access."

"Why did you ask for Michael's police logs?"

John paused; he stared at his tea cup. "The police aren't getting anywhere, Kelly. I just wanted to check, make sure they didn't miss anything."

"John—"

"Don't say it. I know. I *had* to check. Anyway, I remember an entry about an old man . . . killed . . . shot. Michael and Ray were the first cops on the scene. The man's name may have been Peter Olgov. Sound familiar?"

"Right. I remember now. The old man—his name could have been Olgov—reminded Michael of your father."

John ignored the reference to his father; he wasn't worth remembering. Michael had always felt differently, John knew, said he had vague childhood memories of an earlier time, when Mom lived, and his father laughed. John discounted Michael's vague memories in the face of his own more concrete ones.

"What'd he tell you about the old man? Do you remember?" John asked.

"Not much, really. Mainly he just talked about the old man's photos."

"Photos?"

"Yeah . . . Michael had a whole box of them."

"How'd Michael get them?"

"Let me think. He said, I think, a woman . . . an elderly woman who lived in the same building as the old man, gave them to him. The old man had left the photographs in her apartment . . . I think that's right . . . and she wanted to make sure relatives could claim them."

"Where are the photos now?"

"Come to think of it, I'm not sure. Michael looked at them in the den the night before . . . before . . . that last night, but I haven't come across them since. Is it important?"

"I doubt it, but . . . do you think you could find them?"

"I'll see," she said as she got to her feet.

Kelly returned a few minutes later, empty-handed. "We've gone through almost everything, I don't know how we would have missed it. It's a fair-sized wooden—blond wood—box. I don't know where else it could be, unless of course Michael took them to work with him that morning."

"Do you remember the photos?"

"Never even looked at them. I went to bed; Michael stayed up and went through the box alone. We talked about them, though. He said they were family photographs mostly, but get this: he found some sort of false bottom to the box. Underneath, there were photos of a Nazi concentration camp."

"A Nazi concentration camp? You're sure?"

"That's what Michael said; I'm positive. He asked me if I wanted to see them, but I really didn't. Evidently, they were pretty graphic. Now I remember, Michael thought you might be interested in the story."

John remembered Michael's call the morning of his death—Michael had mentioned having a story for him.

"Michael said the pictures were graphic; did he elaborate?"

"No."

"He didn't find anything else in the box?"

"He mentioned only the photographs."

Why hide photos? Either they embarrassed someone, or had sentimental or monetary value. Did this *mean* anything? Unlikely, John decided, although it aroused his curiosity. In any event, giving this Greene a call to see what he had wanted couldn't hurt.

Kelly watched John as he stared off into space, finally interrupting. "What is it, John? What are you thinking?"

John picked up the message from Greene. "I was just thinking I might give this Jacob Greene a call, see what he wanted, but his phone number's not written on the message. Do you have a Brooklyn phone book?"

"Yes, it's over there, on the counter." Kelly pointed. "But how do you know the call was to Brooklyn?"

"I don't," John said as he set the phone book in front of him on the kitchen table. "We'll just see if there are any Jacob Greenes listed."

John flipped through the phone book toward the "G's"; one page flopped open immediately, marked by a card with the name Jacob Greene and a phone number written on it. Michael must have put it there, John realized. He pulled the card from the book.

"John."

John raised his eyes from the card to Kelly. "Hmm?"

She pointed at the card. "The back."

When John turned what he had thought to be a card over, he saw a concentration camp prisoner, deathly thin, in loose rags, a tattooed number clearly visible on his forearm. Kelly moved behind John's shoulder, and he held up the photo to her. "One of the photographs Michael looked at the night before his murder?" he asked.

"I guess so," she said, clearly shaken by the photo.

John continued to study the photo. Sometime during the last day of his life, Michael had stuck it in the phone book. *Why?* John knew one way to try to find out. He reached for the phone and dialed the number on the back of the photo. The line responded with a recorded message from the phone company—the number was no longer in service. A dead end.

"No answer?" Kelly asked, seated again across the table from him.

"Line's disconnected. No forwarding number."

"Do you think the photo means something?"

"I don't know, but I'm guessing Michael asked himself the same question. I'll bet he found the photo, then tried this Greene."

John reached again for the phone book. He started down the list of "Greenes" and found a phone number matching that on the photo. J. Greene, 4422 Newbauer Street. The address went into his pocket along with the photograph.

"You *do* think this means something," Kelly said.

"To be honest, no. It probably doesn't mean a thing. Just curiosity." He changed the subject. "Hey, I enjoyed our walk today."

"Me too." She smiled. "I didn't realize how much I'd missed exercise. Maybe I'll start jogging again. Next time you can join me."

"The shape I'm in, I think I better stick to walking." The two laughed.

When Kelly saw John to the door a quarter-hour later, her reserve finally broke. "John . . . I miss him all the time. I can't sleep; I can't eat. How do I get over this? How do I get on with my life?"

"I don't know. I feel the same way, but it'll get better. I know it'll get better," John lied.

23

A block from Kelly's house John pulled to the side of the road. There was nowhere he had to be, nothing waited for him at home, and his curiosity was aroused. He reached for the memo in his pocket with the address of Jacob Greene. Newbauer Street. He knew where that was. A glance at a map confirmed it. Not too far away; easy enough to drive by. If this Greene didn't live there anymore, so be it. At least he'd have satisfied himself. Probably a wild-goose chase, but a harmless one.

The photograph of the concentration camp prisoner lay next to him on the car seat; his mind turned to it as he drove. More than a lead, it made him strangely uneasy. Concentration camps, the Holocaust, atrocities that shaded the temper of the questions still running through his mind. Why would the dead man from the rooming house, Olgov, hide the photo? Could Michael have struggled over the same question and followed up by calling Greene? Then the biggest question: why was John letting himself believe any of this had something to do with Michael's murder?

The address took him to a lower middle-class section of Brooklyn. Small two-story frame houses with side windows peering four feet across into their neighbors. John consulted the map. Just a few blocks away now. He counted down street numbers and saw what from a distance appeared to be an empty lot ahead.

Not quite empty, he saw as he drew closer. The charred remains of a house stood on the lot. Its address, judging by its neighbors on either side, was that of Jacob Greene.

John parked his car across the street and examined the lot on foot. A total loss.

The fire had not been recent—the lot was cordoned off, and work was well under way clearing the debris. There were no workers present, however, and John decided to find out what he could about the fire from a neighbor.

John pulled a Dictaphone from his coat's inside breast pocket. He always carried one, a micro cassette model, small enough to fit in a palm. He had bought it years ago, absorbing one of the first lessons of an investigative reporter: record your thoughts, and better, if you have the opportunity, record interviews. Recollections rarely mollified editors, but recordings made them ecstatic.

John was well versed on the legalities of taping a conversation—when you needed permission from the person you taped and when you didn't; when you could legally wear a hidden mike; when you could tape a phone conversation. John unwound the microphone lead, clipped the recorder's small mike to his lapel, and replaced the Dictaphone in his pocket, ready to snap it on when he talked to the neighbors.

John started with a house immediately to one side of the burned house. A short, pudgy man with a half-eaten cheeseburger in his hand answered the door bell.

"Sorry to bother you," John said. "I have some business with Mr. Jacob Greene. The last address I had was next door. Could you tell me what happened?"

"Sort of obvious, ain't it. Burned down." The man took a large bite of the cheeseburger.

"Mr. Greene?"

The man didn't bother to swallow. "Went up with the house. They wheeled out what was left of the body the morning after the fire. Too hot to get in there before."

John was startled. *Was this the same Greene Michael talked to?* Another death. "Do they know what caused the fire?"

"Do I look like the fucking Fire Department? Who knows. These old places are fire traps, every damn one of them. Lucky this whole row of houses didn't go up."

"When did it happen?"

"Three, four weeks ago. Something like that."

Michael died four weeks ago. "Can you remember? It's very important."

The man took another bite of his burger before answering. "I said, I ain't the fucking Fire Department. Check with them."

"Are there next of kin? Someone I could talk to about Mr. Greene, a good friend perhaps?"

"Why you asking me? I hardly knew the old man."

"Yeah, okay, I thought since you were neighbors . . ."

"Ask the lady across the street." The man pointed to a small yellow house. "She's the neighborhood busybody. Probably knows what time I take my shits. Okay? Now, is there anything else?"

"No, I guess not . . . thanks for your time."

The man shut the door.

John started across the street, hoping the man was right about the lady being a dedicated snoop. As he walked up to the yellow home's front porch, he saw someone, female he thought, duck behind a curtain. Good, he thought, she must have been watching him from across the street. He rang the doorbell.

"I'm not buying anything, mister," came from behind the door in a high-pitched voice.

"I'm not selling anything ma'am," John replied.

"What was that you're selling?"

John barely heard her through the heavy oaken door. "No ma'am. I said, I'm not selling anything," John shouted.

"Then what do you want? I saw you at Bill Haverdy's."

"Yes ma'am. I had some business with Mr. Greene across the street. I've been trying to reach him by phone for the last week. I just found out from Mr. Haverdy about the fire. Terrible. Mr. Haverdy suggested you might be able to tell me more about it."

The oaken door creaked open. A screen door, which the woman did not open, separated them. She was pencil thin, barely five foot one, and bent over. Her eyes darted swiftly from side to side, never looking at John directly.

"What's your business with Mr. Greene?"

John thought quickly. The truth was convoluted and would probably lead to the door being slammed in his face. He fell back on a cover he'd used many times before in investigative reporting. "I'm a paralegal, ma'am. The attorney I work for sent me to contact Mr. Greene. Our client bequeathed a portion of his estate to Mr. Greene, and we've been trying to get in touch with him to let him know."

"Well, you're too late. He can't use the money now."

Michael contained a black-humored laugh. "No ma'am. I guess you're right. Do you know what happened?"

"House burned down," she said matter-of-factly.

"Do you know what could have caused it?"

"The fire?"

"Yes."

"Could have been a match, I suppose. Or a cigarette. Or a gas line could have leaked, that can happen, you know."

"Yes. Do you know when it happened?"

"Few weeks ago, I guess now."

"Could you be more specific ma'am? I apologize, but my boss is going to want to know."

"Yes, I suppose I can. Let's see . . . it was a Monday . . . yes, I'm sure it was a Monday, early afternoon. That's the day the nurse visits Mrs. Mitchell two houses down. I remember seeing the nurse's car out front when all the fire trucks came blasting in here, so that must have been the day. And let's see, it wasn't last week, not the week before. It was . . . four weeks ago. That's it, four weeks ago Monday," the woman pronounced proudly.

John knew the date without looking at a calendar. The same day Michael died; the same day Michael and Greene traded calls. John couldn't ignore the coincidence. Michael dead, Jacob Greene dead, and, John thought glumly, whatever Greene could have told him, if anything, dead with him.

John pumped the old woman about Greene for the next fifteen minutes. She eagerly volunteered information, unfortunately little of it useful.

"He was always quiet. You have to watch those ones, you know. I kept my eye on him. Had to . . . you never can tell. Just up the street, old man Rice, everyone thinks he's a saint. Huh! Want to know something? Every other week a taxi pulls up and a lady gets out, a different one every time. Always dressed pretty snazzy, if you know what I mean. Well, you can only guess what's going on in that house."

"Yes ma'am. But could you tell me anything else about Mr. Greene?"

She glanced both ways quickly and signaled with a crooked finger for John to put his ear against the screen door. "I'll bet you didn't know this." She lowered her voice. "He was a Jew." She backed away from the door, nodding her head, letting the impact of what she said seep into her listener.

John shook his head.

She signaled him toward the screen again. "That's right, a Jew. I'm not saying I have anything against the Jews, not at all, I won't go to any doctor that ain't a Jew, won't even consider it. But who would know with a name like Greene?"

She lowered her voice more. "I've delivered pamphlets in the neighborhood, for Christmas stocking drives, things like that. What do you think I've seen in Mr. Greene's mailbox? A letter from a synagogue, that's what. The one right over on Ulmstead." She pointed out the direction as she nodded her head again. "That's not all. The rabbi's been to visit Mr. Greene. I know the rabbi, Rabbi Sosman, he drives by my house every morning. Now who else would a rabbi visit but a Jew?"

The humor of the old woman's conspiratorial whispers was wearing thin. John changed the subject. "Do you know if Mr. Greene has any close friends in the neighborhood? A Mr. Olgov, perhaps?"

"No friends, no relatives, from what I can tell. Never heard of a Mr. Olgov. And I do keep an eye open on my street . . . the police tell us it's our duty you know. No, nobody ever visited the man, except for the rabbi, as I said. He was the only one I ever saw more than once, and I've lived here for twenty years."

"Ma'am, you can help me with one more thing, if you could. I have a very old photograph that might be of Mr. Greene. Could you try to identify him for me?" John held out the photograph he had taken from Kelly's.

The old woman opened the screen door and clutched the photograph in her bony fingers; her eyes widened in surprise. She hadn't expected a photograph of someone who looked more skeleton than man. "What's this picture about, young man?"

"Just an old photo—can you tell me if it's Mr. Greene?"

The woman looked again. "This must have been taken . . . a long time ago," the woman stammered. "I can't tell you for sure if that's him or not. No, I can't. The way he's dressed . . . the way he looks. I don't know how anyone could. Where was this taken? What's it all about?"

"Nothing, ma'am. Nothing at all," John said. "Just making sure I've found the right Mr. Greene." Deciding he had discovered about all he could from the woman, he added a curt good-bye, taking some gratification in leaving the woman's curiosity unsatisfied.

John spent the next half hour talking to Greene's other neighbors. He stuck to the paralegal cover, and everyone offered the little bits of information they knew. They alternatively described Greene as a kindly old man, a quiet but good neighbor, and a recluse. Greene had no relatives or close friends as far as any of them knew. Greene had lived in the neighborhood for at least thirty years, yet nobody knew more than the most superficial things about him: he had meticulously maintained his lawn, had kept a classic DeSoto in good working condition, had been a member of the neighborhood crime-watch group, and had a habit of walking around the block every evening at 9:00 P.M. Stray facts providing at best a blurry picture of the man.

John threw out the name Peter Olgov at each house; it never raised an eyebrow. When he hinted of rumors that the fire may have been deliberately set, to a person the neighbors expressed shock anybody would want to hurt the old man. He produced the photograph from Kelly's; none could positively identify the pictured man as Greene, but a few noted a similarity.

And no, they responded to his questioning, they did not know whether Greene had been interned in a concentration camp during World War II.

Before driving off, John sat in his car and reviewed what he had learned. Not much, really, but the fact remained Jacob Greene, a man who may have been able to shed some light on Michael's death, was now dead himself. That was worth looking into.

John withdrew the Dictaphone from his coat pocket, deciding to summarize what he had learned to date. Recording his thoughts would ensure he didn't forget details, and had the added benefit of forcing him to lay out the evidence he had uncovered in a logical fashion.

John pressed the record button and recapitulated the sequence of events to date: Olgov's murder, the box of Olgov's photographs and the false bottom, the phone message from Greene, the photo in the phone book, the death of Greene, the interviews with Greene's neighbors.

He summed up his findings: "Theory: my brother believed Greene had information that would prove valuable in the Olgov case. On the morning of his death, my brother called Greene. Motive for killing Michael: to keep him from discovering the damning evidence known by Greene. Motive for killing Greene: someone wanted whatever Greene knew to die with him. Logical course of action at this point: investigate the backgrounds of Olgov and Greene and search for a connection between the two."

John turned off the Dictaphone. The theory sounded almost persuasive, but he was far from convinced. The supposed motive for Michael's murder, the mysterious something regarding the Olgov case that Michael discovered or was about to discover from Greene—pure speculation. Was it surprising that Michael may have called Greene? If he found Greene's number among Olgov's things, thorough police work required a follow-up call. It took a leap of faith, however, to conclude Olgov's, Greene's, and Michael's deaths were related. He was grasping at straws, and given the circumstances, that might not be healthy.

Even as John reprimanded himself, his mind moved on. Peter Olgov, *another* murder victim, had hidden the photo that led Michael to Greene; Greene had died the same day as Michael, only hours after the two traded phone calls. Unhealthy speculation or not, he had to follow up, if for no other reason than to give himself a much needed, if phantom, sense of purpose.

Where to start? If a link existed between Greene and Olgov, nobody in Greene's neighborhood had given John a hint as to what it might be.

John caught a glimpse of the old woman he had talked to earlier ducking behind her living room curtains. Still on the job, he thought, amused, then recalled something she had said: the rabbi of a nearby synagogue—located on Ulmstead, he remembered—visited Greene regularly. He started for his car to check a map.

John found the synagogue's front doors unlocked. A small anteroom led to the synagogue proper, and he hesitated there. He had been in synagogues before, a few times during grade school for classmates' bar mitzvahs, but couldn't remember if tradition required him to wear a yarmulke, the Jewish skull cap, before proceeding. A quick survey of the anteroom revealed a basket of the caps, probably for visitors. He put one on and entered the empty synagogue.

Similar to a Christian church, he thought. Long rows of pewlike benches, high ceiling, stained glass windows flanking a lectern. Different religious symbols—Torah and menorah instead of cross and figure of Christ. A hallway leading off the rear might lead to offices, but

John hesitated to investigate unannounced. He stood waiting, hoping someone would enter and notice him. After a few minutes shuffling his feet, feeling mildly self-conscious, he turned to leave, planning to phone the rabbi, when a voice greeted him from the hallway.

"Good afternoon, may I help you?"

John turned to see a short but powerfully built man dressed in black with a medium-length salt-and-pepper beard. "Yes, thank you," John answered. "I'm looking for the rabbi."

"You have found him. Rabbi Sosman." The rabbi offered his hand.

"John Sarikov." John shook the rabbi's hand and returned the warm smile.

"What can I do for you, Mr. Sarikov?"

"It's regarding Jacob Greene."

Rabbi Sosman nodded gravely and folded his hands in front of him. "You are aware Mr. Greene passed away recently."

"I am. I'm very sorry."

"I am also. He was a good man. I take it you knew Mr. Greene then?"

"Actually, no, I didn't. But I am curious about the circumstances of his death."

Rabbi Sosman's eyebrows raised. "May I ask why?"

John pulled a card from his wallet, and held it out for the rabbi to see. "I'm a free-lance reporter. I have reason to believe Mr. Greene may have had evidence in a capital crime."

"Excuse me?"

"Four weeks ago a police officer, NYPD, called Mr. Greene in connection with a murder investigation. Hours after that call the officer was murdered. The same afternoon Mr. Greene died in a fire."

John caught the rabbi's expression. "The timing of the two deaths . . . you must agree, rabbi, it's quite a coincidence. I want to find out if it's anything more."

"How?"

"By learning all I can about Mr. Greene."

Rabbi Sosman frowned. "I apologize if I seem skeptical, but you've caught me by surprise. Mr. Greene was a devout, solitary man. I find it hard, if not impossible, to believe anyone murdered him, if that's what you're implying."

"I think it's possible someone did."

"I see." Rabbi Sosman paused and interlaced his fingers. "And you've taken your theory to the police?"

"Not yet."

Rabbi Sosman studied John intently. "I'm sorry, Mr. Sarikov," he said, finally. "I'd like to help, but—"

"Just a few questions about Mr. Greene: his background, the circumstances of the fire."

Rabbi Sosman shook his head. "I think I would prefer that you presented your theories to the authorities; I will be happy to answer any of *their* questions."

"Is there something you're hiding, rabbi?"

"No," Rabbi Sosman answered without hesitation.

"Then why won't you answer my questions?"

"To be blunt, Mr. Sarikov, your suppositions seem a bit too . . . far-fetched. Forgive me, but I must consider the possibility that you are more interested in sensationalism than searching for the truth. Now if you'll excuse me . . ." Rabbi Sosman broke eye contact and started back down the hallway.

"Rabbi Sosman," John called.

Rabbi Sosman turned, looking put upon. "Yes, Mr. Sarikov."

"I'm not interested in sensationalism." John paused, searching for the words, deciding on the truth. "The murdered officer was my brother."

Rabbi Sosman lowered his eyes and nodded gently. "I see. You have my condolences." He walked back to within a few feet of John. "But Mr. Sarikov, I repeat, isn't this a matter for the police, not a private citizen, even one trained as a reporter?"

"I think they're about to close down the investigation."

"And you're trying to breathe new life into it?"

"And if I am? Look, I only learned a couple of hours ago of the phone calls between Mr. Greene and my brother. I drove to Mr. Greene's house, to ask him about the calls. I found out he died—how and, more important, when. I *want* to take this to the police, rabbi; I'm just trying to learn if I'm really on to something or not before I do."

Rabbi Sosman's face continued to show uncertainty.

"Maybe this will prove I'm telling the truth," John said as he pulled the photograph from his coat pocket. "I told you my brother was investigating a murder before he died . . . well, he found this in the possession of the murder victim." John showed the rabbi first the side with Jacob Greene's name and address, then flipped it over.

A pained expression crossed Rabbi Sosman's face. He studied the photograph closely, and once again assessed John.

"Three persons dead, rabbi. The murder victim, my brother, and Mr. Greene. This photograph is evidence there is a connection. Is the man in the photo Mr. Greene?"

Rabbi Sosman studied the photograph again, then pointed to the hallway, suggesting they continue the discussion in his office. Once there, the rabbi took a seat behind a large mission oak desk and studied the photograph again. John sat across from him.

After a few moments of silence the rabbi rose to his feet and stood looking out the window. "Mr. Greene . . . Jacob . . . was an inmate of Auschwitz during the war. A very painful period he chose to keep to himself."

"Auschwitz?"

Rabbi Sosman nodded.

"Then this photograph, it *is* of Mr. Greene?"

Rabbi Sosman studied the photo again. "There's a very strong resemblance. This picture must be . . . almost fifty years old. Jacob would have been a young man then. Sadly, he doesn't look it. How did you get this picture, Mr. Sarikov?"

"As I said, my brother was investigating a murder. The murder victim had it in his possession."

The rabbi continued to stare at the photo.

"You wouldn't have a picture of Mr. Greene by any chance?" John asked.

"No, I'm sorry, and unfortunately I understand very little survived the fire."

John nodded. "Just a few questions, rabbi . . . about Mr. Greene. The answers could be important."

The rabbi reseated himself and drummed his fingers on the desk. "I understand your motivation, Mr. Sarikov, and, frankly, admit to being somewhat intrigued by this photograph. Therefore, I'll listen to your questions, but I warn you, my curiosity has bounds."

"That's all I can ask for, rabbi." John paused to put his thoughts together. "The murder victim, the one whose death my brother was investigating, his name was Peter Olgov. Does the name sound familiar to you? Did Mr. Greene ever mention him?"

"No, not that I recall."

"Could he have been a friend of Mr. Greene's?"

"Possibly, but Mr. Greene was a loner, without family or friends I'm aware of."

"Did he ever mention my brother, Officer Michael Sarikov, or say he recently had dealings with the police?"

"No."

"Was he acting strangely before his death?"

"Not that I noticed."

"Do you know how the fire started at Mr. Greene's?"

"Yes. Gas explosion. The Fire Department said the valves on the oven burners were left open. Gas filled the room, and ignited, probably from the oven's pilot light."

John thought out loud. "Maybe an accident, I don't know, but if you wanted to kill someone and make it look like an accident . . ."

Rabbi Sosman fidgeted in his chair. "I find this discussion disturbing, but for the sake of argument let's say it happened that way. One question. Why, Mr. Sarikov? As I have said, I knew Jacob fairly well, and I can say unequivocally no one would have reason to harm him."

Good question. John had another one: how had he gotten wrapped up in fantasy so quickly? A drowning man will grab anything to stay afloat—maybe that was it. "I don't know why. Maybe Mr. Greene knew or saw something he shouldn't have. I admit I'm firing questions in the dark when I don't even begin to know where to look or what I'm looking for, but there must be a connection between Olgov and Mr. Greene; I want to know what it is."

"And I'm afraid I can be of no help."

"You may have answers and not even know it. Tell me what you know about Mr. Greene. Anything might help. Where he's originally from, his past. Something may ring a bell."

"Besides his experiences during the Holocaust, I really know very little."

"Then start there. I repeat, anything might help."

Rabbi Sosman nodded. "Okay, Mr. Sarikov. For whatever good it will do you."

John surreptitiously snapped on the Dictaphone in his pocket as the rabbi began to speak.

"I first met Jacob about ten years ago, right here,

after a service. I could tell he desperately wished to tell me something, but was having trouble voicing it. I began asking him simple questions, where he lived, where he worked, similar things. In the midst of this small talk he blurted out he wanted my forgiveness. For what, I asked. For forsaking his heritage, for his lack of courage, he answered. He obeyed the Sabbath, read the Torah, kept kosher . . . but only things that could be done in private. I asked him if he was ashamed of being a Jew. You know what he said?"

John shook his head.

"He said no, being a Jew made him proud. I expressed confusion—if being a Jew made him proud, why did he hide his faith? He appeared frightened, wouldn't answer. I asked him nothing further, but offered such forgiveness as was in my power to give. Jacob never missed a service after that. Months later, I stopped him as he left the synagogue and commended him for his regular attendance. We began talking, and then he answered the question I had posed a year earlier—why had he hidden his faith. Fear had been pulling at his insides for fifty years, he said. Fear of being found out a Jew. It caused him to turn his back on a part of himself, disavow beliefs he held sacred."

"What was he afraid of?" John asked.

"My question exactly. That's when Jacob told me he survived Auschwitz. Suddenly, I understood. Because he was a Jew, he had been singled out, enslaved, and threatened with death, and lived in dread of the day it would happen again. Even here in America, after all the years that had passed, he feared they would find him, do the same things to him all over again. Never again, he had promised himself, and to ensure his safety he hid his faith."

The rabbi paused, letting his words sink in. "That may sound foolish to you and me, but neither of us can imagine what he went through, what it took to survive those times."

The rabbi looked through John. "We had many talks after that. Jacob was born in Warsaw, Poland . . . let's see, I believe he was in his mid-seventies, which means he was born in . . . around 1920. His family, I gathered, was fairly well off. He had one sister, I think. I don't really know much of his childhood. He had just started college in Cracow . . . it must have been 1939 . . . when the Nazis launched their blitzkrieg into Poland. He left school and returned to Warsaw to be with his family. He told me what it was like to watch endless lines of tall, handsome German soldiers with polished boots and freshly scrubbed faces march into Warsaw when the city fell and wonder how much longer the rag-tag Polish army could hold on. As it turned out, not very long. The entire country fell in less than a month."

The rabbi's eyes refocused on John. "Is any of this helpful?"

John shrugged. "Please continue, rabbi."

"Life changed dramatically for Jacob under German occupation. A quick history lesson for you, in case you didn't know. Warsaw became a separated city— the Nazis stripped Jews of their rights and possessions and forced them to relocate to a ghetto section. A high brick wall was built, dividing free, Aryan Warsaw from the Jewish ghetto. To survive and provide for his family, Jacob took to smuggling food into the ghetto, a crime punishable by death. He took part in the Warsaw ghetto uprising. The Nazis viciously crushed the uprising and worse, from Jacob's perspective, exposed his sympathies, jeopardizing his family. He hid himself and his family successfully for months, but finally the Nazis caught them; other Poles turned them in."

"Do you know who?"

"No idea. Soldiers packed Jacob and his family into

railway cars with hundreds of other families and sent them to a labor camp in the south, the Birkeneau complex of Auschwitz. There, Nazi guards herded them through a gate. On the other side two German officers divided them, a group to the left, a group to the right. They sent Jacob to the right, his family to the left. He never saw them again, but discovered their fate soon enough. Another history lesson: the ones sent to the left, deemed too weak to work in the labor camps, were taken to a large hall, asked to strip in preparation for showers. They were given towels, soap, and calm assurances, then herded into huge cement bunkers. A gas prepared from Zyklon B was poured through openings in the ceiling; within minutes every person inside died. Hitler's final solution."

Rabbi Sosman exhaled. He had grown animated as he spoke and now calmed himself. "Jacob blamed himself. He had stood up and counted himself as a Jew, and because of that his family was murdered. He was lucky, or unlucky, depending on how you look at it, and survived. He preferred not to think about those times, but more than that, he trusted no one, not even in America. He told me when he landed at Ellis Island he literally kissed the ground—finally free. His estimation of the promised land dimmed the first time someone called him a dirty Jew. It was not to be the last time. All the memories and fears came crashing back, and he never rid himself of them."

"And his life in this country?" John asked.

"As I said, I know so little. He settled here in Brooklyn, and spent the last thirty years or so of his life in the same house—the one that burned down. Never married. Didn't drink, didn't smoke, was a complete gentleman from what I could tell. Worked as a cab driver, but had retired by the time I met him." Rabbi Sosman shrugged. "The sad thing is, I don't think there was much to know. The events that shaped his life, that he could not put behind him, happened long ago."

John wasn't sure what to say. In the abstract, he had known how the Nazis implemented the Holocaust, but the rabbi had related an actual testimonial, not cold and distant textbook facts. "I wish I had a chance to know Mr. Greene; it must have taken a man of great courage to have endured."

"Persons of great courage died also, no distinctions were made." The rabbi smiled grimly. "There, done with my soliloquy. I apologize for the long-winded lecture. Now, are there other questions I can answer?"

John answered yes and spent the next fifteen minutes asking all the questions he could think of: who did Greene sit with regularly at the synagogue (answer, nobody); who did he talk to (answer, again as far as the rabbi knew, nobody); what were his hobbies; what restaurants did he frequent; what were his sources of income; and on and on. John learned nothing of interest.

"As I warned you, Mr. Sarikov, I don't imagine anything I said will be of much use."

"To be honest, rabbi, you may be right. Just the same, I appreciate the time you spent. Would you mind if I took your number and called you if I think of anything else?"

"No, I suppose not." The rabbi wrote his number on a slip of paper and handed it to John. John gave his card in return, then left.

As he walked to the car, John admitted to himself what he hadn't wanted to face—he had never held much hope of clearing Michael. And now? As tenuous as it might be, he had a lead to follow and some reason to hope.

After a moment's hesitation, Rabbi Sosman threw the young man's card in the wastebasket. He knew he would never have cause to use it. He could not fault the young man for the devotion he'd shown to his brother, but his energies were being misspent. *Someone killed Jacob? Preposterous. Jacob had no enemies.*

He'd almost made the mistake of mentioning something that had troubled him at the time of Greene's death, but was glad he hadn't. A logical explanation existed, he was sure, and raising it would only have given the young man false hope on a road leading nowhere.

24

Rolf straightened his tie, then flattened his hair with the palm of his hand. He approved of the image reflected in the mirror. Hair cut short, clean shaven, white starched collar—businesslike, professional. The clothes felt alien, but gave him the capable, polished look he desired.

The suit cost seven hundred dollars at Brooks Brothers, the tie another seventy-five, three hundred for the shoes. A Brooks Brothers suit, he laughed to himself at the thought, but knew the attire was appropriate—silk sport coats and gold chains wouldn't do. This meeting was the real thing, all business. Rolf had to show some respect if he wanted to rise within the organization.

Only three years ago, Rolf reflected, he had trouble imagining any future. After twenty years in America things had reached a low point. When he first arrived from East Germany, living on his aunt and uncle's couch, he tried to play it square and quickly discovered there was no percentage in it. Immigrants could get jobs as manual laborers, clerks, or, like his uncle, maintenance men, but that was a line-up for chumps. The real opportunities in the neighborhoods lay outside the law. If you were tough, were a man, you cut yourself a piece of the pie instead of accepting fucking table scraps.

He had started small—street gangs involved in rumbles and petty larceny. That's where you earned your stripes. When you lined up against a black or Hispanic gang from the Coney Island projects, you found out pretty quick who had the balls to make it and who didn't.

He remembered the first time he killed, at seventeen. Rivals trespassed on his gang's territory on the edge of Brighton Beach. All pretty boys, way over their head. They spray-painted gang symbols on buildings, talked up the girls. A few fist fights broke out; they probably thought that was the end of it. No fucking way. No one shit in his backyard and got away with it. Rolf found where the rival leader lived, then waited for him with a bicycle chain. A big motherfucker, well over six feet, a weight lifter. The first blow brought the asshole to his knees, the second flattened him to his back. It was a high Rolf never forgot—the fear in those eyes as the chain came down again, and then again. Word circulated through the neighborhood the next day: the police found the body, almost unrecognizable, flesh slashed to the bone by what the coroner estimated to be over one hundred blows. No one fucked with his gang after that—a lesson Rolf took to heart.

By twenty, he had graduated to the big time: the Organizatsiya, the Russian mafia. It was smaller then, just beginning. Groups of Russian émigrés, many of them Jews, their roots stretching to powerful black marketeers in the USSR, patterned loosely after the Italian mafia. Rolf was the exception, an East German in a minor Russian crime family, but it was a good fit—he became a favorite enforcer. Extortion, gasoline bootlegging, protection rackets, prostitution, numbers—the family prospered until it fucked up and got involved in city contracts. Not that Rolf could blame the family; big money stood to be made. Nobody considered the Italians, that was the mistake. The Italians considered construction contracts their private preserve.

The Italians hit two of the heads of the crime family Rolf worked for, garroted both. That's when the chickenshits he worked with ran, packed their bags and scattered, or laid low in girlfriends' apartments. Only Rolf struck back. He cornered a minor lieutenant from the Italian crime family, beat him unconscious, then nailed him to the floor—five-inch spikes through knees and elbows. He carved him with a knife, leaving him to be found pinned to the floor, half alive and half human. Then Rolf disappeared— he couldn't win the war alone.

That was the low point; then unexpectedly things turned around. Word got to Rolf, holed up in a flophouse, that the heat had been called off. He reacted warily, but his contacts confirmed the rumors—he was off the hook. A few weeks later, eating at a neighborhood restaurant, he found out why. A well-dressed man, an emissary from someone the man referred to only as "my boss," sat down across from Rolf and the story came out. The "boss" had taken an interest in Rolf's career and was dismayed to find it about to end so abruptly. As an act of friendship, he had extended his help—buying out the contracts on Rolf's life and pulling some favors to ensure new ones weren't issued. No strings, the emissary told Rolf, just an act of friendship.

Rolf was no fool; he had offered favor for favor, the emissary's response what he expected: "My boss did mention an opening in his organization. He would be pleased if you considered working for him." And so Rolf began working for Vasili.

In the last three years Rolf's climb in Vasili's organization had been steady. Now, after the incident with Pavel and the two cops, Rolf fully expected his climb to accelerate, and hoped that was the reason for tonight's meeting.

Rolf considered his reflection a last time—perfect. He headed toward the door, expected at Vasili's Plaza Hotel suite promptly at seven.

25

The interview with Rabbi Sosman still running through his mind, John walked into his apartment to see Barbara standing in the middle of the living room. She seemed nervous, surprised to see him. Frankly, he was just as surprised to see her. They both had apartments in the city. Before Michael's death, they spent most nights at one or the other, but that happened less and less. He had instigated the trend—the simplest remedy to the tension growing between them seemed to be space. They hadn't been together for over a week; he hadn't expected tonight to be any different.

"Barbara . . . ?" John noticed the guilty look on her face and followed her furtive glances toward the bedroom. A half-packed suitcase lay open on the bed. They both kept a number of things at each other's apartment, but he could see Barbara intended to change that.

"What are you doing here?" he asked, the answer now obvious.

Barbara took a long breath. "John . . ."

He repeated the question.

Barbara's eyes pleaded briefly, then turned to the ground. "I'm packing some of my things."

"Why?" It should have been hard for him to ignore the things he had been putting her through for the last weeks, but it wasn't. He still knew, deep inside, he needed her, now more than ever. She must know that also, and yet she was about to leave him. He felt a need to hurt her for that.

She dropped to the couch. "I called twice before I came. You weren't home. I hoped to be gone before you got back. I didn't want this."

"Want what?"

"A fight. I don't want to fight."

"You just want to leave."

Barbara shook her head. "No, I don't want to leave." Her eyes met his for an instant, but he didn't soften. "I don't want to leave," she repeated, "but I have to."

"And what? We weren't going to talk about it? Did you just plan to leave a note on the bed? Dear John . . . how appropriate."

"Talk about it, John? Talk about it? That's what I've been trying to do for the last month."

John remained stone-faced.

"You're going through a rough time," Barbara went on. "I know that. I understand that, and I want to help."

"By leaving?" In some way it felt good to hurt; he had been hurt so much lately.

"I want to be here for you, but you're not taking my help; you're pushing me away."

"Who packed your suitcase? It wasn't me."

She wiped her eyes. "John, you've shut me out. You're destroying yourself, and I can't just sit and watch. You've got to stop punishing yourself over Michael. You've got to go on living. This isn't easy for me . . . but you've got to come back to me. You have to face this, get over it, get professional help if you need it. It's eating you up inside. You're angry, and I'm the one you direct that anger at. I'll come back when you're ready to reach out to me, but I won't stay because you need someone nearby to strike out at. I just don't think I can go through it anymore."

No matter how she couched it, no matter the truth of what she said, the fact remained *she planned to walk out on him,* and if she was prepared to do that, then he wasn't prepared to stop her. Michael had left him, everyone was leaving him. Why did he think she would be any different? He would push her to say it. Once she put it into words it couldn't be taken back. "What are you saying?"

"I'm saying . . . maybe . . . maybe it's better if we don't see each other for a while."

Her eyes pleaded once more, but John ignored them. "If that's what you want."

"It's not what I want . . . we need time apart."

"Then there's nothing left to talk about, is there? When should I pick up my things from your place? Or would you rather just send them to me?"

"John . . ." Barbara started, then ran into the bedroom. Tears started in her eyes, but she wiped them away. She flung her remaining clothes in the open suitcase and carried it with her to the front door. John didn't return her gaze. "You need help, John."

"Thank you for your concern, but I'll manage fine. Leave your key on the table."

She fumbled in her purse for the key and laid it on the kitchen table. "Believe it or not, I'm trying to help the only way I know how. I love you," she said.

John didn't reply, and Barbara turned and left without looking back.

The door shut with a finality that echoed through the apartment.

John mixed a drink, feeling rotten, petty, and vindictive. He hadn't even shown a human emotion. He could run after her, but why, to what end? He wasn't going to change, not yet, and he'd just hurt her in all the same ways. Hell, he knew it—she was one of the best things that ever happened to him. Yet he drove her away. Why?

Now he was completely alone. *Did he want it this way?* Maybe. Maybe martyring himself was the only way to approximate what happened to his brother. Maybe suffering alone was the purest form of suffering.

John drained his drink and mixed himself another. He didn't want to think about any of this. He just wanted to put himself to sleep, and wake up tomorrow, and the next day, and the next, and one day not hurt so bad.

He pulled a scrap of paper from his pocket—Detective Hartley's number, the detective the department had assigned to handle Michael's murder investigation. John had found leads today: the photo, Greene's death. This Hartley might listen to him now, relaunch the investigation. Maybe Barbara was right. Maybe the time had come to step back, let the police step in, and salvage what remained of his life. Then he could call Barbara again, ask her to forgive him, make a new start.

John decided to see Hartley in the morning, and in the meantime get good and drunk.

26

Thank God for college students, Vasili thought as he knotted his tie and looked through the mirror at the bed and the fan of blond hair spread over the pillow. Better than whores, they did anything. This one manned the phone bank at Senator Lund's campaign headquarters; they'd met that afternoon at the luncheon fund-raiser. One more wide-eyed volunteer more taken with his position than taken aback by his age. It hadn't taken much persuasion to convince her to check into the Plaza for the night—hell, it hadn't taken any.

He might even break his rule with this one, arrange another rendezvous. He had performed better than he had in some time, and she seemed eager enough. He checked his watch. Ten minutes yet, and his suite was just down the hall. He sat on the edge of the bed and stroked her hair. No hesitation—she agreed. A good soldier.

Back in his suite, Vasili sipped cognac and considered the meeting. He was taking a risk seeing Rolf in person, he knew, but the time had come to up the ante. Before today he had always insisted on multiple layers of insulation, speaking in person only to a handful who relayed his orders to other subordinate agents for execution. He had tried to stay removed from the dirt, but that was no longer possible—a showdown with the Collegium loomed, he could sense it, and he had to prepare. Men like Rolf would be needed.

A bumbling bunch of dinosaurs, the Collegium still ran, ostensibly at least, the remnants of Russia's intelligence presence in America. They couldn't be completely ignored, not yet.

He should be grateful, really, for the new political climate—chaos breeds opportunity, including the one he had taken advantage of. It had been a bit dicey at first, sitting down with the dons of the Brighton Beach mafia, even for him not men to take lightly. The Italian mafia had a saying: "We'll kill you, but the Russians, they're crazy—they'll kill your whole family."

The principal don, Katkov, was a coarse man, but Vasili found his mind anything but ordinary. Not surprising. For two decades Katkov had balanced on a knife's edge, competition from his own ranks on one side, the Italian mafia on the other, the cops and feds, the ones he hadn't bought, chasing from the rear. Through it all he stayed on top, and now, with the Soviet Union no more, with the Russian mafia in complete control of the burgeoning drug trade between America and the former Soviet territories, he had more power than ever.

The don had been direct: "As you know, business has been very good to us lately. We are gratified to learn that you think enough of our prospects to consider offering us your services. Only one question— what can *you* do for *us*?"

Vasili had given his answer—sophistication. He had access to contacts and connections the mob would never have. People in high places cultivated by the KGB over the last fifty years. He had international bankers who could hide money so it would never be found. Better he had political figures, heads of states, who had worked with the KGB in the past, and would, for a price, work with him now. In essence, he offered the mob a tantalizing prize: a direct pipeline into the world's most sophisticated espionage organization, an organization that now looked for a new purpose.

Then his clincher. He had thrown the two-pound package from his briefcase on the table.

"What's this?" the don had asked.

"Pure heroin. Finest quality."

"We bring in thousands of pounds. Are we to be impressed?"

"This package came from a special assistant to a foreign ambassador, a man who has worked for us in the past. He carried it into the country in a diplomatic pouch."

The don hadn't needed an explanation—he knew. Diplomatic pouches aren't subject to customs checks. "You paint a bright picture. Why do you need us?"

"I can import drugs without you. I can launder money without you. Without you, I can deliver drug enforcement agents, customs officers, heads of banks, politicians, both foreign and domestic, bought and paid for. One thing I don't have—access to supply. The KGB never involved itself with that on a large scale, only what they needed for strategic reasons— payoffs, bribes, blackmail—never for the purely capitalistic pursuit of profit. That, sir, is why I need you. I hope I've already made my case for why you need me."

And it had worked. For almost six months now, with impunity, he had used ex-KGB operatives and connections to import heroin and cocaine for the Russian mafia. So far, Katkov was very, very pleased.

The potential profits were staggering—wealth beyond dreams—and it had all been so easy. The Soviet Union would not have allowed it, but then the Soviet Union was no more. Its breakup made everything possible.

Two members of the Collegium had already been

swayed to his side: Aleksei and, just recently, Grichko. *Bought* was perhaps a more accurate description. They had profited from his initial forays into drugs and were eager to continue padding their offshore accounts. As to their loyalty, Vasili had no misconceptions. If the flow of dollars stopped, he lost even Aleksei.

The others? Soon it would be decision time. Two would turn, he was sure of it. They no longer knew or welcomed risk, and had grown fat and complacent. Once Vasili explained the possibilities to them, which of them could stomach war over dipping their hand into the easy flow of dollars? He could hear himself posturing for the record with words that no longer had any meaning: "We can either ignore this source of funding and watch the organization atrophy to nothingness, or we can tap it, keeping the organization alive and healthy for the day the motherland again calls upon us to protect her."

There would be two, Nicholas and Yuri, who Vasili expected would not see reason. Principle, he supposed, in Nicholas's case; brash stupidity in Yuri's. He had to be prepared to resort to more aggressive persuasion with them, proving the strategy he undertook three years ago to be the correct one. He had seen even then the need for his own private army, a group of ruthless, hungry men loyal exclusively to him. With the supply of agents from Russia cut off, new blood was needed, he had argued to the Collegium, and they narrowly approved limited recruitment. Now it was too late for them to object. He had fifty agents in his direct employ, most, as with Rolf, from the cream of the Russian mafia.

Rolf had performed well, his recent usefulness in the matter of Pavel and the two cops an unexpected bonus. His predilection for young boys, a vice uncovered by Vasili's informants, disgusted Vasili, but he could ignore that for now, at least while Rolf's usefulness continued. Besides, the weakness of a subordinate could often be invaluable as a means of exercising control.

There was a knock on the door and Dmitri, Vasili's bodyguard—not much on brains but powerfully built and cat quick—entered.

"Your guest is here," Dmitri announced.

"Very well, send him in."

Rolf was ushered into the suite, clearly impressed by his surroundings, his hands fumbling at his sides. What Vasili saw pleased him—the suit was new, well tailored and expensive, but Rolf clearly wore it unnaturally. That was a good sign—pleasing Vasili had been more important to Rolf than his own comfort.

Vasili strode forward, his arm outstretched, and gave Rolf a warm handshake. "Rolf, thank you for coming." He patted Rolf on the back and directed him to the sofa.

"Dmitri, would you make us drinks? What are you having, Rolf?"

". . . Scotch . . . on the rocks."

"Make it two," Vasili said to Dmitri, then redirected his attention to Rolf. "It's good to finally meet you in person."

"Thank you, sir. I'm honored."

"Nonsense, the honor is all ours, isn't it Dmitri?"

Dmitri nodded.

"He doesn't say much, but believe me when I say he's been quite impressed by your actions of late, and Dmitri isn't easily impressed, are you, Dmitri?"

Dmitri shook his head, then handed the drinks to Rolf and Vasili. Vasili toasted Rolf, then swallowed shallowly from his drink.

"Please leave us now, Dmitri," Vasili said, "Rolf and I have some business to discuss."

Dmitri left the room, and for a full minute Vasili focused his attention on Rolf without speaking.

"I appreciate the way you've handled things for

me," Vasili said finally. "Especially most recently—the matter has blown over with no repercussions."

"I'm glad to hear it."

Vasili nodded, then held up an envelope and tossed it in Rolf's lap. "A more concrete expression of my gratitude."

Rolf stuck the thick envelope in his pocket without comment.

Vasili continued. "I called you here tonight for two reasons. To thank you, but also to meet you in person. I know what you've done for me—impressive—but I wanted to learn more, the things you can only learn by looking a man in the eye and shaking his hand. I like what I see."

Vasili looked away from Rolf to the window, out over Central Park. "I need a man close to me. One who I can trust implicitly. Who will, if necessary, lay down his life to carry out my orders. I thought you might be that man, so I invited you here to see for myself."

"You've found who you're looking for," Rolf said without hesitation.

"You sound quite sure of yourself."

"I am."

"You are prepared, then, to follow my orders unquestioningly?"

"As I always have."

"Even if they were to put you in peril?"

"Yes."

". . . *Even*, Rolf, if my orders conflicted with the Collegium's?"

"Yes."

"I see . . . and if I find the Collegium and I can no longer peacefully coexist—that one of us must make room for the other, what then Rolf?

"I follow *your* orders."

Vasili was pleased. Only a fool would have answered the questions in any other way, but not everyone would have responded so eagerly.

"Good. Very good. You haven't disappointed me. There will be dangers, but there will be even greater rewards. There will also be rules—silence being one of the most important. You must act as if the very walls have ears—because they do, more often than you realize. Everything I tell you, everything you learn, goes no further, do you understand?"

Rolf nodded.

"Very well. You know business is good. After our little run-in with Koenig, I expect it to stay that way."

Rolf nodded again, accepting the unstated compliment. Two months ago a Hungarian attaché named Koenig had clamped down on illicit activities within Hungary's embassies in the U.S. He played crusader, but Vasili got the real message: raise my cut or drugs don't move. As a result, a principal courier Vasili had cultivated within the Hungarian diplomatic corps reneged on a delivery. Too much heat from Koenig, he said. Two days later the courier received a package. He opened it to find a note: "Trust us, Koenig will not object," and, wrapped in white butcher's paper, a severed tongue. The courier did not miss the point; the courier resumed deliveries within the week.

"In summary," Vasili continued, "no problems, save one . . ." Vasili took a long drink from his scotch. "I'm worried about some members of the Collegium. You don't know all the politics, and for now you don't have to. It's enough for you to know there are some who are open to progress, and some who are not. Those who are not may begin prying into our affairs and raising objections. I will, of course, deal with their objections in a reasonable manner, but some may need . . . further persuasion. That's where you'll come in, Rolf. You understand?"

"Yes."

"I will be asking a lot of you, and I want you to be absolutely sure. I saved you from a delicate situation two years ago without strings, and there are no strings now." Of course there were, Vasili knew it and Rolf was smart enough to know it too. ". . . just a question—can I count on you?—and an answer, yes or no."

"Anything," Rolf said, and Vasili was confident he meant it.

27

John checked his machine. Empty. After a day and a half and two messages, he still had no reply from Hartley.

He called the desk sergeant at Hartley's precinct. The guy acted polite enough, probably wasn't giving him the run around when he said Hartley was out on a call. The desk sergeant didn't expect him in until late afternoon.

John grabbed his car keys and started for the door. The only sure way to see Hartley was to sit in the precinct and wait. It hadn't worked with the police commissioner, but Hartley wasn't going to have a secretary to hide behind.

John took up watch on a bench in the precinct lobby. He opened the newspaper he had brought with him and tried to concentrate on the articles, but his mind wouldn't focus, and his eyes kept breaking from the page every time someone entered the precinct house.

A couple of cops he vaguely knew offered their condolences; a number of others he didn't glanced his way, holding their stares uncomfortably long. John read into their expression what they did not say: there sat the brother of the dirty cop who got whacked a few weeks back.

Two hours or so after John arrived, a young cop, late twenties, entered the building. The desk sergeant called him to the desk and nodded slightly in John's direction; the cop peered at John from the corner of his eyes. Brown hair combed to the side in a wave, eyes pinched together on his face, nose far too short for the length of his head. Flashy clothes—out of place next to the staid and ragged dress of most of the other detectives. Hartley, John was certain.

The young cop looked away from John and started to walk quickly past, but John had enough of being avoided. "Detective Hartley?" he called, rising from the bench and cutting off Hartley's escape.

Harley stopped, an exasperated look on his face. "Yes?"

"My name is John Sarikov. I told the desk sergeant I wanted to see you." John saw no reason to politely ignore Hartley's rudeness.

"Yes, he told me." There was no apology.

"It's about my brother, Michael Sarikov. I understand you're heading his murder investigation."

"That's right. I was," Hartley caught himself, "*am* . . . in charge of that case. What can I do for you?"

John expected to be invited back to Hartley's desk, but Hartley offered no invitation. "I wondered how the investigation is going."

"I can assure you we're doing everything in our power."

A line straight out of some policeman's manual of standard responses, John guessed. "Any leads?"

"No, but we have feelers out. We're still hopeful we can turn something up."

"What about the things found at my brother's house? Any idea who could have planted them there, who could have set up the bank accounts in the Caymans, any clues at all?"

"None at this point, but again, I assure you, we're doing everything possible. Now if you'll excuse me . . ."

John hadn't necessarily expected leads; he had expected more than cold indifference. He held up his index finger. "A moment, detective, please. I think I may have come across a few things you might find interesting."

Hartley adopted a costume smile. "Well, we've done a pretty thorough investigation, but if you've come up with something my team and I missed, we'd be glad to have you fill us in. What is it?"

John dismissed the condescending tone. "Two things. One, Kelly, my brother's wife, told me the night before his murder he was looking through a box of old photographs. They belonged to an old man, Peter Olgov, whose murder investigation my brother was involved in. The next—"

"Olgov?" Hartley interrupted. "I think I know that name. You say he was murdered?"

John nodded. "In Brighton Beach."

"Right. Found the old guy in the bathtub. Are you saying your brother had evidence in the case and didn't turn it over to homicide?"

"I only know he had a box of Olgov's photos, and now they're missing. I told you he looked at the photos the night before he died . . . well, we searched the house a couple of weeks later and couldn't find them. It occurred to me, maybe he was taking them to the precinct the morning he died. You guys find a box of photographs with the bodies or in Ray's car?"

Hartley paused, a sour look on his face. "I'd have to check the inventory list."

"Could we do that, now? It could be important."

Hartley rubbed his forehead as if willing his mind to manufacture an excuse. "Let's go to my desk," he finally said in resignation.

Hartley led John to a large room with three rows of desks, each row four desks deep. A few other detectives lounged in the room, one on the phone, two talking over coffee. A relatively neat desk stuck in a back corner of the room belonged to Hartley.

Hartley seated himself behind the desk, then fumbled through a stack of folders piled on a radiator hood behind him. He found the Sarikov file there, buried beneath a thick layer of paper. He scanned the file quickly.

"No. Nothing of that sort was found in the car or van, or on the bodies."

"That's sort of odd, don't you think?"

"Look, Mr. Sarikov, what's odd about losing photos?—people do it all the time. They're probably lying around the deceased's house somewhere, and his wife just couldn't find them."

"I'm not talking about one or two photos; I'm talking about a box full, the size of a shoe box—hard to misplace that. Anyway, hear me out. My brother discovered a false bottom to this box. Underneath he found more photographs. One had a name written on its back, Jacob Greene, and a phone number. I know because that's the only photo we found; my brother had left it stuck in a phone book. I'm guessing the morning of his death he called this Greene."

Hartley reached into his desk drawer for a roll of antacids. He popped one in his mouth, then shifted again through the file in front of him and pulled out a stapled list of names and numbers. "I had the phone company send me a record of every call made from your brother's number for the month preceding his death." He turned to the last page of the list and scanned intently for a moment. "Here it is. The telephone records show your brother called a Mr. Jacob Greene the morning of his death. 6:56 A.M."

John inhaled quickly. "Was that the only time my brother called Greene?"

Hartley checked the list again. A "1" was written next to Greene's number. "That was the only time.

Now, Mr. Sarikov, why should I care that your brother called this Greene?"

"Because a while ago I tried to call him too; the line was dead. I drove by his house; it had burned to the ground . . . with Greene inside. Guess when the fire occurred."

Hartley shrugged. "I wouldn't know."

"On the same afternoon as my brother's death."

"So?"

So? "So . . . doesn't that seem to be a coincidence? The two talked once, and both died the same day. Olgov, my brother, Greene, all linked, all dead."

"Look Mr. Sarikov, we've had someone look into everybody your brother called . . . that includes this Greene. We checked him out. He didn't have anything to do with this."

"What do you mean, *checked him out*?"

"I *mean* we checked him out. Did a background check, ran a rap sheet. If we'd come up with anything, it would be noted here." Hartley gestured toward the list.

"I didn't say Greene was a criminal. Look, I've got a hunch Greene knew something about Olgov's death, maybe knew the killer. Let's say my brother found out what that something was from the photos. He calls Greene; someone finds out about the call; Greene and my brother are killed. Whatever my brother knew, whatever Greene knew, dies with them."

Hartley took a deep breath before responding. "Mr. Sarikov, I'll look into what you've told me. You have my word on it. I appreciate your stopping in, and my condolences on your brother's death. Now I really do have work to get to."

A brush-off? John stared at Hartley in disbelief, then handed him a scrap of paper with two names and addresses scrawled on it. "I've taken the liberty of writing out Jacob Greene's and Peter Olgov's addresses for you." He had copied Olgov's address from Michael's police log.

"What's that?" Hartley said as he looked at the paper. "Right, Greene, the phone call. Why do I need Olgov's address? The man's dead."

"My brother's wife told me an elderly lady residing in the same building as Olgov gave my brother the photos. I thought you might want to try to find her."

"*You* thought I might want to try to find her. Great." Hartley rolled his eyes. "I'll have someone get right on it, and . . . what was it you said, Greene's place burned down?"

"That's right. I'd be curious to know if there were indications of arson."

Hartley threw the scrap of paper onto a pile of papers to the side of his desk. "I'll look into it—now if you'll excuse me."

John rose to leave, but stopped himself. *Was that to be all?* All his work, waiting until he was sure he had enough to raise questions, and the result—nothing.

John slapped his hand over the papers on Hartley's desk. John wasn't excitable by nature, but once his temper flared he had little chance of keeping it in check. "Listen! This is my brother. He's dead, and I want to know why. I don't need a runaround. My brother deserves a helluva lot more."

The outburst was loud enough to create a moment of silence in the office as the other detectives turned their way.

Hartley looked up, startled, then his face contorted, the edges of his mouth curled down. "You listen. Listen good. People have been going out of their way to sugar-coat things for you around here . . . but not me, not any longer. Get out."

"I'm not going anywhere until—"

"The hell you're not. You don't just fucking come in here yelling and giving me orders. This is my investigation, and you know what? It's over. You hear that, Sarikov, you understand now; it's over. You want to know why your brother was killed, he was killed because he broke his oath to uphold the law. That's the bottom line. Now get the fuck out of here.''

The words stung. The other detectives, recognizing John's surname, threw sympathetic glances John's way. To hear the accusation from the detective in charge of the case was crushing. John wanted to make Hartley take the words back, like a child who had been called a name. "It's not true." He backed away from Hartley's desk and said it again. "It's not true."

He walked quickly out of the office and, still shaken, veered into a men's room, went to the sink, and splashed cold water on his face. Dammit, why had his reaction been so dramatic? He had, after all, half expected what the department's position would be. He dried his face with a paper towel and looked up into the mirror to see Steve standing behind him.

Steve glanced quickly under the stalls to see if there was anyone else in the bathroom. There wasn't. "I heard you just had a run-in with Hartley. A couple of the guys came for me, said you gave the jerk what he deserved, but he shut you up with some cheap shots."

John finished wiping his face, uncomfortable talking about the dispute. "No big deal."

"Hartley's not the most well-liked guy around here."

"I can see why."

"What did you come to see him about?"

John turned and faced Steve. "I've been looking into Michael's death. You told me Hartley heads the investigation. I've uncovered a few things, and thought I should fill him in. I found out he couldn't care less."

"What have you come up with?"

"What does it matter, Steve? The case is closed

according to Hartley. You guys backed up Michael all the way, you really stood behind him."

Steve bit his bottom lip. "Just tell me what you told Hartley. What have you found?"

John summarized his investigations, the leads and what he thought they meant.

When John finished, Steve rubbed his face in thought. When he spoke, his voice came softly. "John, I hate to say it, Hartley's a prick, but I can't totally condemn him here. I mean, what do you really have? Some missing photos? Old family photos . . . some of a concentration camp? Those photos could mean absolutely nothing. So they're missing? They could be anywhere. Michael could have thrown them out, they might be misplaced at his house, or they could have been taken by anyone at the crime scene . . . who knows how long the bodies sat there before they were discovered. The call to this Greene . . . is that what you said his name was?"

"Yeah."

"Who knows? Everybody has to make a last phone call and Michael's happened to be to Greene. Greene died. Okay, I'll admit the timing's peculiar and it should be looked at, but that doesn't mean I'm sold on a conspiracy theory. You said yourself the fire was reported to be accidental. Where's the hard evidence?"

John felt his anger rising, but kept it in check—there was no reason to explode at Steve as he had at Hartley. "I don't have any. I only have coincidences, but they could mean something."

"All right, I'll talk to Hartley, try to get him to focus on what you've told me. But John, you're not a cop. Let this go. Christ, I'm as sorry as anyone about Michael and the way the department is treating him, but I'm not gonna change that and you're not either.

You've got to let go and start over. Let me talk to Hartley, then let us do our job.''

"Just talk to Hartley, that's all I ask. Make sure he looks into this—looks for arson in the Greene fire. I gave him the name and address of Greene, and of the old woman. Consider the coincidences. Check Greene's and Olgov's background, find out how they knew each other. There is a connection, I know it. I'd appreciate it, Steve.''

Steve nodded. "I'll talk to him. I'm not sure how receptive he'll be, but I'll give him a kick in the ass as a jump-start. Promise.''

"Thanks.''

"Yeah, but before you thank me too much, I gotta tell you I'm going to be the next least popular guy around here if I make a habit of telling people what to do.''

"I've got a hunch on this one.''

"Remember, this is a police matter. No playing junior cop. You can get into a lot of trouble. Quit it. You got it?

John nodded, but Steve seemed to sense the nod meant very little. "John, I don't know what you're doing, but watch yourself. If you come up with anything else, anything at all, you let me know. Okay?''

"Don't worry. If I learn something, believe me, I don't plan to keep it a secret.''

28

At the stoplight John checked the street map of Brooklyn for Clayton Street—the street on which Peter Olgov had lived. John had tried in good faith to follow Steve's advice, prepared to let the police do their job, or at least give them the chance to show they would try, but his resolution broke down in less than a week. He hadn't heard from Steve; he doubted Hartley had done a damn thing. He wasn't ready to go back to work, not yet, and his chief occupation at home was emptying booze bottles.

He could not simply sit on his hands, not when there was a lead to run down: the woman who gave Michael the box of photographs.

Even though Brighton Beach was small, less than a square mile, and John had been born and raised there, Clayton Street wasn't familiar to him. Not surprising—he had rarely returned since leaving sixteen years ago, just once every three months or so for dinner, on Michael's prompting. Michael liked the idea of two local boys who made good revisiting their old haunts to reminisce. Michael would pick the restaurant, always Russian, one of the many that lined Brighton Beach Avenue. After twenty years in the precinct, Michael knew most of the owners. They liked having a Russian cop frequent their place and gave the brothers extra attention.

The outings were always the same. Michael referred

to John as little brother; they ate Russian food and drank vodka until John's stomach gave out. John would have preferred restaurants on the upper East Side of Manhattan, but had lost that battle long ago. When the Sarikov brothers went out for a meal, Michael insisted, it would not be at some over-priced, nouveau French, yuppie hangout with skimpy helpings.

Michael embraced his ancestry, John did not. He wasn't ashamed of his bloodline, just preferred to think of himself as American, and saw no reason to adopt the traditional Russian trappings. He didn't speak Russian, didn't eat the ethnic food; didn't go to Russian Orthodox church; didn't own a fur hat; and didn't make pilgrimages to Brighton Beach.

Perhaps their ages accounted for the difference. Because their mother had died at John's birth, John had never known life in Brighton Beach with her. They were happy years, according to Michael, and left him warm memories even the later sullenness of their father could not erase. If John had grown up with more laughter than tears, perhaps he wouldn't have been so eager to escape his past, but as it was his days in Brighton Beach had been filled with one obsessive thought—to get out.

Strange to be going back now. Everything looked alien, as far removed from his present life as he had been able to put it, and yet he came from here, and try to deny it or not, part of Brighton Beach was still with him.

He pulled up in front of a dilapidated building and double checked the address. Unfortunately, this was it. Not very attractive. He did his best to put on a confident air.

With a hard tug the front door unstuck, and John walked into the apartment building. The stale air hit his nostrils and caused his nose to wrinkle. He approached an old dried-up man behind a counter who didn't look up.

"Excuse me."

A short appraising glance served as a greeting, then the man resumed reading his tabloid. "Yeah, what is it?" The clerk had a strong Russian accent.

"I wonder if you can help me."

For the first time the man put down the paper and gave John his full attention. "Why not? Why would I have been put on earth if not to help you?" The man raised his paper again.

Pleasant. "I'm looking for a woman."

"Who isn't?"

John ignored the comment. "One of your boarders, I believe. An older Russian woman."

"We have lots of older Russian women here."

John's initial surprise at the rudeness of the man turned to anger. "My brother is a cop. He came here about a month and a half ago to talk with her in connection with the murder investigation of a Peter Olgov. You remember that?"

The man lowered the paper again, his eyes darting quickly to John's, betraying recognition. "You a cop?" he asked.

"No."

The man relaxed. He picked a greasy drumstick from a crumpled sheet of aluminum foil and took a bite, speaking as he chewed. "There are cops in here all the time. What the fuck's so special about your brother?"

John's eyes narrowed. He'd never punched anyone in his life, and had always wondered what it would take to get him to drive his fist into another's face. Not all that much, he decided. "Do you know the old woman or not?"

"Look, son, I know plenty of old women, young

ones too. How the fuck do I know which one you're talking about?"

John bit his tongue. "Mind if I talk to some of your boarders and see if I can find her?"

"You're not selling anything are you?"

"No."

"You can go up, no one's stopping you, but if you cause any trouble, if anyone complains, I kick your ass out of here. You understand?"

John started up the stairs without responding.

He remembered stairs like this from childhood. He would run up and down them, and along the halls, playing tag or cops and robbers with his brother. The only children in the building, the old men cornered them with long rambling stories from their youth while the old ladies spoiled them with ponchiki and vareniky, Russian desserts he once had a fondness for.

A few of the tenants John met on the first floor were more helpful than the desk clerk. They directed him to room 12, where an older Russian woman lived by herself. John knocked at the door. Creaking floorboards preceded a darkening of the door's peep hole.

"Who is it?" came from behind the door.

"My name is John Sarikov."

The door remained closed. "What can I do for you?" the voice asked.

"I'd like to talk to you. I believe my brother may have spoken to you . . . about six weeks ago I think."

"Who is your brother?"

"He is . . . was . . . a police officer. He investigated the death of a Mr. Peter Olgov in room eight."

There was a momentary silence from the other side of the door. "What has that got to do with me?"

"I know the two of you talked, and I believe you gave him a box of photographs belonging to Mr. Olgov. I'd like to find out what you talked about."

"Why don't you ask your brother?"

"I can't; my brother's dead. Killed. I don't know why, but I think it may have had something to do with Mr. Olgov's death."

The door creaked open revealing a round-faced older woman with wispy gray hair. Put her face on a box of cookies—it would fit. Her expression remained noncommittal as she eyed John through thick glasses.

"Yes, you resemble your brother. I remember him. I am very sorry."

"Thank you. Then you gave him the box of Mr. Olgov's photographs?"

"Yes, I did. To hold in case Mr. Olgov had any relatives who came to collect his things. But I don't understand, how could Mr. Olgov be involved in your brother's death?"

"I don't know; I wish I did. That is why I'm tracing my brother's movements before his death, trying to find a motive."

The woman accepted John's explanation and invited him in. She introduced herself as Mrs. Banovich and politely insisted John have something to eat. He started by turning down shchi and stroganoff, and ended by accepting milk and babka. The pastry tasted good, and John surprised himself by accepting seconds.

After serving him, Mrs. Banovich offered to help. "What would you like to know?" she asked.

"What my brother asked you . . . what you said."

"He asked about Mr. Olgov. I told him what I knew."

"Could you repeat what you said?" John turned on the Dictaphone in his pocket.

"I can try. I told your brother Mr. Olgov would come up to my apartment once every month or so to eat dinner, but all he ever talked about were old times."

"Anything you can tell me about Mr. Olgov might be of help, Mrs. Banovich."

Mrs. Banovich rocked back in her chair and rubbed her thighs nervously. "All right, let's see. Mr. Olgov came here from Russia in, oh, maybe a few years after the war, probably the late forties. He escaped from Russia, did you know that?"

"No, I didn't."

"Yes, he told me the whole story . . . it sounded very dangerous. He escaped because he hated the Communists. He didn't always, but he grew to hate them. He fought for them once, in World War II, did you know that?"

"No."

Mrs. Banovich rose to her feet, opened the top drawer of a desk and withdrew a framed photograph. She proudly handed it to John.

"That's Mr. Olgov, from World War II. He's the tall one. He gave the picture to me. Whenever he came over, I put it on the coffee table. I think he liked seeing it here, framed, as if he were part of a family. He didn't have any family you know, Mr. Sarikov, none alive over here anyway."

John nodded, barely listening. He examined the picture—five soldiers lined up in front of a tank. John concentrated on the tall soldier in the middle. Light hair, clear eyes, broad shoulders, handsome. "Good-looking young man."

"He was, then. Didn't age well . . . the alcohol, you know."

"A drinking problem?"

She nodded her head gravely. "Never up here, of course—I don't allow that sort of thing. But I knew he was a man who liked his drink. After the things he'd been through it's no wonder. Did you know he was decorated for valor during the war? Wounded

fighting the Germans in Berlin. A very brave man . . .
but the war changed him."

"How's that?"

"Made him hate communism, as I said. I wish he
were here to tell you. He was always making speeches
to me about Russian war atrocities. All sorts of things.
Things others did, and some things they wanted him
to do, terrible things to innocent people."

John tried to lend some direction. "So he left Russia
for America."

"Yes. He said it wasn't easy for him living in Russia,
being held down by a restrictive government, so he
left. Said he hiked across the border to Finland, to
make his fortune in America."

"What about his life here?"

"As I said, he never told me much. I think he might
have been embarrassed. He was very smart, knew all
sort of things, had great dreams and ideas, but
here . . . He never learned to speak English very well;
you might not have known that."

"I didn't."

"Even smart men aren't always good at learning a
language, you know. He said his poor English held
him back, that and discrimination. He said none of
the big companies, the ones with money, would listen
to his ideas because he was only an immigrant. I don't
know what other jobs he may have held, but I know
most recently he worked as a dishwasher. He didn't
tell me that, but I found out. He said he worked at a
restaurant. I figured as a chef or waiter, but one day
while out walking I stopped, and they told me he
worked as a dishwasher. That happened years ago, but
I never embarrassed him by telling him I knew."

"What's the restaurant's name?"

"The Ukrainian Café. It's a restaurant on Brighton
Beach Avenue."

"What about the box of photographs?"

"They were old photos of Mr. Olgov as a little boy, and of his family, and the old country. I've seen them many times. Mr. Olgov said they were the most valuable thing in the world to him."

"He told you the photographs were *valuable* to him?"

"Yes, in a sentimental sense, I'm sure."

"Why did you have his photographs in your apartment?"

"He left them after our last dinner."

"And you didn't return them?"

Mrs. Banovich shook her head. "He knew I had the photographs, Mr. Sarikov. He was tired after our dinner, said he didn't want to lug the box downstairs. He asked me to take care of them until our next dinner."

"My brother's report on Mr. Olgov's death indicates his apartment was thoroughly searched. Someone was looking for something; may or may not have found it. It occurs to me they could have been looking for the box, and Olgov left it in your apartment because he knew someone might be looking for it. You think that's possible?"

"They were only family photographs."

"No, Mrs. Banovich, actually they weren't. Did Mr. Olgov ever show you photos of a concentration camp?"

"You mean one of the Nazi camps?"

"Yes."

"No, I'm sure he did not."

"How about photos of prisoners in striped uniforms?"

"No, I would remember if he had."

John studied her face; she seemed sincere. "My brother found a false bottom to the box you gave him. In it were photos of a concentration camp—photos of prisoners. Were you aware of the hidden compartment?"

"Absolutely not."

"Have you ever seen this photograph before?" John held up the photograph of Jacob Greene.

She took the photograph from John and held it at arm's length, squinting through her glasses, then frowned. "I told you, the only photos he showed me were of his family. Nothing like this. The man"—Mrs. Banovich pointed toward the photograph, still frowning—"he is one of the prisoners you mentioned?"

"I believe so. Does he look familiar?"

She shook her head. "No."

John believed her. "Do you know if Mr. Olgov ever visited or was posted to a concentration camp? or ever mentioned a concentration camp in any way?"

"No, he never mentioned one."

"Did he ever mention a man named Jacob Greene?"

"Not that I recall."

John spent the next twenty minutes asking Mrs. Banovich to recollect everything she might remember about Olgov—his escape from Russia, his habits, hobbies, the most inconsequential detail she could remember. When they finished, Mrs. Banovich spent another ten minutes talking about herself, and would have dwelt on that subject for much longer if John had not pleaded another appointment, and cut her short.

As he prepared to leave, John asked if he could take the photo of Peter Olgov. He promised to make a copy and return the original to her.

"I don't think Mr. Olgov would like knowing I gave away his picture, but if you're careful with it, you may take it," she replied.

"Thank you, Mrs. Banovich, and thank you for all your time."

Mrs. Banovich's face grew worried. "Mr. Sarikov, who would want to kill Mr. Olgov?"

"Frankly, I don't have any idea. That's what I want to find out."

"Do you think I should worry . . . could I be in danger after what happened to Mr. Olgov and your brother?"

John paused, never having considered the issue before. If his wild theories weren't in fact so wild, someone had murdered three times to protect themselves. *Could* she be in danger? Could *he* be in danger? The possibility seemed too remote to suggest. "I don't think so, Mrs. Banovich. No. No. You are, I'm sure, in no danger."

Mrs. Banovich smiled and opened the door.

The desk clerk watched John pull away in his car, then hurried behind the front desk and shifted through a ragged stack of paper. He swore to himself, sure he had the number somewhere. From one of the stacks he pulled a crumpled piece of paper with a telephone number on it.

Two hundred bucks for reporting the cop's visit; he should at least get the same, or a hundred, he'd settle for a hundred, for the information that the cop's brother was now snooping around, asking questions about— What was the name? Greene. That was it. Jacob Greene.

29

The tall, downy-haired man took the penknife from his pocket and opened the blade with large, strong hands. Now the best part, he thought, as he cut the skin. It sliced easily.

He took a bite and smiled. How could anyone buy those tasteless things the groceries stocked? He'd filled the better part of two bushels. That should keep Dorothy busy canning for a while. Good tomato sauce all winter long, a pleasant reminder of summer.

He moved to the patio and lowered himself into one of the loungers. His eyes swept the yard with satisfaction. Manicured, sculptured. Just a small piece of earth, but very important to him. Here he had created order, things made sense.

He lay back and let the sun beat on his wrinkled and weathered face. Dorothy would yell at him; he'd already had a number of lesions removed. Skin cancer, the doctors said—nothing to play around with. Maybe not, but the sun felt too good to shut out.

He let himself drift. The smell of dirt, grass, and manure filled his nostrils. Until him, his family had worked the soil for generations. Maybe it was in his genes. Tilling fields, watching things grow, fall harvests—a life he would have enjoyed.

Dorothy interrupted his thoughts.

"Cover yourself up this minute!" she scolded.

He smiled and pulled his hat down over his face.

Hadn't taken her long—she watched him like a hawk ever since the doctors removed that first lesion. The first hint she'd ever had that he was anything but invulnerable. It had scared her to death, more so than it did him—he had lived with the possibility of death much longer than she knew.

"You've got a call in the den," Dorothy said.

Under the hat his mouth turned down. His private line, used only for business, it rarely rang anymore. He debated having Dorothy take a message, then not return it. Stupid thought, he knew. They'd just come for him in person.

"Thanks, dear. I'll be right in." His knees protested as he stood—in some way that bothered him more than the cancer had. Knees were basic. How can your knees begin to fail you?

He made his way to his private study and picked up the phone. "Hello," he said.

"Sir, I'm with A-1 Gutter Service. We're offering a fall special in your area . . ."

Even after so long a time, he barely had to think to deliver his line. "If you'll send me an estimate, I'll consider it."

The voice turned official. "Hold one moment, sir."

Then another voice. "Good to speak with you again, Grigori."

The downy-haired man stiffened on hearing the name. "Grigori," his given name, the name he answered exclusively to for his first twenty years, but heard only occasionally over the next fifty and not at all for the last year and a half. He recognized the voice on the other line: Nicholas, an old comrade, now head of the Collegium.

Grigori returned the pleasantry without enthusiasm.

"How are you, old friend?" Nicholas asked.

"Enjoying my retirement."

"I envy you. Unfortunately, I also have need of you."

"You would do well to fill your needs elsewhere. The years have not been kind," Grigori lied.

There was a pause on the other end. "It is a very delicate assignment, Grigori," Nicholas said after a moment. "If I could trust someone else, I would."

Age emboldened Grigori, and he tried again. "It's been a long time . . ."

"I would take your skills, rusty or not, over any other's. I'm afraid I must insist."

Grigori shut his eyes, resigning himself to the inevitable. It meant another business trip away from home and, the worst part, another lie to Dorothy.

"What is it you need of me, comrade?" he asked, finally.

30

John sat on the rocky outcropping to the side of Belvedere Castle, a small-scale stone castle built on a hill in the center of Central Park. He came here often when stuck on a story, sometimes for inspiration, sometimes to clear his mind. The rocks overlooked a small lake, a mosaic of baseball fields, and an outdoor theater. You couldn't actually see the theater's stage from the rocks, but John imagined you could hear at least fragments of any performance. He had never tried to find out, however, because the theater group performed at night, and although certain areas of the park were perfectly safe in the evening, these rocks were not among them.

John smacked his thigh with his fist, for once unaffected by the view. He had been doing everything a good investigative reporter should—running down every lead, doing the leg work, talking to every possible witness. Looking for a break. He had put in the time, now when would there be a reward?

The things he had discovered about Jacob Greene were nothing but ancient history. The same now went for Peter Olgov. What had he learned from Mrs. Banovich: Olgov worked as a dishwasher and had a drinking problem. Earth-shattering revelations. Tie that up with Jacob Greene, a retired Jewish recluse, and what did you have? Anyone could see it pointed to a grand conspiracy leading to Michael's death.

Dammit, it was almost laughable. He wouldn't be able to convince Steve, let alone Hartley.

Rabbi Sosman's and Mrs. Banovich's words came back to him: "Who would want to kill Mr. Greene? Who would want to kill Mr. Olgov?" Based on John's investigations so far, nobody would, which left Michael dealing drugs, and John couldn't accept that. He had to look harder.

He patted his coat and felt the Dictaphone in its internal pocket. The cassette of his interview with Mrs. Banovich would still be inside. He removed the Dictaphone, rewound the cassette, then pressed PLAY. He listened closely, searching for anything he might have missed the first time around.

John had just asked Mrs. Banovich where Olgov had worked, and she answered the Ukrainian Café on Brighton Beach Avenue, when John turned the Dictaphone off. Somebody—a friend, an acquaintance, an enemy—knew why Greene and Olgov were killed. John had to find that somebody. If Greene had any friends besides the rabbi, John hadn't found them, but he might have better luck with Olgov. The Ukrainian Café would be as good a place as any to start.

He started back to his apartment.

John parked his car on a side street off Brighton Beach Avenue. He didn't know the exact location of the restaurant, but the Russian strip was not very long, just ten short blocks or so. It would be easy to walk.

Childhood memories long banished from his consciousness rushed back involuntarily as he stepped from the car. The rumble of the elevated train that ran the length of the avenue echoed off the storefronts on each side of the street. John remembered scurrying up the stairs to the El as a child, ducking under the turnstiles, running along the elevated platforms, playing tag and army and incidentally catching glimpses of the Atlantic Ocean one block to the south and the Ferris wheels and roller coasters of Coney Island only a short distance to the west.

The avenue looked pretty much the same as John remembered—ethnic groceries and cut-rate department stores lined its sides with names like Odessa, Stolichny, Muscovite, and other names in Cyrillic lettering. Stout, middle-aged women scurried between groceries, and squat, stocky men, a few wearing tall fur hats, stood in scattered groups exchanging news in Russian. Every couple of dozen yards street hawkers sold second-hand clothes and household goods. Nobody seemed to notice or to care about the litter, pervasive even by New York standards.

John realized his distaste for the avenue had more to do with an abusive, alcoholic father than it did with the realities of the neighborhood, but he couldn't help that—the two would always be linked in his memory. Blind to the pleasant side streets with rows of small but well-kept brick houses, he couldn't see the community in its historical role: a starting off point for thousands of immigrant Russians who would make a new life for themselves in America. He saw only a dead end he had narrowly avoided.

John scanned the shop signs looking for the Ukrainian Café. He came upon it after walking five blocks, a small corner restaurant, its name painted in red on its window.

On rare occasions, maybe a half-dozen times he could remember, his father took Michael and him out to eat at restaurants similar to this. Somehow his father would have saved enough money from sweeping stores, cleaning windows, and other odd jobs to afford the extravagance. Besides funerals, they were the only times he remembered his father wearing a suit. His father would shower, shave the stubble perpetually adorning his face, don a starched white shirt, a red-

and-blue striped tie, and a brown three-piece suit, and walk proudly with his boys to the restaurant.

Their father allowed John and Michael to order anything they wanted, and John never held back. He devoured huge meals of *shashlyk* and *tseploynok tabaka*. His father would pat him on the back and urge him on to seconds and dessert. Michael, on the other hand, consistently professed a lack of appetite, ate very little, and skipped dessert. Besides these outings, John never remembered Michael having anything but a ferocious appetite; years went by before John understood Michael's small sacrifice.

They always finished their restaurant meals with a shot of vodka, even Michael and John. The waiter poured the two of them only a small amount, maybe a third of an ounce, but John still remembered how his throat burned as their father led them in toasts. Not that he ever minded, for at those times his father would be in a rare mood unlike any John could remember. They became a family, the three Sarikov men, drinking and laughing together, and for a few hours everything made sense. Then his father would pay for the meal with coins and wrinkled dollar bills, and they would leave. When they returned home, his father would hang his suit carefully in the closet and sit in his chair by the window, a picture of John's mother in one hand and a glass of vodka in the other. Soon everything would revert to normal, and those brief and cherished hours when John felt something akin to love for his father faded quickly from his memory.

A few stragglers from the lunchtime crowd and three old men bunched together at one end of the bar stared at John as he entered the Ukrainian Café, clearly marking their territory before returning to their conversation in hushed tones.

John approached the bar at the opposite end from

the old men. The bartender, a large bear of a man with thick black eyebrows that overwhelmed his eyes, took his order. He thumped down a beer in front of John and grunted when John thanked him.

As he paid, John brought up Peter Olgov's name. The bartender went to the cash register, returned, and counted out John's change, ignoring the inquiry.

"My understanding is he worked here," John said.

The bartender grunted again.

"Can you tell me anything about him?"

A half sneer crossed the bartender's face as he turned and disappeared into a back room. When he returned a moment later, a middle-aged man accompanied him. Brown hair swept back from a round, pock-marked face. Tight brown pants; white short-sleeve shirt barely restraining a bulging pot belly. The man from the back room approached John.

"I heard you had some questions?" the man asked coolly.

"Yeah . . . about a Peter Olgov. Do you know him?"

"You mean *did* I know him . . . the Olgov I knew is dead."

"Right—he worked for you?"

"What's it to you?"

"I just have a few questions."

"You have a badge to show me?"

John reached into his pocket and put two twenties on the bar. "Will this do?"

The man left the money on the bar. "Maybe. It depends on the questions."

"Did Peter Olgov work for you?" John repeated as he picked up the money, folded it, and slid it in the man's shirt pocket.

The man shrugged. "Yeah. Scrubbed pots, did dishes, cleaned up, that sort of thing."

John paused to collect his thoughts. He didn't know

exactly what to ask; he was just fishing, hoping some question would elicit information of value. "How long did he work at your place?"

"Off and on, a couple of years. He would work pretty regularly for a few weeks, then disappear for a while. He'd show up a week or two later."

"Where would he go?"

"Nowhere—the streets, his room. Money for booze would run low and he'd come back."

"Why didn't you fire him?"

"He worked cheap—besides, I run my business the way I choose. Olgov was Russian; I'm Russian. I look out for my own."

John took the last sentence as half sermon, half warning. "Did he have any enemies?"

"Nah, not really—he stuck to his own business. He was a bit of a blowhard, but everybody put up with him."

"He was shot in the back of the head three times; someone must not have been too fond of him."

The man shrugged. "Maybe it was robbery."

"Would you rob a dishwasher who saved only enough money for a two-week liquor binge?"

"I don't know anything about it."

"Did he talk about himself, any problems he had?"

"I don't know, I never really talked to the guy—just signed his checks. He didn't have all that much to say . . . you know? Hell, he was drunk half the time."

"You ever see this man?" John held up the photo of Greene.

The man looked at the photo closely. "No, he a convict?"

"Something like that. Did Olgov ever mention to you anything about a concentration camp in World War II?"

"Never. I told you, the man and I almost never

talked. I paid him; he washed my fucking dishes. Okay?"

"Yeah. Was he involved with any shady people?"

"Half the people in this part of town are a little shady. Nothing outside of the ordinary, as far as I know."

"What about the Russian mafia?" John asked.

The man's eyes darted from side to side. "Never heard of it . . . and I think you've about used up your forty bucks."

John slid another twenty onto the bar. "Ever hear the name Jacob Greene?"

The man hesitated, then picked up the bill. "No."

"Olgov have any friends?"

"No idea. I didn't pal around with the guy."

John took another drink of beer. "Anybody here pal around with him?"

The man paused. "Yeah. I know somebody."

"Have a name for me?"

"Another one of my dishwashers—they used to go on a bender together now and then. Who knows, you bring a few more of these," the man patted the bills in his pocket, "and maybe I can get him to talk to you."

"Where is he?"

"Doesn't work tonight. You come in tomorrow night, anytime after six, he should be here."

"You'll be here?"

"I own the place. I'll be here."

"I'll look for you tomorrow then." John didn't bother finishing his beer.

31

Vasili glanced from the figure seated on the park bench a half block away to his watch—12:45 P.M. Their meeting was scheduled for 12:30 P.M., but he would keep the man waiting a few minutes longer. In the meantime, he scanned the report on the Sarikov brother for the fourth time that afternoon.

John Sarikov was seen snooping around the apartment house of the traitor, Olgov, asking questions about Jacob Greene. How he had connected the death of his brother to Olgov and the Jew, Vasili had no idea.

Vasili rarely made a mistake, but clearly in this case he had acted too conservatively. The cop's brother should have been taken out at the start. He had been far too worried about what the Collegium might think—he had let it cloud his judgment.

The Collegium now knew of Sarikov's investigations and the old fox, Nicholas, had personally delivered their instructions: the organization's interests must be protected. Vasili must take no action against Sarikov until meeting with their man, who would help solve the situation to everyone's satisfaction.

Vasili had confirmed the orders with Aleksei—their conversation, even now, irritating to recall.

"I tried my best, but what did you expect?" Aleksei had said. "Nicholas and his stooge, Yuri, made sure to remind the Collegium that you *promised* there would be no repercussions. They can't be ignored, Vasili, not yet."

"*I* will handle the situation."

"*With* the Collegium's help. They insist—no more bungling."

"There has been no *bungling*."

"A lot is riding on your actions, my friend. They haven't been steady lately. I do not care to think I have tied my future to a sinking ship."

Vasili had bit his lip and promised himself Aleksei would pay for that comment. "You know Nicholas's offer has nothing to do with help. It has to do with keeping one of his men close to me, strait-jacketing me, making me lose face in the eyes of the organization."

"Yes. He plays the same game we play, and well. The Collegium members are scared. They'll run from any disturbance that threatens to unbalance their lives. Nicholas simply pushed hardest this time—he created the disturbance they reacted to."

Astute, Aleksei, Vasili remembered thinking, *only why weren't you there to push back?* The question still bothered him.

Vasili accepted his position, he had no choice. Ordering Sarikov's elimination in the face of orders to the contrary, now when he stood so close to his goal, would be foolish. Let Nicholas enjoy himself, his turn would come soon enough. Vasili would wait, bide his time, strengthen his forces, and soon, very soon, deal with Nicholas from a position of unquestioned superiority. Then even Aleksei would toe the line.

Vasili looked again at the park bench. He knew the man sitting there: Grigori Karchenko, planted in the early fifties, one of the old-timers like Vasili himself. Vasili had heard little of him in the past decade, but once his work had commanded the respect of the entire Collegium. Not a man to take lightly.

The two were friends once, a long time ago, when they trained together in Moscow, two young idealists fresh from the countryside, minds full of dreams of preparing the world for the worker's revolution. What a farce that had turned out to be. Vasili had come to America expecting to see great masses of down-trodden, what he found instead were workers with the highest living standards in the world. Couples had a house and two cars, grocery stores brimmed with produce—things only the highest party officials in the Soviet Union could afford. It was obvious where life was better, and it was not the Soviet Union, where the worker's revolution had already succeeded.

Vasili learned quickly the real game being played had little to do with workers' rights or standards of living. The real game dealt with power—its acquisition and its deployment—and there were winners and losers. Vasili wondered if Grigori had learned the same lessons. If he had, perhaps their friendship could be rekindled, their alliance reestablished.

Nicholas's choice of representative had been fortuitous, Vasili decided—perhaps the old man was slipping.

Vasili opened his car door and stepped out. He looked quickly to his left toward the white van parked a half block away, two of his men inside. He didn't expect aggression, but had decided against taking chances—he could feel the weight of the semi-automatic in his coat pocket.

Besides Grigori, the small park stood almost empty. A mother and two children played on the swings; a man threw sticks to his dog. Vasili walked the short distance to the park bench in confident long strides.

Impeccably dressed in a white overcoat and gray three-button suit, his white downy hair combed back from his forehead to reveal intelligent blue eyes, Grigori played with a rabbit's foot as he watched Vasili approach. He had spotted Vasili earlier, in a car on the other side of the park, but hadn't let on, curious to see how long the posturing would go on. He had also spotted the white van parked nearby. Grigori couldn't be sure Vasili's people manned the van, but his operative circling the park in a yellow cab would test his hunch by tailing the van when it left.

Vasili walked on dangerous ground, Grigori knew, but then again so did he. Two days ago he worked in his garden—today he would make an enemy of a powerful man, a man he once, long, long ago, counted as a friend. He had cast the die; he would remain loyal to the old power structure, at least until something better came along, or, preferably, it crumbled all together. Vasili did not represent the "better" he had in mind.

The Collegium had charged him with getting a line on the Sarikov matter, reining in Vasili's more impetuous impulses, and, if necessary, aiding Vasili in removing Sarikov. Nicholas had delivered a slightly more amorphous and infinitely more delicate charge in private: learn Vasili's habits, document his activities, discover his weaknesses. In effect, Grigori was to take the first steps in an undeclared war against Vasili with an aim to eroding his power within the Collegium. "While you're at it," Nicholas had said, "play the grain of sand. Irritate Vasili. See if you can provoke an ill-considered response."

Vasili stopped in front of the bench and waited as Grigori stood and drew alongside, then the two began walking. Grigori spoke first.

"It's been a long time, old friend."

Vasili nodded. "Too long. You're looking fit."

"You are being too kind. My bones ache, my chest droops, my hairline recedes. I'm afraid we are not the men we once were."

Vasili smiled. "It's been over fifty years, Grigori."

"The all-night drinking, the partying, the girls. Were we ever really so young?"

"We were . . . young and naive. Perhaps the wisdom we've gained is worth the hair we've lost."

"Let us hope you are right."

The two walked a moment in silence before Vasili spoke again. "We worked well together once . . . we should give thought to working together again."

Grigori parried the invitation. "And we are . . . that is why the Collegium sent me—so that I might be of service to you."

"I thank the Collegium for their concern, but it is not necessary. I have everything under control."

"The thread is still pulled. The loose end still exists," Grigori said, softly now.

"Sarikov is reaching in the dark. Olgov is dead, the Jew and the policemen are dead; the evidence is destroyed."

"It seems we thought the same thing before."

Vasili's voice took on an edge. "Sarikov is persistent, but knows nothing of consequence."

"Perhaps your moves were hasty. The policeman knew very little."

For the first time Vasili glared at Grigori. "I didn't know for sure how much the policeman understood, but he had the pieces to the puzzle and had only to put them together. I couldn't allow that. He jeopardized my cover. *All risks* had to be neutralized."

"His death has raised questions, has brought attention."

"The Collegium has already passed on my actions."

"After a promise from you that the matter had been put to rest . . . yet now we are dealing with the policeman's brother."

"A minor inconvenience. If the brother learns too much, I will contain things."

"By what means?"

"Elimination would be the surest remedy."

As they passed under a tree branch, Grigori reached up and plucked a leaf. He twirled it by its stem as he spoke. "Perhaps. The Collegium, however, is not so certain. They believe another unexplained death could raise suspicions further."

"No one, other than the brother, questioned the first deaths. If I remove Sarikov, no one will question his."

Grigori's voice lost its tone of diplomacy. "*If* it becomes necessary to remove Sarikov, and let me be quite clear the Collegium will make that determination, I am here, with all deference to your agents' abilities, to oversee the operation."

"I appreciate your offer of help, but—"

"I have not," Grigori interrupted, "made an *offer,* I have passed on Collegium *directives.* You *will* keep me informed of Sarikov's actions and your recommendations. I will apprise the Collegium, the Collegium will decide on a course of action, and I will inform you of their decisions. Those are the Collegium's directives. If you are confused, I can repeat them."

Vasili's face turned red, but he held his tongue. "That will not be necessary. I, of course, will inform the Collegium of my intentions, and am happy to be able to call on your expertise. You may tell the Collegium that."

Grigori nodded. "They will be pleased." The two walked on in silence. "This is not the way I had planned my golden years," Grigori said, eventually. "I was, frankly, glad to give up this type of thing."

"Then perhaps, comrade, it is time you stepped aside and allowed those with vision to lead the way."

"Perhaps you're right. I am old. I do not have the same fire burning in my belly as when I was young . . .

as when we were young. Things were much easier to understand back then."

Vasili pointed to his chest. "Fire still burns here. Times change, powers shift, but the game remains the same. It is possible to adapt and prosper."

Grigori shrugged. "I personally tire of the game, but no matter. Service calls. I have dutifully answered its call too many times to turn my back on it now."

"Do not confuse duty with stupidity, *old friend.*"

An open challenge. Grigori turned and looked Vasili in the eye. "I'll try to remember the distinction."

The two walked again in silence.

"Have you considered the possibility of being compromised?" Grigori asked finally.

"That will not happen."

"The Collegium feels there is a possibility. Obviously, in such a case they would be concerned with containing any damage, ensuring that the finger didn't point in their direction. Have you worked out a contingency plan?"

"No contingency plan is necessary. I will not be compromised."

"Humor me. Assume you are. What are your plans? What identities have you set up?"

"That, comrade, is not your concern. I am in no danger of compromise, and if I was, I would do all that was necessary to neutralize the danger."

"As we all would hope, *comrade.* Regardless, I will report to the Collegium that you have not taken, nor do you intend to take, precautions. Perhaps that will not concern them."

Vasili turned his head and spit, making his feelings clear.

"Forgive me," Grigori continued. "I must be getting too Americanized—I've adopted their annoying habit of rattling on." Grigori stopped walking and Vasili followed suit. Grigori's voice grew businesslike as the two men faced each other. "For the time being I suggest you do the following. Put a tail on Sarikov. Search his apartment. Report anything your people come up with to me." He paused and looked into Vasili's eyes. "And otherwise take no action against him."

Vasili nodded. "It will be done."

The two parted in opposite directions.

32

John played the messages again. The first, from Barbara, was identical to the other two from her this week. "John . . . please call," the entirety of the message. He wouldn't, he knew. It had been two weeks since she walked out on him, and nothing had changed. One thing, and only one thing, mattered now.

An assistant editor of the New York *Post* left the second message. A few months ago John had agreed to write a series on discriminatory housing practices. He'd missed a number of deadlines and could no longer ignore the editor's messages piling up on his machine. The editor and John had a good working relationship in the past, but it was about to end. John scrawled a quick note, explaining he must bow out of the series for personal reasons.

The editor, justifiably, would go ballistic, but John didn't feel he had a choice. Earlier in the week he tried to concentrate on writing, hoping it would draw him out of his preoccupation with Michael's death, but it hadn't worked. He lacked motivation, and no distraction seemed to keep his mind from wandering toward his brother's case, as it did now.

John wrote a personal check in an amount equal to the advance he had received on the series and tucked it and the note in an envelope addressed to the editor.

That cleared his schedule—no assignments, no intentions of seeking one.

John checked his watch. Hours before his meeting with the dishwasher at the Ukrainian Café. And if he learned nothing there, what then? The obvious answer, pounding the streets, didn't appeal to him. It meant visiting every laundry, bar, restaurant, grocery store, or other establishment within a five- or six-block radius of Peter Olgov's rooming house and asking the same question again and again: "Do you happen to know a man by the name of Peter Olgov?" In all likelihood a waste of time, but you never knew for sure until you tried. Steve might be able to get him a photo of Olgov; that would help—someone might recognize him by sight and not by name.

By sight and not by name. *By sight and not by name.* Stupid of him not to have thought of it before. He had learned quite a bit about Olgov in the last few days, things he didn't know when he last spoke to Rabbi Sosman. He reached for the Dictaphone and dropped in the cassette of his interview with the rabbi. As John suspected, he had asked the rabbi only if Greene had ever mentioned a man named Peter Olgov. Hardly thorough questioning.

From his wallet, he pulled out Rabbi Sosman's phone number. Four rings and the rabbi answered.

"Rabbi Sosman, John Sarikov. We talked a couple of days ago about Jacob Greene."

"Yes, Mr. Sarikov. I remember." The rabbi sounded impatient.

"I'm sorry to bother you again, but since we've talked I've had the chance to learn a bit more about Peter Olgov—"

"I'm sorry Mr. Sarikov—Peter Olgov?"

"Yes. The man whose murder my brother investigated. Remember?"

"Yes. I remember now."

"I wonder if can tell you what I've learned of Peter Olgov, see if anything rings a bell . . . if Mr. Greene ever mentioned anybody who matched his description?"

"I think I told you last time, to my knowledge Jacob never mentioned a Peter Olgov."

"Perhaps not by name—"

"Mr. Sarikov, as I told you, I'm reluctant to get involved in what I consider a police matter. Have you gone to them with what you know?"

"Actually, I did . . ." John paused, debating how to paint the brightest possible picture of his meeting with Hartley. "They said the information I brought them was insufficient to reopen the investigation. They needed something more concrete. I'm trying hard to find that something, rabbi."

Rabbi Sosman's voice wavered. "My time is some what limited—"

"It will just take a moment. I promise."

"If you make it quick . . . I suppose. . . ."

John didn't wait for Rabbi Sosman to change his mind. "I'll start talking, you stop me if anything occurs to you."

"Okay."

"His name, again, was Peter Olgov. Age seventy-five. About six-one. Caucasian. Bald with a fringe of white hair. Medium to heavyset. Lived alone in a rooming house in Brighton Beach. Never married as far as I know. No family. He worked part time as a dishwasher at the Ukrainian Café, a restaurant in Brighton Beach. He evidently had a drinking problem. He used to have dinner once every month with a woman named Mrs. Banovich, a Russian woman living in his rooming house. He gave her a box of photographs. Under a false bottom to the box my brother found photographs of a concentration camp, including the one I showed you, the concentration camp prisoner that you thought might be Mr. Greene."

"I remember, yes."

"Peter Olgov came to the U.S. from Russia after World War II. During the war he served in the Red Army, I believe in Eastern Europe, as a foot soldier. Evidently shocked by atrocities he witnessed in Poland, he turn anti-Communist. After the war he escaped from Russia and emigrated to the United States. Life in America was a disappointment—he never developed a full command of the English language and ended up working as a dishwasher . . . That's all I really know."

Rabbi Sosman did not hesitate in his response. "I'm sorry, Mr. Sarikov. You could have saved yourself the call. Absolutely nothing rings a bell."

"Nothing?" How surprised could he be? He'd been grasping at straws. "I might be able to find a picture of him, if that would help."

"Mr. Sarikov, let me repeat. Jacob had no friends I am aware of. None. We talked about almost nothing other than his Jewish faith and the Holocaust. Nothing I know about Jacob in any way connects . . ." Rabbi Sosman paused.

"What is it, rabbi?"

"I hesitate to mention this, Mr. Sarikov," Rabbi Sosman said. "I find it impossible to believe Jacob's death was anything but accidental, and I'm concerned this pursuit of yours will not only be unrewarding, but may be unhealthy as well. I will be doing you no favor, I fear, by adding fuel to the fire."

"What were you thinking, rabbi?" John said.

"I warn you it's absurdly improbable. You said Olgov served in the Red Army . . . the Red Army liberated Auschwitz."

Auschwitz, again. "I didn't know that."

"Yes. The Soviets liberated most of the concentration camps in Eastern Europe. Of course there must have been a million, two million soldiers in the Red Army. The odds . . ."

"Yet it's possible, isn't it? They met as liberator and prisoner?"

"*Possible,* Mr. Sarikov, just extremely unlikely."

The rabbi was right, of course, but it was a lead, and he didn't have many of those right now. "It *would* explain why Olgov had a photograph of Mr. Greene from Auschwitz."

"Granted. Now what else do you want from me?"

John paused a moment to think. "Did Mr. Greene ever mention the liberation of Auschwitz?

"Many times."

"What did he say?"

Rabbi Sosman sounded annoyed again. "What do you want, Mr. Sarikov: the facts? Okay, fact: the day the Soviets liberated Auschwitz most prisoners had already been evacuated by the Nazis and marched to camps within German lines. Mr. Greene was one of maybe . . . eight thousand prisoners remaining—those so weak as to be worthless as slave laborers. Jacob witnessed the frantic activity of the SS: dynamiting crematoriums, torching warehouses, attempting to destroy all evidence of butchery before Auschwitz fell into Allied hands.

"Or would you prefer feelings? When the Nazis guards and the SS left, when for the first time the machine-gun towers stood empty, the front gate went unguarded, Jacob was scared. Perhaps hard for us to understand, but the Nazis, though they starved and murdered, also represented order—told the prisoners when to wake, when to wash, when to eat, when to sleep. When that order disappeared, it unsettled the prisoners. An eerie silence settled over them; they didn't rejoice for a time, until finally it sunk in: they were free. Jacob told me he cried, something he could never afford to do before under the most inhumane of conditions. Does that help you?"

John ignored the question. "And the Soviets?"

"They arrived hours after the SS left. At first the prisoners greeted them with wild cheers, Jacob said, but the cheering stopped abruptly when the Soviet soldiers opened warehouses the SS had not had time to burn and found dresses, suits, and shoes piled to the ceilings. Then the prisoners felt shame, at the way they looked, at their threadbare clothes, the stink. They'd been treated as subhumans, and under the disbelieving gaze of the Soviet soldiers, they felt subhuman. That's the type of thing we discussed, Mr. Sarikov. Now how can any of this possibly help you?"

"I'm sorry, rabbi. If you'll bear with me. A few more questions and I won't trouble you again."

Rabbi Sosman remained silent, so John continued. "How long did the Soviets control the camp?"

"I can't remember for sure. A few months . . . maybe longer. Over time the Soviets released the prisoners to deportation camps for resettlement in their homelands or other countries: Israel, the United States."

"And life in Auschwitz under Soviet control?"

"Liberation didn't mean freedom, if that's what you mean. Not that I know what the Allies could have done . . . just open the gates? These people had no homes to go back to—their property had been expropriated by the German state. They had no shelter, no clothes but the rags on their backs, no food, no money to buy food, no jobs."

"How were the inmates treated?"

"It varied, according to Jacob. He told me the compassion of some Soviets for the Jews was at best skin deep, that they were more interested in the propaganda benefits from the camp's liberation than anything else. There were some atrocities, but not nearly of the magnitude as under the Nazis. Some women raped; some prisoners intimidated. On the whole, though, treatment was good; relationships between the prisoners and soldiers, excellent."

"And Mr. Greene?"

"Experienced the good and bad. He told me he made one great friend among the Soviets."

"Did he mention a name?"

"If he did, I don't remember it. An officer."

"And the bad experience?"

"A local Pole came to camp on a regular basis to barter with the Soviets—eggs and fresh vegetables for fuel oil and vodka, that sort of thing. Jacob recognized the Pole, a tanner who used to work for his father before the war. The Pole, now wealthy by the standards existing at that time, in that place, began looking after Jacob, bringing him food and clothing. Evidently a Soviet soldier took note of Jacob's new friendship and used it to extort money from the Pole."

"How?"

"The Soviets shipped prisoners from Auschwitz by rail to deportation camps in the West. Jacob was scheduled to be on one of those trains, but a week before its departure the Soviet soldier took Jacob aside. The Soviet command, the soldier said, had decided to quietly execute certain prisoners accused of aiding and abetting their Nazi captors. He knew, he said, because they had ordered him to carry out one of the executions—Jacob's."

"*Did* Mr. Greene aid and abet the Nazis?"

"He would have welcomed death before doing so. No, whether the soldier told the truth or bluffed, Jacob never knew, but his purpose was clear. For the right incentive, the soldier hinted he might be inclined to ignore his orders. Jacob pleaded with the Pole, the Pole negotiated with the soldier."

"What happened?"

"The day the train arrived, the soldier took Jacob aside, into the woods outside the camp. Jacob feared the soldier intended to renege on his deal, but once in the woods the soldier let him go. Jacob traveled by foot for two days before catching a deportation train to Austria. He never knew how much the Pole had to pay to buy his freedom."

John bit his tongue. Why was it that so often a person professed to know so little, but under questioning filled volumes? "Do you know the soldier's name?"

"No."

"Anything about him? A description? Rank? Anything?"

"Sorry."

"Rabbi, the soldier's name couldn't have been Peter Olgov, could it?"

"I don't know," he said.

"What about the Pole?"

"Again, Jacob gave no name, no details."

"Mr. Greene said this man was a tanner who worked for his father. Was Mr. Greene's father in the leather industry?"

"I really don't know."

"Do you know the name of his father's business?"

"No."

John asked a string of other questions, but learned no more.

"Thank you, rabbi, for your help," he said, finally. "I appreciate the time you took."

"You're welcome," Rabbi Sosman said, and then, after a pause, he spoke again hesitantly. "One last thing, Mr. Sarikov."

"Yes?"

"I . . . I guess I find this whole thing sort of hard to swallow. I just can't believe anybody would want Jacob dead, but . . . well, I'm sorry for the way I acted, and I thought you should know. Something occurred to me after the fire. I almost told you the last time you were here."

"What is it, rabbi?"

"I told you the Fire Department said open gas jets on the oven started the fire?"

"Right."

"Jacob didn't cook."

Rabbi Sosman paused, letting the revelation settle, then continued. "I've been to his house a number of times. He always ordered out or picked things up from the deli, but he never cooked. Told me he hadn't in years. When I heard the cause of the fire, I thought perhaps Jacob had tried to light the oven for the first time . . . got confused, or forgot about the jets being on, didn't realize the danger . . . I don't know. His concentration wasn't what it was."

Michael felt fingers of excitement grab his stomach as he hung up the phone. With plenty of time left before his meeting with the dishwasher, he reached for his Dictaphone to paraphrase the conversation. *A Soviet soldier, bribed to release Greene. Greene, a man who never used his oven, killed in a fire caused by open jets on that oven.* John felt better than he had in weeks.

On entering the Ukrainian Café, John's eyes took a few moments to adjust to the darkened interior. He recognized the bartender, the same one who served him the last time. As John leaned against the bar, the bartender greeted him with his now familiar grunt.

John asked for the owner. The bartender betrayed a hint of a scowl before disappearing into the back room. He reappeared a moment later with the owner, who recognized John immediately.

"Yeah, the dishwasher's back there." The owner gestured over his shoulder toward the kitchen. "You buy him a few drinks, pay a little for his time and a little for mine. . . ."

John got the message and slid two twenties across the bar.

The owner picked it up. "He's got a break in fifteen minutes. I'll say you're here. I can't guarantee he's got anything worthwhile to say, but he'll sit down with you."

John nodded and ordered a beer. The same group of old men as yesterday occupied the end of the bar. They had hushed when John walked in, shot him cool stares, and now began to whisper among themselves again in Russian. Same old neighborly place.

A half an hour and two beers later, the bartender grunted again in John's direction. He pointed out a gray-haired man in a white T-shirt and smock who was taking a seat at one of the restaurant's tables.

"That the guy?" John asked, and the bartender nodded.

"Name's Bersch." It was the first time the bartender had spoken. The low grumble of a voice fit him.

John snapped on the record button of the Dictaphone in his shirt pocket as he walked to the table.

John's initial impression was of an elderly man, but as he neared the table, he realized his mistake. Bersch's face looked weathered and tired, and red puffy pouches underlined each eye, but his arms and hands looked strong and powerful. The web of red veins highlighted on his nose and cheeks indicated a heavy drinker; he smoked a cigarette.

"May I sit down?" John asked.

Bersch shrugged and John took a seat.

"I talked with the owner yesterday; did he tell you?"

Bersch nodded.

"He said you knew Peter Olgov."

Bersch studied John without speaking.

"You remember Olgov?" John asked. "He worked here, as a dishwasher."

"Many have worked here," Bersch answered in a thick Russian accent.

"C'mon, Mr. Bersch, not that many." John slid forty dollars into the center of the table. Bersch made no move to pick it up.

"Look, I'm trying to help . . . someone killed Olgov, you must know that." He slid across another forty. It was only money.

Bersch looked straight ahead, expressionless.

"I'm trying to find his killer."

"Why?"

"Because I think whoever killed Olgov may also have killed my brother."

Bersch snubbed out what remained of his cigarette in an ashtray and lit another one. John didn't recognize the brand, but it smelled like Turkish tobacco.

"Who was your brother?" Bersch asked.

"A police officer."

Bersch's eyes narrowed, his caution evidently aroused. "You police too?"

"No, I'm not."

Bersch relaxed only slightly.

"I need your help." John's Russian was never that good, and it was rusty, but he tried. *"Pozhalyista."* It meant *please*.

John thought he saw some brightening in Bersch's eyes, some hint of warmth.

John spoke again. "I didn't know Olgov, but no one who came to this country lacked courage and dreams. Your friend didn't deserve to die in a one-room apartment in a flophouse, facedown in a bathtub."

Bersch remained impassive. After a few moments, he offered John a cigarette.

John didn't care to smoke, but decided to accept nonetheless. The cigarette was short, no filter, a light brown, coarse paper wrapper. He lit the cigarette, inhaled, and restrained a cough. Exceedingly harsh, probably a product of Russia, John thought.

"You are Russian?" Bersch asked.

"My mother and father were."

Bersch nodded. "They taught you to speak some."

"Only some," John agreed.

The two looked at each other for a few moments in silence.

"I knew Olgov," Bersch said, finally.

John nodded.

"We work here together, go out for drink now and then."

"How long did you know him?"

"Five, six years . . . long time."

"You were good friends then?"

"We drank together, had laughs together. Friend? I guess friend too."

"Did you ever hear him mention the name Jacob Greene?"

Bersch shook his head. "No."

"An older Jewish man, maybe he came in here sometime?"

"No."

John withdrew the photo of Greene from his pocket and placed it in front of Bersch. "Look familiar?"

Bersch scanned the photo without expression. "No," he said, and slid the photo back in John's direction.

"Do you have any idea who might have wanted to kill Olgov?"

Bersch words came quickly. "Almost everybody."

John was shocked at the reply. "What do you mean?"

"Oh, not really kill him . . . but Peter full of shit most of time. We go out and many times he start fight. He make everybody mad sooner or later . . . he talk so big. Big man, big plans, very smart he said, but he full of shit."

The description of Olgov did not match the picture John had developed in his mind. "I understand he was a war hero."

"Peter?"

"Yes, decorated for valor."

Bersch laughed. "I hear him tell that story. Killed many Germans he say. Big hero. Phooey. Peter not war hero. He deserted."

"Deserted?"

"Yes. From Russian Army in Second World War. Peter not interested in being hero."

"Why? Why did he desert?"

"He met Americans. They have money, girls. Everybody in America rich, Peter thought. Peter have nothing. Plus Peter always disobeying orders, lying. He worried his lies catch up with him if he stay in army or go back to Russia. So he desert and come here."

Always disobeying orders; afraid his lies would catch up with him if he stayed in the army—the soldier who released Greene would have precisely those worries. "I was told he escaped Russia after the war because he hated communism."

"No. I tell you. He desert and come here, never went back to Russia. He did not hate communism; he hate being a pig farmer. That's what his family do in Russia, you know?"

"No, I didn't."

"Yes. Peter did not want to be pig farmer."

"Did he ever mention to you he was afraid of anybody here, that somebody was after him?"

"Peter, scared? No. Not for long time. You must know something about us who came here, many scared at first. Here not as safe as you think. The KGB here, secret police here, they track you down from Russia and poof, you disappear. Russia has very long memory."

"Were they after Olgov? Did they kill him?"

Bersch took a drag off his cigarette. "I talk only of very old history. Peter here many years. If they had wanted kill him, he would be dead long time ago. No. I think not. What would they care about dishwasher? Especially now, with USSR no more."

"All ancient history?"

"All very old."

"What about the present? Did Olgov have other sources of income? Did he . . . do you know if he was involved in drugs?"

"No drugs."

"Other income?"

"He was poor man. Always asking for money. No."

"Any enemies?"

"No, as I say, sometimes we all want to kill him, but we all like him too. He was good talker. Always planning what he would do someday. Full of bullshit, but fun to drink with. He told me, before he die, he worked on something big, something make him rich man."

John straightened in the chair. "Do you know what he was working on?"

"No. A dream, like everything with him. Nothing ever become of them."

"Maybe something did of this one."

Bersch shrugged. "Two years ago he going to open fishing charter service, a year ago he invent new type of wrench. Always crazy ideas."

"What about the last one, what was it?"

"He did not say."

"Wasn't that unusual? It sounds as if he liked to brag about what he was going to do."

Bersch paused. "Yes, he like to brag. But this time he say he could tell no one."

"Do you know why?"

Bersch hesitated. He glanced quickly toward the bar, then hunched forward in his seat, closer to John. "He said it was secret, old secret, from the war, that only he knew. As long as it remained secret he would make lot of money off it. That is all he say." Bersch suddenly looked anxious; he glanced at his watch. "And now my break is over. I must get back."

"Wait. A few more minutes."

"I am sorry. Must get back to work."

John slid another twenty across the table. "Just a few more questions."

Bersch sat down reluctantly.

"Olgov must have known something," John continued, "something he wasn't supposed to know. Do you have any idea what that something was?"

Bersch now spoke at barely a whisper. "No, I don't. I have no idea."

"He said the secret was worth a lot of money to him. Did he ever say how much?"

"No. But he said he might buy restaurant and put owner to work washing dishes." Bersch laughed. "But that was Peter. That was the crazy way he talked."

"Do you think his secret was crazy?"

Bersch shrugged. "Hard to tell with Peter, but all his other schemes—"

"What about *this one*? Could his secret have been the reason he was killed?"

Bersch fidgeted in his chair. He snubbed out the cigarette he smoked and lit another. Beads of sweat broke out on his forehead. "You give me more." Bersch's hand scratched at the table and he held up four fingers. "Four, huh?"

John counted out three twenties and put them on the table. "That's all I have left," he said.

When Bersch reached for the bills, John covered

them with his hand and spoke. "Why was he killed? For his secret?"

Bersch slid close to John and continued in a whisper. "I don't know." John started to say something, but Bersch interrupted. "But I tell you this, and then we done. There was man, thin, but strong-looking, you know—black hair, mean look. He come to restaurant a few days before Peter killed. He ask questions about Peter. He talk to me. I say nothing. My English very bad that day, you understand. The owner talk to him for a long time."

"Do you have a name? A way of contacting this man?"

John noticed Bersch broke eye contact before answering that he did not. John felt sure he had lied and pressed the question again. "This is very important to me. Are you sure?"

Bersch's eyes flared as they met John's. "You call me liar?"

John backed off. He could pursue the question later, but couldn't afford to scare Bersch off at this point. "No. I . . . just wanted to make sure you didn't get his name."

"I didn't ask yours; I didn't ask his."

"What did the man want to know?"

Bersch calmed. "About Peter? Everything . . . like you."

"You're scared of this man?"

"I scared of very few things in life . . . but, yes, I scared of this man."

"What . . ." John began, but stopped when he saw the concerned look on Bersch's face as his eyes locked on the bar behind John.

"I must go back to work now," Bersch said as he stood.

John looked back at the bar and saw the restaurant

owner glaring in Bersch's direction. "A few more questions," John said.

"No. I go back to work," Bersch insisted. He picked up the money from under John's hand and put it in his pocket. "No more talk. Don't come back. I am dishwasher, that is all. That is all I want to be." Bersch spun around and walked away from the table and into the kitchen.

John sat, stunned, realizing he had actually uncovered something. Olgov may have been killed because he planned to use a "secret" from World War II to get money, perhaps through extortion. John could not help thinking the "secret" pertained in some way to the concentration camp photos Michael had found.

John looked back over his shoulder. The owner still stared in his direction. He could see the bartender in the kitchen talking to Bersch; the bartender's facial expression looked far from pleasant.

John decided it might be wise to leave. He stopped first at the bar and signaled the owner who moved across the bar from him.

"Was he helpful to you?" the owner asked.

John was on guard. Things didn't feel right. He remembered Mrs. Banovich's fears and downplayed their conversation. "No. Struck out. A waste of money."

The owner smiled. "Too bad."

John nodded, then reached for his wallet and handed the owner one of his cards. "That's my home phone. You or anybody else remembers anything about Olgov, you can call me there. I've got plenty of cash to spread around for information."

"Okay, but like I said, there's not much to tell about the old man," the owner said as John walked out of the bar.

At his car, John admitted to himself, for the first time, that somewhere, deep inside, he *had* harbored doubts about Michael. Steve's words came back to him, "I've known cops, good cops, who have taken some money. It happens." Now John had the ammunition to face those doubts.

The pizza had cooled by the time John got it home, but he didn't care. He ate ravenously, finishing three-quarters of the pie and putting the last quarter in the refrigerator for breakfast. To say John's diet had been suffering lately was an understatement. He'd never eaten well, but now there were times he didn't eat at all, preferring a liquid diet to solid food. Tonight, however, his appetite had returned with his rising spirits. Pizza, even for breakfast, was an improvement.

John sat at the kitchen table with a pad, the names Olgov, Greene, and Michael arranged in a triangle on the top sheet. John drew a line between Michael's name and Olgov's and wrote above it: "murder investigation, box of photographs"—the connection between his brother and Olgov. Next he drew a line between Michael's name and Greene's and wrote "photograph, telephone calls" above it. Last he drew a line between Olgov's name and Greene's and wrote "photograph, Auschwitz? Olgov's secret?"

The common denominator: the concentration camp photographs. They were the key to everything.

Where to now? The police?

No, he decided. Not yet. He hadn't a sound theory, never mind hard facts.

He lined up his cassette tapes, played them one by one, then listened to them again. Auschwitz, Auschwitz, the name kept popping up. The more he learned, the more fingers pointed to the distant past, with the concentration camp the recurrent focal point. Did Greene and Olgov meet there? If they did, what happened between them and how could he find out?

A thought occurred to John; he reached for the

phone book and found the number for Penn Station. As he asked the Amtrak representative for the following morning's D.C. train schedule, a wave of doubt crossed his mind. *Why was he immersing himself in things over fifty years old?* He pushed the thought from his consciousness. What other avenues of investigation were left to him?

From the bus stop across the street, from around the newspaper he held, Rolf saw John leave his apartment and hail a taxi. Rolf watched the taxi until it disappeared into the turbulent stream of morning traffic, then tossed the newspaper into a trash basket and crossed the street.

He didn't foresee any problems. It wasn't a doorman building, and, as expected, the lock on the ground floor delayed him only momentarily. He checked the two rows of mail slots for Sarikov's name. Apartment 19C. He took the elevator up to the nineteenth floor.

The apartment's lock picked as easily as the lobby's. He entered and shut the door behind him, leaving the lights off—there was enough light from the apartment's windows to comfortably see.

Vasili had given Rolf his instructions the night before, stressing the assignment's urgency—Sarikov was moving fast, faster than Vasili thought possible. First, according to reports Vasili had received, Sarikov was seen nosing around Olgov's apartment building, then, just yesterday, at the restaurant where Olgov had worked. "How?" Vasili had asked Rolf, then proceeded to answer the question himself. "Have we once again failed to recover all of Olgov's evidence? Could it be some of that evidence is now in Sarikov's hands?"

To Rolf's mind, an obvious solution existed: take

Sarikov out, quickly and cleanly. Rolf would have gladly volunteered for the duty; unfortunately Vasili forbade it. It seemed a representative of the Collegium's old guard had passed a message to Vasili: for the time being Sarikov was not to be touched. Declaring it would be premature to force a confrontation with the Collegium, Vasili ordered Rolf to search the apartment, nothing more.

Chickenshits, all of them. Even Vasili. Old men with shriveled balls. If Rolf were in charge, he'd have sent his own message to the Collegium by slicing off Sarikov's head and delivering it to their representative.

Rolf searched the kitchen thoroughly and found nothing. The same result in the living room. He started on the bedroom. On the dresser sat a picture of Sarikov's brother, the cop, and a hint of a smile passed Rolf's lips. He wished John Sarikov would come home now, unexpectedly. "It was very unfortunate, but what choice did I have," Rolf would tell Vasili.

On a desk in the corner of the bedroom was a personal computer surrounded by piles of paper. Rolf shuffled through them quickly, finding nothing. A stack of small cassette tapes caught his eye, and he turned one over. "Interview with Mrs. Banovich" its caption read. Rolf knew the name: the tenant, the one who lived in Olgov's building, the one both Michael and John Sarikov had gone to see. The next tape read "Interview from Ukrainian Café." Olgov's workplace. There were other tapes and names Rolf didn't recognize.

Rolf searched the desk's drawers and found a Dictaphone. He inserted a tape, the one from the restaurant, rewound it, and pressed PLAY. Briefed sufficiently by Vasili to understand the import of what he heard, his lips curled as he listened.

After a few minutes he popped in another tape,

then another, until he had reviewed short segments from each. Taking the tapes would alert Sarikov; Rolf decided to return with another recorder immediately and make copies.

Sarikov had been a very busy boy. He'd discovered all sorts of evidence: the dishwasher, the old lady, the rabbi, the cop's widow—sources of information Vasili couldn't ignore, sources of information Vasili might want to disappear before the Collegium learned of them. Rolf's services would be needed again soon, that was obvious.

He felt the excitement spreading in the very pit of his stomach.

The place was still, somber. People walked with their hands behind their backs; families shuttled through arm in arm, whispering among themselves only occasionally.

Strange, that this memorial steeped in inhumanity should bring out the very best in people. It gave John hope, until he looked back at the displays: piles of toothbrushes, bent glasses, and worn shoes; mock-ups of ovens that had made these items superfluous. Then he wondered.

John wasn't sure what he hoped to find here, but had come nonetheless—every clue, every coincidence he had uncovered seemed linked somehow to the happenings commemorated within the walls of this building, the Holocaust Museum in Washington, D.C.

The morning train ride had taken only a few hours. The time had past quickly; he'd stopped at a B. Dalton on the way to Penn Station and picked up two books, one on World War II, the other on the Holocaust. He read the references to Auschwitz with particular interest.

John had come to the museum to learn, not feel, but couldn't avoid the latter. On entering the museum, one of the staff issued him an identification card, to simulate the treatment of Jews in Nazi Germany. His was for a Chaim Rubinstein, born in Gabin, Poland, in 1901. The last page of the I.D. revealed his fate; he and his family perished at Treblinka in 1943.

The elevator took him to the fourth floor. He wound his way downward, as if toward hell, from Hitler's ascendancy to the extermination camps. John found himself stopping to absorb every exhibit: eye and hair color charts for identifying non-Aryans, calipers for measuring skull diameters to weed out the mentally unfit, a cattle car used to ship prisoners to death camps.

So many faces looked back at him from the walls of the memorial. Photographs of long dead strangers who came to life in this setting. Each reminded John of the photo he kept in his pocket. The eyes, always the eyes, looked the same.

Back on the first floor, in a room set aside for introspection, John's hands played absently with the I.D. card he had been issued. He had learned nothing of value, at least as far as his investigations were concerned. He read the inscription on the wall in front of him, the gist of it that we must never forget. He wouldn't forget either, and rededicated himself to clearing Michael's name.

He looked again to the I.D. card in his hand. He flipped through it, then stopped; his eyes jumped to the picture of Chaim Rubinstein and the short description of his life underneath. I.D. in hand, he made his way to the information desk and caught the attention of one of the women behind it.

"Excuse me," John said. "The identification cards,"—he held up the card as he spoke—"how did the museum collect the information that's included inside?"

"You mean the names?" the woman asked.

"And the histories, the pictures."

"I think it varied, person by person. Sometimes the information came from relatives, sometimes from books and other records. Are you interested in researching a victim of the Holocaust, sir?"

"A survivor, actually."

"Then you might want to talk to someone in our library, up on the fifth floor." She pointed to a corner of the building. "The elevator's through there. They might be able to help you."

John nodded and started for the elevator. If the museum had a picture and brief history of Chaim Rubinstein, might they also have them of Jacob Greene? As the elevator rose, he pulled his wallet from his pocket and extracted his *New York Herald* identification card—people usually went the extra yard for the press.

John spent a few minutes wandering the library, a series of large, light-filled public rooms with long tables and carrels. Thousands of books filled the shelves. Uncertain of where to start, he approached a young man behind the main counter. He explained briefly what he looked for, then flashed the *Herald* card. The card did the trick—the young man picked up a telephone and a few moments later led John to the office of Dr. Amy Davis, the chief archivist.

A small, lean woman, she sat poised behind a desk that seemed to dwarf her, that is until she spoke. Her commanding presence made John somewhat ill-at-ease, resurrecting old doubts. Was he simply wasting her time, his time, on an obsessive wild-goose chase into the past?

After introductions, John smiled and took her hand. "Thank you for taking the time to see me."

"No problem." She indicated a chair. "Please, take a seat." After John sat, she continued. "Now, I understand you had some questions about searching records for a Holocaust survivor."

"That's right."

"What is it exactly I can do for you?"

Brief and to the point, John told himself. "I'm investigating a story. It comes down to this. I have two names. One, a Jewish prisoner of Auschwitz, the other, a Russian soldier who may have taken part in Auschwitz's liberation. I think the two may have met in Auschwitz. For purposes of the story, I need to learn all I can about the prisoner. It would also help if I could confirm the Russian soldier helped liberate Auschwitz. I hoped you might be of help, in both matters."

"I see. Unfortunately, Mr. Sarikov, the information you're seeking may not be available . . . but I think I am getting ahead of myself. Before we get to specifics, may I ask why you need this information?"

For a second he considered starting in on the convoluted truth, then realized Dr. Davis would more than likely dismiss him as paranoid if he did. "I'm sorry, Dr. Davis, I'm not at liberty to go too deeply into the facts at the moment."

"I see. . . ."

John pushed on. "I'm here conducting basic research on the story. The identification cards, the ones you issue on entrance, include a history and picture. That got me to thinking—maybe records exist for the Jewish prisoner I'm researching. The Russian soldier, I know, is a slightly different matter."

"What's the prisoner's name?"

"Jacob Greene."

"G-r-e-e-n?"

"G-r-e-e-n-e."

"Just a moment." Dr. Davis picked up her phone and punched in four numbers. "Aaron, could you do something for me?" she said a moment later. "Could you check the computer, see if we prepared a mock identification card for a Jacob Greene. G-r-e-e-n-e. Or something close to that spelling." Her eyes jumped to John's, and she spoke to him as she waited for an answer. "We've been surprised by the tremendous demand for tracing victims and survivors. We hadn't expected it, not fifty years after the war. Frankly we're not geared to handle all the requests, but—"

Dr. Davis broke her eyes from John's and spoke again into the phone. "Okay, thanks for checking." She placed the receiver on the cradle, then shrugged. "A shot in the dark, Mr. Sarikov. We never prepared an identification card for Jacob Greene. Obviously the I.D.'s cover just an infinitesimal fraction of Holocaust victims and survivors, but I thought it was worth a try. So let's see, where do we go from here? Let's get the Russian soldier out of the way first. I don't have access to Soviet troop rolls, and, unfortunately, I don't have any idea who might. A number of the books in our library deal in part with Auschwitz's liberation; the name of a Russian soldier could, I suppose, be mentioned in passing, but . . . well I doubt if you'd find what you're looking for. The prisoner? There I know where to look, but I'm afraid you still might find yourself disappointed. After the war millions of dislocated Jews tried to locate one another—ripped apart by the Holocaust, some were sent to camps, some had just disappeared. Unfortunately, the Nazis destroyed many of the camp records; it took years to collect the surviving information and organize it in a useful form. The Captured German Records Division of the National Archives has copies of the death books and registration books for most of the concentration camps liberated by the Western Allies. After the war the Red Cross established an international tracing service in Germany specifically for the purpose of tracing survivors of the Holocaust. But your situation is somewhat more difficult."

"Why is that?"

"Because Auschwitz was liberated by the Soviets."

"Which means?"

"Which means the Soviets carted off all records from Auschwitz that the Nazis didn't have time to destroy. They have been less than forthcoming about opening those records."

"Even now?"

"I suppose there are differences of opinion about that. Between 1991 and 1992 they released forty-six volumes of the *Sterbebüchern* to the Auschwitz Memorial Museum in Oswiecim, Poland."

"*Sterbe,* what?"

"Death books." Dr. Davis reached across her desk to a stack of three books on a shelf, pulling out the center one. "We just got these in recently." She handed the book to John.

He read the title: *Death Books from Auschwitz.*

"They contain excerpts from the volumes the Soviets delivered to the Auschwitz museum. *Sterbebücher* means *death book* in German. Here, let me show you." She rose, made her way around the desk, and stood over John's shoulder. She flipped quickly through the book, then laid it open on the desk for John to see.

A page from a death book, in German. John couldn't read it.

"Let me translate it for you," Dr. Davis offered. "It says a bookseller, Richard Israel—the Nazis made all male Jews adopt the middle name of Israel—Lanyi, died in Auschwitz on May 28, 1942, at eight forty-five in the morning. He was born on December 9, 1884, in Wien—that made him . . . what? . . . fifty-eight. His father was Leopold Lanyi of Wien, and his mother was Johanna Lanyi, maiden name Spitzer. He was married to an Anna Lanyi, maiden name Bartos. The Auschwitz doctor certified the cause of death as sudden heart failure."

John stared at the page for a few seconds, then turned to the next, and to the next after that. Each displayed a copy of another page of a death book. Prisoners, one after the other, indexed in typically efficient German style. He imagined forty-six volumes' worth—pages of names, books of pages, stacks of books. The cold organization of Hitler's "final solution."

Dr. Davis continued. "The Russians say what they released, forty-six volumes of death books, represents the full complement of records they took from Auschwitz. There's another school of thought, however, that says they've got all sorts of Auschwitz records tucked away in their archives—other volumes of death books, and, more important from your point of view, the Auschwitz registration books."

"Registration books?"

"On a prisoner's induction, the Nazis recorded various information. Name; place and date of birth; work assignment—Auschwitz, Birkenau or one of the many area work camps; and of course the registration—tattoo—number. Ultimately, they listed the prisoner's final disposition. "Selected," was frequently written in this last column—a euphemism for the gas chamber."

John thought of the tattoo number on the forearm of the prisoner whose picture he carried. The Auschwitz registration books, if nothing else, would tell him for certain if that tattoo number belonged to Jacob Greene. "All prisoners were registered?"

"The Nazis didn't bother to register prisoners sent immediately from the trains to the gas chambers. Otherwise, yes."

"But there is no way to access the registration books?"

Dr. Davis shook her head.

The finality of the answer silenced John, prompting Dr. Davis to continue. "I'm sorry, but if they exist, to my knowledge they're just not available, and believe me, if the Soviets released them it would be pretty big news—I would have heard about it."

"I see . . . looks like I've wasted your time then, Dr. Davis. Any suggestions?"

"Yes. I'm going to give you a name. He's a scholar connected with Yad Vashem, the Holocaust research center in Israel. Hold on . . . I know I have his name here somewhere." Dr. Davis flipped through a stack of publications on her desk. "He just wrote an article in . . . yes, here it is. Ready?"

John pulled a pen from his sport coat pocket. "Go ahead."

"Okay. It's Isaac Lieberman. That's L-i-e-b-e-r-m-a-n. I don't have an address or phone number, just a name, but you should be able to get them from Yad Vashem." Dr. Davis gave John Yad Vashem's address and phone number. "Two things he can do for you. First, Yad Vashem has managed to collect some information on Auschwitz survivors. It won't hurt to check whether they have any records on this Jacob Greene. Lieberman can assist you there, that's part of his job. Second, he's *the* authority on German records captured by the Soviets. Your question about the Russian soldier, maybe he can help. And if there has been any news, any rumors, concerning the release of Auschwitz materials from Russian archives, he's going to be the one to know about it. He seems to have developed some sort of pipeline into Moscow—he's published some pretty startling material in the last couple of years."

John nodded appreciatively. "I'll call him. Any other suggestions?"

"Not that I can think of."

John rose from his chair. "Then thank you. I appreciate all your help."

Dr. Davis smiled. "Glad to be of service, Mr. Sarikov, and good luck to you."

                    *   *   *

It was eight o'clock when John got home from Penn Station. He started a pot of coffee, lit a cigarette—a habit he had again fallen into—and opened the book he bought that morning about World War II, all the while trying to ignore the tremors in his hand and the bottles in the kitchen that could make them go away. He had to stay sharp for tonight.

Pursuing stories for ten years had taught John a number of things, one of the most important being to doggedly follow through. Sit on the phone and call everybody, chase down every lead no matter how un- promising it might seem—it cost only time and a sore ear, but once in a while the payoff was tremendous. Israel lay seven time zones east of New York. That meant John had to wait until tomorrow morning to call Lieberman at Yad Vashem, or stay up and start calling at 1:00 A.M. John had chosen the latter—he wouldn't have been able to sleep anyway.

The intervening hours passed slowly.

At 1:15 A.M. John called Yad Vashem and was put through to Lieberman's office. He was away from his desk. Rather than leave a message, John mentioned the *New York Herald* and asked if he could hold. Five minutes later Lieberman picked up the phone.

Hebrew turned to English after John's bumbling "Hello."

"I am told you are with the *New York Herald.*" The connection was clear, Lieberman sounded anxious to help.

"That's right. Dr. Davis of the Holocaust Museum in Washington, D.C., suggested I give you a call."

"I'm afraid I don't know Dr. Davis, but what is it I can do for you?"

"I'm researching a story." John gave Lieberman the same thumbnail sketch of his investigation he had given Dr. Davis.

"I'm afraid Dr. Davis may have been overly optimistic," Lieberman said after John finished, "at least as far as the Russian soldier. I won't be able to tell you anything about him. We do collect information regarding Holocaust *rescuers,* people who kept Jews in attics, or secreted them out of harm's way, but that doesn't include the Soviet troops who liberated the camps . . . except of course for officers in charge, we might have something on them. Was this man an officer?"

"Not based on what I've been told." John thought of the photo of Olgov Mrs. Banovich had given him. "If you can wait just a second, I have a picture of him in uniform." John raced to his bedroom to collect the photo. "I'm looking at the picture now," he said, back on the phone, "and no, there's no indication he was an officer."

"No garland, no stripes, no identifying marks on his hat?"

John studied the picture again; Olgov's uniform wasn't decorated at all. "No."

"Well then, I won't—"

"One thing though," John said, interrupting Lieberman. "I hadn't really paid any attention to it before. There's a tank in the background of the photo with an insignia on it: two digits, a six and a zero, you can make it out pretty clearly. Sixty. Does that help?"

"It could, I'm not sure. Look, why don't you give me the soldier's name and I'll see what I can do. I wouldn't get my hopes up though."

John spelled Olgov's name.

"Now the survivor. Did Dr. Davis fill you in on the problem with researching Auschwitz survivors?"

"Yes. She said most of Auschwitz's records were either destroyed or are in Russian hands."

"Exactly. We have reconstructed some records here based on testimonials from survivors and their families. I can check them for you. I can also put in a call to the Auschwitz Memorial Museum in Poland. They, however, also have only limited records. Could you give me the survivor's name, please."

John did.

"That was his given name?"

"As far as I know.

"What can you tell me of Jacob Greene that may be relevant?"

"I have his tattoo number."

"You do? Excellent. Could you read that off for me?"

Again, John did.

"Anything else?" Lieberman asked.

John explained that, unfortunately, he knew very little. What elements of Greene's personal history he did know he related to Lieberman, who then asked the same question regarding Peter Olgov, and again John painted a very sketchy picture.

"All right. I'll see what I can do for you. If you'll give me your number—"

"Excuse me, Mr. Lieberman," John interrupted. "Dr. Davis intimated that . . . well that you might have developed some sort of pipeline into the Russian archives . . . might be able to access records kept there."

John noted Lieberman's delay in answering, and the undertone of suspicion when he did. ". . . And why would she intimate that?"

"I'm not sure, really. She said you were *the* expert on records captured by the Russians, and that if their status had in any way changed, you'd be the man who would know about it. She also mentioned something about your having published some fairly startling material in the last couple of years."

"I see . . . I'm sorry, Mr. . . . it's pronounced Sarikov?"

"Right."

"Mr. Sarikov, if I ever meet Dr. Davis, I will have to thank her for her vote of confidence, but I can't work miracles. *If* the Russians still hold Auschwitz records in their archives, the status of those records has not changed; they simply aren't available. Now, if I can have your phone number, I'll check the records that *are* open to me, and give you a call as soon as I know something."

John passed on his number, then wound up the phone call, expecting very little to come from it.

35

Mrs. Banovich couldn't imagine who would be sending her flowers. She took another look through the peephole—Sulty's Florist, the patch above the man's breast pocket said. He held a large centerpiece of roses and carnations.

She tried to remember the last time she had received flowers: maybe thirty-five years ago, when she dated Howard, the car salesman from Queens. My God, she thought, such a long time ago, yet the memories lingered sweetly. Forgotten were Howard's crass mannerisms, the revelation of his marriage, the ensuing bitter breakup. She held onto only the good: dinner for two at candle-lit restaurants; his desire for her, hers for him; the feel of coarse, masculine hands.

She opened the door.

"Mrs. Banovich?" the pleasant-looking man asked.

"Yes?"

"I have a delivery for you."

"Oh my, for me?" she said, excitement clear in her voice.

"Yes ma'am. It's sort of heavy . . . can I put it somewhere for you?"

"Why yes, thank you . . . could you put it over there, on the table," she said, pointing, eager to read the card dangling from the arrangement.

As the man stepped past the door, another taller man appeared behind him and followed him into the apartment. Mrs. Banovich was momentarily frightened by his appearance, but he also wore a florist's uniform and smiled warmly at Mrs. Banovich as he shut the door behind him. He placed a clipboard and pen on the table next to the flowers and asked Mrs. Banovich to sign for the delivery.

As Mrs. Banovich reached for the pen and clipboard, the taller man grabbed her wrists. She looked into his eyes, which had lost even the hint of warmth, and prepared to scream. The sound rising from her throat never escaped; the man behind her threw a heavy-gauge clear plastic bag over her head, tightening it around her neck with one hand and clamping it to her mouth with the other.

In slightly less than a minute Mrs. Banovich had stopped her struggles. In three minutes her veins began to stand out in blue along her temples. After five minutes the man securing the plastic bag around her neck removed it, and the man holding her hands dragged her limp body across the room and set it gently on the couch. They picked up the flowers, pen, and clipboard, scanned the room quickly, and left.

36

Kelly set the phone back on the cradle and sat in quiet repose. After a few moments, her mind still lingering on the phone call, she cleared her breakfast dishes—an oatmeal bowl and tea cup—loaded them into the dishwasher, and sponged down the table. The kitchen looked spotless when she finished, a rarity when Michael still lived. Then dirty dishes flanked the sink, mail, books and pencils dotted the counters, and stray footprints betrayed Michael's disregard for doormats. In those days Kelly hadn't been keen on spending her spare time cleaning. Now she had nothing but time, and cleaning had become a welcome chore—it filled an hour or two with purpose every day.

The phone call had been from Barbara. After small talk, Barbara had brought up the real reason for the call—she and John had broken up a few weeks back. The news only got worse. John always sounded fine when Kelly talked to him—positive and comforting—but according to Barbara he put up a front. John was self-destructing. Barbara had provided details hesitantly, troubled over breaching his confidences but convinced she no longer had any choice—she just couldn't get through to him. Kelly was the only person he would listen to, and he needed to listen, Barbara said, before it was too late.

Kelly never noticed, never thought to look, too worried about her own problems. John had hidden things from her, that was obvious now, but she should have guessed—like Michael, he locked his emotions inside.

Kelly hesitated, John's phone number in her hand. She never thought she had to worry about him. He had been the strong one since Michael's death; the one who had comforted her, whom she had leaned against. He could get through this, there had never been any doubt, or at least she had thought. What did she intend to say to him now? Don't punish yourself any longer, get over your brother's death, and get on with your life. How could she sound convincing when she hadn't been able to convince herself of those very things?

Kelly dialed John's number and got his answering machine. She left a short message asking him to call. A few long hours later he did, sounding upbeat. Kelly suggested they meet at a restaurant for lunch; she needed to get out, she lied. They chose a place in Manhattan.

Kelly spotted John at the bar when she entered the restaurant; she immediately noticed the dark circles under his eyes. His weight seemed down, and his face had an unhealthy pallor.

As they ate their meals and made small talk, Kelly examined John through different eyes. He laughed, smiled, told jokes, the same old John, but his hands fidgeted, and he rarely looked her straight in the eye. He appeared preoccupied, or perhaps a better description would be guilty, but guilty of what?

Kelly decided to give him a chance to come clean. "How's everything going with you and Barbara?"

"Fine. Great. Couldn't be better." John looked away as he spoke.

"John . . . Barbara called me this morning."

An embarrassed half smile crossed John's lips. "Okay, so-o-o-o, maybe not that great."

Kelly didn't smile. "How about the two of you broke up."

"Okay . . . not good at all."

Kelly's fork played with a piece of broccoli on her plate. "Barbara's worried about you."

"*Maybe* Barbara should mind her own business. I'm fine."

"Is that the truth?"

John didn't meet her eyes. "Yeah . . . the truth."

"She says you haven't gone back to work."

"Work's never been a problem for me. I'll start again when I'm ready."

"She says you won't take her calls; you don't talk to any of your old friends."

John pulled the napkin from his lap, used it to wipe his mouth, then threw it, crumpled, on his plate. "Can we change the subject?"

"No. Barbara's really worried about you, and frankly, so am I."

"If she's so worried why'd she walk out on me?" The words sounded bitter.

"She said you'd been drinking, every night, all the time. She said she couldn't get through to you . . . and . . . she said . . . she said you started to scare her."

"Kelly, look, that's crap." John's index finger stabbed the table for emphasis. "And anyway, it's between Barbara and me."

"What goes on between you two, yeah, I care, but it's your business. But your work, the drinking . . ."

"Is this an inquisition? Sure I've been a bit down, but—"

Kelly had no intention of letting up. "Is she telling the truth, John?"

". . . Maybe, sort of, but I'm all right . . . really I am. I'm just not ready to see a lot of people yet."

"The drinking?"

John dropped his head forward and ran his fingers

slowly through his hair. "Some. Not as bad as all that though. Hell, I always drank, now it's suddenly a terrible thing? Maybe I've had a bit more than I should . . . you know better than anyone it hasn't been a great month."

Kelly nodded, then placed her hand on his. "Since Michael's death I've sunk lower than I ever thought possible, but you've been there for me, and that's helped. Now it's my turn to be there for you."

"I'm fine."

"Well, I'm not. That's the truth, and I'll face it, because that's the only way I'm ever going to get better, and I want to get better. I want to get beyond the pain and start healing. And then I'm going to do everything Michael would want me to do: I'm going to smile again, I'm going to laugh again, and someday I may even love again. Someday I'll focus on all Michael gave me instead of what someone took away. That's what he would want for me, and that's what he would want for you. Not for our lives to end with his. Never that."

"I'll be okay, Kelly; I really will."

"Promise me. Promise me. I know I've been selfish . . . talked only about my problems. I needed to lean on you, but now it's your turn. Tell me when it's tough. Talk to me when you're down."

John nodded once unconvincingly.

"Another thing. Barbara says you've been investigating Michael's death on your own. She's worried, frankly, that you're obsessed with it. Isn't it time to let go, to let the police handle it?"

"Like they've handled it so far?" he asked, his fists now clenched.

Kelly didn't respond.

"I'm serious," John said. "They haven't done a damn thing. They've swept the whole thing under the rug. I won't let them do that. I don't care what Barbara or anybody else thinks. I won't let them get away with it."

"But you're not the police. What can you do?"

"To tell you the truth, I don't know, but I'm going to keep trying. I talked with a detective named Hartley the other day; he's handling Michael's case. Do you know what he said to me?"

"No."

"He said they've closed Michael's case. He said . . ." John hesitated, then continued under his breath. "He said Michael was a dirty cop who broke his vow to uphold the law and got what he deserved."

Kelly's hand went to her mouth. At that moment she wanted to tell John to ignore everything she had said, to find Michael's killers and prove once and for all the only thing Michael deserved was to be cherished.

"I can't let that be how Michael is remembered. I just can't. I can't walk away."

"*We* know the truth, isn't that enough?" she asked John, and herself.

"*No*. Michael would never have turned his back on me. Besides, I've found some things, some things that might be important."

"John—"

"I *can't* stop now."

"Okay . . . okay. What kind of things? What have you found?"

"You'll listen? With an *open* mind?"

Kelly lied. "Yes."

John leaned in toward her. He filled her in on his investigations, ending with the revelations from Bersch, Rabbi Sosman, and Lieberman.

John paused, allowing the information to sink in, then pressed on. "That's not all. Kelly, you told me about the photographs of the concentration camp Michael found under the false bottom of the box. Those photographs have disappeared—you can't find them, the police can't find them. Couldn't those photos have been compromising to someone? Couldn't they have been taken from Michael? Couldn't Michael have been killed because he saw them, the same for Olgov and Greene? Michael's police log says Olgov's apartment was ripped apart. Someone had searched it looking for something. The photos?"

"But, John—"

"It all ties together. There are too many coincidences. I just haven't figured out the key to the puzzle yet."

"You're so wrapped up in this it's scary. You should see yourself. It's just not healthy."

"I think I can find something on this. There's a chance, just a chance, I can clear Michael, and that's enough for me to keep trying. I'd do anything for you, Kelly, you know that, but I beg you not to ask me to stop."

"And you've taken this to the police?"

"Most of it."

"They can't ignore the things you've discovered. Let them handle it—they'll come up with something," Kelly tried once more.

"How? They've closed the case, remember. They don't want it reopened. It was a political embarrassment to them. I told you Hartley's response when I brought information to him; let me repeat it: 'Michael was a dirty cop who broke his vow to uphold the law and got what he deserved.' I need harder evidence before I go back."

"Go to Steve; he'll listen."

"I've talked to Steve so many times he's sick of me. He did listen, but wasn't convinced either, and I can't totally blame him. What do I really know? I've got some strange coincidences, but what motive? Who's responsible? I've got to find some answers before I go back to him. Don't worry, okay? I'm an investigative reporter, remember?"

Kelly gazed blankly at her food. "I don't know. I just don't know," she whispered. "Maybe you have to try. Maybe it would be wrong to ask you to stop, it's just . . . I didn't want you throwing your life away . . . banging your head against the wall. I'm ashamed to say it, God forgive me, I'm ashamed because I've thought . . . part of me, a part I don't like very much, wasn't sure you would . . . could . . . find anything to clear Michael. There've been times I've . . . I've had doubts."

John reached out his hand and set it on hers. "It's all right, Kelly. It's all right. How could you not have doubts? Maybe I have too, but doubts or not, I know you believe in him, that's what's important. I do too, and that's why I'm going to get to the bottom of this."

Kelly sat silently for a moment. "I don't want ever to doubt him. I came here to tell you to move on, but I don't have the right, and selfishly, maybe I don't want you to. I don't know what to do, I don't know what you should do, but you've got to realize one thing, if you stop now, or tomorrow, or the day after, you haven't betrayed Michael. Just promise me you'll remember that and take care of yourself."

John promised.

37

After eyeing the meats behind the deli counter, Rabbi Sosman chose a beef roast. He had invited his brother and sister-in-law for dinner that night, and decided a roast would probably not strain his limited cooking abilities. Perhaps it was simpler fare than his brother, a bond trader on Wall Street, normally ate, but with the rabbi's limited ability as a cook also went a limited budget. Besides, the rabbi thought, his brother often took far too much relish in parading his poor but selfless brother the rabbi in front of countless shallow uptown friends in the city's finest restaurants. Tonight it would just be the three of them—a simple meal among family, the way it ought to be.

As the rabbi queued up to place his order, he felt a prick on the back of his neck, like a bee's sting. He turned to find a middle-aged woman fighting with two large packages and an umbrella.

She apologized immediately. "Oh, I'm sorry, I was just shifting packages and I'm afraid I caught you with the point of my umbrella."

"That's quite all right," Rabbi Sosman said reflexively, as he rubbed the back of his neck. He wiped the resultant small smear of blood from his fingers with a handkerchief. The stab of pain passed quickly, forgotten by the time the butcher handed him the neatly wrapped roast.

Three blocks from the deli the rabbi began to feel

strange. A light sweat coated his forehead, temples, and upper lip; the sound of traffic echoed in his ears. He felt dizzy. He put a hand to his chest and discovered his heartbeat had increased dramatically.

Up ahead he saw a bench, a place to rest.

Rabbi Sosman had taken a half dozen steps toward the bench when a look of fear crossed his face. His heartbeat continued to race, its pounding now ringing in his ears. There was no explanation; he exercised regularly and the walk from the deli had not been trying.

The bench was now less than a half block away. The rabbi began hyperventilating; his breathing matched the rapid thumping of his heart. Blood surged rhythmically just under the surface of his face, his eyes, his fingertips. Faster, and faster.

Three feet from the bench he fell and rolled onto his back. He felt no pain; on the contrary massive amounts of adrenaline coursed his system pushing his senses to a knife's edge. His eyes widened, their pupils dilated, almost obscuring the irises.

The heartbeats climaxed at an almost constant drumming, then stalled, his heart ripping itself apart. Tremendous pain came then, but it was short-lived. Rabbi Sosman was dead within minutes.

38

John replayed the messages from his answering machine. Two of them, each potentially a positive development. The owner of the Ukrainian Café had left the first. He suggested John be at the restaurant tomorrow at 1:00 P.M. if he wanted to talk to someone who had information about Olgov. Potentially no more than a shakedown for additional cash, but John saw no reason not to pursue the lead.

Isaac Lieberman of Yad Vashem had left the second message. They had talked only four days ago; John hadn't expected a return call so soon. He checked his watch—early evening in Israel, but maybe Lieberman would still be at his desk. John dialed Lieberman's number, hoping for good news. A secretary took his name and put him on hold. The next voice he heard was Lieberman's.

"Mr. Sarikov?"

"Yes," John answered. "I got your message. Have you been able to find out anything?"

"Yes and no, with, I'm afraid, an emphasis on the latter."

"Oh." John couldn't hide the disappointment from his voice.

"Let me tell you what I did find first. You wanted to know whether a Red Army soldier, Peter Olgov, participated in Auschwitz's liberation. I can't tell you for sure; as I suspected, we don't have that informa-

tion. However, you described the photo you have of
Olgov . . . the tank in the background with the digits
six-zero on it. I did some checking. I'd guess the 'sixty'
represents the Soviet 60th Army, a branch of the 1st
Ukrainian Army Group under Marshal Konev. The
60th Army group liberated Auschwitz."

"Olgov *was* there."

"That seems likely."

Olgov dead, Greene dead, and finally he'd established the connection. John's momentary excitement
ebbed quickly. "What about Jacob Greene?"

"That's a different matter. I've checked our files
and those of the Auschwitz museum. I uncovered no
evidence a Jacob Greene was ever interned there. As
I've told you, however, that's not surprising—our records in regard to Auschwitz are spotty at best."

"What do you suggest, Mr. Lieberman, are there
any other sources to check?"

"No, to be blunt. I tried every variation of 'Greene'
I could think of. After the Holocaust it was not unheard of for Jews to change their names, especially
when they left home and emigrated to America.
Afraid of being recognized as Jews, of being singled
out again, of having the Holocaust repeat itself, some
Jews Americanized their names—shortened them to
lose a readily identifiable Jewish suffix, or changed
their names completely. After all 'Greene' is not a
terribly Jewish name."

"And you didn't find anything?"

"No. Besides, even if I missed a variation, or
Greene changed his name from something totally unrelated, I had the tattoo number you gave me. I
couldn't match the number to any of the records we
have. I can tell you, however, that numerically the
tattoo number makes sense—in other words some
prisoner in Auschwitz did have the numbers 1-7-6-1-

3-4 tattooed to his forearm. The tattoo was on his left forearm, right?"

"I think so, why?"

"The Nazis tattooed most Jews in Auschwitz on their left forearms, on the forearm's top side."

John pulled a picture from his chest pocket. "I'm looking at a photo of Greene right now. He's holding up his arm. The tattoo's on the left, top forearm, just as you said."

"And you're not mistaken about the number."

"No, the picture's old, but it's still clear. He's wearing a grayish blue vertical striped shirt, his sleeve is pushed up, and—"

"*What was that*, Mr. Sarikov?"

"What?"

"You said vertical striped shirt?"

"Yes."

"This photo you have, it was taken *at* Auschwitz?"

"I assume so. Why?"

"I *never* imagined. . . ." The excitement in Lieberman's voice was clear. "Do you have more photos, Mr. Sarikov?"

John paused to think before answering. Why had Lieberman's tone changed so dramatically? What was John missing? "I have the photo of Olgov."

"Could that have been taken at Auschwitz also?"

"I don't know; it could have been."

"Any others?"

"Photos?"

"Yes."

"Why is it so important, Mr. Lieberman?"

"*Important*, Mr. Sarikov? Do you have *any* idea how valuable photos from Auschwitz are? And I don't mean monetarily. Very, very few exist—the Nazis, for obvious reasons, didn't allow cameras in the camps. It would mean a *great* deal to me, to my work, to get my hands on Auschwitz photos."

EXPOSED 259

"I only have the two."

"Where'd you get them?"

John again rejected the idea of telling Lieberman the truth. "The story . . . it's complicated. I have two, out of an original . . . I guess maybe a dozen."

"A dozen? Where are the rest?"

"I'm trying to track them down."

"Who has them?"

"I don't know, not yet. Again, I can't go into detail, but the information I sought from you, on Jacob Greene, I was hoping it would lead me to the photos."

"You're saying if you knew more about Jacob Greene, you might be able to get your hands on those photos?" Lieberman's voice was almost desperate now.

"I might." John sounded much more confident than he felt.

"Are the chances *good,* Mr. Sarikov?"

Something told John he should lie. "I think so."

"Describe them, please."

"What . . . the photos I'm trying to find?"

"Yes."

"I haven't seen them. I understand they're graphic. Upsetting."

The other line went momentarily silent. "Let me ask you something, Mr. Sarikov. Could you send me the two photos you have?"

"I could send you copies."

"And the other photos, if I could get you the information on Greene you wanted, and if you tracked down the other photos, you could send me copies of those also?"

Suddenly, this sounded like a bargaining session—what did Lieberman have to offer, John wondered. "You just finished telling me there were no records left to check."

"Yes, but . . . there are . . ." Lieberman stumbled

over his words. "I may be able to find out something for you."

A light went on in John's head. He remembered Dr. Davis of the Holocaust Museum intimating Lieberman may have developed some sort of pipeline into the Russian archives. Understandable that Lieberman would want to keep such a source secret, so the Russians didn't cut off his access. "The last time we talked, I mentioned some think you have developed a source within—"

"Mr. Sarikov," Lieberman interrupted, "I repeat, if I can get you the information you want, and you can track down the other photos, *will you* send me copies?"

"Yes."

"Good. Let's leave it at that. No questions, I insist. The two pictures you have now, when can you get them to me?"

"A day or two, I suppose, if I used an air delivery service."

"Please do, Mr. Sarikov. And please, please, be diligent in your search for the other photos. If they are what you say they are, we *must* make sure nothing happens to them."

"I will. You'll be calling me, then?"

"Yes, in a day or two. I hope with good news. Thank you, Mr. Sarikov, now I must go."

John said his farewell, then hung up the phone, pleased that what he once thought a dead end suddenly showed promise.

Lieberman reached for his address book. A phone number was there, encrypted in a simple code. The rumors were correct, of course; he had developed a conduit into the Russian archives. Since the fall of the Soviet Union, enough money waved in the right corners could buy almost anything—cosmonaut space suits, Fabergé eggs, jet fighters—the Russians were turning out be very good capitalists. The phone number in his address book would connect him directly to the chief archivist of state military history in Moscow. Hitting upon the archivist had taken months of well-placed bribes, but they were worth it, though the archivist steadfastly refused to deliver wholesale documentation, leaking information only in dribs and drabs to protect his new-found annuity. Perhaps the bribes were about to pay off again.

39

Bersch searched his pockets—only three dollars and change, not much, but plenty for another bottle of Thunderbird. He gained his feet unsteadily.

Noon, and already he'd been through one bottle, here in the alley a few blocks from the Ukrainian Café. That was usually enough drink for him, but not today. Thirty years ago today he had married Tatyana. Beautiful Tatyana, barely more than a child when he married her, a gift from heaven he had taken for granted. He had expressed no desire for children, no desire for romance, and after ten years she left him. He hadn't seen her since, but time had not killed his memories.

Bersch stumbled down the alley. Maybe he would buy a better bottle of wine to celebrate. The liquor store owner knew he was good for it. Yes, he decided, a celebration was called for.

A garbage truck rumbled into the alley and Bersch pressed himself against the brick wall to allow room for it to pass. The truck, however, stopped short of Bersch and two men in coveralls and blue stocking caps got out. They walked toward the garbage cans in front of Bersch.

The shorter and stockier of the two looked Bersch in the eye. "Hey, I know you, don't I? You work at the Ukrainian Café, right?"

Bersch didn't recognize the man. "Yes, I do," he

slurred, growing uneasy as one of the well-built men moved to each side of him.

"I thought I recognized you," the man said, smiling. "You're the one that doesn't know when to keep his fucking trap shut."

With these words Bersch's head exploded in a flash of white light. He knees buckled, but he caught himself and circled his powerful hands around the neck of the man who spoke. Another second and the man's neck would have snapped like kindling, but Bersch didn't have another second. A second powerful blow from behind crushed his skull and Bersch crumpled to the ground.

The man to Bersch's left returned the blackjack to his pocket and with the help of his companion dragged Bersch by the shoulders to the truck. Together they hoisted the limp body into the truck's trash compactor and emptied the two trash cans from the alley on top of the body.

One man flipped the hydraulic lever engaging the compactor, then both entered the truck and started for a landfill on Staten Island.

Bersch never made a sound.

Rolf lit another cigarette as he leaned against the streetlight and kept watch over the sidewalk. He had assigned others to take care of the old woman, the dishwasher, and the rabbi, but he wanted this one for himself.

The plan was simple and tantalizing. The dead cop's widow regularly took a jog sometime between twelve and one in the afternoon, completing an approximately three-mile circuit that included a loop along the park sidewalk Rolf now watched. He would see her in plenty of time to intersect her path, would walk calmly in her direction, and if, as now, no one was within sight, he would hit her hard across the face as she passed. If she attempted to scream, he'd hit her again, until she stopped. Thick bushes were only twenty yards away.

Someone would find her body in a day or two, and the papers would give the story a brief but high-profile run. Another lesson for their female readers: never jog alone, never jog in isolated areas.

Rolf glanced at his watch. Past one now. She was either very late or she wasn't coming at all. He hit the lamppost with the palm of his hand in anger. He could deal with her tomorrow, or the next day, but had wanted it to be today. Vasili would be happier, but more important, the idea excited him. First her, then later today her brother-in-law, within hours of each other.

Rolf dropped the half-smoked cigarette and ground it underfoot. No more time to wait. He had to meet Grigori at the warehouse, to deal with him and Sarikov. Depending on how it went, maybe he'd alter the plan. Maybe he would visit her in her home tonight. He could make it appear to be a break-in turned violent. The idea took the edge off his frustration, and he headed toward his car with renewed anticipation.

Ten minutes later, Kelly walked past a streetlight encircled by a half-dozen cigarette butts. She made a feeble attempt to resume jogging, but it was short-lived. For some reason she didn't feel much like running, and decided to walk the rest of the way home.

40

Grigori ordered a second vodka, straight up, no ice. He took a slow drink, appreciating its undiluted flavor. It was one of the rare occasions he drank before a job. His life had many times depended on split-second decisions and reactions, and usually he couldn't afford the handicap of alcohol. The assignment this afternoon, however, entailed little risk—one male, a non-professional, unlikely to be carrying a weapon, unlikely to be looking for a trap. A very easy mark, low degree of danger, so Grigori allowed himself the drinks, hoping they would make his assignment easier to stomach.

Vasili had presented Sarikov's tapes to the Collegium. The evidence was clear—Sarikov knew far too much—and the Collegium's decision, though not the one Grigori had hoped for, had not surprised him. Vasili had drawn the line on this one, and the Collegium backed down without a fight. In a not-so-close vote—Yuri voting no, Nicholas abstaining—a motion passed: one of Vasili's men, aided by Grigori, would remove Sarikov.

Grigori mentally reviewed what he had learned of Sarikov: a newspaper writer, usually investigatory work, used to asking questions and finding answers; a potentially dangerous man with the bit between his teeth. Grigori's orders were to abduct him—the Collegium did not want a repeat of Vasili's bungling—ques-

tion him, then hand him over to Vasili's man, Rolf.
Nicholas had called him personally to apologize. "I'm
sorry," he had said, "that you have to play a part in
this . . . it's not what I wanted or promised, I know,
but the Collegium's orders must be carried out; the
time has not yet come to confront Vasili."

At least, Grigori thought, Sarikov would not die by
his hand—Vasili had insisted Rolf have the honor.
Grigori hadn't killed a man in almost ten years and
was glad his record would remain intact.

He remembered the last: a CIA agent operating in
Afghanistan, instrumental in molding the Afghan
tribal bands into an effective fighting force, who, with
rifles and hand-held rocket launchers, had held the
great Soviet Army in check. The USSR's Vietnam. An
embarrassment the Kremlin wanted crushed.

The KGB ordered Grigori to liquidate the CIA
agent. Little chance of getting to him in Afghanistan,
so Grigori waited until he returned to Washington, D.C.,
for a holiday. He tailed the agent for a week, searching
for patterns in his movements, and incidentally and
unfortunately putting faces to his wife and children.
The rest was simple. He used a connection the KGB
had developed with one of the D.C. street gangs. The
gang didn't know they dealt with the KGB, maybe
they would have cared, probably not—what mattered
to them was someone had an awful lot of money to
spend and some problems to take care of.

The gang dispatched a youth of fifteen to handle
the matter, having learned a juvenile convicted of a
crime, even murder, would at most serve a few years
in prison. When the CIA agent left his apartment for
his regular morning jog, Grigori, parked in a car across
the street, flashed his headlights twice, a signal for
the gang member to approach the agent, then busy
stretching, stick a gun to his spine and pull the trigger.

The .45 caliber hollow-point slug blew a fist-sized whole in the agent's abdomen.

The Washington, D.C., papers reported the incident as one more case of random street violence. Even the CIA didn't seem overly suspicious.

It was so easy in the United States—everyone seemed to be armed, everybody was shooting everybody, how could anyone sort out a street murder from an assassination?

Just a few weeks later, the Soviet Union announced its withdrawal from Afghanistan. Grigori knew all the arguments: the CIA agent knew he was in harm's way; the CIA had taken out Soviets, including friends, in similar fashion, but guilt preyed on him nonetheless— he remembered the faces of the CIA agent's family.

The survival of the Soviet Union had not been at stake; given the withdrawal, the Soviet Union's vital national interest wasn't even in question. Just the game being played for the game's sake.

Now the Sarikov brother. He must once again bloody his hands, not for Russia's sake, not for the sake of justice, but to appease a madman and prop up an organization that now stood for nothing but its own survival. Couldn't the Collegium see, appeasement would only fuel Vasili's mania, not satisfy it. Even Grigori, as tired of conflict as any, would prefer they face the enemy head-on.

Grigori straightened his right leg, then massaged its knee. Dorothy had packed liniment; he reminded himself to apply it that evening at the hotel room. His joints had reacted poorly to the cool fall air of New York. Sore knees. Sore joints. What was he doing here?

When the Soviet Union had split into sovereign republics, Grigori had felt a great release. Overnight TASS and Pravda transformed the evil Americans into friends, terminating Grigori's mission, or so he thought. In fact, Russia had allowed its clandestine operations in the United States to linger on, feeding Russia with a steady, if markedly reduced, stream of information. Sources of control had weakened, the power structure showed signs of stress, the sense of purpose waned, and most important, the stream of funding had dried up, but the organization hadn't dissolved as the Soviet Union had, and the Collegium, despite internal power struggles, still wielded power.

Grigori's dream of riding off into the sunset as the organization died peacefully remained no more than that—a dream. Nicholas, he knew, felt as he did, but the power hungry were not about to see the most efficient clandestine organization the world had ever produced rust away, not with so much money to be gained from subverting its power to their own purposes.

The bartender's glance and nod interrupted Grigori's thoughts. He looked toward the doorway. He recognized Sarikov from his picture: handsome, strong-featured, and somewhat naive-looking.

Grigori had been right, this would not be hard. He took a healthy sip of vodka, finishing the glass.

John approached the bartender, who, without a word, pointed toward a man sitting by himself at one of the tables. John started toward the man cautiously. He looked harmless enough, fatherly if not grandfatherly—white hair, nicely dressed. Clearly nobody to worry about, which perhaps explained the hint of foreboding John felt. The man appeared too capable, too confident, hardly what you would expect of an informant in a place like this.

John stopped in front of the man. "My name's John Sarikov. The owner said you had some information for me."

Grigori rose and shook hands with John. "Yes, my

name is Grigori . . . I heard you are interested in Peter Olgov."

"How did you hear that?"

"People."

"What people?"

"It was talked about. My understanding is you started the talk, then left word where you could be reached if anyone had information. Am I mistaken?"

John hesitated momentarily. "No . . . no, you're not mistaken." He pointed to the other chair. "Mind if I take a seat?"

Grigori waved his hand in invitation and sat down himself.

John began. "How did you know Olgov?"

"Please, Mr. Sarikov. What I have to tell you, I do not reveal lightly. I am very uncomfortable. First, we order some vodka, yes? It will help us to talk about things it would otherwise be hard to discuss."

John shrugged. "Sure, if you want. I'll buy." He left for the bar and returned to the table with two glasses of vodka on the rocks.

"The bottle. The bottle would be better, Mr. Sarikov."

John gave Grigori a sideways glance, wondering if he wasn't about to buy a drunk his dinner. He left the glasses on the table and walked back to the bar and purchased the bottle.

"Now, Grigori . . ."

"Now, we drink. A toast, to Russia, our mother country."

"My country is America."

Grigori laughed softly. "Of course, of course, America is a great country, but my fire, my blood, flows from Russia. You are not Russian?"

"My father and mother were."

"Ah, then you are lucky. You will always be Russian, in America or not." With that Grigori took a healthy drink from his glass.

John joined him, but took a much smaller drink, leading to a disapproving look from Grigori and another more generous swallow.

Grigori smiled. "Now, first, before I tell you what I know, you must tell me why you are interested. Why do you ask questions about Olgov?"

"Someone murdered him. I want to know who and why."

"People are murdered every day in this city, Mr. Sarikov. Why, specifically, are you interested in Peter Olgov?"

John shook his head. "I didn't come here to answer your questions, remember? I've told you my purpose; the message said you could help. *Can you?*"

Grigori ran his index finger around the rim of his cocktail glass. "Yes," he answered after a moment. "But that doesn't mean I will." He took a swallow from his glass and urged John to do the same.

"If you want my help," Grigori went on, "I must know more about you. I insist, for my own safety."

Grigori used cautious words, but seemed coolly logical. Was he a frightened man looking to protect himself as he collected a paycheck, or someone with an agenda of his own, John began to wonder as his sense of unease grew.

"What is it you do, Grigori?" John asked.

"I'm retired."

"You haven't asked me for money. That surprises me."

"At the appropriate time, rest assured I'll make my demands known."

John scratched his cheek as he considered the answer. "And you live where?"

"Bay Ridge."

John took a sip of his drink, his eyes never leaving

Grigori's. "I couldn't help noticing your tan. Nice, for Bay Ridge, this time of year." John watched Grigori's face for a reaction; there was none.

"As I said, I'm retired. I have plenty of time to travel . . . but, please, the conversation has turned to me. I must know who you are, or our discussion ends."

John considered his options. Clearly Grigori expected a give and take, though for what reason John could only imagine. He nodded, and Grigori started in on a string of questions.

At some point in the questioning John began to feel light-headed.

"Why are you looking into Olgov's death, Mr. Sarikov? Why not the police?" Grigori asked.

Why not the police? It took John a few moments to come up with the answer, and even then his mouth did not seem to want to form the words. His tongue felt heavy and clumsy. He'd had only one drink—with the practice he'd been having lately that was nothing. In halting language, John told Grigori he had a personal stake in finding Olgov's killer.

"If what you are doing is outside the law, Mr. Sarikov, if it's illegal, I'm not sure I want to get involved."

John found his head slowly drifting downward and snapped it upright. "Excuse me, I seem . . . very tired . . . all of a sudden."

Grigori stared intently into John's eyes. "You probably just had too much to drink, that's all."

John heard the sound of the words, but they entered his brain garbled. He felt himself falling to the side, but couldn't keep himself up as the room spun and his vision blurred. Everything moved in slow motion as he slid from the chair and hit the floor. His shoulder absorbed the initial impact of the fall, but his head followed with a thud, his limp neck providing no resistance to his body's momentum.

The spinning grew faster and faster, pulling John

into its black vortex. He heard, far off in the distance it seemed, the voice of Grigori, calling to him from the edge of the whirlpool. *What was happening? The vodka? Illness?*

Through his garbled thoughts, John brought one to the forefront—stay conscious. He was at risk here, in this place, with this stranger whom he had been uneasy about to begin with. He thought of Kelly, Michael, and Barbara, any thought he could hold on to. The spinning whirlpool, however, convoluted his thoughts, making it harder and harder to think.

He remembered the hernia operation he had as a child. He had done his best to fight the anesthesia, not out of fear, but because consciousness meant control, and he had not wanted to lose that edge. His thoughts now, over two decades later, as the spinning pool took him under, were the same.

41

John woke much as he went under, trapped in a spinning blackened world, consciousness slowly returning. His head began to pound. When he opened his eyes, he shut them quickly, the light searing deeply, magnifying the pain. A monster hangover, he initially thought, but that quick glance revealed something that made his heart race—Grigori, the man from the restaurant, sat in front of him, and they were not in the restaurant any longer.

"Mr. Sarikov. Good, you are awake."

John shook his head, attempting to clear it. How did he get here? What had happened at the restaurant? Struggling to speak, a sudden urge to vomit overtook him. He gagged twice and opened his eyes involuntarily to see Grigori holding a wastebasket before him.

"Use this, Mr. Sarikov," Grigori said.

John tried to reach out and brace the wastebasket with one hand, but his arm wouldn't move. He bent forward and emptied his stomach.

Grigori wiped John's mouth with a napkin before feeding him a glass of water. After a moment John began to feel better, but resisted the temptation to offer thanks. As the haze continued to lift from his mind, John suddenly realized why his hand hadn't moved—his arms were tied behind him to the chair on which he sat, his legs to the legs of the chair. He pulled against the ropes to no effect. "What am I doing here?" he asked, too drowsy to voice fear or anger.

"I wanted to talk with you."

John scanned his surroundings. Boxes piled on pallets, concrete floor, twenty-foot ceilings, cold. A warehouse. "You drugged me?"

"Yes. When you went to the bar to get the vodka bottle. I apologize. An effective drug, but with the unfortunate side effects you experienced on waking. They will go away soon. I convinced the bartender you could not handle your vodka, and he helped me carry you to my car."

John fought panic only half successfully. "Who are you?"

"My name, as I told you, is Grigori."

John coughed, his stomach still unsettled. "What do you want?"

"We'll get to that."

John felt the heat rising in his face. Again he wrestled with his bindings, and again they held firm. "Christ, what the hell am I doing here? Why am I tied to this chair?"

"I apologize for your treatment, Mr. Sarikov. Unfortunately, you must be made to understand your position."

John's anger turned inward. What a fool he'd been. His investigations had evidently hit a nerve—someone wanted them terminated. Three people murdered, and yet he hadn't considered the possibility, let alone taken precautions.

"Then there's been some mistake. You've got the wrong person."

"No mistake has been made. John Sarikov, brother of Michael Sarikov, deceased New York City cop. Freelance reporter; address: 148 East 84th Street, Apartment 19C. Age: 34. Father, Viktor Sarikov, died of cirrhosis of the liver at 55; mother, died bearing you. Do you want me to go on?"

"This is insane."

Grigori shrugged. "It's an insane world, I sometimes think." He leaned forward in his chair. "Mr. Sarikov, you've been piecing together a puzzle that, unfortunately, could be embarrassing to the people I work for if completed. That is why I must find out how much you have learned . . . but first, where are my manners. I'm afraid we never got a chance to finish our drinks. Vodka?"

John was beginning to feel better physically, the pounding in his head now just a dull knocking, but had no desire for vodka. "No thanks, I seem to have a bad reaction to it."

Grigori smiled. "Really quite good, Mr. Sarikov. But don't worry, no additives this time. It'll make you feel better and I do hate to drink alone." He left John's side, walked into a small glassed-in office, and returned with a bottle and two glasses. He then undid one of John's wrists from behind the chair.

John debated struggling, but feared the effort would be futile as long as his other hand and his feet remained bound.

"One of the few true benefits of Russia's Communist state, vodka, very good vodka, for just dimes a bottle." Grigori poured two glasses and handed one to John. "Nothing like the rubbing alcohol you make here."

A benefit of *Russia's Communist state*? Nothing like the rubbing alcohol *you* make *here*? John was struck by Grigori's words.

"I apologize, I do not have ice," Grigori continued. "I know Americans like to dull the taste of everything they drink or eat with ice, ketchup, salt. It is a failure, one I do not know if I ever will get used to, but I keep trying."

What the hell was happening? He had been drugged, kidnapped, but his abductor prattled on as if at a dinner party. And why the talk of Russia? "Who do you work for?" he asked.

Grigori shrugged. "Interested parties."

"Who?" John repeated.

"You haven't guessed, Mr. Sarikov?"

Should he have? "No."

"Then perhaps you haven't learned as much as some feared. Would it surprise you to know I work for an arm of the Russian government?"

"That's bullshit."

A knowing smile passed Grigori's lips, as if he expected John's answer. "You Americans are odd. In Russia we know the CIA has infiltrated. We are suspicious of everyone. Americans, on the other hand, ignore reality. Your press convinced you long ago that any talk of Soviet operations in America should be dismissed as right-wing Communist witch hunting. That's what makes it so easy for us. Believe me, we play much harder and dirtier than the CIA ever did. Hundreds of us are here, whether you will accept it or not."

Inwardly John reeled, but he maintained a facade of control. If Grigori told the truth, what in God's name had he stumbled on? "I don't buy a thing you're saying."

"I would advise you to believe me, Mr. Sarikov. Believe me, then consider who you are dealing with, what you are up against. I have told you who I am for a purpose: so you will understand the utter hopelessness of your situation if you don't cooperate."

John found himself falling into the surreal conversation. "You really expect me to believe that you're . . . you're what . . . KGB?"

"With the fall of the USSR the KGB no longer exists. Officially, I'm now assigned to a special international branch section of Russia's Federal Security Service. I've been stationed here, in America, for many years, have grown to love it. I do so want to become a real American; such a remarkable country, even with its idiosyncrasies."

John's stomach muscles pulled tight.

"Do you find my statement surprising, Mr. Sarikov? Every Russian who has seen anything of this country accepts America's greatness. But I am also Russian, and Russia and America were at war, or, as Americans say, a cold war, and one does play hard for one's side, doesn't one?"

"If it's the right side."

"Right side, wrong side, who is to say? I was born in Russia, raised in Russia by Russian parents, on food raised from Russian soil. I played in the fields of Russia, in the shadows of the great Ural Mountains. I kissed my first girl, a Russian girl, in a barn in a small town in Russia. There is a line from a famous Russian poem that goes: 'Even the smoke of our Motherland is sweet and pleasant to us.' Russia was, will always be, my home, and I fought for her. Would you have done differently? . . . How is your vodka?"

"Needs ice."

Grigori laughed. "A few more years and I will probably be drinking light beer and Chardonnay."

"The KGB planted you here?"

"Yes, long ago. I own a small import-export business now. It is doing well, actually. There were some rough times after the changes in my mother country, but I've expanded my base of legitimate business and tightened control of my cash flow. I've found I am quite a good capitalist. My two sons work for me. They have married lovely girls from good families. I even have two grandchildren. I hoped to put this type of thing"—Grigori gestured toward John—"behind me."

If John was not expendable, would Grigori tell him any of this? "Then why did you drug me? Why not let me go?"

". . . Orders."

"And after the questioning?"

"I won't harm you."

John looked Grigori straight in his eyes; they didn't waver. "And my brother, did you promise not to harm him either?"

"You'll have to believe me, I am sorry about your brother. I was not involved. It was a mistake to . . . what happened was a mistake."

Anger displaced fear. "My brother's dead, and you call it a *mistake*?"

Grigori closed his eyes for a moment, as if in thought. "Yes, a gross and inexcusable overreaction. My comrades, myself, we can't go back to Russia— we are a political embarrassment—and very few of us want to. Most of us are successful, some extraordinarily so. Why would we want to leave this for bread lines? No one is hunting us now; we want it to stay that way. Your brother—"

"Threatened to expose you?"

"No, not me . . . somebody else. Someone powerful, with a much higher profile than me."

"And so he killed my brother?"

Grigori nodded. "As I said, his actions were inexcusable. If I had been consulted . . . well, that is hardly worth discussing now, but I would have preferred handling the matter differently. I'm sorry."

John bowed his head. His brother was real—flesh and blood—not just an abstract matter that had to be *handled*.

Grigori continued. "If you compromised the identity of this man, the one who fears exposure, and he talked to authorities, he could ruin many lives. That can't be allowed to happen. Now you understand why I must talk to you. To find out how much you know, and who else you have told."

"And then you'll kill me?" John's heart pounded out the question.

"No. As I said, I will not harm you. Now I have answered your questions honestly and to the point. I ask you to do the same. We know much of what you have discovered already, therefore I suggest you do not lie. You were seen visiting a Mrs. Banovich at a rooming house in Brighton Beach. Why were you there?"

"You had me followed?"

Grigori shrugged. "We paid a few dollars to the desk clerk to keep his eyes open and pass on information."

"I asked her about Peter Olgov."

"Yes, and what did she tell you?"

"Who is Olgov to you?"

"You had your turn to ask questions, Mr. Sarikov, now it is mine. What did she tell you?"

"Nothing, just that she and Olgov had dinner now and then."

"Be more specific, Mr. Sarikov, tell me everything you know, and include the photographs. Yes, we know about the photographs."

John took a deep breath. *What could he say to keep himself alive? What might he say that would ensure he was silenced?* Roughly cover what he had found, he decided; it was probably in his interest to at least appear to be cooperating. He knew nothing worth dying for, though he wouldn't mention Kelly.

Grigori listened closely, interrupting often with sharp questions that forced John to elaborate in greater detail than he had intended. Grigori knew about Greene. He knew about the rabbi, somehow. He knew what John thought, what his theories were.

John could have added little to Grigori's knowledge if he had wanted to.

When John finished, Grigori pressed his fingertips together and sat silently in thought. Finally, he spoke. "Have you told me everything?"

"Yes." Almost, John thought.

Grigori's eyes again pierced John's. "I believe you."

"So you'll let me go?"

The edges of Grigori's mouth dropped. "No. I am sorry. That I cannot do."

John narrowed his eyes. A bad gamble; if he had held back information, then he'd still have something to bargain with. "What are you going to do with me?"

"I will not harm you, as I promised, but I must deliver you to an associate. Actually, he is coming here . . . should be here momentarily." Grigori's eyes broke from John's. "I apologize for my deception, and what may befall you. . . . I have no stomach for it anymore, but I'm still a soldier taking orders."

Grigori's voice had been calm, almost soothing, but the import of what he said fanned the fear burning in the pit of John's stomach. "I *am* to be killed?"

"If it makes any difference to you, a number of us, myself included, did not wish to harm you. When a sweater is unraveling because someone is pulling a thread, there are two ways to solve the problem. Stop the pulling or cut off the thread. My superiors decided to stop the pulling, which unfortunately meant stopping you. I personally would have chosen the latter solution. The man you were threatening to expose lives today because I was overruled."

The pleasant words Grigori chose to couch the pronouncement did not change its meaning: a death sentence, the end of life. John strained against his bindings. "Am I supposed to forgive you? For this, for my brother's death, I pray you burn in hell."

"If there is a hell, I will surely burn there. Meanwhile, I live in a private hell of my own making."

"If you know what you're doing is wrong, for God's sake let me go."

"I cannot. I would be killed, perhaps my due, but they would also revenge themselves against my family—that is how loyalty is enforced in my business."

Grigori pulled a rabbit's foot from his pocket and fingered it with his large hands. "I can," he said softly, "offer you an alternative, Mr. Sarikov."

"What?"

"I shoot you now, in the head. I will say you were trying to escape. You do not deserve the death that otherwise awaits."

John's found it hard to hear over the heartbeats resonating in his ears. "One way or the other, I die?"

"Unfortunately, that is certain."

John glanced wildly side to side. There had to be a way out of this. He was a news reporter, an average person who was supposed to grow old surrounded by grandchildren and friends, not die strapped to a chair for reasons he less than half understood. *Crazy. Unbelievable.*

John looked to the glass of vodka in his free hand. If he threw it hard at Grigori's face, the glass might stun him, the alcohol perhaps blind him. Then John could flip his chair on its side and crawl to Grigori, pull himself with his one arm until he could grab Grigori's neck. And if he moved fast enough—

"I think I'll skip your offer," John said.

"As you wish. This may be hard for you to believe, but our goals were noble once. We employed ruthless means, perhaps, but we had a code and we lived by it. I'm afraid that nobility is over—some of my comrades are opening our ranks to little better than street scum who kill as much for pleasure as for survival."

John was ready. He tightened his grip on the glass.

Grigori stood only five feet in front of him. The screech of a fence being swung open interrupted his thoughts. He hesitated momentarily, and Grigori rose and walked to the door.

Out of range. A lost opportunity.

Grigori looked back at John, his eyes saddened. "My associate has arrived."

The appearance of the man who walked through the door a minute later chilled John. The man smiled at John, but the smile held no warmth. He was wiry, with a thin face that highlighted his cheekbones and long chin. Dark hair lay slicked back from his forehead. He displayed none of the class Grigori had shown. It took a moment before John remembered Bersch's description of the man asking questions about Olgov—the same man.

With Grigori, John felt he had at least been dealing with a human being, but with this one—John's breath came shallow and quick.

Grigori addressed the man, but did not shake his hand. "He's yours now, Rolf," Grigori said.

Rolf nodded dismissively.

"I'd suggest there is nothing left to question him about; he does not know anything we haven't already learned," Grigori added.

"What's he fucking drinking and why's his fucking hand untied?" Rolf snapped.

Grigori walked to John and took the glass of vodka from his hand. John didn't resist. With the two of them here, his plan didn't make any sense. Besides, he had lost any desire to hurt Grigori, who seemed a protector compared with this new man, Rolf.

As Grigori retied John's free arm to the back of the chair, Rolf moved to Grigori's rear, then narrowed the distance between them. Rolf slid his hand noiselessly into the pocket of his black leather coat.

Grigori, from a squatting position, spun suddenly,

in one motion pulling a 9mm from a shoulder holster and squaring up to Rolf, now less than two paces away.

A surprised look passed over Rolf's face, replaced by momentary fear, and then, when Grigori made no further move, a smile. His hand eased from his pocket, empty.

Grigori, his face registering intense distaste, stared at Rolf a long moment before lowering his handgun. He didn't reholster it.

"Mr. Sarikov," Grigori said, facing John now, "if there is a life after this one, take pleasure in the torment in store for me and my friend over there." Grigori gestured toward Rolf. "I am sorry." He then turned, his unguarded back contemptuously directed at Rolf, and exited the warehouse.

Rolf sat in a chair and locked his eyes on John's, saying nothing.

John finally broke the silence. "What do you want?"

Without warning, Rolf rose and clubbed him hard in the ear. "First lesson," he said, devoid of emotion, "I ask all the questions; you answer them."

"Why are you—" John began.

Rolf clubbed him again on the same ear. "I ask *all* the questions." He turned and sat down again. "You and Grigori became friends?"

John glared at Rolf. "No."

"Will you and I become friends?"

"No."

Rolf grinned crookedly. "I think you're right, but I don't want your friendship; I want your obedience. Like a dog. Will I have that?"

John sat mutely and Rolf rose again. He grabbed a broom leaning against the wall, and returned to hover over John with it, the broom head in his hands. Rolf then swung the broomstick hard at John's shins.

John gritted his teeth but couldn't entirely squelch his groan.

"Will I have that?" Rolf repeated.

John hesitated, and Rolf's face lit with cruel fury as he swung the broomstick again and again at John's shins.

John's determination to deny Rolf the satisfaction of screams was short-lived. He broke into a series of animal groans, timed to the rhythm of the broomstick; only when the beating stopped, when the stick mercifully cracked, did he reclaim some measure of control.

"I will ask you again," Rolf said, more emotional now. "Will I have your obedience?"

"Yes." John bit his tongue to keep from saying more.

"That's better." Rolf's face calmed. "You've been a busy boy, haven't you, Sarikov?"

"Yes."

"Asking all sorts of questions that don't concern you. Just like your brother. The person I work for isn't very happy about that."

With the mention of Michael, John abandoned his reserve. "The hell with the person you work for."

Rolf smiled. "You know, I'll tell you something: you think you can fuck with me, you think you're a fucking big man, don't you? But I don't really mind when you say something like that. You know why? Because I've explained the fucking rules, you've broken them, and now I set the punishment."

Rolf approached the chair John was tied to, then reached for one of its legs and toppled the chair on its side. John's shoulder took the impact of the fall. Rolf stood over him, his grin vanishing as his foot struck out and connected with John's ribs. John held back a cry of pain, which incited Rolf. He unleashed a flurry of kicks to John's ribs and stomach.

When Rolf stopped, John fought for breath, his

senses overloaded with pain. At the mercy of this madman, for the first time he realized he wasn't going to escape. Here, on the cement floor of this warehouse, for reasons he would never completely know, he would die.

Rolf left John on the floor and reclaimed his chair. "Now you are going to answer some questions for me. You will answer promptly, and you will answer truthfully. If you don't . . . well, I just explained myself to you. I trust I've convinced you."

Rolf began to ask John questions about Olgov, Greene, Mrs. Banovich, all similar questions to those asked by Grigori. The questioning differed, however, in that whenever John hesitated with an answer or attempted to hide something, Rolf lashed out.

John told Rolf everything, withholding only Kelly's involvement. There was no reason to hide the rest; he had already told Grigori. Besides, Rolf seemed to know almost everything before John revealed it.

Even John's cooperation did not alleviate periodic blows. His face was soon a mass of pain; his ribs hurt when he breathed. Blood dripped from above his eye.

"I think you're holding out on me, Sarikov. You've never mentioned the pretty young widow's involvement in all this. No matter . . . I'll just have to get that information from her directly."

"Bastard," John spit at Rolf, only to bring a rain of blows to his head. By the fourth he lapsed into unconsciousness.

Rolf kicked the limp body in front of him. It didn't move. He bent down and felt Sarikov's wrist. There was still a pulse. Good, Sarikov would regain consciousness. He had learned all he needed to learn, in fact had known most everything from the cassette tapes he had taken from Sarikov's apartment. Nothing else to get here. He would wait, then finish it. In the meantime, he must make a phone call. He entered the small, glass-paneled office, picked up the phone, and dialed a number. Vasili answered.

"It's Rolf."

"Yes."

"I've questioned Sarikov; I learned nothing we didn't already know. I will dispose of the body."

"Excellent, and Grigori? Is it done?"

Finishing Grigori, as well as killing the old lady, the dishwasher, the rabbi, and the cop's widow, was to have been Vasili's signal to the Collegium—an unmistakable slap at their authority. First Rolf had failed to remove the cop's widow, now Grigori. Vasili wouldn't be happy with the news of this second failure. "It was impossible."

"You *should* have found a way."

"His hand never left his gun," Rolf lied.

"You alerted him to our intentions?"

"I think, somehow, he guessed."

The line fell silent; Rolf could hear only his own breath echoing from the receiver. Vasili's next words carried a thinly veiled threat. "You've disappointed me, Rolf. You've shown weakness when it was important to show the Collegium our strength. I can't have that."

"I can eliminate Grigori tonight, the cop's widow too."

"You couldn't handle Grigori with his back turned; what makes you think you could do it face on?"

Rolf's hand tightened on the receiver. He would *gladly* confront Grigori face on, would force fear into those fucking cold blue eyes. "Grigori will not be a problem."

"Perhaps. Where are you calling from now?"

"The warehouse."

"The warehouse? You know never to call from there; it's not a scrambled line."

"The Grigori matter, I knew you'd want to know immediately."

"Not from there, not ever. Never again, do you understand?"

"Yes." Rolf forced himself to add words he almost never used. "I'm sorry."

"Be more than sorry, Rolf, be scared enough of the consequences never to do it again, do you understand?"

Rolf bit his lip to keep from saying what he felt: no one, not even Vasili, could talk to him this way. ". . . Yes, sir."

"Enough on this line. Call me later, from a pay phone or a scrambled line, and we will decide what must be done about Grigori. That's all."

The throbbing in John's head, ribs, legs, and jaw told him he still lived. He opened his eyes and saw Rolf, in the small office, on the telephone. John could make out most of the words, but focused on one phrase: Rolf's promise to dispose of the body.

John struggled against his bonds—perhaps his last chance. He kicked his legs, again and again, and suddenly one came free. Looking down to his ankle, he realized what had happened: Grigori had tied each of his ankles to a chair leg, but with the chair overturned, a loop of rope had slipped off the end of one of those legs. If he could do the same with the rope binding his other ankle before Rolf returned—

John looked up again to see Rolf's smoldering glance through the office window. A moment later, Rolf stood in front of him, and John abandoned his struggles.

"Awake again . . . good," Rolf said. "You've caused me a lot of trouble; trouble I don't need. I wanted to make sure you felt what comes next."

John thought of Grigori's offer. He wouldn't hesitate to accept it now—the idea of more pain was unbearable. He prepared to die.

Rolf kicked him hard in the stomach, then once in the shoulder. The throbbing lessened as John felt a new warmth flowing through his body. He barely felt the next two kicks to his chest as a light enveloped him, protecting his senses. He smelled grass, and trees, and lost feeling in his extremities, no longer fearing what was to come.

Rolf tilted John upright in the chair. Angry when his eyes didn't open, he slapped John's face repeatedly with the back of his hand before grabbing the hair on the back of John's head and pulling down hard.

John's head snapped backward; his eyes opened, slowly, and he tried to focus on the ceiling, but his vision blurred, and his eyes rolled back revealing their whites. His breath came labored in short gasps.

"You have the face of your brother, but you're weaker," Rolf said as he bent down. He pressed his lips to John's, then poked the blade of his stiletto between the buttons on John's shirt, pressing its tip to the skin directly beneath the rib cage. He watched John's eyes as he slowly applied pressure.

Rolf's words and the knife's pressure stirred John's mind, and pulled it from the light and warmth it bathed in. The pain returned. Every limb, every muscle, felt on fire. Death was about to come, and in some ways that was a relief, but something within him refused to surrender, appreciated the gift of life too much to let it end.

He felt Rolf's lips on his, but hadn't the strength to struggle. Hot moist breath; suffocating pressure. *Macabre.* He used the revulsion to clear his mind.

A thought forced its way to the surface of John's mind, something Barbara told him from a self-defense class she once took: during a rape, with your life in immediate danger, there were ways to fight back. It had made him cringe when he'd first heard it: her instructor told her to bite the rapist's bottom lip as hard as she could, then rip. No halfway measures—bite and shake her head as violently as possible.

A desperate measure, the instructor said, but very effective for two reasons: there are no ligaments, tendons, or other connective tissue securing the lips to the skull, and all face wounds bleed profusely, the lips especially so. Chances were the attacker's lip would be torn from his face, he'd lose a tremendous amount of blood quickly, and go into shock.

John felt the knife break the skin on his chest. He must do it. Now. Summoning his last reserves of energy, he sunk his teeth deep into the flesh of Rolf's bottom lip.

Rolf let out a high-pitched scream and tried to back away, but his lip remained firmly locked in John's teeth.

Blood poured into John's mouth, and he bit harder, then swung his head powerfully from side to side, the way a shark shreds a fish to pieces.

Rolf's head came with John's at first, until one end of the lip tore free as John's teeth ripped through the soft tissues and met to grind together. Still John shook his head, Rolf's lip now stretched in a thin red line between them. One last violent shake of John's head tore it free.

Rolf, stunned and horrified, the bottom row of his teeth momentarily exposed then covered in a rush of blood from the torn tissues, sank to his knees. John, the lip hanging from his mouth, continued to shake his head from side to side, the entire incident having taken at most two seconds.

In the absence of pressure from Rolf, John realized what had happened and opened his eyes to see Rolf on his knees, trying unsuccessfully to hold in the blood streaming from his mouth. John let the piece of flesh tumble free from his teeth.

Rolf was hurt, badly hurt, but hadn't gone into shock. Dazed, he wiped his chin of blood with his shirtsleeve, then attempted to focus on John, his hand still gripping the stiletto.

John had only a fraction of a second to react. He remembered his one free leg, and kicked outward, his heel driving into Rolf's unprotected throat, crushing his windpipe. Rolf's head snapped back; the force of the kick knocked him to the floor, where he lay unmoving, the only sound coming from him a soft gurgling noise that died after a few seconds.

Rolf lay on his back; the stiletto a few inches from his right hand. John had to act quickly—he had no way of knowing how long Rolf might be down. He strained at his bonds; they held tight. He spotted Rolf's knife on the floor and with his one free leg managed to slowly pull and scoot his chair to the spot. He tipped himself and the chair over, falling sideways, wincing in pain as his weight crashed on his arm. Rocking the chair twice for momentum, he pushed hard off the concrete with his free leg, flipping the chair onto its back. He had hoped the fingers of his bound hands would find the stiletto, instead they found Rolf's arm. The ropes kept his hands from recoiling.

John gathered his breath for a moment, then rocked again, after two tries flipping the chair back on its side. He craned his neck to locate the stiletto, then inched his body and the chair forward with his free leg, and flipped the chair again. This time John's fingers touched the cold metal of the blade; he slid the stiletto toward him with his fingertips until he could grip it, then flipped the chair back on its side and attacked the ropes.

Rolf coughed then through a blood-clogged throat.

John's back faced Rolf; he couldn't see what was happening. Chilled, John ripped through the last strand of rope binding his hands. Another cough from Rolf, then a groan, then John's hands were free. One of John's legs remained tied to the chair, but that only affected his mobility minimally. He spun to his knees to find Rolf on one elbow, staring at him, dark eyes over a crimson mouth. Without hesitation, John drove the stiletto into Rolf's chest.

Rolf's eyes widened in surprise and pain, then he sunk to his back, his body shuddering for a few seconds, like a fish, before lying still. The eyes stayed open, staring at John, the mouth hideously agape.

John cut the ropes binding his leg to the chair, then stood. He bent over the dead man—the man who had killed Michael and had tried to kill him. A momentary urge to bash Rolf's head in with his foot vanished at the sight of Rolf's face—hideously twisted, blood everywhere.

John went through Rolf's pockets. Empty except for car keys and a wallet. The wallet contained a few credit cards, a driver's license, some cash, a Social Security card—all in the name of Yevgeni Malinovsky. Rolf's real name? He put the wallet and keys in his pocket, then patted down Rolf's shirt and pants and discovered a small revolver in a holster strapped to his ankle. John took the gun and holster and strapped it to his own ankle. He found another handgun in Rolf's coat, a silencer affixed to its barrel; he appropriated it as well.

John started to walk to the door of the warehouse, but stopped after a few steps, hunched over and coughing.

His ribs protested with each breath; his jaw ached dully and shot strings of pain up toward his eye sockets. His arms and legs were okay, bruised but not broken. After a moment of rest he found the energy to propel himself forward and staggered the rest of the way to the door and looked out its window.

He was in a brick building set back from a row of other two-story brick buildings. A high fence capped with coiled barbed wire separated him from the street. The fence had a lock on it. John remembered Rolf's key chain and prayed the key to the fence was included. One car sat in the lot, probably Rolf's. He saw no one.

John recognized two imperatives. First, get out of the warehouse, out of danger. Second, call the police. He recognized a problem with the second—he didn't know the location of the warehouse. He turned and looked back toward the office. There would be papers inside, something with the name and address of the warehouse on it. He unsteadily made his way there, hoping not to regret the extra minutes he delayed his escape.

The office was stark, just a metal desk, a wooden chair, a wall of steel file cabinets, and a mirror on the wall. John involuntarily gasped as he caught a glimpse of his face in the mirror. He used a stack of napkins lying next to a coffee urn to dab away the blood, then turned his attention to the desk. A scatter of invoices and bills of lading covered its surface. One name linked them all: Best Import Company, 4556 Wilson St., Brooklyn, N.Y. He stuffed an invoice in his pocket, knowing he could not afford the time to search the file cabinets.

As he turned to leave, the phone on the desk caught his eye. Something about it made him hesitate. A friend came to mind—Herb Mueller. *Why was he thinking about Herb Mueller now?* Herb worked for the New York *Daily News* and had a reputation for sleeping around. His wife was clueless until . . . *Until what? and why did he care?*

Herb's story flashed through his mind. His wife had

been trying to reach their daughter at an upstate college one Sunday morning, but her line was continuously busy. Leaving Herb at home, she walked to the corner grocery and tried her again when she returned. She pushed the redial button, but it wasn't her daughter who answered. She recognized the voice, a friend of theirs, a female copy editor from the *Daily News*. A few months later Herb agreed to a high six-figure divorce settlement.

John picked up the phone's receiver. It was there— a redial button. He remembered most of Rolf's last call. Rolf had been talking to someone important, someone he took orders from. They were talking about Grigori and about John. Rolf had initiated the call, so the number should still be stored in the phone's memory.

John pressed the redial button. He heard a rapid sequence of tones and the beginning of a ring before he killed the line. He wasn't ready to talk to whomever had answered on the other end, not yet, not without a plan.

John was about to unplug the phone when he stopped—the phone's memory would probably not be erased when he unplugged the phone, but he couldn't be sure. Near Rolf's sprawled body lay John's neatly folded coat, his Dictaphone to its side where Grigori had evidently left it for Rolf. John retrieved the Dictaphone and held it up to the phone's receiver. He pressed the record button, then pressed the phone's redial button, this time hanging up before the phone rang. The Dictaphone went back in his coat pocket, and the phone, unplugged now, under his arm.

The walls of the warehouse felt as if they were closing in. No time to call the police from here. No more delays. He had to get away, now.

John looked out the front door window again—still nobody in sight. He walked to the front gate. The third key on Rolf's ring opened the lock, and he swung open the fence. Rolf's car keys fit the parked car. He started it and exited through the gate.

John drove desperately for a few minutes, continuously checking his rearview mirror, not caring where he was or where he turned, just distancing himself from the warehouse. Then he came upon a familiar street and soon merged onto the Brooklyn-Queens Expressway, heading for Manhattan and safety.

42

Fifteen blocks from his apartment, John pulled over abruptly to the side of the road, prompting a chorus of horn blasts from behind. *What was he doing?* As soon as Rolf's body was discovered, Rolf's associates would begin hunting him, and the first place they'd look would be his apartment. He should have driven to Steve's precinct house, only a short distance from where he had been held in Brooklyn, but hadn't been thinking. Manhattan had seemed distant and safe then, less so now.

John pulled the car back into traffic and found a parking space down the street near a pay phone. He'd played investigator, but there was a dead body to deal with now and somebody had tried to kill him. He had to lay everything on the table—Steve would know what to do.

John rummaged through the glove compartment for tissues, found a paper napkin, and scrubbed his face of blood, using the rearview mirror. He zipped his jacket to hide his bloodstained shirt, then walked to the phone. He dialed Steve's number with an unsteady hand, praying he'd be there to answer the call.

"Hello." It was Steve.

"Steve, it's me," John said barely above a whisper. He knew his voice sounded strange—his jaw muscles were already starting to swell.

"John . . . that you?"

"Yeah . . . I found something. I've got a lot to tell you. I—"

Steve interrupted. "Hold it for a second, let me shut my door." The line went silent for a moment before Steve spoke again. "John, forget that stuff now, you are in trouble, big trouble, my friend. I shouldn't be telling you this—they'd strip me of my badge—but hell, I'm going to anyway. The department's about to issue a search warrant for your apartment."

John was stunned. "What are you talking about? Why?"

Steve answered, his voice barely more than a whisper. "I'm telling you this, buddy, so you have a chance to get in there before the cops and clean up whatever needs to be cleaned up. You got it?"

"No. What the hell's going on?"

Steve paused. ". . . Nobody ever knows I told you this, you understand?"

"What is it?"

"Hartley received some information this morning from the Cayman Islands bank where Michael had an account."

"Where an account was planted . . ."

"Yeah . . . sure. It showed two accounts in the name of Sarikov."

"Two accounts in Michael's name?"

"The other account's in the name of John F. Sarikov."

Dumb-struck, John said nothing. His breathing turned shallow. Like fighting an octopus, whoever killed Michael kept coming at John from different directions, even after he had chopped off one of its arms.

"John, speak to me. You got something to tell me, you better do it now."

"It's a lie. I never opened any account in the Caymans. How much is in it?"

"$30,000."

John thought out loud. "They're trying to frame me . . . like they framed Michael. I'm too close . . . they're afraid. They planned to get rid of me, and no one would have cared because I'd have looked as dirty as Michael. One more supposed drug killing. That was their plan."

"Get rid of you? What are you talking about?"

"Listen, Steve, someone tried to kill me."

John paused, waiting for a reaction. None came, so he continued. "I followed up a lead in Brighton Beach—"

"What do you mean a lead?"

"Michael's murder."

"Dammit, John, I told you to lay off."

"C'mon, you knew I wouldn't. I talked to someone who said he had information regarding Peter Olgov, the guy whose death Michael had investigated. I met him at a restaurant, and he drugged me. I woke up in a warehouse. They questioned me, then tried to kill me. I managed to . . . it was self-defense. . . ."

"What was self-defense?"

"I killed a man. I had to, before he killed me."

"A dead man? You killed him?"

"Yes."

"Where?"

"At the warehouse . . ." John pulled the invoice from his pocket. "Best Import Company, 4556 Wilson, in Brooklyn. That's why I called you, to tell you to send the police."

"Are you there now?"

"No. I'm in Manhattan."

"Why didn't you stay put, dammit! You don't flee a crime scene."

"I couldn't stay there. I had to get away. They almost killed me, and they could have come back. I needed to put some distance between us."

"Okay, John, sorry. You hold on. I'm going to get some cars to that warehouse. Just stay on the line, okay?"

"I'll be here."

Steve was off the line for a couple of minutes; John nervously surveyed the passersby, an act of irrational paranoia, but he couldn't help himself.

"Still there?" Steve asked, finally.

"Yeah."

"Good. We should have cars on the scene in a few minutes. I want a little more information from you, then we've got to bring you in. When did this happen?"

John looked at his watch. "I left the warehouse . . . maybe twenty-five, thirty minutes ago."

"You keep talking about 'they.' 'They' are after you. Who are 'they'? Give me a quick rundown. What happened? Why did someone want to kill you?"

"Like I said, I had looked into Michael's death on my own. And I found some things. No hard evidence, but I think I was getting close. I think I scared someone."

"Who?"

"I'm not sure. . . ." John paused before going on. "This guy in Brighton Beach who supposedly had some information about Michael's death, the one who drugged me, his first name was Grigori. The other one, the dead man, he called himself Rolf." John pulled Rolf's wallet from his pocket. "But his driver's license, all his I.D., is in the name of Yevgeni Malinovsky." John spelled the name. "I have his driver's license with me. He lived at 2396 N. Congress in Queens."

"What did they want?"

"Information. They wanted to know what I'd uncovered—"

Steve interrupted. "This was all about Michael's death?"

"Yeah, and Peter Olgov's."

"Okay, go on."

"That's it, just what hard evidence I had, what conclusions I'd drawn, who I'd told. Jesus! Kelly! This Rolf, he said he was going to go after Kelly."

"Why would he do that?"

"He thought Kelly knew what I'd uncovered. They are trying to plug all the leaks."

"But you say Rolf's dead now."

"Yeah, but there's Grigori, and who knows who else."

"Okay, don't worry about Kelly. I'll assign a man to watch her as soon as I get off the phone with you. All right?"

"Yeah . . . yeah. Thanks, Steve."

"No problem. I care about Kelly too, you know that. She'll be safe. Now these two, Rolf and Grigori, were they drug dealers?"

"I don't know."

"What's your guess?"

"I only know what they told me."

"Yeah?"

John hesitated. "You're going to find it hard to believe."

"Cut the crap. What did they say?"

"They said they worked for Russia."

"Jesus Christ, John, the KGB?"

"That's what Grigori—the guy who drugged me—told me, only since the breakup of the USSR, I guess they call it something else."

"All right, I'm guessing he lied. Fed you a line to scare you. Our files are scrammed with reports of Russian mob violence; they're heavily into drugs and they operate out of Brighton Beach. That's what I put my money on."

John coughed, a sharp reminder of the state his ribs were in. "That makes sense, only . . ."

"What?"

"You had to see this guy . . . cool, professional. I told him to his face I didn't believe him, but in truth, I don't know why, but I do."

"C'mon, John. Why in the hell would the KGB be after you?"

"Grigori told me Michael had stumbled onto evidence that could expose one of their agents. That's why he was killed. And I . . . I guess I just did too much digging. The same thing almost happened to me."

"Drug dealers killed Michael."

"Grigori said they just made it look that way. Look, I know how this must sound, but that's the way it happened; I'm just trying to make sense out of being kidnapped and beaten half to death. You should see my goddamn face. I can hardly breathe my ribs hurt so bad. *You* make sense out of the account Hartley found. *You* make sense of what this Grigori told me. He's a drug dealer, part of the Russian mob . . . fine—*you* track him down."

"Easy, easy. First things first. The important thing is to get you in here, then we'll talk some more."

"I'm all for that. Can you come get me?"

"Can't you move?"

"I don't want to. I've got the dead man's car. Someone might spot it or me. And, frankly, I'd rather have you take me into custody personally than turn myself in to some cop I don't know in a precinct around here."

"Okay. I can arrange to get there. Now, John, about the first thing, the account down in the Caymans. Are they going to find any surprises in your apartment if they go in there with a search warrant?"

Still don't trust me, huh friend? "I never had any dealings with drugs, period."

"So you're clean?"

"Of course." John thought of his Dictaphone tapes. "Look, Steve, I just thought of something. In my apartment . . . I left some evidence there that may help my case. I'll let you, the cops, in . . . you won't need a search warrant. On my desk, in my bedroom, are Dictaphone tapes. A record of everything I've learned . . . everybody I've interviewed. I want those safely in police hands."

"All right. After we pick you up, we go there. Where are you exactly?"

John looked at the street signs. "Corner of 45th and 7th."

"Where should I pick you up? That corner?"

John thought for a moment. "No. I'd like a few more people around. Let's say 42nd Street. On the north side of the street . . . how about between 7th and 8th. I'll find you."

"Why the cloak-and-dagger stuff? Why don't I just pick you up on the corner?"

"It's nuts, but I'm scared. They'll be looking for me, I know they will."

"Okay. We do it your way. We just want you in safe and sound. It's six o'clock now . . . I can be there . . . let's say seven, make it seven-fifteen. That good?"

"Great. At seven-fifteen, start walking west from 7th. I'll be looking for you. And Steve, don't forget to get a man over to Kelly's."

"Consider it done."

"You don't know how happy I'll be to see you."

"Likewise, buddy. The cavalry's on the way; don't go anywhere."

There was no place left to go, John thought as he hung up the phone.

Captain Kevin Bacall looked young for his age, but when he finished the phone call with the commissioner, he looked each of his forty-six years and then some. Mayer wasn't going to like this, and Bacall couldn't blame him. Bacall didn't know John Sarikov, but had known his brother, Michael, and he believed Mayer when he said John was not a threat. He didn't know why the commissioner had taken such a strong interest in this case, but he had, and Bacall's protests fell on deaf ears.

Bacall caught Steve as he prepared to leave the station and held out a receiver/transmitter unit. "Put this on."

"Why?" Steve said, confused. "I'm going alone. You checked off on that. A black-and-white on each end of the street, me in the middle. That's the plan. This is an old friend, we're not going to need that."

"Things have changed. I talked to the commissioner. He wants more people there. They're on their way now."

"Who's on their way?"

"SWAT." Bacall didn't meet John's eyes.

"Why the hell . . . this isn't a hostage situation, this isn't a sniper, this is a friend of mine. He's turning himself in, for God's sake. There's not going to be a problem. *No SWAT.*"

"Dammit, Steve, I'm not holding a debate here. The commissioner says we have a SWAT team there, we have a SWAT team there."

"Why, dammit? He's turning himself in."

"You heard the report from the warehouse in Brooklyn. There's a man lying down there with a knife up under his ribs, his face torn apart, and your man admitted responsibility. We have the evidence of the drug tie-in. The commissioner is of the opinion Sarikov should be considered armed and dangerous. He doesn't think we should take any chances. If Sarikov does what he said he's going to do and turns himself in peacefully, he's got nothing to worry about."

"I promised John—"

"You promised a murder suspect. Remember that, detective."

Steve's face reddened; he wasn't going to win this argument. "How many?"

"Four, placed on roofs along the south side of 42nd. They'll be strung out to cover the street between 7th and 8th. You'll be in contact with the SWAT team and their chief, Chuck Nelson, with this receiver and transmitter. He'll tell you when they've spotted Sarikov."

"I don't like it. This arrest is getting too much play. Why four SWAT members for a case like this?"

"Commissioner's orders, that's all I can tell you."

"I'm surprised the commissioner even knows about this case, let alone has taken a personal interest."

Bacall started to say something, then stopped. Mayer had mirrored his own thoughts, but that didn't change the situation. The commissioner had asked to be fully informed of any and all developments in the Sarikov matter; Bacall was just doing his job. "Surprising or not, he has. I'm in the same boat you are, Mayer. He's the commissioner, I'm a captain, you're a detective. That means I take orders from him, you take orders from me. Have I made myself clear?"

"Tell that team to keep their fingers off the triggers. I don't want to haul in a corpse."

"Neither do I, detective."

Steve took off his jacket, strapped the receiver to his chest and ran the microphone up along his shirt, clipping it to his collar. He put the small transmitter in his ear.

"When you get out of your car at 7th, Nelson should be set up and ready to receive you. The receiver's set at the correct radio band." Bacall glanced at his watch. "His men should just about be in position.

They'll keep you informed of what they see as **you** **walk** down 42nd."

Steve put his jacket back on and headed out of the **building** to join the uniformed officer waiting to drive **him** to 42nd Street.

John looked at his reflection in the mirror. He had **just** finished washing his face of all remnants of dried **blood**, but hardly looked better for it. The bruising was more pronounced than ever—shiny black—and the swelling had stretched his facial skin taut. He looked like hell, felt like hell. Gingerly touching his hand to one of his swollen eyes, he winced in pain.

He was in a hotel on 43rd Street, halfway between 7th and 8th, in a rest room off the lobby. Paper clogged the toilet of the one stall; graffiti covered the walls; if the floor or sink had been cleaned in the last month, John would have been surprised.

After talking with Steve, John had walked 42nd Street, a street in transition—triple-X theaters and empty storefronts slowly giving way to renovated buildings catering to out-of-state tourists. Halfway down the block he came upon a small marquee—"Excelsior Hotel, Low Rates, Use 43rd Street Entrance." Underneath the marquee, a brick propped open a glass door. The hotel, from what John saw in the lobby, attracted a mix of transients and young student travelers; thick, bulletproof plastic protected the registration desk. Given the makeup of the clientele, no one had taken particular notice of John's face.

The doorway onto 42nd Street would be a perfect place to wait for Steve—the escape route to 43rd Street put him at ease, though he had no logical reason to believe he'd need it.

John tried to swallow, but there wasn't enough moisture in his mouth. His hands shook, and he fought to calm them. Hard to look at this afternoon as a blessing, but in some ways John saw that it was. He'd been kidnapped, almost killed. The police, even Hartley, would believe him now; they'd have to. They'd drop the drug charges against him, and reopen their investigation of Michael's murder. They'd hunt down Grigori, and the truth would come out, finally.

A glance at his watch showed seven-ten: time to watch for Steve. John started for the hotel's entrance on 42nd Street.

The street was crowded, the wind biting cold. John retreated back into the entranceway out of the wind's path. Mirrors covered each side of the entranceway, enabling John to watch pedestrians approaching from the east without being fully exposed. He would see Steve in plenty of time to walk out and greet him.

Steve exited the squad car after adjusting the receiver in his left ear. 42nd and 7th; seven-fourteen. Time to arrest an old friend.

He glanced at the building tops, but couldn't see any of the SWAT team. God, they made him nervous. A bunch of high-powered rifles trained down at him. It didn't make sense, not in this case; there just wasn't enough risk to justify it.

Before setting off down the street, he spoke into the microphone. "Nelson . . . do you read? This is Detective Steve Mayer."

"Gotcha, detective Nelson here."

"I'm at 42nd and 7th, about to head west on 42nd, on the north side of the street. You all set up?" Steve asked.

"You've got a green light, detective. My men are in position, four shooters. They've got the street covered like flies on shit. We've already spotted Sarikov."

"Where is he?"

"Halfway down the block, tucked back in the entranceway to a hotel. Alone. No sign of a weapon.

My men report having clean shots—crosshairs dead on the temples."

Nelson sounded a bit too much the cowboy. Steve took him down a notch. "Tell your men to rein it in, Nelson. This guy's a friend of mine. He's a good kid."

"My orders say he's armed and dangerous; wanted for possible drug dealing and murder."

"That's bullshit. All of it. There's not going to be any trouble, and I don't want any accidents. Got it, Nelson? Nobody fires. He's turning himself in, and I want him alive. Are we clear?"

"We're on the same wavelength, detective. If Sarikov plays it by the book, he walks in with his brains intact."

The man slumped against the wall below the window, his chest heaving. He looked fiftyish, a nondescript everyman with a receding hairline and a comfortable overfed look to him. The latter characteristic and three flights of stairs taken at a run accounted for his long wheezing gasps.

He too wore an earphone and before rushing the stairs had heard the conversation between Detective Mayer and the SWAT commander. As he struggled to catch his breath, he peered from the window, hoping he wasn't too late. He spotted the detective first, walking slowly west on 42nd Street directly across from him. He scanned the street and spotted the mark a little farther on, just where the SWAT commander said he would be.

The man had to hurry—in only a few moments the detective would take the mark into custody. He unzipped a large tennis bag, withdrew and opened a plastic case, exposing the barrel and stock of a rifle, the same model the SWAT team used. He hurriedly assembled the weapon.

The man had received the call only a short time ago: a rush order requiring gathering the necessary equipment, crossing town to 42nd Street, and locating a vantage point, all within slightly over an hour. Luckily, the traffic flowed smoothly and finding a vantage point hadn't turned out to be as hard as he feared. The rooms above the last remaining triple-X theaters on 42nd Street were readily available for a price, although it raised a few eyebrows when he said he wanted a room by himself.

Now he had to make the hit, and he had only seconds.

The earphone kept feeding him information; the hit's contractor had told him what radio band to receive on.

"You're within ten yards now, detective . . . he's just up ahead," the earphone crackled as he slapped the clip of bullets onto the rifle. The bolt slid easily, inserting a bullet in the chamber.

The man turned on the microphone that hung from his neck, thrust the tip of the rifle barrel out of the window, and looked through the scope. *Only seconds.* He sighted the detective, then quickly swung the rifle left along the storefronts until the mark filled the scope. He wet his lips as he lined the crosshairs on the mark's forehead, just above the bridge of the nose. It was a long shot, but he was paid well to be accurate at long shots.

As he began to gently squeeze the trigger, something gnawed at his brain, told him the shot wasn't right, and he hesitated, but then heard another voice in the earphone.

"He's coming out, detective."

He had to act now. He tracked the mark's slight movement forward, the crosshairs still trained on their target, and yelled into the microphone, "Take him out, he's got a gun!'' as he smoothly pulled the trigger, confident of a kill.

The mirror exploded in front of John's face. He jumped back instinctively into the protection of the entrance an instant before a storm of rifle shots rang out, tearing into the walls on both sides of him. In a panicked run he retreated into the hotel.

One moment the scope showed the mark's forehead, the next a shattered mirror. Sure of his aim, the man was momentarily confused, then realized what had happened. He realigned his sights, but caught only a glimpse of the mark's reflection ducking into the hotel. He swore under his breath—a damn stupid mistake. The first job he ever failed, and the timing couldn't have been worse. This was a big-time hit and would have paid well. The contractor would not be pleased by his failure.

Steve stopped in his tracks, momentarily stunned by the heavy volley that ripped the air, then regathered his wits and yelled into the microphone, "Stop firing! Hold your fire, dammit!"

The rifle volley sputtered to a stop and Steve ran forward, praying he wouldn't find John's body sprawled on the ground, bloody and bullet-riddled. Steve turned the corner and found the entranceway clear. He charged into the hotel, holding his badge in the air, but saw no sign of John.

Two hotel clerks cowering behind the registration desk pointed at the front door in response to Steve's shouted entreaty. Steve bolted past the door, which fronted on 43rd Street. He snapped his head in both directions. A dozen or so people strolled the street; Steve didn't see John among them.

*   *   *

John disappeared down the first subway entrance
he found. He bought a token and waited nervously
for a train to arrive. The first went to Brooklyn—
anywhere would have done. His breathing didn't slow
even after the doors closed and the train left the station. His hands shook uncontrollably. He felt un-
hinged, had almost been killed.

*Why? Who had fired? Who knew he was meeting
Steve?* John glanced at the other passengers on the
car, paranoid he would find them staring back, somehow able to guess instantly he ran from the police. In
truth, the passengers couldn't have cared less who he
was. They stared blindly forward, careful to mind no
one's business but their own, having learned in New
York City a nervous man with fresh bruises was to be
ignored, not studied.

John got off the train at Brooklyn Heights, across
the East River from Manhattan, and walked the
streets frantically, uncertain of where to go, what to
do. He still shook uncontrollably an hour after leaving
42nd Street.

John checked his pockets—less than ten dollars. He
would need more. He stopped at an automatic teller
machine, fed in his card and punched in his pin number. His request for cash was denied. The machine
showed his balance to be nine thousand dollars, but
allowed no withdrawal. No available funds, it insisted.
John fared no better at the next two machines he
tried, the meaning clear—the police had frozen his
accounts.

A few months ago his life was ordered, his biggest
worries: deadlines. How had it come to this? He
needed help, but who could he turn to now? The same
question kept rising, did Steve set him up? He refused
to believe it, but then who?

Only one person had answers for him. He must talk
to Steve, but not on the phone. Phone calls could be

traced, and more important, John wanted to confront Steve face-to-face; it had to be in person.

Steve lived only a dozen subway stops away. John checked his watch. 8:40 P.M. When Steve came home, John would be there waiting for him.

43

Aleksei Denisov stared out over the city as the red diode on his phone flashed in regular one-second intervals. Vasili held on line two. Aleksei hadn't picked up the phone for a simple reason—he had yet to decide what to say.

He could see the crowds of people thronging Fifth Avenue twenty stories below—scurrying ants, tens of thousands of them. Normally, the view made him feel on top of the world—not tonight.

He picked up the photo of Joan and the kids. Ned, a high school sophomore, reserve goalkeeper on the school's soccer team. Maggie, eleven, her birthday next week. They had invited all the neighborhood kids and most of the relatives to her party; he'd planned to pick something up for her tomorrow morning at F.A.O. Schwarz.

What the hell had he been thinking?

The nightmare had almost been over. Within his grasp, finally, a chance to live day by day without the constant fear of compromise—the awful dread that one day a federal agent would walk through his office door and take everything away. And he had thrown that chance away.

It had seemed so safe, so simple, in the beginning. Vasili had made all the arrangements and taken all the risks. Aleksei had only a decision to make: would he like an account established in his name in the Cayman Islands, monthly deposits of $100,000, or not? He took the money; only later did he recognize the attached steel wires.

Drugs *were* the future, others on the Collegium saw that; he wasn't the only one. And the money had come with little work. But then came the requests for small favors, then the enforced advocacy, and soon the realization that Vasili didn't just want to make some money on the side; he had much grander aims—control of the Collegium, power. And Aleksei was just a tool to help him realize his ambitions.

Now this mess. Aleksei hadn't signed up for all-out war, especially a war he had a significant chance of losing. Vasili remained powerful, still had the ear and muscle of the Russian mafia at his disposal, but things must be made clear to him. Unfortunately, that job fell to Aleksei.

His mind made up, Aleksei picked up the phone and pressed line two.

"Aleksei?" Vasili demanded, clearly irritated.

"Yes, I'm here."

"You left me waiting five minutes."

Aleksei purposely skipped an apology. "I was in the middle of something important."

The other line fell silent. Aleksei imagined Vasili's internal debate, to snap back in anger or move on to business. Vasili chose the latter. "I need you to do something for me."

"What?"

"Nicholas phoned Grichko a short time ago. Grichko then called me, agitated by the half-truths and mindless speculations. I'm concerned Nicholas intends to similarly upset every member of the Collegium. I need you to calm things down if necessary."

"You've a right to be concerned; Nicholas *has* talked to everyone."

"Including you?" Vasili asked, clearly surprised.

"Yes. About an hour ago." Nicholas's words had dominated Aleksei's thoughts and soured his stomach ever since.

"And you didn't inform me?" Vasili's surprise turned indignant.

"I intended to, after I took the Collegium's pulse. I've already talked to Grichko and Popova. Kozlov was out. I didn't bother to speak to Yuri."

"Good. Then you're ahead of me. You have assured them all I have things under control."

"Do you?"

The challenge incensed Vasili, as Aleksei knew it would. "Are you questioning my actions, Aleksei?"

Aleksei said nothing. He walked a dangerous line, but Vasili's actions gave him no other choice.

"I said, are you questioning my actions?"

"Nicholas said you had three people, all peripherally involved in Sarikov's investigations, removed. Is that true?"

"Not *peripherally* involved. All had evidence incriminating me. You heard the tapes. There is a fourth, the cop's widow, I have yet to deal with."

"You'd do something like that without consulting me, without orders from the Collegium? After killing the two cops, with the problems that caused us, you would do that? That is what you call under control?"

"The Collegium *must be* taught it can not dictate to me. The matter is concluded; the Collegium has no other choice but to accept my actions."

"And Grigori, the Collegium's representative, what of him? Nicholas tells me your man made an unsuccessful play to eliminate him. A direct challenge to Nicholas, Vasili? Is that wise?"

"The old man hasn't the energy to do more than gnash his teeth and vent his spleen."

"You may underestimate him, Vasili. Backed into

a corner, I'm afraid we'll find he's lost neither the will nor the capacity to fight."

"I look forward to it."

"Your alliances might not be as strong as they were a short time ago."

"Are you speaking for yourself, Aleksei, or for others on the Collegium?"

Aleksei sidestepped the question. "I am stating fact. The last bit of news Nicholas passed on to me, to the Collegium, was that you twice tried to remove Sarikov and twice failed. Is *that* true?"

"We will have Sarikov soon enough—there is no place he can run."

"You argued vehemently before the Collegium that Sarikov had information that could compromise you. You convinced the Collegium; they declared Sarikov a risk and ordered his removal. Now the Collegium members are told one of your people is in the police morgue and Sarikov remains alive, knows more than ever, and is being hunted by the police. Can you guess what's going through Grichko's, Popova's, and Kozlov's heads, Vasili? I can. They see a time line: the police find Sarikov, the police question Sarikov, Sarikov implicates you, the police begin to investigate you, the investigation broadens. Don't you see? *You* are the threat Grichko, Popova, and Kozlov will fear if you don't get Sarikov out of the way, soon."

"Sarikov is a gnat, no more. He will be taken care of."

"*Before* the police get to him, Vasili." Aleksei tempered his voice. "I speak to you as a friend now, as an ally. Grichko and Popova said nothing specific, but what they didn't say was revealing. Trust me, you must eliminate Sarikov before doubts begin to snowball. *Forget* Grigori, *forget* the cop's widow, make Sarikov your first priority; he must not be allowed to tell the police what he knows."

The other line went silent for a long couple of seconds. "As you wish. Sarikov will be my first priority, and don't worry, he'll be dealt with shortly. In the meantime, you sit with the old men you are so worried about and hold their hands."

"Even they have their limits."

"As do I, Aleksei. You would do well to remember that." Vasili punctuated his comment by killing the line.

Aleksei stared again over the city, long after placing the receiver back on its cradle. He decided to make two more calls before heading home: the first to Nicholas's man Yuri—the time had come to hedge his bets; the second to a reliable bodyguard.

44

John recognized the car first. He ducked back behind a line of bushes as the older model station wagon rumbled past and pulled into an open spot just short of Steve's house. He fingered Rolf's gun in his pocket. He didn't plan to use it, but was glad to have it just the same.

Stepping from behind the bushes, John walked quickly along the sidewalk toward the station wagon. The driver turned off the engine and opened the car door. It was Steve. John hurried his steps and, when five yards distant, stopped and called out.

Surprise turned to relief as Steve turned. "*John*! *Thank God* you're all right. Christ, I'm sorry."

Steve took a step forward, but John's words stopped him cold. "Get back in the car, Steve."

Steve's eyes traveled to John's arm tucked in his jacket pocket. "You pulling a gun on me, John?"

"I just want to talk, but out of sight. You've got nothing to worry about. If anyone sees you get in the car, you can honestly say you were forced."

"We can talk at the station."

"I was ready to try that, remember. Humor me. Let's do it right here, right now. Slide over to the passenger's seat." Steve shook his head, but reentered the car. John sat on the driver's side and shut the door, his left hand still gripping the gun.

"What the hell happened, Steve?"

"I'm not sure. . . ."

"Who fired the shots?"

"I don't know."

"Did you have some of your people there?"

Steve stared out the car window, frozen for a moment in thought. "I couldn't stop it. I tried to tell the captain you weren't dangerous, but . . . Four SWAT sharpshooters were on the buildings across the street."

"I thought you were coming alone."

"The commissioner was breathing down the captain's neck on this one. He gave the orders himself."

"*But why?* Why'd they shoot?"

"I talked to them afterward, and they all said the same thing. Over their earphones they heard someone yell to take you out, that you had pulled a gun. One shot came first, then they all fired. Each denies giving the order or taking the first shot."

"I *didn't* pull a gun."

"I believe you. None of the four sharpshooters would admit *broadcasting* the order, but they all *heard* it. They did what they were trained to do."

"One of them's lying."

"For the life of me, they all seemed sincere. I know you're right, but . . . These are some elite cops, they just don't screw up that often."

"Maybe they didn't."

"What do you mean?"

John rubbed his forehead with his free hand. "I mean I've had a lot of time to think. Call it paranoid, but what if I was set up? Someone tried to kill me in the warehouse and failed . . . maybe they tried again."

"This is a SWAT team we're talking about."

"One of whom is lying. Look, Steve, all I know is someone fired a shot at me in a no-risk situation. Maybe someone doesn't want me in custody where I can talk."

"Screw your fucking head on straight, John. It was

an accident. A horrible accident, but an accident, and we can correct it by taking you in now."

"I'm not sure if I believe in accidents anymore—there's been too many of them. The coincidences mean something. You say you believe your people, then who took the first shot? Why are they lying about it?"

Steve shrugged. "One of them fucked up, okay, and he's covering his ass."

"You said these guys are the elite."

"You've got some questions, I can understand that. Come in now. We drive in . . . together . . . no one else has to know."

John shook his head.

"You don't have a choice anymore, John. They're going to issue an arrest warrant for you in the morning. There's an APB out for you already."

An arrest warrant? For him? John's mouth gaped open. "For what?"

"Drug trafficking—"

"I didn't open any account in the Caymans."

"It's gone beyond that. I *told you* the cops were going to search your apartment. They found an eighth of a kilo of heroin in your closet."

John let his head fall to the headrest. "Shit." He pulled his left hand from his pocket, leaving the handgun inside.

"It gets worse," Steve went on. "Suspicion of murder."

John snapped his head toward Steve. "What?"

"Homicide has concocted a neat little theory. Everyone knows you've been trying to track down Michael's killer. They figure he was either a supplier to Michael and you, or a rival. You finally found him, at the warehouse this afternoon, and rammed a knife up under his ribs. Fits neatly, huh?"

"And what? Then I called the police to turn myself in?"

Steve shifted uncomfortably in his seat. "Yeah, but you got scared. The official stance on tonight's meeting is you pulled a gun. The SWAT team was justified in opening fire."

"But that's not true!"

"Hell, John, it doesn't matter if it is or not—that's the department's position. Let me give it to you straight: the next time a cop sees you, he's not gonna ask a lot of questions, he's gonna blow your ass away. Another reason you gotta come in with me now."

John knew Steve was right, but on a gut level he resisted. "I'm supposed to turn myself in, huh? I'm supposed to trust the department after what happened on 42nd Street, after the trumped-up charges you just told me about? And what if I'm onto something, what if whoever's after me has someone inside the department, how long will I last in custody?"

"You're talking crazy, John."

"Maybe, but I'm scared shitless. Whoever's after me, they're not going to quit until I'm dead; I'm sure of it." John stopped in thought. ". . . Kelly. Did you put the man on Kelly?"

"She's covered. No one's getting near her. You better start thinking of yourself, buddy. What do you want? You gonna stay on the run? How far do you think you'll get? How guilty do you think you'll look when they catch you?"

"I have to know a few things first. I've got to know where I stand."

"Where you stand is the shit house. You turn yourself in, and maybe, just maybe, you get out of it."

John didn't respond.

Steve softened his voice. "What the hell happened to your face?"

"I told you. In the warehouse . . . I was beaten. You should see my ribs."

"What happened in there, John? The guy had his mouth ripped off, a knife sticking in his chest."

"He tried to kill me."

"Why?"

"Like I said, to shut me up. It had nothing to do with drugs. I'm getting too close to whatever happened to Michael, and they wanted me silenced."

"Goddammit, I wish you had stayed at the crime scene and waited for the police. . . . Okay, get this through your thick head. You killed someone. You got that? That's reality. If it was self-defense, you'll get your chance to prove that. Same thing goes with the drug charge. I can back up your story on 42nd Street. But if you stay out here, no one's going to believe a word you say."

"And if I come in now, then will they believe me?" John asked. He took Steve's silence as his answer. "They wouldn't, would they? They'd all think I'm either crazy or a liar. You don't believe me either, do you?"

Steve hesitated again, but this time John let the silence linger, forcing a response. "Let me have the whole story again, slowly. We've got time."

John did. He followed the chronology of events culminating at 42nd Street, summarized his interviews, laid out the evidence he had collected.

When John finished, Steve nodded solemnly. "Look, I'm not going to dispute anything you've told me, but I can't help thinking maybe you got caught up in this thing, let your imagination run a little wild. Your theories, what ifs, talk of Russian illegals and police conspiracies—I don't care if you're onto something or not—aren't going to change the fact that the department has hard evidence against you. Becoming a fugitive isn't going to either. You want to prove your innocence, you come in with me now and answer the charges. Your face, the beating you obviously took, is going to help. So is my testimony. And we've got leads to pursue—tracking down this Grigori, tracing the background of the dead guy, Rolf."

"I don't know . . . I . . . I have to think," John stammered. "What about Rolf, you find anything about him so far? I gave you his real name, his address."

"The address was phony. No one by that name lives in the apartment building."

"You run a rap sheet on him?"

"No record locally. Tomorrow I'll check with the FBI."

"What about the cassette tapes at my apartment?" John asked, desperately. "You remember to have one of the cops pick them up?"

"No tapes, John. The cops went through your place top to bottom. They found heroin, but no tapes."

"But they were there . . ." John began and then stopped. It was obvious what had happened to them. "You got a piece of paper, something to write with?"

Steve pulled a pen from his shirt pocket and handed it to John. Paper, the back of a gas receipt, he scrounged from the glove compartment.

John spoke as he wrote. "You heard my story. I know what you think of it, but consider this: someone must have taken my tapes when they planted the heroin. If I've been operating on crazy theories, letting my imagination run wild, then why would someone bother to take the tapes?"

Steve raised his eyebrows but said nothing.

John handed him the paper. "I've written down the name of the restaurant where Bersch works and the name of Rabbi Sosman's synagogue. Mrs. Banovich lives in Brighton Beach on Clayton Street; I've written that down, but can't remember the exact address—

you can get it from Michael's police log. You talk to these three, you can reconstruct what was on the tapes. I'll let you reach your own conclusions as to why someone wanted to keep them from falling into police hands. You might get somewhere talking to Bersch. He told me somebody was nosing around the restaurant, asking questions about Olgov a few days before he was murdered. If I'm not mistaken, he'll be able to identify Rolf's body."

"Same guy who asked about Olgov?"

"I'd put money on it—descriptions matched."

"Okay, John, that's worth checking."

"One more thing."

"What?"

John pulled out his Dictaphone. "When I was in the warehouse, tied to the chair, Rolf made a call from the warehouse office. I overheard it. It sounded as if he were talking to his boss, the one he took orders from. After I escaped, I noticed something. The phone had a redial button." John pointed to the Dictaphone. "I taped the number."

John pushed the play button, and the eleven tones sounded in quick succession.

Steve's face brightened. "Good thinking. That could get us somewhere."

John handed Steve the tape.

"Sound quality's good," Steve said as he put it in his pocket. "I should be able to trace it. Anything else?"

"No."

"Then let's go."

John shook his head slowly. "I'm getting out of the car." He held up his hand as Steve prepared to interrupt. "I know you're giving me good advice, and I appreciate it, but I'm not turning myself in, not yet. There's too much that doesn't add up about 42nd Street. Sorry, Steve, but I'm trusting my instincts on this one. In jail, I'm trapped; out here at least I have options."

"You're a fucking idiot, John. I'm trying to help you."

John put his hand on the door handle. "Help me by following up on the things we talked about. Give me time to think; I'll be in touch."

Steve nodded reluctantly. "Sleep on it, John. See a good lawyer in the morning; he'll tell you the same thing I have. . . . I'd invite you in, but . . ."

John smirked. "Thanks . . . I've involved you enough. I'll be okay." He opened the car door. "I'd appreciate it if you didn't follow me."

"I should. I should follow you, knock you on your dumb-ass head the first chance I get, and drag you to the station."

John smiled and stepped from the car.

"John," Steve called as he reached into his pocket. "How're you doing on this stuff?" He held up a thin wad of bills.

"Not too well."

"Take it. I'm sorry it isn't more," Steve said as he threw it on the driver's seat. "Just don't tell anyone where you got it from."

John nodded, and shut the door.

Steve remained in the car for a few minutes before making his way to his house, entering quietly so as not to wake his wife. He mixed himself a scotch and water and sat in an easy chair in the den, leaving the lights off.

The kid was in big trouble and headed for more, but there was nothing else Steve could do for him. He would have a hard time explaining the things he had done already. *Why wouldn't John turn himself in?*

Logic kept pointing to one answer: John had something to hide.

* * *

Counting the money Steve had given him, John had a total of fifty-eight dollars and change. Even if he could find a room for the night for fifty-eight dollars or less, an unlikely prospect, he couldn't afford to part with what he had. That left only one good option for the night, which is why he had joined a group of men in a line outside the Holy Family Congregational Church in Brooklyn, the basement of which served as a homeless shelter for men.

John had done an article on shelters in the city less than a year ago; he never imagined he would put to use what he had learned in such a practical manner.

John looked at the other men in line—wild hair sticking out beneath skullcaps, tangled unkempt beards, downcast eyes with their spirit sapped, and darting eyes guarding their host's few possessions. Heavy long coats all of the same color, the color of dirt ground in layer by layer, day after day. There was a smell also, strong and pungent, of urine, sweat, and rot.

John stuck out. He hadn't fallen as far, not yet. His clothes weren't as dirty; he had shaved that morning. *Was it only that morning?* It seemed so long ago.

The line moved quickly when the church doors opened. Two men at the doorway asked each man to sign in, and checked their eyes and speech. They didn't take men high on drugs or alcohol, but John's battered face didn't elicit comment—evidently it wasn't news when a homeless person was beaten. John signed in with an alias and passed through the doorway and down a flight of stairs to the shelter.

He heard the man's voice behind him: "That's all for the night." Only a few of the long line of men behind John had been allowed in—it was a cold night outside, and shelter space was at a premium. He had been lucky, and laughed to himself at the thought.

A short, businesslike man pointed out a cot with clean sheets and a heavy, although somewhat moth-eaten, wool blanket.

"If you need to use the bathroom, do it now, because the lights go out in twenty minutes. The lights will come back on at 6:30 A.M., and you're to be out of the shelter by seven," the man said, expressionless. "Any questions?"

"No."

John looked around. A number of the homeless seemed to know each other; they talked in small knots, laughing and flashing warm smiles revealing yellow and missing teeth. Others seemed not to have any laughs left in them, and huddled on their beds in the fetal position. Still others seemed unbalanced and yelled out swear words and curses intermittently at no one in particular.

He, as with these men, had nowhere else to go. *How could he live like this? If he ran, moved to a different city and tried to start over, would it be any different? And if he stayed and turned himself in, how long would he live?*

John's whole body throbbed with pain. He lay back on the cot and the questions didn't seem to matter anymore. Mercifully, a deep sleep came swiftly.

45

As the phone rang again, Barbara squinted in frustration at the clock by her bedside. 7:30 A.M. Another ring. It wasn't going to stop. Why didn't she get a bedside phone, she asked herself, as she threw the covers to the side.

She kept her eyes half closed, hoping to be able to fall asleep again after the call, and hurried across the room to the phone without bothering with a robe. She'd left the blinds on her studio apartment's windows open, but as far as she was concerned if some nut had the dedication to train a telescope on her apartment at seven-thirty in the morning, he deserved whatever view he got. She picked up the receiver and sprawled on the couch. "Hello."

"Barbara."

Barbara sprang to an upright sitting position and wiped the sleep from her eyes. Relief and anger hit her at the same instant.

"John? Is that you?" She knew, of course, that it was, but his voice sounded different somehow—not drunk, but remote.

"Yeah," John said. "It's good to hear your voice."

Barbara felt the same way. They hadn't talked since she moved her things out of his apartment over two weeks ago. She had waited a week for him to call before breaking down and phoning him, but she never got anything but his answering machine. Thankful for whatever led him to break his silence, she let him lead the conversation.

"I . . ." John started

"What is it, John?" she prompted.

"I don't know where else to turn. I . . . I've no right to ask, but I need your help."

Something told Barbara this was not the time to reopen old wounds. "Anything, John. Anytime. I hope you know that."

"Barbara, I've made such a mess of things. Of us, my life, and now . . . I never meant to hurt you."

"I know."

"Something's happened . . . I'm in trouble."

"What is it, John? What's happened?"

"I can't tell you right now, but I need your help. I know I have no right to ask—"

"Quit it. You have every right to ask."

"I don't want to involve you."

"You're scaring me. Involve me in what? If you want me to help you, you've gotta tell me what's going on."

"Can't, not this time. You've got to trust me."

Barbara's indecision lasted only a fraction of a second. "What is it you need?"

"Money and a car."

"Now you're really scaring me. What happened to your car? Your money? Are you in some type of trouble with the police?"

"I can't answer that; I've involved you enough just by calling."

"I don't mind being involved, but I'm worried about you. Tell me what's wrong."

"No. Like I said, you'll have to trust me."

She always had. "Okay."

"Barbara . . . whatever happens, whatever people tell you about me, remember, you know me better than anybody. I'm not capable of certain things . . .

you'll know that in your heart. The other thing I hope
you know is . . . is I put you through a lot and I'm
sorry, but . . . I never stopped loving you."

Barbara's eyes moistened. "I wasn't sure anymore.
I didn't think things could change, but . . . Tell me
how I can help."

Against John's orders, Barbara hesitated before
walking out of her building. Curiosity got the better
of her, and she scanned the length of the street. There
was a man by a pay phone across the street, a woman
window shopping, a man reading the paper at a bus
stop, and scattered strollers. Nothing suspicious.

Barbara opened the lobby door and turned right,
toward midtown Manhattan.

She resisted the temptation to glance back over her
shoulder to see if anyone followed—John had told her
to act completely natural. She was to go to a café,
order a cup of coffee, read the newspaper, then shop
at Bloomingdale's before coming home. John said she
might be followed, or she might not, but not to worry,
they weren't after her. But she did worry. For him.
And for good cause.

She wished John would have taken her into his confidence, but wasn't surprised—John would take on the
world by himself if he felt he had to.

The driver of the yellow cab parked on the corner
put down his coffee cup when he saw Barbara leave
the apartment building. He glanced across the street
to the cop who had been pretending to read a newspaper but whose eyes now followed the young woman.
Stationed at a bus stop since sunup, the cop had stuck
out like a sore thumb. Two hours ago an unmarked
police car had delivered him breakfast. An easy spot.

After a half minute or so the cop fell in step a block
behind the woman. The driver hesitated. He had seen

the young woman stop inside the doorway and peer out, looking for something. Maybe, he guessed, trying to spot a tail, and yet she did nothing to evade being followed. That raised the possibility she wanted to be shadowed, one of the reasons he decided to stay put. The other was the curious episode earlier that morning when she hurried out to a cash machine around the corner, withdrew money, then went directly home.

He took another sip of coffee. His instincts were correct more often than not—the mark would show up.

John checked his watch. Close to an hour had passed since he called Barbara. That should be long enough—anybody who had been watching Barbara's apartment would now, he hoped, be trailing her.

He covered the three blocks to Barbara's quickly, stopping at the corner of her street to survey. He saw a few knots of people on the sidewalk—nothing out of the ordinary. After flipping up his collar, he walked casually to Barbara's building. No one appeared to take notice of him.

John entered the building, fingering his key to Barbara's apartment. Forty-five minutes later he exited. Freshly showered and dressed in slacks, shirt, and sport coat, he carried a small gym bag of clothes, all things he had kept at Barbara's but never picked up. Barbara's car keys and four hundred dollars in cash, from the cash machine Barbara visited that morning, were tucked in his pocket.

Barbara's car was parked where she said it would be, and he started it, merged into traffic, and headed for the Holland Tunnel and New Jersey. He hadn't decided on his next move, but felt safer, somehow, to be heading out of the city.

He didn't notice the yellow cab that had pulled into traffic behind him.

46

When he woke, John noticed the ceiling first—stained by water and cigarette smoke, hosting spiders in each of its corners. The second thing he noticed was the sheets—frayed, wrinkled, dirty, certainly not cleaned after the last occupant. The third thing he noticed was his head and ribs ached worse than ever. It hurt to sit up in bed. He lifted his shirt carefully, finding it painful to lift his arms above his head. Whatever fractured ribs looked like, they couldn't look much worse than his—large blackened knobs stood out from his rib cage; every inhalation hurt.

John walked gingerly to the bathroom, soaked a hand towel with cold water, and held it to his jaw. A look in the mirror showed a patchwork of black bruises framed in yellow. One eye was almost completely swollen shut.

He had taken a room in a lousy little motel, the Starlight, off Highway 17 in New Jersey, approximately five miles from Manhattan. He'd been to the place once before, to interview a Teamster on the run from union thugs about a contract kickback scheme. John figured any place the International Brotherhood of Teamsters couldn't find had to be relatively safe.

The clerk could not have helped but notice John's bruised and battered face, but had asked no questions, which was what John had counted on.

He had parked Barbara's car in the back of the

motel, away from the road. Keeping the car was dangerous, John knew, but he needed transportation. Hotwiring a car was a mystery to him, and he feared the police would have circulated his name and description to the car rental agencies.

John glanced at his watch—a little after 2:00 P.M. Almost three hours of sleep, though it felt like minutes. He stepped into the shower, ignoring the mold that had overrun most of the grout. The warm water felt good, easing his battered body and giving his mind a chance to think.

He swallowed the acid creeping up his throat. *What the hell was he doing?* He'd gotten himself in tight spots before, but running from the law? Yes, he'd almost been killed, and yes he had every reason to be scared, but the futility of his situation was obvious. He had Barbara's car, the clothes on his back and in the gym bag, and four hundred dollars, less now that he had paid for the room. That was it. He wouldn't get far, and when the police caught him, how could he blame them for assuming his guilt?

The sliver of soap slipped from John's hand into the brackish water that pooled around his feet—the result of a slow drain. Rather than fish for it, John cut the shower short and reached for a towel.

No matter how many times he ran the arguments through his head, the quandary remained: he wanted to turn himself in, to face the charges against him, to prove his innocence, but every nerve in his body screamed in unison that someone had purposely set out to kill him at 42nd Street.

John dried himself and moved to the bedside phone. He attempted unsuccessfully to calm his nerves with long slow breaths. He would call Steve, then take things one step at a time. Perhaps he worried for nothing. Maybe Steve had already gotten a line on Grigori, maybe he'd traced the warehouse phone number, maybe he'd discovered some way for John to get out of this mess.

Steve answered the phone on the first ring and recognized John's voice immediately. "John, thank God, I've sat by the phone all day hoping you'd call. Where the hell are you?"

"Never mind that now, Steve, I need to talk. Are you tracing this call?"

"No."

"Anyone else on the line?"

"Just you and me."

John paused. "I . . . I owe you an apology for last night. Things were crazy."

"Don't worry about last night, no one's ever going to know about it."

"I was scared . . . still am. Don't know what to do today anymore than I did last night. I know all the arguments, but when I consider turning myself in . . . Steve, something stunk to high heaven last night."

"Yeah . . . I think you may be right."

Steve's reply caught John by surprise. "What do you mean, I may be *right*?"

"Look, John, I don't think I made too much of a secret of what I thought last night. A police conspiracy sounded crazy, still does, but . . . maybe not quite as crazy as I thought. I've found some things that don't add up."

John's heartbeat accelerated; his feelings of defeat momentarily lightened. "What things?"

"The way things went when you tried to turn yourself in . . . it bothered me. Two possibilities. Either the SWAT team screwed up real bad, which I found hard to believe . . . or it was a setup, which I found even harder to believe, so I leaned on the captain, got him to assign a team to pick up every damn bullet they could find at the scene. They were there starting at six this morning. They found fourteen. All the same caliber. Problem is, the SWAT team was interviewed, their rifles checked. They all started with full clips; they fired a total of only thirteen rounds. Thirteen from fourteen leaves one. Where'd the extra bullet come from?"

"Jesus—"

"There's more. The SWAT commander had ballistics do some rush tests this morning—he wanted to know if one of his men had lied, had popped an extra bullet into his clip before turning in his rifle. The preliminary results are in. The crime lab checked each bullet's striations against the SWAT team rifles—"

"Striations?"

"Yeah. Every rifle barrel leaves a unique set of scratches on a bullet . . . unique as a fingerprint. One bullet didn't match any of the four barrels."

"There was *another* rifle?"

"That's what ballistics says."

"It *was* a setup."

"I don't know what else to think. Like I said, I'm starting to believe your story, and that is scaring the shit out of me. The SWAT commander doesn't know what to make of the ballistics report; he's not looking for any publicity. I didn't, for obvious reasons, tell him about our little meeting last night."

"Who knew we were meeting at 42nd Street?" John asked.

"Me. The SWAT team. A handful of patrol officers. The captain. The commissioner."

"One of them?"

"I don't buy it. I know most of those guys . . . it doesn't fit. I'm guessing the leak's somewhere else— someone who learned about our meeting indirectly. I don't know how exactly but it's not hard to imagine. We didn't exactly treat your pickup as a state secret— we didn't see any need to."

"So if I tried to turn myself in again?"

Steve hesitated. "As things stand now, without special arrangements, it might be too risky."

"What special arrangements?"

"I've been working on them all day, hoping you'd call. I've got an appointment with the police commissioner this afternoon. I'm going to lay out your whole story, everything you told me. I'm bringing the ballistics report with me. That's hard evidence, John. The commissioner has the power to request special protection—federal agents. You stay put, then call back tonight, and between me and the feds, and only between us, we'll have something arranged. We'll bring you in safely, and keep you safe."

"The commissioner'll go for that?"

"I think so—he can't ignore the evidence. Besides, he wants you in as badly as anyone. He'll go for it."

"I don't know."

"What the hell do you mean, you don't know? I'm talking the FBI. You're not going to make it on the outside on your own. You gotta come in; I'm guaranteeing your safety."

"You and the commissioner are going to be the only ones that know?"

"Yes."

"Okay, let's agree on this. I call you back, you tell me the arrangements. No promises, but if the commissioner's willing to play ball, I guess I'd be a fool not to."

"I'll second that."

"When should I call you?"

"I've got the appointment at four-thirty, so let's say six."

John looked at his watch. Three hours and maybe, just maybe, the nightmare would end. He sighed audibly in relief. "Thanks, Steve. I'm almost at my wits' end. I appreciate having someone on my side. Maybe I can get out of this thing okay after all."

"It's going to be an uphill battle, John. There's some other things I found out. Not all of them good."

"What?"

"The three persons you had taped, that you wanted me to question . . ."

"Yeah?"

"If they were important to your story, I think you better forget it."

"What do you mean?" John asked, tension gripping his stomach.

"The old woman . . ." John heard a rustling of papers. "Mrs. Banovich . . . is dead. Respiratory failure the coroner says. Found her in her apartment. No sign of foul play. The dishwasher . . . Bersch . . . couldn't find him. Owner of the restaurant said he was a drifter . . . had talked about heading to California. His apartment was cleaned out. We've got people looking, but he may be hard to find. The rabbi—Rabbi Sosman—died of a massive heart attack yesterday."

John struggled to absorb the news. Mrs. Banovich dead. He remembered his words to her: *No. No. I'm sure you're not in any danger.* Rabbi Sosman dead. Bersch missing, probably dead. All good people, whom he had involved, and now— They were wiping the slate clean, and obviously weren't going to let anybody stand in the way.

"You okay?" Steve asked.

"To tell you the truth, I'm sick to my stomach."

"Yeah . . . you're right—something stinks . . . something fucking stinks real bad."

"They killed them. Anybody that knew a hint of the truth—dead."

"Anybody else on those tapes we should be worrying about?"

John thought of Davis and Lieberman, then realized he never taped their conversations. His heart stopped. "Kelly. Her name's scattered all over them."

"Take it easy; she's fine. A cop's still watching her. Frankly, the department thought you might try to contact her."

"I almost did. Make sure a cop stays on her till this is over, will you, Steve?"

"Already taken care of. No one's going to give her any trouble, okay?"

"Okay."

"Now, something else," said Steve.

"What?"

"I called an old friend at FBI headquarters in D.C., asked him to do a background check on Yevgeni Malinovsky, the dead guy from the warehouse who went by the name Rolf. Our check had come up negative, and I was looking for something to pull your ass out of the fire. The guy did a rush job for me. No record at all, no offenses, but because I'd mentioned KGB in passing, he did some additional checking, things I hadn't requested, things they sometimes look at when foreign agents might be involved. He checked the name against the Social Security records and found something sort of peculiar."

"What?"

"Yevgeni Malinovsky died thirty-four years ago."

"What are you talking about?"

"Yevgeni Malinovsky died at the age of six months."

"Steve, I don't know what you're getting at. Are you talking about a different Yevgeni Malinovsky?"

"Yes and no. My friend explained it to me. It's a way of getting an identity. Let's say this Rolf was thirty-four and wanted a new name and all the I.D. that goes with it. He goes through the death records, finds a child. Yevgeni Malinovsky, who died about thirty-four years ago. He applies for a birth certificate in the child's name. Anyone can get one. Simple. Using the birth certificate he applies for a Social Security card in the child's name. Chances are if he picks a kid who died young enough, a card was never issued. The wheels of the bureaucracy turn, and he's assigned a Social Security number. A card is sent to him and the hard part's over. As far as the government is concerned he has become the child. Once he has a Social Security number, getting other I.D. is simple, risk free—driver's license, passport, credit cards, employment, everything. A nine-digit Social Security number was his passport to another identity."

Something clicked in John's mind. "Say that last part again, Steve."

"What? A nine-digit number was his passport to another identity?"

"Yeah . . ." The phrase kept going through John's mind although he couldn't explain why. "What about the kid's death records?"

"Never checked by the Social Security agency—it takes time and effort, and they're not set up for it. Whoever Rolf really is, in the eyes of the government he's Yevgeni Malinovsky, the little kid who died thirty-four years ago."

John absorbed the information and moved on. "Anything on Grigori?"

"No."

"What about the telephone number I recorded with my Dictaphone? Were you able to trace it?"

"Yeah."

"Whose is it?"

"I'm not going to tell you that."

"Why?" John asked, surprised.

"I don't know what you've got by the tail, but one big fucking fish belongs to that number. I can't have you knocking on his door. I'll take it to the commissioner with the other things. When we have you safely in, we'll figure out how the phone number works into all this. Then, if it's appropriate, we'll go after him, big fish or not."

"If it's *appropriate*? The guy behind that phone number may have ordered my execution!"

"Trust me. I've got to go through channels on this one."

"Goddammit, Steve—"

"It's not open for debate, John."

John had chosen another swear word before he stopped himself from using it. Steve was on his side, he reminded himself. "Then go through your channels, but if they're blocked, I'm going to want that name."

"No one's gonna block me, not on this."

"All right. what do I do now?"

"You sit tight. Don't call anybody, don't move. After six I should be back in my office. Phone me then, and I'll lay out the plan."

"You're the boss."

"Hang in there, pal."

47

Vasili signaled impatiently for his secretary to shut his office door, then picked up the phone. "Richard, good to hear from you. To what do I owe the pleasure?" His voice came smooth and practiced, devoid of any hint of the anxious expectation he actually felt.

"That Sarikov matter we've talked about, I think we'll have it cleared up very soon," Commissioner De-Luca said, obviously pleased with himself.

So the old windbag was actually good for something besides information. "Good. That's excellent news. How did you manage it?"

"Detective Mayer just called. You remember my mentioning him, the one who was to meet Sarikov on 42nd Street."

"Right. The one Sarikov pulled a gun on."

"Well, as I told you, there was some confusion on that point—"

Vasili cut DeLuca off. "Confusion is something the public doesn't want to hear about, not when the election's going to be as close as it is. I think we're better off supporting our boys, don't you, Richard? I'm sure if more than a dozen shots were fired by one of your crack teams, they had a reason."

"Of course, but—"

"But nothing. Let's not get ourselves mired in details. Sarikov pulled a gun, and the SWAT team took the appropriate action. Now what did Detective Mayer say?"

"Sarikov called him again. He still wants to turn himself in, but he's afraid . . . thinks there's a leak in the department and what happened on 42nd Street wasn't an accident. He thinks it was a deliberate attempt to kill him."

Vasili removed his glasses and set them on the desk in front of him. "That's ridiculous, obviously, but as long as we get him in, it doesn't really matter how paranoid he is. What else did Sarikov say?"

"Mayer's coming over this afternoon to fill me in. All sorts of crazy allegations about his brother being framed, agents of a foreign government, witnesses disappearing."

Vasili forced the angst from his voice. "What does he want from you?"

"Added protection. Sarikov's story sounds like fantasy land to me, but Mayer doesn't dismiss his claims of a leak in the department. He said he's uncovered evidence of a political bigwig's involvement and is bringing me some sort of proof . . . wants me to call in some federal agents to orchestrate Sarikov's pickup and provide protection. Mayer will deliver Sarikov to them and we'll have our man."

Vasili took a moment to gather himself. *What evidence? Could it implicate him directly?* If the evidence convinced Mayer, it could convince the commissioner, then others. And if the feds got involved— "That's terrific news, Richard. Now this cop, Mayer, can we trust him? What's his background?"

"Yeah, we can trust him. Twenty-year veteran. Excellent record. He was a friend of Sarikov's brother, the cop on the take, but there's no indication he was involved in that mess."

"Which precinct does he work out of?"

"Brighton Beach."

Vasili jotted down the name, then the precinct, on a sheet of paper. "Good. Sounds like he's the man for the job. What time did you say he planned to meet you?"

"Four-thirty."

He added the time to the list. "At your office?"

"Yes. I'll listen to what he has to say, and if it pans out, I'll call the feds. One way or the other, we should have Sarikov in by this evening."

"It sounds as if this entire affair will soon be behind us. I commend your handling of the matter."

"Thank you, though I've got to say the whole thing mystifies me. Sarikov may be messed up in drugs, may even be a murderer, but his case just never seemed politically explosive to me. You really think this thing could have fouled up the next election, huh?"

Vasili regurgitated what DeLuca needed to hear, but his mind had already moved on to other things. "Believe me, Richard, it wouldn't have helped. I've seen it before. Look at the bad press the administration's already received—payoffs, dirty cops, Caribbean bank accounts, street justice. The papers had a field day. Readers ate it up while the mayor's poll numbers took a nosedive. Now you have the brother of one of the dirty cops on the loose, guilty of drug dealing and murder, and he's eluding arrest, pulling guns on police officers. It becomes too high profile, and suddenly the papers have a second chance to rake your department over the coals. I'm having a hard enough time lining up the big donors for the mayor's campaign as it is."

"That bad?"

"Possibly. Why take the chance? But don't worry— the mayor's going to win, and he'll keep you in your job for a long, long time. Just keep me up to date, and I'll be able to handle the fallout."

"Thanks, I appreciate your help."

"That's what I'm here for, Richard."

48

The man in the conservative blue suit glanced to his right and met the eyes of the truck driver parked at the edge of the intersection with his emergency flashers on. The truck driver nodded his head once.

The man in the conservative blue suit glanced to his right and met the eyes of the truck driver parked at the edge of the intersection with his emergency flashers on. The truck driver nodded his head once.

This was their mark then, the man with the reddish brown hair who had just passed by, headed, as expected, across the street to the building that housed the commissioner's office. The man fell in step behind the mark, eyes darting from the crosswalk lights to the truck driver. The light showed a stale WALK, and the truck idled in perfect position. It was going to be easy.

They started across the street in the midst of a small crowd, maybe ten pedestrians. Time to separate the mark from the herd. The man threw a ten-dollar bill to the ground, then tapped the mark's shoulder and pointed to it.

"Excuse me," he said. "You just dropped some money."

"Thanks," the mark replied, then bent over to pick up the bill.

The man checked the light. Blinking WALK now. Good. He withdrew the stun gun from his pocket, bent over the mark as if to aid him, and surreptitiously touched its contacts to the bare skin of the mark's arm. Thousands of volts jumped across the two leads.

The mark hit the ground, shaking uncontrollably as

if in epileptic seizure. He wouldn't regain control of
his muscles for at least ten seconds, plenty of time.

The light changed to DONT WALK, and the man
waited till the truck surged forward toward the prostrate body before running, leaving the mark alone in
the crosswalk, convulsing and helpless.

As he disappeared into the stream of pedestrians
on the other side of the street, he heard the dull thud
behind him, and then the screams.

49

After talking to Steve, John made a fruitless effort to sleep, but couldn't calm his racing mind, and ended up staring at the ceiling, wide-eyed, wondering how things had gotten to this point and where it all would end. The thoughts weren't comforting, and he flipped on the television to quell them with a mindless telecast. An afternoon talk show should have done nicely, but John grew antsy, turned the set off, and paced the room, considering Steve's proposal.

He couldn't trust the local police, not after 42nd Street, but the FBI? The tentacles of whoever chased him couldn't stretch that far. Besides, he had evidence now—solid evidence—the ballistics report and the phone number from the warehouse. If he turned himself in he'd have a fighting chance, Steve was right about that, but doubts lingered. His opponent, like a shark unseen beneath the waters, struck swiftly, unexpectedly. The warnings had sounded—there *were* sharks in the water—and John couldn't shake the feeling he was about to take a swim.

6:00 P.M. came slowly.

John waited only a few minutes after the hour before dialing Steve's precinct number.

"Hello," a voice answered. It didn't sound like Steve.

"Detective Steve Mayer, please," John said.

"May I ask who's calling?"

"A friend," John answered tentatively.

"Can you hold a minute, I see him coming."

"Sure."

Forty-five seconds went by and alarm bells began ringing in John's head. Something didn't feel right. Another fifteen and John killed the line. A few minutes later he threw the motel key on the bed and walked out of the room. He'd put at least half an hour between himself and the motel, then put his suspicions to the test.

The half-hour drive took him to a diner west of Newark. White paper hats, bow ties, fifties retro. Drinking a shake and eating a turkey sandwich, he monitored his watch and finally fingered a quarter and headed for the pay phone in the rear of the restaurant. He pulled a book of matches he'd taken from the Starlight Motel from his pocket and read off the phone number, then plunked in the quarter and made the call.

"Starlight Motel," a voice answered.

John deepened his voice. "Sergeant Andrews, NYPD, I'd like to speak to one of the officers on the scene please."

There was no hesitation on the other line. "Sorry, sergeant, they've all left . . . maybe ten minutes ago."

He'd have been in custody by now—a close call. "Did they get him?"

"The man in room 4?"

His room. "Yeah."

"No. He cleared out before they got here."

"Dammit," John said, stalling as he considered what other information might be valuable. "Were you able to get a description of his car? his license number?"

"Sorry, as I told the officers, I didn't see him drive up, didn't see him leave."

John hung up the phone, his worst suspicions confirmed. *What did it mean?* Had the commissioner listened to Steve and rejected his request, then ordered someone to monitor Steve's line waiting for John's next call? Possibly, which meant dealing with the police, at least on the basis John had counted on, was out for now. His hopes, once again, crashed upon him. Back to square one.

John fished for more change; his own number this time. Maybe Steve had tried to reach him.

His machine turned on, and he tapped in his four-digit code. Kelly had left the first message. Sounding on edge and distressed, she asked him to call her as soon as he could.

Lieberman had left the second and final message. "Mr. Sarikov, Isaac Lieberman of Yad Vashem calling. I just received your package with the two photos, and I can't tell you how happy I am. They're excellent quality, just excellent. If the others are as good . . . Anyway, I've got a preliminary report on your requests. Some luck—I got nowhere tracing the name Jacob Greene, however I *have* been able to trace the tattoo number you gave me. The Nazis assigned it to a Jacek Gruenbaum. That's J-A-C-E-K G-R-U-E-N-B-A-U-M. I assume Greene and Gruenbaum are one and the same. I should receive additional information on Gruenbaum within the week. I hope it'll be helpful, Mr. Sarikov. I can't tell you how important it is to find those additional photos. I'll be in touch."

Jacek Gruenbaum. What had Lieberman said the last time they spoke, it was not unheard of for Jews emigrating to America to Americanize their names. It fit: Jacek to Jacob, Gruenbaum to Greene. Didn't "gruen" in German translate to "green" in English? He thought so.

Interesting, but irrelevant, at least for now. No time to call Lieberman, no time to follow up. He tucked the information away, then focused on the immediate.

Restocked with change from the diner's cash register, this time he called Steve's home number. If Steve wasn't at his desk, if he'd been pulled from duty, he might be home. Of course his home line might also be tapped, but John would keep their conversation short. He'd get a message across—go to Paddy's tonight, I'll call you there—without identifying himself, then hang up.

A man answered, his voice strained.

"May I speak to Steve?" John said.

There was a pause, then a stuttering reply. "I'm . . . sorry . . . but . . ."

"Or Nancy, if Steve's not available."

"Nancy is . . . can't come to the phone right now. This is her father. May I help you?"

Fred Jacobs. John had met him a few times, though not often enough to be on a first-name basis. "Mr. Jacobs, this is John Sarikov. . . ." John paused; no reply. ". . . Michael Sarikov's brother," he added.

"Yes, yes . . . John." Mr. Jacobs's voice sounded strange, distant somehow.

"I've been trying to get ahold of Steve. . . ."

"I'm sorry, I'm afraid I'm not very good at this. It hasn't quite sunk in yet. . . ."

The alarms again, ringing loudly this time. "Is everything all right?" John asked.

"No . . . there's been an accident. . . ."

The way he said it, John knew immediately. He didn't say anything, and Mr. Jacobs continued. "A rather bad accident. Steve . . . passed away this afternoon."

The words hit home, and the room swam in front of John's eyes.

"It . . . it's so hard to believe. Just yesterday . . ." Mr. Jacobs's voice trailed off and the line fell silent.

John tried to collect himself. "What type of accident?"

"Excuse me?" Mr. Jacobs murmured.

"How was he killed?"

"Hit and run. They didn't even get the guy. He

killed my Nancy's Steve, and they don't even know who he is."

John cursed himself.

"I've got to go now, John. Nancy is . . . she needs me. I've got to go."

"Of course, sir. You can't know how sorry . . . how very sorry . . . I am . . . for you, Nancy, the family."

Mr. Jacobs mumbled a thank-you, then hung up.

John sunk to the nearest booth, eyes glazed. He didn't even consider the possibility of it being an accident. The string of bodies now included Steve, a friend since childhood, who died trying to help. He thought of Nancy and swore to himself. If he could get his hands on the people who did this—but he couldn't; they were winning and he wasn't even in the ball game.

Steve, I'm so very sorry, he thought as he smashed his fist on the table.

John thought of the gun strapped to his ankle. What had he done on this holy quest of his but cause pain? It would be so easy to end things before he caused another death. *What difference would it make anyway? How long could it be before he joined the list? What good did it do to run when they'd proven they could get anybody?*

Anybody. John stopped at the thought. They had taken out Steve because he knew too much. John had confided in one other person, and Steve couldn't protect her any longer.

John pulled himself together and more change went into the phone. On the fifth ring John muttered, "Come on," and on the seventh Kelly answered.

"Kelly, it's John."

"*John.* Thank God. Where are you? The police were here earlier, asking all sorts of questions. They said—"

John interrupted her. "I know what they said; it's not true."

"But they said you *killed a man,* John."

"Someone tried to kill me, Kelly, that's the truth."

"Then you've got to turn yourself in to the police. Barbara said you took her car and some money and—"

"You've talked to Barbara?"

"She's here now."

"She's there *now*?"

"Lying down—I hope sleeping—in the back room. She's been here all afternoon, ever since she heard about the charges against you. She's beside herself, John. I told her about your investigations, how wrapped up you were getting; she thinks she let you down."

John held his emotions in check, focusing instead on Kelly's words: *I told her about your investigations.* Only one thing mattered now, making sure the two were safe. "Tell Barbara I was the one that let her down."

"I better wake her up. She's going to want to talk to you."

"No. I want you to do something for me first. It's important. Steve told me he was going to provide you with police protection."

"Yes, he did, but I want to know about—"

"Just listen. *Please.* A cop's been watching your house around the clock?"

"Three different shifts, but yeah, since yesterday, across the street in an unmarked car. What's this all about? Steve wouldn't tell me and now you're—"

"I want you to check something for me. I want you to check and see if a cop is out there now." John spoke slowly, deliberately, but couldn't conceal his sense of urgency.

"You're scaring me, John. Of course he's out there—I brought him coffee, maybe an hour ago."

"Just check for me, okay?"

"Okay."

John's heart froze, waiting for her return. He balled

his free hand into a fist, the nails biting into the flesh of his palm.

"John," Kelly said, "he's still there."

John mouthed a silent thank-you to Steve. His heartbeat slowed.

"What's going on?" Kelly asked.

"Too long of a story to explain, and someone might be monitoring this line."

"Monitoring this line? What—"

"I . . . I was worried. I wanted to make sure you were okay."

"Why wouldn't I be?"

"Because—" John started to explain, then stopped himself. The less Kelly knew the better off she'd be. "I just wanted to make sure you were okay. I don't trust the police, Kelly. Not anymore. I wanted to make sure your protection wasn't called off."

"Steve said they'd be with me for a week; besides, Carl couldn't leave without telling me."

"Carl?"

"Carl Nicholsen. He's on duty now. I'm sure you've met him before. A friend of Michael's and Steve's. He was at our wedding. Carl and the other two cops watching the house, they're all friends, John. I'm not the one in trouble—*you* are. Now where are you?"

John ignored the question. Friends of Michael's and Steve's could be trusted—a reason for John to feel some relief—but he had to get the two out of that house. "Kelly, I want you to do something else, and I don't want an argument. I want you to wake up Barbara, pack a few things, and spend a couple of days at a hotel. Both of you. Pick an anonymous, out-of-the-way place. Nothing close to where you live, nothing on a main drag. *Don't* pay with a credit card, use cash. Park your car in the back of the hotel, out of sight of the road. Stay inside. If you absolutely have to go somewhere, don't travel without other people around you. Don't tell *anybody* where you are. Call your parents periodically; I'll get a message to you through them in a day or two."

"John—"

"Listen to me, Kelly. I want you to leave as soon as I hang up. Do whatever you have to do to make Barbara come along. Have her call in sick to work. . . . You say this Carl Nicholsen's a *good* friend?"

"Of Michael's and Steve's. Yes."

"Then I want you to ask him a favor. Steve assigned him to you personally, so he'll come along to the hotel, but I want you to ask him and the other two cops to keep the fact that you've moved quiet. Ask them to keep it out of their reports. For a few days, anyway. That's important."

"I'm not going to do *anything* until I know what's going on."

"Kelly—"

"Not until I know what's going on."

John paused, then decided he needed to be blunt. "Steve's dead, Kelly," he whispered.

"What?"

"He was killed."

"No. *No.*"

"Stop, Kelly. I told you so you'll know I'm serious. They're after me; they got Steve. I'm worried about you and Barbara now."

"My God . . . Steve . . . Nancy. *They*? *Who, John*?"

"I don't know. Listen, you and Barbara pack and go to a hotel, now, with Carl providing an escort. Then you ask Carl to keep the move quiet. You tell him Steve's dead and you're scared, and he'll understand. Promise me you'll do that, okay? . . . Promise me, Kelly."

". . . I promise."

"One last thing: remember where I put Michael's service revolver?"

"Yes. In the closet in the study."

She was regaining control. A tough woman, John thought. "Get it. There are bullets in the gun case. Load it; carry it in your purse. I know you know how to use it. Keep it with you."

"John. *Please. Talk to me.* Are you okay?"

"Sorry, Kelly, I've got to go."

"But what about you?"

"I'll be okay."

"Barbara will want to talk to you," she tried again.

"Make Barbara understand. Tell her I'm sorry, and I never wanted to cause her pain, but . . . I don't think I have the capacity to love anybody anymore, Kelly. Now do what I asked; no questions. For Michael, for me, take care of Barbara and yourself. I'll call as soon as I can, okay?"

John hung up the phone without waiting for an answer.

Eyes closed, John rested his forehead against the pay phone. Barbara and Kelly were safe, but for how long? Stopgap measures weren't going to be effective forever, not if Michael's killers had the two on their list. That realization and the weight of Steve's death enveloped John as he pulled himself from the restaurant and started toward Barbara's car. Steve had been his last hope—now what? Another lousy motel, another shelter, waiting to be caught or get the news that another friend had died? It was up to him alone, and he hadn't a clue.

He started east, considering staking out Kelly's house. She would be gone, but Grigori or whoever might come looking for her wouldn't know that. If John spotted Grigori before Grigori spotted him—

A thought hit John, a less desperate plan. There *was* a clue left to explore. Steve had traced the phone number Rolf called from the warehouse; he said it belonged to "one big fucking fish." John had made

only one tape of the phone's signal tones, the one he
gave to Steve, but the phone itself, the one Rolf used
in the warehouse, should still be in Rolf's car where
John had parked it—on 45th Street in Manhattan. He
still had the car keys. If a battery backed up the
phone's memory, the number would still be stored.
That was his clue. That was his chance.

John continued east, toward Manhattan, praying
Rolf's car hadn't been towed or found by the police.
And how would he trace the number if it *was* still
there? He had no good answer to that one. Not yet.

It was close to ten when John turned onto 45th
Street. He clenched the wheel, knuckles white, trying
to remember exactly where he'd parked—somewhere
between 7th and 8th, he thought. Then, up ahead, he
saw it, Rolf's car, multiple parking tickets on its windshield. Thank God the tow trucks hadn't gotten to it
yet. He parked around the corner and walked back
toward it, then past it, concerned with the possibility
of a police stakeout. After verifying the other cars
parked on the block were empty, he returned to Rolf's
car. The phone he found where he'd left it, under the
passenger seat.

On the way back to Barbara's car, rising above the
Broadway theaters, John saw the Marriot Marquis,
and the obvious occurred to him—a way to trace the
number stored in the phone. He took his gym bag of
clothes from the trunk of Barbara's car, tucked in the
warehouse phone, and started back to the hotel.

Unlike many of the overdressed tourists in the hotel's lobby, the well-mannered Marriot desk clerk
avoided staring at his face. After registering and part-
ing with a good chunk of cash, John headed for the
elevator bank.

Once in his fifth-floor room, John moved quickly to
the bedside table. He unplugged the hotel's phone,

substituted the phone he'd taken from the warehouse, then rubbed his hands together. If the warehouse's phone still had the number stored in its memory, John could hope for any one of three possibilities after he pressed the redial button. One, someone answered and gave their name. Two, a machine answered and its message revealed a name: "You have reached the something or other residence," something like that. Or three, a machine answered and gave a number: "You have reached so and so number, we're not home now." Any of the three would do.

John crossed his fingers and pushed the redial button. Eleven tones rang off in rapid succession. Still there—thank God. John waited for a ring, but none came. He hung up, pushed the redial button again, with the same result. Puzzled, he examined the dialing instructions mounted on the desk, and had his answer—he needed to dial a nine for an outside line.

John's finger hung poised above the digit nine when he stopped himself. His heart leapt to his throat, and his hand went to his forehead. Pushing nine would have erased the number stored in redial. Close—two inches—to a disastrous blunder. Somehow he needed to both access an outside line and preserve the number stored in redial. He searched the wall next to the bed and found what he looked for: another wall jack— this was the computer age after all: faxes, personal computers, all feeding off the phone lines.

A bellhop appeared a few minutes later in answer to John's call to the front desk. He handed John a phone cord as requested before being shuttled out the door with a tip.

John hooked the hotel phone to the second jack, then picked up both receivers—each had a dial tone. This should work, he told himself, but he nonetheless spent an extra minute checking his logic before punching a nine on the Marriot's phone. That brought another dial tone—an outside line—on both receivers. He set down the Marriot's phone and grabbed the one from the warehouse. A quick prayer, then he pressed the redial button. The sequence again rattled off, then a pause, then a ring. *Jackpot.* John wiped perspiration from his forehead with his shirtsleeve.

His relief was short-lived. A machine answered the line with none of the three possibilities he hoped for. A grumbling monotone voice spat out the message: "No one is available to receive your call. Please leave your name and number at the tone and someone will get back to you."

John swore. Every time he moved forward, every time it seemed as if he might get somewhere, he was stymied. No exception here. Now what? John racked his brain and hit upon a simple, if unlikely, solution.

He pressed the redial button on the warehouse's phone again and counted the rapid sequence of dial tones. The phone connected to nothing, since he hadn't pressed nine first. Eleven digits—a long-distance number. He penned eleven dashes on a piece of paper and, above the first, the numeral "1," then pressed the redial button again, listening, noting the pitch of the second note sounded slightly higher than the first.

He next lifted the Marriot's receiver and pushed its number "1," listened to the resultant tone, then played with the phone's keypad, searching for a number that corresponded to the second tone on the warehouse's phone. His confidence evaporated rapidly. One of his father's few extravagances had been to insist John learn piano, part of the great Russian artistic tradition, but the task John had set for himself seemed beyond his abilities. The notes called by the redial button came too fast and, to his ear at least, sounded all too similar. Nonetheless, he continued to experiment with the keypad, willing himself to distinguish every tone, refusing to admit defeat.

After an hour he threw his hands up in the air. Who was he trying to kid? He looked at the four numbers he had jotted down—at best wishful thinking. He swore, then swore again when he realized he hadn't asked for a key to the room's wet bar.

He sat on the bed, the now familiar question taunting his brain: what now? The phone from the warehouse held a valuable clue, but how to make use of it? The police had machines that could do the job, but what could he use? No answer came to mind, no magic this time.

In the early morning he would start off to Kelly's house as he had originally planned. He'd break from surveillance later in the day to find someone, maybe an electronics hack, who could pull the number from the phone. If that didn't work, he'd hook the phone up again, dial the number repeatedly until a person answered, then improvise, perhaps flim-flam the speaker into volunteering his or her identity.

He knew he should get some sleep, but couldn't. He was wired. He called the front desk and asked for another bellhop—the skimpy shot bottles in the bar wouldn't do. The bellhop showed up with bottom-shelf whiskey, though John paid him top-shelf price for it. It burned going down, but that didn't stop John from downing glass after glass until the bottle was almost half empty, then he stumbled toward the bed.

He lay down and the room spun; the pain from his ribs and face soon dulled, as did the news of Steve's death. The booze took its desired effect as John passed from groggy to an uneasy sleep.

50

The don of Brighton Beach, Katkov, settled his not insubstantial weight into the chair next to Nicholas. His smile was warm; his eyes dark and unreadable. "Thank you for seeing me on such short notice. I'm sorry for interrupting you at your home, at this late hour," he said.

Nicholas nodded. To refuse would have been like pre-Nixon America refusing to recognize China; it would have ignored reality.

Katkov had arrived at Nicholas's Greenwich estate in two cars with a total of four bodyguards. Not many, considering he entered hostile territory. It showed either he trusted Nicholas or had a good appreciation for Nicholas's intelligence—only a fool would so openly declare war with the Russian drug lords.

Nicholas proffered a box of Cuban cigars. "How can I be of service?" he asked.

Katkov accepted one and lit it before continuing. "I think men of our standing should meet, at least now and then. If there is no communication, unfortunate . . . misunderstandings . . . can occur. As we have now."

So this was why Katkov had come? To make threats? "As we have now?"

"Yes. I've been giving a lot of thought lately to one of our mutual associates. As you, I'm sure, know, the two of us have had certain . . . business dealings . . . that have been extremely lucrative. It occurs to me, given this fact, that you may have the wrong impression of my relationship with this man."

Nicholas's face remained passive—it was Katkov's show—but inside his heart sank as he waited for the ultimatum: you raise arms against Vasili, you've raised arms against me.

Katkov puffed his cigar, then continued. "You see, my business has been lucrative for a very long time; with or without this man, it will remain so."

Nicholas's face twitched. Not what he expected.

"A successful businessman realizes the bottom line is important, but not all important," Katkov said. "At times he must consider the broader picture. For instance, I'm comfortable now. I've cut out a niche that my competitors respect. Suddenly, I work with this man, and I have worries."

"Such as?"

"Some have nothing to do with this man, I'm sure. Just two days ago in Uzbekistan, the military shut down a business concern I have a stake in. I thought the authorities and I had reached an agreement as to the concern's operations, but suddenly, unexpectedly, they changed their stance. Strange, wouldn't you say? And very unfortunate. Maybe it is wrong of me to blame this man, but I am a believer in karma, good and bad."

A business concern? Try a five-hundred-acre opium farm. It had meant calling in old favors; it had meant risking Katkov's ire, but the message had obviously been received. Nicholas still had pull within Russia and the former states of the USSR, and now the don knew it.

"Not a calamity, but disheartening," Katkov continued. "My primary concerns, however, deal with the man himself. He's gotten himself into, perhaps the best way to put it is . . . an embarrassing situation. I prefer, as I'm sure you do yourself, to stay out of the limelight. I insist my associates do also, especially the ones that, how should I say, have intimate knowledge of the details of my business operations."

Nicholas nodded.

"Then there are the personality flaws. He is a very ambitious man. It's worried me, at times. I like to keep my people content; however I'm not certain this one can ever be content as a subordinate."

Nicholas made a mental note: never take the don lightly, he had a facile mind. "I have found the same."

"I have a good friend from a very large bank on Wall Street, a mergers and acquisitions expert. He tells me that sometimes mergers work out, sometimes they don't. Corporate cultures complement each other, or clash. Executives cooperate with each other, or compete. I've been thinking, the same can be said of our businesses. Sometimes mergers have to be dissolved. Perhaps it would be best for us both if . . . shall we say a bright line existed between our separate enterprises."

More than Nicholas had ever hoped for. His turn to enjoy a cigar. "That, I believe, would be a wise decision," he said as he lit it.

"Which brings me to our acquaintance. What to do with him? Perhaps I'll leave it in God's hands. If something were to happen to him, an accident perhaps, I think my period of mourning would be short-lived. I wanted to make sure you knew that."

Nicholas drew deeply on the cigar. "Unfortunately, there are some who are suspicious even of the hand of God."

Katkov nodded. "Perhaps, with your permission of course, I can make my views known to a few of your associates I've had the opportunity to meet."

"That would be appreciated."

"Good. Here," the don said, pulling a stack of documents from a briefcase.

"What's that?"

"Detailed documentation of certain activities of questionable legality our friend has been involved in. You might find a use for them." Nicholas raised his eyebrows, and Katkov added: "If a rat hole's not plugged, my father used to tell me, count on more rats sneaking through."

51

The alarm rang at three. John sat up in bed with a start. Beads of sweat stood out on his forehead. He raced for the bathroom and emptied his stomach in long agonizing retches. A cold glass of water caused him to bend over the toilet again, before wobbly legs carried him back to bed.

A worthless drunk, just like his father. Under stress, when he was needed, his father had never failed to turn to the bottle. Like father, like son. The thought spurred him to the shower. He left the hotel room a short time later for the front desk, planning to arrive at Kelly's well before first light.

When John announced he was checking out, the man at the front desk, the same one who checked him in less than five hours earlier, gave him a questioning look.

"Is there any problem, Mr. Thompson?" the man asked, using the name John had checked in under.

"No, just a change of plan. You've got the key, and I believe I'm all paid up. Good-bye." John had started for the door before the desk clerk called after him.

"*Just a moment, Mr. Thompson.* Our computer shows you made a long-distance phone call."

". . . A long-distance call?" Of course, the answering machine he reached. "Yeah, right, I'm sorry." John walked back to the desk. "How much do I owe you?"

"Just a moment, sir, and I'll give you a receipt." A printer spat out a bill, and the clerk handed it to John. "Just one dollar and fifty cents, sir."

John reached into his pocket to pay as he absently reviewed the receipt. His heart stopped. "What's that?" John pointed at the string of numbers next to the charge; he thrust the receipt in the clerk's direction.

The clerk turned his head so he could read. "That's the number you called, sir."

"That's the number I called?"

"Yes, sir."

"Your computer keeps track of every number dialed from one of your rooms?"

"Yes, it does. Is there a problem, sir?"

"No, absolutely not." John threw two dollars on the desk and picked up his two quarters change along with the receipt. "Is there a pay phone here?" John asked, excited now.

"Just around the corner, sir."

"Thanks." John found the phone and dropped in one of the quarters. The number he knew from memory. A groggy, obviously just woken, man answered—Walt Donaldson's voice. Good, he had worried the *Herald* might have him on nights.

"Walt?"

"Speaking. Who's this?"

"John Sarikov."

"John, what the fuck, it's . . . it's almost four in the fucking morning."

"Yeah, that's what my watch says too."

"Is something wrong?"

Walt obviously didn't know of John's troubles. Good—John wouldn't have bet on his help otherwise. "You could say that."

"What is it?"

"I need a favor."

"No, really? I'll get out the party hats and blow up the fucking balloons."

"Okay, I admit it; I take advantage of you now and then, but this is important."

"It always is. I'm going back to bed, buddy. Call me at a civilized hour. Good night."

"No, don't hang up." It came out louder, more emotional, than John intended.

". . . All right. You've got me. I'll listen, but it better be good. I need all the beauty sleep I can get. Hold on while I take a piss, then tell me what you want." The phone was silent for a long minute before Walt's voice returned. "Now what is it?"

"Remember working on the Decker story?"

"This is your emergency? Calling about a story that's a year old?"

"Do you remember it, Walt?"

"Yeah . . . what about it?"

"Remember, you had a phone number, one you thought linked Decker with the sanitation commission, but you had to trace it—see who it belonged to."

"Yeah."

"How'd you do it?"

"Easy. A reverse trace on CD-ROM."

"Huh?"

"Get with it, Sarikov. You know what a CD-ROM is?"

"Yeah; I'm not that out of it."

"Then you know a CD-ROM stores information digitally; it's read by laser. A few CD-ROMs can store an incredible amount of information—the data from the phone books for the entire U.S., for example."

"And something like that—the phone book data—is available on CD-ROM?"

"Sure, for a number of years now."

"And that's what you searched?"

"Yeah, you type in a name and it will spit out a

telephone number, or, in the Decker case, I put in a number and a second later out popped the name and address that correlated to it."

"That's what I thought; what I need. Walt, if I give you a number, can you give me a name?"

"Yeah, but not right now. The *Herald* has the CD-ROMs; I don't."

"Can't you access them from home?"

"Nope, don't have the CD-ROMs, don't have the necessary software."

"But the *Herald* has what we would need? We could do the trace, tonight, if we went there?"

"What do you mean *we*?"

"So I admit, I'm a little bit behind the times. I like books, paper; I wouldn't have any idea how to use CD-ROM."

"It's simple. Learn. I have no intention of zipping off to the *Herald* in the middle of the night. . . . Oh, by the way, that one got Charlotte up, and she's shaking her head at me . . . vigorously."

"I'm a selfish son-of-a-bitch sometimes, but I really need you on this one. I *really* need you. I can't take the chance of fouling this up; I've got a real tight time frame. I'll owe you, seven ways to Sunday, or whatever that saying is, and I'll pay off, anyway you ask. Besides, I dealt you a square on the Senator Wilcox case, didn't I? I saw your article two weeks ago—good stuff; you probably got all sorts of pats on the back."

"A few . . . Okay, so maybe you're right; for once maybe *I* actually owe *you,* though it doesn't seem possible . . . but does it have to be at four in the fucking morning?"

"I'm afraid it does."

"Well, fuck, you've convinced me, but Charlotte's now *glaring* in my direction. I'm afraid you still lose."

"Let me talk to her."

Charlotte's voice came strong and determined. "John, before you say anything, the answer is no."

"Charlotte, look, it's a ploy. You let Walt go, five minutes later, buzz me up. We'll have at least an hour before he makes it back. What do you say?"

Charlotte laughed, then spoke to Walt in mock excitement. "I've changed my mind, Walt, you can go." She directed her next words back at John. "Now really, John, is it that important?"

"It really is, Charlotte."

"It can't wait until morning?"

"I'm afraid not. I'm in a hell of a tight jam, and only Walt can get me out of it. I might bother Walt anytime, but I wouldn't bother you unless I meant it."

"Anyone who is looking to my husband to save them must be desperate. . . . Okay, John, you can have him. I won't object . . . this time."

"Bless you, Charlotte."

"Good night, John. Here's Walt again."

Walt sounded awestruck. "How'd you do that? I've lived with the woman for twelve years, and I've never gotten her to back down that easily."

"She's crazy about me."

"Yeah, and I'm just crazy. What time do we meet?"

52

The streets were nearly deserted; even the majority of nightclub patrons had finally called it a night. Trucks owned the streets now, an army of them, delivering the goods that fueled the city before disappearing at first light, leaving the streets to cabbies and cursing commuters. John felt a kinship to the truckers—he, like them, now moved at night, in the shadows.

John parked four blocks from the *Herald* building. A chilly night, he pulled his collar tight at the neck as breath shot from his mouth in white. He passed a group of men lined up across a hot-air vent sleeping under ratty blankets. *Was that his destiny if he failed tonight—the only sure way to drop out and never be found?*

As a frequent free-lance contributor, John had been granted an access pass to the *New York Herald*'s building. He might nonetheless have a hard time getting in tonight—he didn't look much like the smooth-skinned, youthful-faced man pictured on the I.D. John had done what he could in the hotel room, showered, put on a fresh shirt, but could do nothing about the black, swollen eyes and cheeks.

The front entrance to the *Herald* was open. John started for the elevators; the night guard came out from around his desk to intercept him.

"Bill, hey, how're you doing?" John, luckily, knew the guard from long nights spent publishing articles.

They'd shared drinks now and then at 7:00 A.M., the end of Bill's shift and John's sometime copy deadline.

No sign of recognition registered in Bill's face. John held out his *Herald* I.D. card and tried again. "It's me . . . John Sarikov."

The guard squinted. "Johnny? Johnny, that you? What the hell happened?"

"A long story I don't have time for now. How do I look?"

Bill pressed the elevator's up button. "Like shit."

"Yeah. That's nothing compared to how I feel."

Bill laughed as the elevator doors opened and John stepped in. "You gotta learn how to take care of yourself."

"Now you tell me," John said as the doors closed.

The copy room was almost empty—just a few young reporters, bleary-eyed after a long, sleepless night. Rumpled shirts and blouses, loosened ties, straggly hair. John didn't recognize any of them, and none gave him more than a single swift glance as he crossed to a small room stuffed with computer terminals. Walt was already there.

"Jesus, John, your—" Walt started before John interrupted him.

"I know, Bill already told me. I look like shit."

"With a capital 'S.' What happened?"

"Shaving accident."

"My ass. Looks like you pissed the shit out of the wrong person."

"Yeah, something like that."

John sat down next to Walt after clearing away two half-filled coffee cups and an ash tray of bent butts. "You set here?"

"CD-ROMs are loaded; I'm all logged on. Just waiting on you, buddy."

John pulled the hotel receipt from his pocket. "Okay, here's the number." He read it off.

Walt punched in each number then pressed the ENTER button. "It'll just take a second," he said.

A name flashed on the screen almost immediately.

"Is that the name you were looking for?" Walt asked.

John stared at the name. *Jacek Gruenbaum.*

"Well? You recognize it?" Walt persisted.

"It can't be . . ." John started. Lieberman traced the tattoo number to Jacek Gruenbaum, he was sure of it.

"What?"

"He's dead."

Walt swiveled on his chair and faced John. "Who's dead?"

"Jacob Greene; Jacek Gruenbaum."

"Who are they?"

John, locked in thought, didn't answer.

"Yoo-hoo, I asked a question. Who are they?" Walt repeated.

"Not 'they,' 'he.' Just one guy; one and the same. Died in a fire a couple of months ago." *Did he?* The rabbi said he saw the body, but would it have been identifiable?

"So, he could still have a phone in his name, couldn't he?"

No, that didn't make any sense. The phone number began with a five-one-eight area code. Five-one-eight was assigned to upstate New York, the Albany area, John had checked. Rolf speaking to Jacob Greene? Jacek Gruenbaum? in Albany? He couldn't get a handle on it.

Walt watched John's puzzled face in silence for a few moments, then turned back to the keyboard. "You've got me very curious, old buddy." He clicked in a series of commands.

"What are you doing?" John shook himself free of his shock to ask the question.

"Since you won't tell me a damn thing, let's see if I can find out anything for myself."

Walt logged onto a newspaper database with practiced ease. "What files do you wish to search?" the computer prompted. Walt typed a response: New York City newspaper articles for the last year. Then another prompt: "Please enter your search request."

Walt typed "Jacek Gruenbaum," and pushed the ENTER button. The computer completed its task, searching hundreds of thousands of pages of text for the words "Jacek Gruenbaum," in seconds. "Your search has identified 0 items" blinked onto the monitor's screen.

"Nothing," Walt announced. "So, I'm stuck with getting an answer out of you. Who was this guy?"

John remembered asking Steve about the trace on the warehouse phone number. "One big fucking fish belongs to that number," Steve had said. *How big, John wondered? Big enough to make the papers?* "Do it again," John said.

"Huh?"

"But go back further this time. Let's say fifteen years."

Walt shrugged. "Whatever you say, captain." He modified the search request and pressed ENTER.

John's heart skipped a beat as he stared at the screen. "Your search has identified 6 items," stared back at him.

"Display them," John directed, barely breathing.

The first article appeared; John devoured it and moved on to the next.

More than one article referred to Gruenbaum as a "king maker" in New York State politics. He held no elected or appointed office, had no title, but was evidently well connected and extremely influential, counting various foreign governments as well as a number of Fortune 500 corporations, as clients. He ran a boutique consulting firm out of Albany, JG Consultants, which had been phenomenally successful in lobbying state and national elected officials with promises of more than generous campaign contributions. If Jacek Gruenbaum turned his thumb down at a candidate, one article said, the money spigots closed tight and the writing was on the wall, hence the title "king maker."

This *couldn't* be the Jacek Gruenbaum he knew of. *How would it be possible? Two separate identities? A Brooklyn recluse and power broker?* It didn't make any sense.

And yet what had Grigori said: Michael was killed by someone powerful, someone with a high profile. It fit.

"Hey, you're dealing with big-league stuff here," Walt said, gesturing toward the screen. "What's this guy to you?"

John ignored the question. "Go back a little further, Walt. Widen the search. Let's see if we missed anything."

It took a little playing with their search field before they found it, a 1974 society column from the *New York Times* regarding a dinner for Holocaust survivors in the New York area held by the American Jewish Congress. One name leapt from the list of attendees: Jacek Gruenbaum. A parenthetical note after his name read "survivor of Auschwitz concentration camp."

"Jesus," John whispered.

"Is that important?" Walt asked.

This *was* his Jacob Greene? How was it possible? "It just doesn't make any sense," John whispered.

"Start talking, boss. What doesn't?"

"I know this guy's history; it doesn't jive with the things I'm reading."

"Maybe you don't know as much about this guy as you thought."

John shook his head.

"You say this Gruenbaum you knew died a couple of months ago?" Walt asked, rubbing his temple.

"Yeah."

"Funny."

"What?" John asked.

"This guy's obviously a pretty important player."

"Seems so; what of it?"

"This database is current; articles are input within a week. Why didn't we pull up an obituary?"

Good question. John had no answer.

"You sure you got the right guy?" Walt asked.

John's mind raced. Two Jacek Gruenbaums? Both Auschwitz survivors, both wrapped up in his brother's murder? How many coincidences could he accept? There must be some other explanation. What did it mean?

John felt a rush of adrenaline as something in his mind clicked.

"I said you sure you got the right guy?" Walt repeated.

John didn't answer, instead he ran a hypothesis through his mind and the scattered, jumbled bits of evidence he had uncovered careened neatly into place. His fists clenched; pupils dilated. It explained almost everything; the reason someone had killed Michael; had tried to kill him; the identity they wanted hidden. The picture was nearly complete; *it had to be.*

"What is it, John?" Walt asked.

"I think I figured something out, Walt. Something incredible."

"What?"

"Can't tell you now," he muttered, his mind moving on.

"Hey, come on, give your old buddy who got up in the middle of the night, out of the goodness of his very large heart, a piece of the action."

"When it breaks, I'll let you in on it."

"Promise?"

"Yeah. When it breaks."

It came to John suddenly, in a moment of extreme lucidity—there could be no more running, no more hiding, no more turning to the bottle as his father had throughout life. It was up to him to bring things to a head, and he could and would do so. No one left to rely on, no one left to trust. On his shoulders alone, to win or to lose, to walk away or die, anything but the indeterminable agony of guarded existence.

John became focused, and the primal hunter in him stirred. From the first he'd tried to run and gotten nowhere. Perhaps the time had come to counterattack. They, he reminded himself, were afraid of him. Afraid *he* could destroy *them*. And he would, he told himself, now that he had a weapon, now that he had discovered, he hoped, the truth.

John Sarikov, the last of the Sarikov men, would face them down. One way or the other this had to end.

John inhaled audibly and jumped in his chair as he felt a tap on his shoulder.

"Woow, John boy. It's just me," Walt said. "You looked like you were in some sort of trance."

"Yeah . . . thinking."

"Sorry to interrupt that kind of brain power, but I think you should know you're starting to gather a crowd." Walt pointed to a small group of people who were glancing furtively in their direction. "You know what that's all about?"

Dammit, John thought, he knew exactly what that was about. The paper's employees had begun arriving for the workday, and one of them must have recognized him and known the trouble he was in. Word would spread, and soon, inevitably, the police would appear. Time to leave; just a couple of last things to do.

"No. I guess it's my face. Look Walt, two more things, then we're out of here, okay?"

"You don't have to twist my arm—a nice warm bed has my name on it."

John now had a theory and a name; he needed more. First, he hoped, a picture. He hurried to the *Herald*'s vertical files, leaving Walt to stare after him quizzically. He opened the drawer marked "G" and thumbed the folders inside, stopping at one marked "Gruenbaum, Jacek." The folder contained a half-dozen file photos. John pulled the best, a four-by-six color photo, before replacing the folder in the drawer.

He raced back toward Walt, to his jacket draped over a chair, and pulled out the photograph of the concentration camp prisoner. He stared at it, compared it with the photo from the vertical file.

No way, even after fifty years, could these be the same man. Not possible.

As John stared at the concentration camp picture, something gnawed at him. Something said to him within the last few days; something he knew might be important. He tried to remember, and lost all touch with the memory. He stopped trying, relaxed, and it came. Steve's face. The memory rushed back and gripped his gut. He remembered Steve's words— something he had said about Rolf.

Stirring excitement and a rush of energy swamped all pain and fatigue as another piece of the puzzle fell into place. *Proof.* He would need proof if anybody was going to believe him, and he thought he just might have found a way to get it.

The beginnings of a plan coalesced in his mind.

Now he needed an address. The *Herald* kept a library of current phone books, and John hurried to it. He found the phone book covering Albany and looked up Jacek Gruenbaum. No listing. He had bet-

James Koeper

ter luck with JG Consultants and copied its Albany business address and phone number.

John turned to leave when a thought occurred to him. He remembered his second discussion with Rabbi Sosman, when he learned of the Polish man who had bribed the Russian guard and secured Greene's freedom. He ran back to the vertical files, took a stack of folders from the drawer and scanned them rapidly, one after the other, finding an acceptable photo after a few minutes: a black-and-white, from the forties or fifties, of a young man in a suit and tie.

He looked up to see that the group of persons glancing in his direction had grown. He grabbed Walt and they made their way quickly to the elevator.

53

John surveyed the woods a last time. Beautiful—the floor a canopy of reds, oranges, and yellows, the almost naked limbs of the trees branched in graceful design. Hard to imagine what would take place here in only a short time if things went according to plan.

John refocused on the location's merits. Only a short distance from Albany and yet isolated—not a house for a mile in either direction—and there was an old logging path a car could be turned into and hidden from view. Chance of running into anyone unexpectedly—remote. The sound of a gun, especially one muffled by a silencer, should go undetected.

Perfect, John decided.

John had left Walt standing outside the *Herald* building with a string of unanswered questions, and had driven north toward Albany. JG Consultants had its office in Albany; Jacek Gruenbaum had a number with an Albany area code. If John wanted answers, he'd find them there.

He had left Manhattan with only a rudimentary plan, but had fleshed it out on the way. Surprisingly, he thought, the plan had a reasonable chance of success. Risky, but it passed John's primary criteria—it would bring things to a head quickly, and with absolute certainty.

With the discovery of the wooded area, he had now completed the first step of that plan: locating an isolated area close to Albany. John started Barbara's car and began the short drive to Albany, ready for step number two.

A renovated turn-of-the-century building in downtown Albany housed the offices of JG Consultants. John drove around the building a half-dozen times, making mental notes. A couple of security guards in the lobby. Maybe he could get past them on the way in, but what about on the way out? Back entrance locked, didn't seem to get much traffic. A parking garage connected to the building. Better. The second level provided a perfect vantage point over the garage's entrance. A good, anonymous place to spot, and confront, Gruenbaum.

John stopped at a street-side stand and bought a newspaper, then drove back to the parking garage, parked Barbara's car on the garage's second level, and took up a position over the garage's entrance between two parked cars. Prepared to feign interest in the newspaper and his wristwatch should anyone pass, he hoped to leave the impression of an impatient man waiting on a lunch partner.

He glanced at his watch. 12:48 P.M. It could be a long wait. He had no way of knowing whether Gruenbaum had come to his office today, or whether he used this garage, or if he even drove to work. John put the maddening string of questions out of his mind. He would start surveillance here, and, if need be, consider other vantage points. Sooner or later, by some means, Gruenbaum had to show up at JG Consultants.

He held the *Herald*'s file photo of Gruenbaum in his hand. Every feature of the man had been burned into his memory, yet each time a car pulled into the parking garage, he went through the same process, his eyes traveled from the face of the driver to the photo and back again.

At 2:20 P.M. John found his man.

A black Mercedes, first two letters of its license plate "L-D"—that was all John had time to catch before being drawn back to Gruenbaum's face: dignified, authoritative, yet wrinkled and adorned with a thick pair of glasses and folds of useless white flesh dangling from a weak chin. Stripped of his car, his clothes, his position, just an insignificant, feeble old man, and yet, if John was right, he had ended Michael's life—snuffed it out and probably never had a sleepless night.

John shuddered thinking of what this man had done to Michael and what John must now do to him.

The Mercedes climbed the parking ramp, passing John on the second level and continuing upward. John soon lost contact with the fading drone of its motor.

He waited fifteen minutes before following its trail. He found a black Mercedes, first two letters of its license "L-D," on the garage's fourth level. The hood of the car felt warm to his touch.

There were empty parking spots near the Mercedes, as John had hoped. He eased Barbara's car into one of them and waited, his palms sweating, but his mind focused on his plan and his eyes on the door leading from the garage to the office building.

The minutes slipped by, each taking with it another chance for John to act on his second thoughts and abandon his plan. For two and a half agonizing hours he watched person after person exit through the door, and then, finally, Gruenbaum walked through.

John gripped Rolf's gun, the one with the silencer, and choked down stomach acid. No going back now; things were coming to a head. He forced himself from the car and cut a path intersecting Gruenbaum's.

Gruenbaum stood ten yards away, digging car keys from his pocket beside the Mercedes, when John called out, his hand still locked around the gun in his pocket. "Mr. Gruenbaum." His voice cracked slightly.

Gruenbaum turned in John's direction, squinting in the semidarkness of the garage. "Yes?" John noticed only the slightest hint of apprehension.

"I wonder if you could do something for me, sir?" John asked as he walked forward, footsteps echoing off the concrete. He switched to Russian, hoping to get it right. "Look behind you," he yelled.

Gruenbaum started to, until he caught himself. When he turned back around, his face reddened and his eyes flew from side to side. One hand inched toward his coat pocket.

Only a few yards separated them now. "Please raise your arms," John commanded as he pulled the gun from his pocket and pointed it from his hip at Gruenbaum's midsection.

Gruenbaum's hand hesitated, frozen in a moment of indecision, then rose slowly with its partner. "Who are you?"

"Someone with a request." John drew to within three feet of Gruenbaum.

"My wallet's in my back pocket."

"I don't want your money."

"What do you want?"

"To talk."

"Then talk . . . I'd like to get on with my business." Gruenbaum spoke coolly, with the practiced air of command.

Gruenbaum's eyes drifted above John's shoulder. Instinctively, John's mind registered danger. He spun, but too slowly. Something slammed into the back of his shoulder and knocked him to the ground between Gruenbaum's car and the next.

For a moment John felt nothing, then a burning sensation spread from his shoulder; a sick feeling rose from his stomach. His hand went to the pain and touched the growing stain of blood.

He heard footsteps, someone running toward him

from around the line of cars. They didn't come from Gruenbaum's direction, and they weren't far away. He had fractions of a second to act. He was wounded, but alive; in a moment he wouldn't be.

John's gun had landed a few feet in front of him. He lunged for it, stretching out his hand, his fingers grasping its butt as a squat, powerfully built man in a black trench coat turned the corner of the car. Two things registered in John's mind simultaneously: the weight of the handgun as he spun it upward toward the man, and the barrel of the man's gun dropping to John's eye level.

John fired first. The pop of the silenced gun sounded like a toy.

The man's face froze in surprise. One hand went to his gut, the other still held the gun pointed at John. Then John's second shot hit the man in the chest, dropping him to his back.

John remembered Gruenbaum, spun quickly on his knees, and drew down on him just as Gruenbaum's hand cleared his coat pocket, revealing a small revolver.

"Stop!" John yelled, and Gruenbaum froze. "Drop it and stay where you are," John commanded, and Gruenbaum obeyed.

John rose to his feet and backed toward the man on the ground. The man's eyes stared upward unblinking, two growing stains of red centered over his heart and stomach.

"Dammit," John swore, then forced his eyes from the body and motioned to Gruenbaum, an edge of panic to his voice. "Get in the car. Through the passenger side door."

"You shot him. . . ."

"Now!"

"Can I get the key out of my pocket?"

"Hurry." John tensed for any sudden moves, but

none came. Gruenbaum unlocked the door and opened it.

"Now slide in to the driver's side," John commanded. "I want to see your hands at all times. Put them on the steering wheel. If you reach for anything, make any sudden moves, I shoot to kill."

Gruenbaum did as told.

A wave of nausea hit John as he settled into the passenger's seat. His breathing came hard. He reached under his coat and winced as he touched the perimeter of the exit wound. Blood had already soaked a large section of his shirt, and his fingertips came back crimson.

"We've got to call an ambulance," Gruenbaum said. "That man is going to die without help."

"He's dead already." The simple statement concealed John's actual thoughts: what type of game did he play that called for him to kill a man—maybe an innocent man?

"And you?" Gruenbaum said. "You're badly hurt. You'll bleed to death without attention."

John realized Gruenbaum could be right; the bullet had exited just below his collarbone to the side of his left shoulder joint, and the wound bled like a son-of-a-bitch. John had no experience with gunshot wounds, and for all he knew without medical treatment the bleeding would continue. It didn't matter; he had to save his plan, improvising as necessary—he had gone too far to turn back. If he called an ambulance now, his life was just as surely over.

"Start the car and drive," John ordered.

"To where?"

"Start the car and get us out of this garage. *Now!* I'll tell you where to go."

"And if I refuse? I don't think you're prepared to shoot me."

"Tell that to your friend on the ground. I've got nothing to lose now. You have. *Now go!*"

Gruenbaum started the car and eased it from its parking spot, clearing the sprawled body on the garage floor by a few feet. At the garage's exit John buried the silencer-tipped gun barrel in Gruenbaum's side as Gruenbaum inserted an electronic access card that raised the exit's gate. Then they were out.

John directed Gruenbaum to make a left on the street. A few more streets and they merged onto the expressway headed south. Anther twenty minutes and they would exit the expressway only a short distance from the wooded area John had found that morning.

John gently touched his wound. He knew he should put pressure on it to reduce the blood flow, but found it impossible—his right arm trained the gun on Gruenbaum, and his left, although it had limited mobility, was too weak for the task. He had to hope the wound would clot on its own.

Gruenbaum spoke again. "Before I drive any farther, I insist on knowing what you want. Do you plan on killing me?"

"No. If I wanted to kill you, you'd already be dead. I want to strike a bargain, and I want money, a lot of it. I hadn't counted on this." John pointed to his shoulder wound.

"Who are you?"

"You'll find out soon enough. My turn to ask a question. Who was that man back there? The man I shot?" John asked.

"A bodyguard."

"Police?"

"No, private. Where are we going?"

"A place where we can talk and not be disturbed. It won't be long now. Keep driving."

Blood pounded at John's temples, adrenaline coursed his veins, but his mind stayed clear and sharp.

He closed his eyes momentarily to clear the pain, then opened them to catch Gruenbaum eyeing him slyly, as if waiting for an opportunity to pounce. In that moment John hit upon a strategy. Maybe, just maybe, he could still salvage the situation.

They passed a sign for the exit—four miles, not long now. Off the expressway, John followed the markers he had memorized. The street signs, the train crossing, the farmhouse, and there, up ahead, the woods he had scouted.

"Slow down," John said. "On the left, see the logging road? Pull into it."

Gruenbaum did. John directed him forward until they had traveled a few hundred yards into the woods, then John ordered him out of the car.

"What now?" Gruenbaum asked as the two men stood next to the car, facing each other.

"Roll up your shirtsleeve."

"What?" Gruenbaum's face showed surprise.

"*Roll up* your shirtsleeve."

"Why?"

"Because I've asked you to, and I'm holding the gun. Do it."

Gruenbaum removed his overcoat and suit coat and placed them on the car's hood. He took off a gold cufflink, slipped it in his breast pocket, then slowly rolled up the right sleeve of his shirt. John's eyes focused on Gruenbaum's forearm. It had to be here, or he could add charges of murder and kidnapping to the list of felonies he was wanted for.

Steve's words about Rolf's bogus Social Security number came back to him: "Whoever Rolf really is, in the eyes of the government he's Yevgeni Malinovsky, the little kid who died thirty-four years ago; a nine-digit number was his passport to another identity." In this case it would be only six.

Gruenbaum rolled the sleeve up above his elbow

and stopped. Nothing. The blood drained from John's face. *Mistaken? About everything?* Then, with relief, he recalled—the left forearm.

"Roll up the other one."

Gruenbaum paused before obeying, regarding John through narrowed eyes. Finally, he slowly turned up his left shirtsleeve until, on the upper forearm, John saw what he looked for. A brown tattoo, six small numbers: 176134. John knew the sequence by heart.

"Who are you?" Gruenbaum asked.

"Walk down the logging road. I'll tell you when to stop."

A hundred yards later John directed Gruenbaum off the road and into the woods.

"Sit down. Against the tree." John pointed to a tree behind Gruenbaum.

Gruenbaum sat in fallen leaves, which crackled under his weight. John followed suit, leaning against a tree a few feet from Gruenbaum and sliding to a sitting position.

Gruenbaum repeated his question, a trace of fear in his voice. "Who are you?"

"By now I thought you would have guessed." John studied Gruenbaum's face, searching for recognition. "But you haven't, have you? That's how insignificant I was to you. Maybe you'll recognize this." John reached into his breast pocket with his left hand, ignoring the pain radiating from his shoulder, pulled out Michael's shield and threw it in Gruenbaum's lap. "I've been carrying it around for a couple of months now. It was my brother's."

Gruenbaum looked at the badge, then his eyes rose slowly to John's.

"I think you're starting to get the picture. My name is John Sarikov; I had a brother named Michael. Ring a bell?"

Gruenbaum said nothing, but his eyes held the answer.

"But you can't answer, can you? Not without admitting guilt, but you *do* know me. Maybe not my face, but the name. I think you knew my brother too. I think you killed him."

"I don't know what you're talking about."

"You're lying."

"What do you want from me?"

"I told you, money, lots of it."

"For what?"

"My silence. But be patient, we'll get to that. I've planned this all out—everything I'm going to say. Word for word. To tell you the truth, half of me wants to pull the trigger right now and forget the money. If you interrupt again, I might."

Gruenbaum's face turned red, but he remained silent.

John pulled the photograph of Jacob Greene from his coat pocket and threw it in Gruenbaum's direction. "I want you to look at that."

Gruenbaum picked it up. "I'm looking."

"Recognize the man?"

"No."

"He's a concentration camp survivor . . . interned at Auschwitz. Sure you don't recognize him?"

"I'm sure."

John searched Gruenbaum's face unsuccessfully for a twitch, perspiration, averted eyes, anything that betrayed guilt—the man lied well. "You were interned at Auschwitz also, weren't you?"

"Yes."

"When?"

". . . Late 1944 . . . into 1945."

"Odd coincidence—same with the man in the photograph. Sure you don't recognize him?"

"From over fifty years ago, among tens of thousands of prisoners?"

"Hundreds of thousands. It would have been a logistical nightmare for the orderly Germans, I guess, if they hadn't come up with a typically efficient, albeit inhuman, means of keeping track of them all. Every Auschwitz prisoner received a tattoo on the forearm—a registration number, each unique. Isn't that right?"

Gruenbaum answered hesitantly. "Yes."

"That's why I thought it odd you didn't know the prisoner in the photograph. The two of you have something in common."

"What's that?"

"You didn't look at the photo closely. Look again . . . look at the prisoner's arm."

Gruenbaum looked confused for a moment, then the color drained from his face.

"That's right. There's a tattoo on his left forearm. Take a good look at the number branded there—you can make it out—same number as on your forearm. Curious you both should have the same tattoo, and the Germans being so organized about things and all. How do you think it could have happened?"

"I . . . don't know . . . a mistake, perhaps."

"Perhaps. Maybe you would recognize the name he went by. Jacob Greene."

"No."

"No? 'J-G,' same initials as you, did you notice? Jacob, Jacek, pretty close. The last name's not all that different either. Take Gruenbaum, cut off the suffix, Americanize it, and what have you got?"

Gruenbaum sat mute.

"How about a hint? I'll give you the benefit of my high school German. 'Gruen' translated into English is 'green.' . . . Still no guesses, huh? Or aren't we in the mood for games?"

Gruenbaum's breathing turned heavy.

"Then let me give you the answer. Jacob Greene was once named Jacek Gruenbaum. Talk about coincidences. How about another name? Peter Olgov. Recognize it?"

"No."

"You're lying again. Not nice. You know who Peter Olgov was, who Jacob Greene was, who my brother was. You also know a Detective Steve Mayer, a Rabbi Sosman, an old lady named Mrs. Banovich, and a dishwasher from the Ukrainian Café. You had them all killed."

"You're crazy. Understand? Crazy. I don't know what you're talking about."

"You don't? Then let me explain." John spoke boldly, masking his alarm at his blood-soaked shirt. The pain he could bear, the dizziness had passed, but how much blood could a person lose before they lost consciousness? "I just put the puzzle together, so forgive me if my rendition isn't polished. I think this is a story that goes back fifty years. To the Second World War. I've been reading up on it lately. Interesting. Makes me think I should have paid more attention during school. Do you know many historians think the Soviet Union was the clear winner of World War II?"

Gruenbaum glared.

John continued. "Perhaps you did; I didn't. But the logic's compelling—think of what the Soviets had gained by the end of the war: East Germany, Poland, the Baltic states, Czechoslovakia, Hungary, the Balkans. The West had gone to war to keep those countries free from fascist control, but in peace they abandoned them to communism on a silver platter. And that's not all. While we longed for peace, Stalin positioned the Soviet Union to fight the cold war. And you know, I've a hunch he recognized early on the importance espionage would play in that war." John paused, drawing a comment from Gruenbaum.

"What does any of this have to do with me?"

"I'm coming to that. Another thing I didn't know: the Red Army liberated most of the concentration camps of Eastern Europe. Here's my guess: Stalin recognized a golden opportunity—a made-to-order means of planting an agent in the U.S. Look at the facts. The Red Army controlled the camps and the prisoners; they controlled the documentation left behind by the Nazis; they were in charge of shipping the survivors to deportation camps for relocation to the West. What if a Soviet agent was substituted for one of the prisoners?"

John watched Gruenbaum's eyebrows twitch as the last question struck home.

"What if a Jewish prisoner were selected, one who had not been in camp very long, whose family had been eliminated by the Nazis. Then a willing and loyal Soviet soldier is found. He befriends the prisoner, exhaustively explores and records the prisoner's past under guise of this friendship. He takes the prisoner's name, memorizes the prisoner's past, even"—John paused and pointed with the pistol's barrel at Gruenbaum's tattoo—"gets the same tattoo on his forearm. The Soviet soldier takes the Jew's place and is sent west to a deportation camp. The Jewish prisoner's fate: execution. Taken to the woods to be unceremoniously shot. Less than a year later the Soviet agent finds himself in the United States. So simple. Who would ever suspect him, he who had supposedly endured so much, sacrificed so much, of being a KGB mole? Instant credibility and stature. A brilliant plan but for one slip—the prisoner isn't shot. He arranges to bribe the soldier charged with carrying out his execution. He is released and emigrates to America. *Two* Jacek Gruenbaums in *one* country. Quite a potential embarrassment to the impostor, don't you think?"

John stopped, his silence again prompting a response from Gruenbaum.

"You dare suggest—"

"I do."

"Madness. Check your facts. . . ."

"Then let me. How did you leave Auschwitz?"

"I was shipped by train to a deportation camp in Italy."

John nodded. "Ever see this man?" From his pocket he pulled the black-and-white photograph of the young man he had taken from the *Herald*'s files. He tried to look confident as he held it up to view, hoping a living witness, even a fictitious one, might rattle Gruenbaum.

"I don't . . . remember him. No, I don't think so."

"It's a picture from the late forties, a long time ago. Are you sure?"

Gruenbaum didn't bother looking back at the photograph. "I don't remember the man."

"Strange, he remembers you clearly. Or I should say he remembers Jacek Gruenbaum clearly. He's Polish. Today he lives in . . . but no, perhaps it would be foolish of me to tell you where he lives . . . you might wish to pay him a visit. In 1945 he delivered five hundred American dollars to a Peter Olgov, a Russian soldier who served in the Soviet 60th Army, the unit that liberated Auschwitz. It was a payoff, for Olgov's release of an Auschwitz prisoner named Jacek Gruenbaum. Funny, though, when I showed him your photo, he didn't recognize it at all. Said you were too heavy-set, a whole different face from the Jacek Gruenbaum he remembered. Then I showed him another photo of an Auschwitz prisoner, the one you're holding. That, he said, was Jacek Gruenbaum. He sounded quite certain. Why do you think that was?"

"You are crazy," Gruenbaum said as he removed his glasses and wiped his forehead with his hand. "An old man is confused after fifty years, and now what, I'm a spy?"

"Old people can become confused, I suppose, though this man seemed quite sharp to me. He says Jacek Gruenbaum escaped from Auschwitz; you say you were sent by rail to Italy. He says you don't look anything like Jacek Gruenbaum, but positively identifies the man in the photograph, who happens to have a tattoo identical to yours. Who, I wonder, is confused?"

Violence showed in Gruenbaum's eyes. "Nothing but lies."

"Are these lies too? Turn over the photo of the prisoner. You see what's written there? A name: Jacob Greene, one of the men you don't remember. I have witnesses who can testify the photo is of Jacob Greene. Jacob Greene, the real Jacek Gruenbaum. I've already mentioned the similarities in the name. Greene altered it just enough to put anyone trying to track him down off the scent. My brother, the cop, found that photo and a number of others from Auschwitz while investigating the murder of Peter Olgov. A day after he found the photos, my brother and Jacob Green were killed. The photos disappeared, all but this one and the one of the Pole, that is."

"This is absurd."

"Is it? I think during Peter Olgov's time at Auschwitz he determined you were KGB and pieced together your plan. Then I think he took pictures of the real Jacek Gruenbaum and the Pole, thinking they might be useful someday. What happened then, I can't be sure . . . he happened upon a newspaper article about you, perhaps. A penniless failure himself, he discovered you were rich and successful. But you also had a secret, one he hoped you would pay to keep buried. He tracked down the real Jacek Gruenbaum, now going by the name of Jacob Greene, then he blackmailed you. Poor Peter Olgov didn't know what a ruthless man he dealt with. You had him killed."

John paused. Gruenbaum said nothing.

"But you screwed up, didn't you? You didn't recover the blackmail evidence," John waved the photograph in his hand. "But my brother did. And he unwittingly led you to Greene. It took me a long time to figure it out, put the pieces together, but I have it now. That's why you killed Olgov, Greene, Mayer, and my brother. How things change . . . now I'm in a position to kill *you*."

"You can't kill me, because that evidence is nothing, *nothing*! I've never heard of your brother, the other people you mentioned or this *real* Gruenbaum."

"You're lying, but you're right about one thing. I want to kill you, but that would be . . . impractical. It wouldn't bring my brother back."

"Then why bring me here? Why not go to the police with your fairy tale?"

"I've tried that, remember? I was almost killed."

"I don't know what you're talking about."

"I'm talking about options—I don't have many of them. I go to the police, and I'm betting you'd make another attempt on my life. Even if you failed, there's no guarantee the police would buy my story. I'm a fugitive, remember, and I find the prospect of a long jail term unappealing. On the other hand, if I stay on the run, with no money and the cops and your people chasing me, I'm not going to last long. I could force a confession out of you, but it wouldn't hold up in court. I considered killing you, but I'd still be hunted by the police, maybe by your organization as well. I see only one way out: a deal between you and me."

Gruenbaum looked puzzled. "A deal? For what?"

"I keep quiet about everything I've learned; you give me money, a *lot* of money, enough to leave the country and live comfortably for the rest of my life.

You killed my brother, you've ruined my life, now I expect to be compensated; I know you can afford it."

"Why should I pay you to keep your lies quiet?"

"I will not play games, Mr. Gruenbaum. If you will not pay, first I'll visit my friends in the press, then I'll go to the police. Forgive me if I leave you here. I'll need your car." John held out his hand for the keys.

Gruenbaum didn't move. "You said yourself they won't believe you," he said.

"No, what I said is they *might not* believe me. Then again, they might—I do have evidence; I do have a witness. I'll have to roll the dice—I can't run without money. One way or the other, my story's bound to cast plenty of attention your way. I'm guessing there may be others who won't be happy with you for that development. Can you take the chance, Mr. Gruenbaum?"

"You're forgetting my bodyguard. You'll face murder charges."

"I'm already facing murder charges. Besides, he fired on me first, from the rear. I've got the wound to prove it." The statement drew John's attention back to his shoulder—the bleeding had subsided, the pain hadn't. . . . It's your decision."

"Your threats don't worry me."

"Then you are very brave, or very stupid." John held out his hand again, and again Gruenbaum left it empty.

Gruenbaum pointed at John's wound. "You'd never make it back to the city."

John wondered if Gruenbaum might be right. His mind was still clear, but he wondered for how much longer. He had to move his plan along, before it was too late. "I'd make it."

Gruenbaum frowned. "This talk of revenging your brother . . . all lies. You're nothing but a common blackmailer, aren't you?"

"I recognize the reality of my situation. Do you?"

Gruenbaum's visage turned shrewd and, after a moment, he spoke. "I do have access to limited sources of capital. Some arrangement could be made . . . if only to save myself the embarrassment your lies might bring."

"I don't care why I am paid, only that I am paid, but there will not be *some* arrangement; there will be *my* arrangement, without debate. Five million dollars wire transferred to the bank of my choosing in the Caribbean."

"That is an awful lot of money. I don't think . . ."

"Don't waste my time. I said it's not up for debate. You will send it, or I go to the papers and police with all the evidence I have. The photographs, the Polish witness, the background information, the ex-KGB agents who abducted me, everything."

"And if I pay?"

"Simple. I don't."

"And the information?"

John took a long breath. As he spoke, his voice came noticeably slower. "It will remain safe, but out of the public eye. Just before I met you in the parking garage, I put copies of the evidence, and a long letter explaining how it all fit together, in an envelope and posted it to an old journalist friend of mine. Don't bother trying to find him, you never will. But this guy loves a good story, and he's good at digging. As long as I stay alive and check it periodically, my friend is instructed to sit on the information. Anything happens to me, he's to run with the story, make the most of it. My insurance policy. It just might keep me alive."

"How do I know you'll keep your end of the bargain?"

John shrugged. "Honor among thieves?"

"Five million dollars is too much."

John aimed the gun at Gruenbaum's forehead, then

moved the barrel slightly to the right, at the tree trunk. He squeezed the trigger.

Gruenbaum flinched at the dull pop of the silenced gun.

John continued. "If I thought I couldn't deal with you, it would be a toss-up—would I rather see you rot in jail, or would I rather kill you here and now. Right now, I'm leaning toward the latter. How does the old story go . . . we've determined what you are, now we're just talking price."

John paused, his breathing now clearly labored. "Considering what you are, and the funds you have available to you, I've come to the conclusion I'm setting a fair price. In fact, it's my firm price—my last and only offer."

Gruenbaum appraised John. "If I agree, you'll let me go? Just like that, you'll let me go?" he asked.

John slurred his answer between wheezing snatches of breath. "Yeah. Just like that. I leave you instructions where to wire transfer the money . . . I take your car . . . and drive off. Not that . . . I don't trust you, but I'll stay out of sight for . . . three days. By the end of the three days . . . I'll expect the wire transfer."

It was a few moments before John continued. "If the money comes . . . I go live a life of . . . leisure somewhere in South America or the Far East, never . . . to bother you . . . again. If it doesn't, I release . . . everything. I would . . . recommend you be . . . prompt in payment." John slumped forward when he finished, taking quick shallow breaths.

Gruenbaum's eyes narrowed. He watched John's labored breathing for a few seconds before speaking. "You trust me?"

"No . . ." John said, his head falling toward his chest before snapping upright. "But you aren't . . . stupid. What choice do you have?" John's head bobbed downward again before he caught it. "Five . . . million isn't . . . much . . . isn't much. . . ."

"No, I suppose it isn't, not for one's freedom, for one's life." Gruenbaum spoke in a slow, steady cadence, his eyes glued to the stain of blood on John's shirt.

John made a weak and unsuccessful effort to get to his feet. "I have . . . must get to the hospital."

"Of course you do," Gruenbaum said soothingly. "I'll take you there, if you want, just as soon as we've worked out our arrangement. I've got a lot at stake, after all."

John again made an effort to rise with the same result.

Gruenbaum smiled, then rambled on about the money, about his political career, his service to the people, the senators and governors he counted as friends.

John didn't seem to have the power to interrupt, and his eyelids sunk slowly closed. Finally, his head slumped to his chest and stayed there. His arm fell limply to his side; the gun slipped from his fingers.

Gruenbaum moved quickly, his arm swinging out and pushing John to the side as he grabbed for the gun. John moved sluggishly as if coming out of a deep fog as Gruenbaum snatched the gun and stood, pointing the pistol at John.

John's eyes widened as his head rose slowly to meet Gruenbaum's cruel stare.

"You are a stupid amateur, Mr. Sarikov! An amateur who should have stayed out of this from the beginning!"

John shook his head as if to clear it. "Nothing's changed. You know . . . what I have. You cross me . . . you go to jail."

"I couldn't disagree more. Everything's changed. I'm holding the gun."

John let his head fall back against the tree trunk. "Five million is . . . a cheap price . . . to pay."

"I agree. Five million is nothing."

"Then we have a deal?"

"No," Gruenbaum said definitively. "You look shocked, Mr. Sarikov. You're a fool. Even if I paid you the five million, don't you see I'd still have a problem?"

"What . . ."

"Others, Mr. Sarikov. Others. As long as you're alive, as long your evidence is out there, I'm a liability. *You* have evidence implicating *me*; I have evidence implicating two organizations. Names, dates, enough to put people away for a long time. I might trust you not to run to the authorities, but would they? Letting word of your evidence leak, letting you live, either would sign my death warrant."

"Then I was right . . . about everything. You're guilty."

"Right? Yes, I congratulate you. But guilty? Guilty of what? Being a Russian patriot who was willing to do what had to be done for his country? Guilty of self-preservation? Guilty of removing Olgov, a traitor to his people?"

"And my brother . . . Mayer, O'Hern, and Greene, a host of others . . . and trying to kill me."

" 'Guilty' is a concept to control the masses. I don't believe in it. I do what is necessary. Needs and advantages are what determine power—'guilty' is for little people."

"But you killed them?"

"Just as I'm about to kill you, or watch you bleed to death. Now you *will tell me* who you mailed the evidence to."

"I'm not going . . . to tell you a thing. Five million, that's my price. You kill me . . . and you're finished."

"You're wrong. You're going to tell me who has

the evidence, and it's not going to cost me a thing. You want to know why? Because if you don't, I'm going to blow one of your knee-caps off. And if you still don't tell me I'll blow the other one off. Then you'll tell me, unless you're very strong, in which case I'll blow your fingers off below the knuckles, one by one. I have experience in these matters. Believe me, you may think you're in pain now, but you're just scratching the surface. It wouldn't be long before you'll scream everything I want to know. Then you'll beg me to put this gun to the side of your head and pull the trigger to end the awful pain. *Now tell me.*"

John shook his head weakly. "We can work something out . . . I know we can. There's no need . . . for this. We can make a deal."

Gruenbaum laughed. "A deal? For what? I want only one thing—the evidence. You *will* tell me who has it . . . and if you don't, or you die before you can, then I will have to live with that fact. The others? You'll force my hand, I admit, but in the final analysis you're just accelerating the inevitable—I'll take care of the others a bit earlier than I had planned, that's all. The police? Your evidence will sound too fantastic to be believed. You're a wanted man, Sarikov; I'm a respected citizen. All you have are a few coincidences, nothing more. I will suffer some minor embarrassments, but will I go to jail, Mr. Sarikov? I don't think so."

Gruenbaum raised the gun and aimed it at John's kneecap. "Where's the evidence?"

"I can't tell you."

Gruenbaum's mouth turned down at the corners as his finger tightened on the trigger. "Then we will discover the answer the hard way."

The crack of a gunshot and the round hole in Gruenbaum's forehead came at the same instant. Then came a stream of blood, and Gruenbaum tumbled backward.

John sat, stunned for a moment, then reached under

the fallen leaves to his side. His fingers grasped the cold metal of the revolver he had left hidden there hours earlier. He spun to his knees and swung the revolver in the direction of the sound.

"Police. Drop the gun!"

John froze. His heart beat strongly; his mind raced. The police? How? He looked at the hole placed squarely in the middle of Gruenbaum's forehead—whoever was there, he wasn't about to shoot it out with them. He let the gun drop from his fingers.

"Hands up. We won't miss from this range."

John's eyes frantically searched the trees in front of him but could see nothing. He slowly raised his hands. A moment later, he caught movement that defined itself into two men walking toward him. One looked unfamiliar—short, stocky, wearing a waist-length plaid jacket and training a rifle on John. The other, an older man with flowing white hair and intense blue eyes, wearing a white overcoat, John recognized instantly—Grigori.

John toyed with the idea of reaching for the gun he had just dropped, but Grigori and his companion were less than twenty yards away now.

Grigori spoke first. "Mr. Sarikov. We are, as you see, not the police. You know me, of course, and this is Yakov. Yakov, John Sarikov. We had the pleasure of sharing a bottle of vodka once."

As Yakov tipped his head, John fell back to a sitting position against the tree.

"It wasn't all that pleasurable, as I recall," said John.

Grigori kicked the gun lying to John's side out of reach, then shrugged. "It seems you have a penchant for putting yourself in unpleasant situations."

Grigori walked to Gruenbaum's prostrate body and crouched down, examining the bullet wound. The shot appeared to have been perfect—the bullet had entered the middle of the forehead and exited just above and behind the left ear. Grigori felt for a pulse.

"Yakov, you surprise me," Grigori said. "You are usually one hundred percent." He donned a pair of black gloves and searched Gruenbaum's body, removing his wallet and car keys. He pulled the gun with the silencer out of Gruenbaum's hand, then stood and spoke, looking down at the body.

"His given name was Vasili. I knew him long ago when we were both young and naive. I considered him a brave man once. I condemn him for what he became, but will remember him for what he was."

Grigori pointed the gun at the back of Gruenbaum's head and pulled the trigger. There was a click. He pulled the trigger again. Another click. Then another.

Grigori popped the clip from the gun. He looked to John, his mouth gaped open. "Empty. But I *saw* you fire into the tree. Why would you fire your last bullet—" He stopped, then looked again at the clip before searching John's eyes. "You had an extra gun hidden by your side. Convenient."

John said nothing.

Grigori motioned to Yakov, who shot Gruenbaum once in the back of the head with his rifle. John cringed involuntarily.

"Have I underestimated you, Mr. Sarikov?" Grigori asked.

John remained mute.

Grigori's eyes narrowed. "I have, haven't I?" He bent down and patted John's chest carefully, avoiding the gunshot's exit wound. He felt something, what he knew would be there.

He smiled. "My compliments, Mr. Sarikov. Brilliant. You wanted more evidence, needed a confession, and found a way to get it. Let me see if I've got this right: you empty the gun into a tree by Vasili's . . . Gruenbaum's . . . side, then exaggerate the effects of your shoulder wound—wheezing, halting speech—and finally pretend to lapse into unconsciousness. The gun falls from your hand; Gruenbaum picks it up. You know it's empty, and another gun is hidden by your side; he doesn't. He thinks he's in control and admits his guilt."

Grigori nodded appreciatively. "I commend you on your plan, although I wonder how you would have allowed the empty gun to be taken from you if you hadn't been wounded. No matter, you improvised well—even I was convinced you were three-quarters dead."

Grigori undid the buttons on John's shirt and carefully peeled back the coat and then the blood-soaked material of the shirt, revealing the Dictaphone strapped to John's chest.

"I'm afraid we can't let you keep this." Grigori pushed the stop button, then popped the cassette tape from the Dictaphone and put it in his pocket.

John swore to himself.

Grigori pointed to John's wound. "May I?" Grigori asked, but didn't wait for an answer. He peeled John's shirt farther back. John winced as Grigori probed the wound's perimeter. "Not too bad. The bullet passed cleanly through. I myself have been shot three times. My shoulder tells me when the rains are coming . . . perhaps yours will do the same."

Grigori took a handkerchief from his pocket, folded it neatly, and held it against John's wound. "Hold this tightly. It seems you will live."

"Perhaps," Yakov corrected.

Grigori nodded. "You have made things difficult for us, Mr. Sarikov. We were hoping you would take care of our embarrassment for us." Grigori gestured toward Gruenbaum's body. "That didn't happen. Unfortunate. Then our second disappointment." Grigori pointed toward what looked like a long microphone that hung from Yakov's belt. "We were able to listen to a good portion of your conversation. You've uncovered more than we thought possible. Worse, you've mailed the evidence you've collected to another party—that creates a problem."

Of course it did, John realized. They couldn't kill him, couldn't afford to let Gruenbaum kill him, until they recovered it. Anything that incriminated Gruenbaum had the potential to incriminate Gruenbaum's associates. Still some bargaining power, just no tricks left.

Yakov interjected. "If you wish to live, you *will* tell us who you mailed it to."

John pointed at Gruenbaum. "I've seen how you deal with potential embarrassments. Why would I tell you anything?"

Yakov picked up a fallen tree branch and broke it in half. He held its jagged end a half foot from John's wound. "Why, Mr. Sarikov?" he asked, then jabbed the stick forward.

John doubled over; an animal groan escaped from his clenched teeth.

"Now that you have your answer, let me try again," Yakov said. "Who did you mail the evidence to?"

John didn't reply, and the stick jabbed forward again. Then again. John soon lost count.

"I ask you again," Yakov said finally.

When he regained his breath, John spat out a response. "I'll die before I tell you anything. On my brother's grave, I'll die first."

Yakov's face hardened. "Then you will die."

Yakov thrust the stick forward, but Grigori interceded, grabbing his arm before it struck. Yakov's eyes flared.

"We must talk, comrade," Grigori said and pulled Yakov with him away from John.

John caught snatches of their heated conversation before his mind turned inward, and their voices gave way to the pounding of blood in his ears. He looked to the sky and saw a bird cut swiftly through the bands of gray clouds above the tree branches. He shut his eyes then, longing for a final sleep to liberate him from pain. Instead, his eyes snapped open at a loud, angry voice.

Yakov glared at Grigori. "It is on *your* head. I take no responsibility."

"I will accept full responsibility. It *can* be done, comrade."

"But the risks . . ."

"I know this man," Grigori responded. "He *will* die before he talks."

"But if he's alive—"

"And if he's dead? You heard him—he has mailed his evidence to a journalist. What will killing him have accomplished if that evidence comes to light? Won't his death only lend credence to his story? On the other hand, we have an opportunity to silence *all* questions, to wrap up *all* loose ends. We *will* take it. I speak for the Collegium."

"And you, *comrade,* will have to answer to them."

Grigori took the rifle from Yakov's hands. He popped out the clip, removed the bullet from the chamber, then wiped its exterior clean with a handkerchief. He did the same to the handgun with the silencer that lay next to Gruenbaum.

Grigori stood over John. "We have made arrangements to explain Gruenbaum's disappearance. If you would agree to cooperate with us on certain matters, it would be possible, with minimal effort, to alter those plans to our mutual advantage. In such a case, I could offer you your life."

Grigori held out the rifle. "Are you interested?" he asked.

John looked him in the eye and nodded. What other answer was there?

"Good." Grigori dropped the rifle, and it fell into John's hands.

54

John watched Yakov speed from the fourth level of the parking garage in disbelief. He was alive. And free. He tottered down the garage's stairs toward street level, wondering how much blood he'd lost, and how much more he could afford to lose.

His breathing came in shallow gasps, and a warmth spread through his body masking the pain of his shoulder. He fought a desire to sink to the ground and let the warmth envelop him—now was not the time to give up.

He stumbled out onto the dark street. No sign of Yakov, no sign of Grigori. No tricks.

John staggered toward a tall, gaunt-faced man in blue jeans and flannel shirt passing on the sidewalk.

"Yup?" the man said, then noticed the red stains on John's shirt and whispered, "Oh my God."

John stood still for a moment, not sure what to say, then his eyes rolled up into his head and everything went black.

55

When the minister finished the prayer, John raised his head and looked again at his brother's gravestone. To his left a line of seven police officers in dark blue dress uniforms raised their rifles, prepared to fire the first of three volleys into the air. To his right stood Kelly, and to her right Steve's wife, Nancy. A small group of friends and relatives stood behind them. Ranking officers of the police force, including Police Commissioner DeLuca, huddled together farther back near a ring of reporters from the New York papers and the Associated Press.

John flinched as the first rifle volley ripped the air. The second two came in quick succession, each report echoing once loudly, leaving thin ribbons of smoke curling from the rifle barrels.

Kelly squeezed John's hand and looked up into his face. Her eyes held no tears. Her mourning was far from over, John knew, but today's ceremony was to honor Michael—his vindication—and whether he was some place where he knew or not didn't matter. John and Kelly owed him in memory all that they had owed him in life.

John had demanded the ceremony and the department had not resisted—a burial with honor was the entitlement of every cop who died in the line of duty, and Michael had, no one questioned that any longer. John felt good for Kelly's sake, but felt only minor satisfaction himself. He did not feel whole yet, and was not sure he ever could again.

One by one, starting with Kelly, the attendees approached Michael's grave and set a single yellow rose on the grass. John then steered Kelly and Nancy toward the parking lot, Kelly's parents and their friends following in a long, slow line.

Commissioner DeLuca intersected their path and, with news photographers poised, held out his hand to John, who stopped and looked the commissioner in the eye. John swore he saw compassion there, but knew better. An upcoming mayoral election and sinking approval ratings concerned DeLuca, nothing more. John's story had made headline news, and DeLuca's involvement severely embarrassed the city's administration; the press hinted the mayor would dump him within weeks if he didn't resign first. DeLuca knew a handshake with John pictured prominently in the papers would lessen the political fallout.

Without comment John ignored DeLuca's outstretched arm and escorted Kelly and Nancy toward a waiting limousine. He wasn't in a forgiving mood.

The battery of news photographers recorded the snub and the unfaltering blend of anger and humiliation fixed on DeLuca's face.

John walked with his right arm around Kelly, his left arm in a sling. It was a clean wound, the doctors said. The bullet missed his lungs and shoulder joint, causing only muscular damage. With a few months of physical therapy, they assured him, the shoulder would be as good as new. His blackened eyes and cheeks, and the bruises along his fractured ribs, were still noticeable, but becoming less so every day. Externally, he was healing fine.

When they reached the limousine, John gave Nancy a last hug and turned to Kelly.

"Thank you," she said simply.

No reply seemed necessary to John, and after a moment's pause Kelly continued. "This helps me . . . let's me . . . begin to move on. I hope it does the same for you."

John said nothing.

Kelly turned to enter the limousine, thought better of it, and faced John again. "I've talked to Barbara. She wanted to be here today, but felt, without an invitation . . . Why don't you call her, John?"

John nodded unconvincingly. How could he? What right did he have to cause her more pain. Things hadn't changed.

Kelly's half smile mirrored dear and tragic memories. She reached out to give John a last hug. "Like your brother. Too strong for your own good. There's nothing more you can do for him, John. *Nothing* more. Let it go and get back to your own life."

John watched the limousine and then car after car depart the cemetery until he stood alone in the parking lot. Kelly was wrong—he could do one more thing for Michael. He took a last fleeting glance in the direction of Michael's grave, then checked his watch. It was getting late and he had a long drive ahead of him.

56

Heading south on the New Jersey Turnpike, John's mind drifted to the recent past. He remembered Grigori's words. "Tell the truth, just leave out those things we might find embarrassing." John had. He spat out answers, details, facts, lies, just as rehearsed. And the police swallowed them all, as Grigori said they would.

Four times the police had him go through his story, and each time John had followed the script, played the charade perfectly, trusting Grigori to keep his end of the bargain.

No one had believed him that first day—John, after all, was a wanted man, Gruenbaum a respected citizen.

The first major bit of evidence supporting his story turned up the second day. The police, unable to locate Gruenbaum, had issued an APB, half expecting Gruenbaum's body to turn up as a result. Instead, a flight entry from Kennedy Airport came to light. According to American Airlines' records, Jacek Gruenbaum boarded a jet bound for Colombia less than five hours after John collapsed on the Albany street. Ticketing agents and passengers confirmed Gruenbaum's description.

By the end of a week the flow of evidence became overwhelming—the police found everything Grigori promised.

With Gruenbaum's whereabouts unknown, the police searched Gruenbaum's residence. They made their first discovery in a laundry basket in the basement: wrapped in a towel, a .45 caliber handgun affixed with a silencer. Next, hidden in the closet of Gruenbaum's study, they found a wooden box of photographs matching John's description of Olgov's missing box. From Gruenbaum's safe, they removed for review a thick stack of documents; the detective in charge scanned them quickly and noticed the name Best Import Company, the warehouse where John said he had been held captive, scattered throughout.

An overnight examination of the evidence taken from Gruenbaum's lent further credence to John's story. The .45 bore Gruenbaum's prints. The wooden box had a false bottom under which the crime lab detected trace amounts of high-grade uncut heroin. The documents taken from Gruenbaum's safe revealed two things: Gruenbaum, through shell corporations and nominees, owned Best Import Company; and Gruenbaum had been laundering huge sums of money, close to $5 million a month for the last half year, through a Cayman Islands corporation, Carson Moffit, Ltd.

The police returned to Gruenbaum's residence the following day to continue the search. From the trunk of his car, they collected hair and fabric samples which the crime lab matched to Michael and Ray. They also searched the Albany parking garage and pried from a wall on its fourth level a .45 caliber slug—in all probability the same slug that passed through John's shoulder, the crime lab said. Ballistics matched the slug to the .45 found at Gruenbaum's.

At that point the police issued an arrest warrant for Jacek Gruenbaum.

Two agents from the Federal Drug Enforcement Agency then flew to the Cayman Islands to investigate Carson Moffit, Ltd. A stream of payments from Carson Moffit, Ltd. to a Cayman Islands bank led them to an assistant account representative who admitted to falsifying accounts in Michael's, Ray's, and John's names.

Last came the details. Forensics experts determined the shape and length of Rolf's stiletto blade was consistent in all respects with the knife wounds inflicted upon Michael and Ray. The desk clerk of Olgov's rooming house admitted to alerting someone he knew only as Rolf of Michael's and John's investigations. A similar admission came from the owner of the Ukrainian Café. After the police examined Gruenbaum's phone logs and discovered a string of calls to Commissioner DeLuca, DeLuca admitted to unwittingly feeding Gruenbaum sensitive information on the Sarikov investigation, including the 42nd Street rendezvous.

Everything fit snugly. The truth of John's story became inescapable, and the conclusions reached by the police were what Grigori had predicted, as a front-page summary of the story—Walt Donaldson got the byline—in the *New York Herald* proved:

Lobbyist Linked to Murder and Drugs in Odyssey Involving Police Commissioner

Jacek L. Gruenbaum, an Albany-based lobbyist and top power broker in New York State politics, is being sought today by local and federal authorities on murder and drug-related charges.

Law enforcement officials have uncovered evidence indicating that, over the last year, Gruenbaum orchestrated the import of over fifty million dollars worth of cocaine and heroin, and ordered the execution of three New York City police officers who threatened to uncover his growing drug empire.

The unlikely string of events culminating in the arrest warrant for Gruenbaum began with the murder of Peter Olgov, a small-time drug courier who is believed to have been skimming drugs from Gruenbaum. Gruenbaum allegedly ordered the execution of Officers Michael Sarikov and Raymond O'Hern after the two, while investigating the murder of Olgov, discovered evidence linking Gruenbaum to the crime. Based on evidence allegedly planted under Gruenbaum's orders, the Police Department erroneously concluded the two officers were corrupt and had been killed in a drug payoff gone violent. There the story would have ended if not for the efforts of Officer Sarikov's brother, John.

John Sarikov, a free-lance newspaper writer, undertook an incredible investigatory odyssey, surviving repeated attempts on his life to vindicate his brother and topple Gruenbaum, and perhaps New York City Police Commissioner Richard DeLuca as well.

Police Commissioner DeLuca, who has called a press conference for next Thursday at which some political analysts expect he will announce his resignation, has admitted to unwittingly apprising Gruenbaum of John Sarikov's investigations, facilitating both an attempt on Sarikov's life and the murder of Detective Steve Mayer, who aided John Sarikov in his investigations.

Gruenbaum's current whereabouts are unknown, although he reportedly fled the country for Columbia after an attempt on John Sarikov's life. John Sarikov was recently released from a hospital in Albany, where doctors treated him for a gunshot wound to the shoulder.

Political leaders from both parties have expressed shock at the allegations surrounding Gruenbaum and DeLuca. (*Continued on page 6*)

The story went on to track John's investigations: his review of Michael's police log and the resulting interview with Mrs. Banovich; his theory that Michael had discovered incriminating evidence under the false bottom to Olgov's box of photos; his interview of Bersch at the Ukrainian Café; his abduction and torture at the hands of Rolf; his tracing of the redial number with Walt's help; his confrontation with Gruenbaum, which left him wounded on the floor of the parking garage and led to Gruenbaum's flight. It made great copy.

The lie became fact. Frightening, John thought, that Grigori carried out the deception with such ease.

The body of Gruenbaum's bodyguard had been disposed of immediately after John and Gruenbaum left the parking garage. The .45 he had used to shoot John had been wiped clean, and later pressed to Gruenbaum's fingers. Keeping hair and clothing samples from the earlier killings, Grigori had explained, was standard procedure—Yakov had only to sprinkle them in the Mercedes's trunk after planting the .45 in Gruenbaum's basement, the documents in Gruenbaum's safe, and Olgov's box, plus the heroin traces, in Gruenbaum's study.

The documents planted in the safe were genuine—Gruenbaum, Grigori had told John, *had* smuggled drugs and laundered money. Yakov simply placed evidence of Gruenbaum's activities where the police would find it.

The assistant account representative of the Cayman Islands bank was guilty of exactly what he confessed to, as were DeLuca, the desk clerk, and the owner of the Ukrainian Café. The ballistics and forensic records—again real. John's story to the police and the papers—95 percent accurate. That was the key to a successful deception, Grigori had told John: you mixed plenty of truth with just enough lies to distort conclusions.

Jacek Gruenbaum, of course, never caught a plane for Colombia. Grigori and Yakov had probably dumped him much closer to home, in a landfill, under the foundation of a building, or at the bottom of some large body of water. As for the man who looked very similar to Jacek Gruenbaum and used Gruenbaum's passport to fly to Colombia, John assumed Grigori had paid him a handsome sum of money and helped him to disappear.

The police attributed Mrs. Banovich's death and

Bersch's disappearance to Rolf. As for Jacob Greene and Rabbi Sosman, John never mentioned their names and the police never connected them to Gruenbaum. John never heard from Dr. Davis. Isaac Lieberman called, asking about the concentration camp pictures, and John broke the bad news: the photos had been destroyed by someone totally unaware of their value. An anonymous donation to Yad Vashem somewhat assuaged John's feelings of guilt.

Steve, Hartley, and Kelly were the only ones, besides him, who had known bits of the truth. Steve was dead. Hartley, transferred to the parking division for his mishandling of Michael and Ray's murder investigation, had never believed John's stories to begin with. And Kelly? John convinced her his theories involving Greene and Auschwitz were crazy hypotheses that never panned out.

While John now knew the whole truth, Grigori had made his situation quite clear. "Let me tell you what will happen if you double-cross us," he had said. "First, the police will receive an anonymous phone call telling them where to find Gruenbaum, Gruenbaum's bodyguard, and a rifle and handgun. Ballistics will show the rifle fired the bullet that killed Gruenbaum, and the handgun fired the bullet that killed Gruenbaum's bodyguard. Each gun will bear your fingerprints. The police will also receive segments of the tape you recorded. After editing, only your threats on Gruenbaum's life will remain. Then your body will be found. You'll have committed 'suicide.' A few years after that, your sister-in-law, your girlfriend, will have fatal accidents. To summarize: if you tell the story as I've devised it, you go free, vengeance against Gruenbaum in hand, and your brother is vindicated. If, on the other hand, you tell the truth, you won't be believed, you, your sister-in-law, and your girlfriend, will all suffer terribly, and your brother's epitaph will remain: 'crooked cop.' I trust you'll make the right decision."

Grigori had built a neat box. KGB spies, grand conspiracies, and Auschwitz prisoners, versus fingerprints on murder weapons and very real threats.

John let his mind drift from the past back to the future. Grigori's plan had worked almost to perfection. It had only one major flaw—John had no intention of fulfilling his end of the bargain.

57

With the pair of binoculars John could clearly make out the well-kept white colonial. A picket fence encircled the manicured lot, and an American flag fluttered beside the front door. *Americana; Norman Rockwell; one more charade.*

A lean gray-haired woman, dressed in a daisy print blouse, worked in a garden in the front yard. He swept past her, not wanting to put a human face on this family.

John put down the binoculars and lit a cigarette—he could wait. Tucked in a stand of trees and bushes in a park across the street, he stood maybe three hundred yards from the house over a broad lawn.

Finding the house hadn't been difficult. Grigori had told John he owned an import-export business with his two sons—not much to work with, but it proved enough. After John's story hit the paper, no shortage of police officers felt they owed John a favor, and with little difficulty he gained access to Best Import Company's files. He made a list of every import-export business the company had dealt with, and began calling them. From then on it was just a matter of leg work, as every good reporter knew.

John used the same cover each time: a Polish leather goods manufacturer interested in marketing his wares in the United States. Then the setup. "I may have met your owner a few years back at a convention. Long white hair swept back from his forehead, blue eyes? I think his two sons work with him?"

Two-thirds of the way down the list, after three hours of calls, John received the answer he looked for.

"Yes, sir, that sounds like Mr. Rostov," the receptionist said.

"Rostov . . . Rostov . . . I can't say the name sounds familiar," John had replied.

"Sandford Rostov?"

"Hmm. No, I don't think so. I remember a short man, only about five-seven."

"No, I'm sorry. Mr. Rostov is quite a bit taller. At least six foot one."

A phone book and map had led John to the home of Sandford Rostov, the owner of Georgia Trading Co., in a well-to-do suburb of Atlanta. He lived in the white colonial across the park from where John now sat.

Two cigarettes later, the door to the colonial opened. An Irish setter rushed out, speeding into the lawn and into the arms of the old woman.

A man followed the dog.

John stiffened. He recognized the mane of white hair first. Sandford Rostov. *Grigori.* Dressed in khakis and a windbreaker.

John tried to slow his heart. Stay cool, this was for Michael, and would soon be over. The right opportunity would present itself, if not that day, then the next day, or the day after that, or next week. He had nothing but time.

When the lights in the house went off at ten-thirty, John left the small clearing and followed the road a dozen or so blocks to a grocery where he had parked his car early that morning. He drove toward Atlanta, stopping for the night in a budget motel on the city's outskirts.

He slept for an hour or two sometime between two

and four in the morning then returned to the park across from the white colonial by five. He settled against a tree with a large mug of coffee from a local convenience store, waiting for an opportunity that didn't come.

Four days later, tucked in the same clearing, John prepared for another long and uneventful evening when Grigori exited the house. He led the Irish setter by a leash, and the two started across the street toward the park.

John held his breath. A quick scan of the park revealed it was empty—no witnesses. He slung an empty gym bag over his shoulder and placed the gun inside, then waited.

Grigori was a hundred yards in front of him now, moving toward the small lake to the rear and right of him.

John took long slow breaths as the seconds dripped by. In a few more yards Grigori would be shielded from the street by trees—a few yards after that and John would be able to cut off any retreat.

He wrung his hands, trying to clear his head of his heart's pounding. Then it was time. He started in Grigori's direction, his hand in the gym bag tightly gripping the gun inside. Beads of sweat stood out on his forehead.

A dozen yards away now—no going back. John forced himself to call out. "Grigori!"

Grigori halted, remained motionless for a moment, then turned slowly. He took in John and the gym bag slung over his shoulder without expression, his hands remaining motionless by his sides.

John lifted the gun far enough from the gym bag for Grigori to see, then lowered it back inside. Grigori stood still, and warily John closed the gap between them, stopping a few feet away, searching unsuccessfully for fear in Grigori's eyes.

"I wondered if, someday, we might meet again," Grigori said in an even tone.

"You have your answer." John surprised himself, expecting his voice to crack, but the words came easily.

Grigori nodded. "Your move. What do you want?"

John's eyes darted across the park. Still no one in sight, but if he was spotted, so what, they would only see two men talking, one with a gym bag over his shoulder. He refocused his attention on Grigori. The man was cool, John had to admit. "Names and addresses. You can start by telling me who killed Detective Mayer."

"So you can take revenge?"

"I can't go to the police to get justice; you saw to that."

"And if I refuse?"

John gestured toward the gun in the gym bag. "I'll use this."

"Murder, Mr. Sarikov?"

"I've had plenty of time to debate the moralities, and I decided, frankly, that I don't care. I see it as an execution, not murder. I *will* pull the trigger, make no mistake."

Grigori searched John's eyes momentarily. "I've nothing to say."

"I'm not playing a game."

"Perhaps not, but what would stop you from shooting me once I have talked."

"You tell me everything I want to know, and you have my word."

Grigori shook his head. "Even if I could believe you, let me make my position clear: I betray my loyalties, my family will pay the price. I will die before I let that happen."

"Don't think I'm bluffing."

"Whether you are or aren't is irrelevant to my decision."

Now what? Could he see this through? Sitting in the clearing, the answer was easy. Now— *One step at a time,* he reminded himself. He'd do what he must when the time came. He pointed at a small lake a few hundred yards further. "Let's walk down to the water. Tie your dog here."

Grigori looped the leash through a tree branch, then bent and rubbed the dog behind the ears. He straightened and faced John.

John pointed again at the water's edge.

They walked in silence, John to the left of Grigori and a half step behind. When they reached the water, the two faced each other.

"If you thought I might come after you, why didn't you run?" John asked.

"I'm old . . . my roots run deep. Would you have me give up my sons, my granddaughters, my wife? No . . . they are, I have found, the only things worth living for."

"I felt the same way about my brother."

"Then you understand."

John steeled his nerve. "I don't want to kill you, but I will. I'll have my answers."

"For what we did, God forgive us, but it's over now—Vasili . . . Gruenbaum . . . is dead. Let it rest in peace, Mr. Sarikov."

"No. It's not over. My brother's never coming back."

"And you want your pound of flesh?"

Yes, John wanted to yell. *From you and everyone in your goddamn organization.* "It was my brother."

"I'm sorry about your brother, Mr. Sarikov. Gruenbaum ordered it, I had nothing to do with it."

"Nothing to do with it! His blood is on your hands,

and on every other person's that had anything to do with that butcher."

"Blood on my hands? Layers, Mr. Sarikov. But your brother's?" Grigori shook his head. "You don't . . . can't . . . understand."

John's eyes swept across the park—still no one. "Try me."

Grigori paused, then nodded. "All right, Mr. Sarikov. Then imagine you led my life, and tell me how you would have done things so differently. Imagine being born in a small village in Russia. Your father works in a co-op growing potatoes, your mother in a shirt factory. You live hand to mouth in a small apartment, parents, brothers, sisters, grandparents . . . believing the promises communism holds for the future. Your father is a loyal party member, and you love him, and you accept every word he says about the evils of capitalism and the coming worldwide workers' revolution. How can you think differently—teachers, neighbors, newspapers, all say the same thing." Grigori's face grew animated; the words rushed out.

"You are a bright boy—too bright, perhaps. You attracted the attention of the secret police and you are chosen, recruited, a boy of seventeen, called to Moscow to serve your country. What an honor it is. Your mother and father are so proud. You join a group of young men chosen from across the Soviet Union and your training begins at once. A young idealist out to change the world. You are anxious, after all. There is a war going on; young men your age are winning medals. The country is galvanized; her very existence threatened. Heady, terrible, magnificent times.

"As the war winds down, after four years of training, finally your teachers tell you it's time to fight. The real war, they say, is about to begin—the war with the West, the war against exploitation, the war to set the proletariat free. Your mission: to infiltrate a designated foreign country, rise to a position of power, and await the call of duty. Spies. Secret agents. How excited you are . . . here is the danger and the adventure you have been craving.

"Then the reality, and a trap you cannot get out of. A mad game played by mad nations, Russia *and* America. And all you can do is try to play by some sort of civilized rules."

"Like killing innocent people?"

Grigori shook his head. "You're the type of man who wants justice, Mr. Sarikov. All I was able to give you was your life."

"You *gave* me nothing, Grigori. I bargained for my life. Luckily, I had something to bargain with, or I wouldn't be around to bother you now."

"The evidence?"

"Yes."

"An empty bargain, Mr. Sarikov. You held nothing in your hand."

"What are you talking about?"

"Your threat was the release of evidence by a journalist friend. There *is* no journalist friend—I knew that all along."

A guess, John told himself.

"How do you think Yakov and I found you in the woods?" Grigori asked.

"You staked out Gruenbaum's office."

"Wrong. You were followed from New York City."

John shook his head. ". . . I don't believe you. If I was followed from New York City, you could have killed me at any time."

"Exactly, Mr. Sarikov."

Grigori paused, letting the implications sink in, then continued. "A man in my employ had been following you since you drove away in your girlfriend's car from her place in the city. A light blue Buick, if I remember correctly. The motel in New Jersey, a diner, the Marriot in Manhattan, the *New York Herald* building. He planted a transmitter on your car, then tailed you north, on the expressway to Albany—it was then I knew you had figured things out, were going after Gruenbaum. He tailed you right into the parking garage. Yakov and I met him there, then followed you to the woods."

Grigori paused to add emphasis to his next words. "You told Gruenbaum you had evidence . . . that you mailed a copy of it to a journalist immediately before confronting him . . . remember? A lie. My man watched you the entire time. You bought a newspaper, you took up watch in the parking garage, but you never came near a mail box. *There was no evidence; no insurance policy.*"

Grigori was bluffing; he had to be. Yet he knew about Barbara's car, the New Jersey hotel, the diner, the Marriot, the visit to the *New York Herald* building. *How could Grigori know those things unless he told the truth?* "If that's true, why would you spare my life?" John asked.

"I told you. I did what I could to play by civilized rules."

"This from the same man who delivered me to Rolf for execution?"

"I was under orders then, ones I could not ignore. But no one knew that my man had picked up your tail in Manhattan. No one knew I had it in my power to kill you at anytime, and I chose not to tell them."

"Why?"

"Some of us did, once, naively perhaps, think our goal a noble one. But our time is over, and our organization should have faded away. Gruenbaum wouldn't have let it. He would have subverted our entire organization, kept it from dying its natural death. A cancer, he had to be cut out."

"And I was going to do that for you?"

"As long as you remained alive, you stirred the pot. Not all in my organization saw eye to eye on what to do with Gruenbaum. Gruenbaum scared some, seduced others, but they couldn't ignore you. You were loose; you knew things that incriminated Gruenbaum, yet he failed in repeated attempts to remove you. When he started to act erratic, to attract attention through his actions, even his friends and allies deserted him. He became a liability Yakov and I were ordered to remove. You know the rest. The cancer is gone."

John's mind fought to digest the information, to find the flaw in Grigori's story. "If you knew I hadn't mailed any evidence, why the charade?"

"*I knew* you hadn't mailed any evidence, but Yakov didn't. He heard and saw everything. My charade, the threats, were for his benefit. *He* believed you mailed the evidence. *He* believed the evidence could incriminate Gruenbaum and the entire organization. If he hadn't, he would have killed you no matter what I said. And after our *combined* testimony, and the playing of our Dictaphone tape that included your threats to Gruenbaum concerning the evidence, all factions of our organization accepted your claims. For that reason you remain alive."

Grigori let the words linger, and then: "As I said, Mr. Sarikov, we were both stuck in a mad game. Justice isn't in the rules. But I had an opportunity to save you, and I took it. I did what I could, Mr. Sarikov. God forgive me, I did what I could. It was time for the madness to end."

John's mind raced. Lies and truth and right and wrong, meshed and tangled. But one feeling he could not shake: Grigori spoke the truth.

Grigori lowered his head. "If my death would bring back your brother, Mr. Sarikov, I would pull the trigger myself. I live only for my children and grandchildren now . . . they are my only chance for redemption."

A long silence followed, the gentle lapping of the water on the shore the only measure of time. The sun began to set; the first shades of purple climbed from the east. Grigori's steady gaze neither challenged nor pleaded—he seemed reconciled to whatever followed.

John started the handgun upward twice, steeling himself to finish the act quickly, but each time something stopped him—perhaps fear of what he would become if he spilled the man's blood, or perhaps a realization that revenge was not always justice, that justice was not always attainable.

Perhaps the time had come, if not to forget, if not to forgive, at least to let live, and, in Grigori's words, to end the madness.

He turned, finally, in silence, and started back toward his car. He stopped by the Irish setter, who strained against its tether, tail flashing side to side. He rubbed its flank before untying the leash. The dog circled John once and streaked for its master, who remained unmoving by the water's edge, staring blankly in John's direction.

John resumed walking. He knew he would never return.

58

Hours later, well after midnight, the roads empty, the drum of a late night radio talk show and the hypnotic procession of center stripes his only companions, John's mind skipped through time.

He thought of Michael. Saving quarters to ride the Coney Island roller coaster; skipping rocks in the ocean; names, places, adventures. Memories only the two of them could share. Things never to be again.

He thought of Kelly. She had announced plans to reenter college in Virginia to pursue a master's degree. She needed to move on with her life, she said, and didn't think she could in a city that constantly reminded her of Michael. "Michael showed me just how much life has to offer," she had told him. "I'll never stop missing him, but I won't throw this gift away. It's time to live again."

And he thought of Barbara. He had picked up the phone to call her a half dozen times, but always set it back on its cradle without dialing, uncertain things could be different as long as tracking down Grigori dominated his existence. And now? Now that the lust for revenge had exhausted itself? How could things be different as long as he remained mired in the never-to-return past.

No present, no future, not that John could see. Everyone he had cared for, every emotion worth feeling, relegated to yesterdays. He would endure, would keep Michael's memory alive, but saw no room for anything more.

He reached under the car seat for the bottle he stowed there. Recently Michael's face had become harder to conjure up—a betrayal that terrified him—but the bottle always brought it back clearly. A ticket to the past, with all the accompanying bittersweet memories. He unscrewed the cap, but didn't drink, his mind once again tripping in time.

The bottle made John think of his father, and his mind, against his will, summoned him to one of the last times they spoke, the night before John left for Cornell. He had been sleeping, and woke with a start, sensing someone in his bedroom. Light from the bedroom window lit the room dimly in violet hues, and John saw his father's form in an old rocking chair in the corner. Their conversation came back clearly.

"What are you doing?" John had said, startled.

His father hadn't answered for a moment, and when he did, his voice had a faraway quality. "You remind me so much of your mother. Same eyes, smile . . . She was so beautiful."

"Geez, Dad, waking up, seeing you there, it gave me the creeps. What're you still doing up?"

The rhythmic creaking of the rocker broke the ensuing silence, then his father's voice had come again from the dark. "Your mother was such a frail thing . . . so delicate. She'd put her hands against mine, and they'd seem so small and white." He had rocked a few more moments in silence before continuing. "The doctor told her she wasn't strong enough . . . but I wanted another son."

"What are you talking about, Dad?"

"I killed her. The doctor told her after Michael not to have another child. Said it was dangerous. She did it for me—to make me happy—and I killed her. If I had known Johnny; if I had known—"

"Dad, why don't you go to bed. Sleep it off. You didn't kill anyone."

"I did. I killed her . . . and a part of me started to die."

"Dad—"

"She never would have wanted things to turn out the way they have. Michael gone. Now you're leaving too—both gone for good. I just couldn't see—"

"It's late, Dad; get some sleep."

"I thought, all these years, I was keeping her memory alive, but I can see now I wasn't. I betrayed her in death as well as in life. Johnny. For everything I've said and done . . . I . . . I'm—"

"Come on, Dad. We'll talk in the morning, okay?"

His father hesitated, then rose and left the room.

They never did talk in the morning. John left for Cornell the next day, and three months later his father died.

He had never told that story to anyone, not even Michael. During life his father had given him nothing. He cursed; he drank; he abused. His father should have been the one ashamed, but on that last night, from that darkened corner, his father had reached out and John ignored him. He still lived with the guilt.

And now Michael was gone, the only one who would have understood, who offered forgiveness in every word, every slap on the back. A better person. It wasn't jealousy, or blindness, just the truth. Michael *was* better, and just being his brother, just sharing his friendship, made John feel worthwhile, more so, perhaps, than he had a right to.

Why had Michael been taken? There was no justice in that. Compared with the scores who mourned Michael's passing, who would mourn John's own? If he could offer his life in place of Michael's, he would do so, in the blink of an eye, but he couldn't—

John stopped in thought. Or could he? Is that, in

fact, what he was doing? Sacrificing his life for Michael's sake? Forsaking happiness, turning inward and bitter, in the pursuit of suffering—the only tribute left to offer Michael? *Just like his father.*

John repeated the thought. Just like his father. Like father, like son; the words pulled at his chest. His father drank, swore, abused—would he follow the same path? make the same offering to a loved one? And the result, would it be the same too? Would he push away all who loved him and ultimately drink himself to death? And for what? Who would it bring back to life? Not Michael. Someday would he sit in a darkened room and realize, as his father had, that he had betrayed Michael not in life, but in death?

John thought of Grigori's words: "If my death would bring back your brother, I would pull the trigger myself. I live only for my children and grandchildren now . . . they are my only chance for redemption."

On that last night, did his father realize what Grigori knew, that no amount of penance would bring back his wife? That redemption came only through love?

John saw his father again in his mind's eye, silhouetted in the bedroom doorway, repeating his last words: "Johnny. For everything I've said and done . . . I . . . I'm—" before John cut him off. Sixteen years later, on a near empty interstate south of New Jersey, John completed his father's sentence. "For everything I've said and done—I . . . I'm . . . *sorry.*"

John forgave his father as tears welled in his eyes. Then the harder part: he forgave himself for wanting to live.

It *was* over. Only one more thing he could do for Michael—*not* allow his memory to be linked only to pain, misery to be his only legacy. The madness had to stop.

As warm tears streaked his face and washed away the guilt, his thoughts turned again to Barbara. It's what Michael would want for him—no, *no,* it's what *he wanted for himself.* He would drive into the city and knock on her door. She would open it to him, or leave it closed, but he would try. And if she let him into her life once more, things would be gloriously different.

In Kelly's words, it was time to live again.

As John neared New York City, the first hints of orange chased the darkness from the eastern horizon. He would be at Barbara's in less than an hour.

Epilogue

On a humid summer day, less than a month after her husband had succumbed to skin cancer, Dorothy Rostov, with the help of a cane, made her way to the mail box at the end of the driveway leading from her home in suburban Atlanta. There, mixed with the flyers and bills, she found a letter with no return address. She returned to her house, sat down in her favorite room, its walls covered with pictures of family and its windows overlooking the small but well-manicured backyard, and opened the letter.

"I have never had the pleasure of making your acquaintance," the letter read, "but knew your husband once, long ago. Though I knew him for only a short time, I still think of him often. I am happily married, with three children, and it is no stretch of the truth to say all I have, all I have become, I owe in some part to him. The memories of your husband, like those of loved ones I have lost, have grown old, but not distant. They call to me now, from across the years, one thought, above all, linked forever to my memories of your husband: no matter our beliefs, no matter our allegiances, we are all, every one of us, our brother's keeper."